Praise for **The Killing II**

'As with Hewson's first Killing novel it both illuminates and expands on the series, as well as being equally compelling'
Choice

'British author David Hewson is making a brilliant job of bringing the acclaimed Danish TV crime drama *The Killing* to the literary market place'
Lancashire Evening Post

Praise for **The Killing**

'A very fine novel, which is more of a re-imagining of the original story than a carbon copy – and with the bonus of a brand new twist to the ending'
Daily Mail

'David Hewson's literary translation is far more than a cheap tie-in . . . the book allows the characters more room to breathe . . . Hewson's greatest achievement is that it's compelling reading'
Observer

'Not just a novelisation. Hewson is a highly regarded crime writer in his own right; he spent a lot of time with the creators of the original to ensure that he did not offend its spirit and mood, and he has provided his own, different solution to the central murder mystery'
Marcel Berlins, *The Times*

'A fast-paced crime novel that's five-star from start to finish'
Irish Examiner

'As gripping as the TV series.
It will keep you pinned to the very last page'
Jens Lapidus

THE KILLING
III

Also by David Hewson

The Killing

The Killing II

Nic Costa series

A Season for the Dead

The Villa of Mysteries

The Sacred Cut

The Lizard's Bite

The Seventh Sacrament

The Garden of Evil

Dante's Numbers

The Blue Demon

The Fallen Angel

Carnival for the Dead

Other titles

The Promised Land

The Cemetery of Secrets
(previously published as *Lucifer's Shadow*)

Death in Seville
(previously published as *Semana Santa*)

DAVID HEWSON

THE KILLING
III

BASED ON THE BAFTA AWARD-WINNING TV SERIES

WRITTEN BY SØREN SVEISTRUP

MACMILLAN

First published 2014 by Macmillan
an imprint of Pan Macmillan, a division of Macmillan Publishers Limited
Pan Macmillan, 20 New Wharf Road, London N1 9RR
Basingstoke and Oxford
Associated companies throughout the world
www.panmacmillan.com

ISBN 978-1-4472-4623-7 HB
ISBN 978-1-4472-4624-4 TPB

Based on Søren Sveistrup's *Forbrydelsen III* (*The Killing season 3*)
– an original Danish Broadcasting Corporation TV series
co-written by Torleif Hoppe, Michael W. Horsten

The right of David Hewson to be identified as the
author of this work has been asserted by him in accordance
with the Copyright, Designs and Patents Act 1988.

1 3 5 7 9 8 6 4 2

A CIP catalogue record for this book is available from the British Library.

Typeset by SetSystems Ltd, Saffron Walden, Essex
Printed and bound by CPI Group (UK) Ltd, Croydon, CR0 4YY

Visit **www.panmacmillan.com** to read more about all our books
and to buy them. You will also find features, author interviews and
news of any author events, and you can sign up for e-newsletters
so that you're always first to hear about our new releases.

Acknowledgements

I'm indebted to Søren Sveistrup, the creator of the series, and my editor Trisha Jackson for their insights and support. Once again this is an adaptation of the TV original story, not a scene-by-scene copy. The changes along the way are mine alone.

David Hewson

Principal Characters

Copenhagen Police

Sarah Lund – *Vicekriminalkommisær, Homicide*

Lennart Brix – *Head of Homicide*

Mathias Borch – *Investigating officer, Politiets Efterretningstjeneste (PET); the internal national security intelligence agency, a separate arm of the police service*

Ruth Hedeby – *Deputy Director*

Tage Steiner – *Lawyer for internal affairs*

Asbjørn Juncker – *Detective, Homicide*

Madsen – *Detective, Homicide*

Dyhring – *head of PET*

Politics

Troels Hartmann – *Prime Minister, heading the Liberal Party*

Rosa Lebech – *leader of the Centre Party*

Anders Ussing – *leader of the Socialist Party*

Morten Weber – *Hartmann's political adviser*

Karen Nebel – *Hartmann's head of media relations*

Birgit Eggert – *Finance Minister*

Mogens Rank – *Justice Minister*

Kristoffer Seifert – *former Socialist Party worker*

Per Monrad – *Ussing's campaign manager*

Zeeland

Robert Zeuthen – *heir to the Zeeland business empire*

Maja Zeuthen – *Robert's estranged wife*

Niels Reinhardt – *Robert Zeuthen's personal assistant*

Emilie Zeuthen – *the Zeuthens' daughter, aged nine*

Carl Zeuthen – *the Zeuthens' son, aged six*

Kornerup – *CEO of Zeeland*

Others

Vibeke – *Lund's mother*

Mark – *Lund's son*

Eva Lauersen – *Mark's girlfriend*

Carsten Lassen – *a doctor at the university hospital*

Peter Schultz – *deputy prosecutor*

Lis Vissenbjerg – *pathologist at the university hospital*

Nicolaj Overgaard – *former Jutland police officer*

Louise Hjelby – *girl in Jutland*

THE KILLING
III

One

They always gave her the young ones. This time he was called Asbjørn Juncker, twenty-three years old, newly made up to detective from trainee, now gleefully sorting through the skeletons of wrecked cars in a run-down scrapyard on the edge of the docks.

'There's an arm here!' he cried as he rounded the rusting husk of a long-dead VW Beetle. 'An arm!'

Madsen had a team of men moving out to sweep the area. He looked at Lund and sighed. Asbjørn had turned up at the Politigården from the provinces that morning, assigned to homicide. Fifteen minutes later while Lund was half-listening to the news – the financial crisis, more about the coming general election – the yard called to say they'd found a body. Or more accurately parts of one scattered among the junk. Probably a bum from the neighbouring shantytown in the abandoned dock. Someone who'd scrambled over the fence looking for something to steal, fallen asleep in a car, died instantly the moment it was picked up by one of the gigantic cranes.

'Funny spot to take a nap,' Madsen said. 'The grab sliced him in half. Then he seems to have got cut about a bit more. The crane operator choked on his coffee when he saw what was happening.'

Autumn was giving up on Copenhagen, getting nudged out of the way by winter. Grey sky. Grey land. Grey water ahead with a grey ship motionless a few hundred metres off shore.

Lund hated this place. During the Birk Larsen murder she'd come here looking for a warehouse belonging to the missing girl's father.

Theis Birk Larsen was now out of jail after serving his sentence for killing the man he thought murdered his daughter. Back in the removals business from what Lund had heard. Jan Meyer, her partner who got shot during that investigation, was still an invalid, working for a disabled charity. She'd gone nowhere near him, or the Birk Larsens, even though that case was still unsettled in her own head.

She looked across the bleak water at the dead ship listing at its final anchor. Ghosts still hung around her murmuring sometimes. She could hear them now.

'You're not really going to take a job in OPA, are you?' Madsen asked.

The Politigården was always rife with gossip. She should have known it would get out.

'I get a medal for twenty-five years' service today. There's only so much of your life you can spend out in the freezing cold looking at pieces of dead people.'

'Brix doesn't want to lose you. You're a pain in the arse sometimes, but no one does. Lund—'

'What?' Juncker squealed, clambering through the wreckage. 'You're going to count paper clips all day long?'

OPA – Operations, Planning and Analysis – did rather more than that but she wasn't minded to tell him. Something about Juncker reminded her of Meyer. The cockiness. The protruding ears. There was an odd, affronted innocence too.

'They said I was going to work with someone good . . .' the young cop started.

'Shut up Asbjørn,' Madsen told him. 'You're doing that already.'

'I'd also like to be called Juncker. Not Asbjørn. Everyone else gets called by their last name.'

They'd recovered six pieces of a half-naked, middle-aged man's body. Juncker's was the seventh.

There was an old wheelbarrow next to the Beetle. She asked the scrapyard manager for a price. He seemed a bit surprised but came up with one quickly enough. Lund handed over a few notes and told Juncker to put it in the boot of her car.

His hands went to his hips.

'Is someone going to look at my arm or not?'

Stroppy young men. She was getting used to them. Mark was

supposed to come round for dinner that evening with his girlfriend. First visit to her new home, a tiny wooden cottage on the edge of the city. She wondered if he'd make it or invent one more excuse.

Juncker nodded at the photographer now taking pictures where he'd been, then stuck a finger in the air like a schoolboy counting off a list.

'There's no ID. But he's got a gold ring and some tattoos. Also the skin's wrinkled like it's been in water.' He pointed at the flat, listless harbour. 'In there.'

Lund looked at the scrapyard man, then the derelict area beyond the nearest wall.

'That used to be warehouses,' she said. 'What's it now?'

He had a sad, intelligent face. Not what she expected in a spot like this.

'It was one of Zeeland's main terminals. The warehouses were just a favour on the side to the little people.' He shrugged. 'Not so many little people any more. And just a few containers going through. They shut up most of it the moment things turned bad. Almost a thousand men gone overnight. I used to manage the loading side of things. Worked there ever since I left school . . .'

He didn't like talking about this. So he lugged the wheelbarrow over to Lund's car, opened the boot, and set it next to a couple of rosebushes waiting there in pots.

'He's been in the water. He's got tattoos,' Juncker repeated. 'There's marks on his arm that look like they came from a knife.'

The shantytown next door was a sprawling shambles of corrugated iron and rusting trucks and caravans set on the car park to the old dockyard. That was never there when she was hunting the murderer of Nanna Birk Larsen.

'He was a bum who wandered in here looking for something to nick,' Madsen cut in. 'We'll take the photos. You can try writing up the report if you like. I'll check it for you.'

Juncker really didn't like that.

'There'll be trouble if we don't look busy round here,' he said.

'Why?' Lund asked.

'Politicians on the way.' He nodded at the scrapyard manager who was looking closely at Lund's plants, seemingly unimpressed. 'He told me. They're doing a photo opportunity with all them homeless people.'

'Bums don't have votes,' Madsen grumbled.

'They don't have gold rings either,' Juncker pointed out. 'Did you hear what I said? The big shots are going to talk to the men left in the dockyard. Troels Hartmann's coming they reckon. Here in an hour.'

Ghosts.

This place had just acquired a new one. Hartmann had been a suspect in the Birk Larsen case, one whose ambition and arrogance almost ruined his career. *Pretty boy*, Meyer called him. The handsome Teflon man of Copenhagen politics. As soon as he was cleared he scored an unlikely victory to become the city's mayor. Then two and a half years ago, after a campaign racked by vitriol about the collapsing economy, he'd emerged victor in a general election, becoming the Liberals' Prime Minister leading a new coalition.

'Hartmann was in that big case of yours,' Juncker added. 'I remember that.'

It seemed like yesterday.

'Were you here then?' she asked without thinking.

Asbjørn Juncker laughed out loud.

'Here? That was ages ago. I read about it when I was in school. Why do you think I joined the police? It sounded—'

'Six years,' Madsen said. 'That's all.'

Long ones, Lund thought. Soon she'd be forty-five. She had a little place of her own. A dull, simple, enclosed life. A relationship to rebuild with her son. No need of bitter memories from the past. Or fresh nightmares for the future.

She told Madsen to keep on looking and make sure nothing untoward came near the media or the approaching political circus. Then she drove back to the Politigården, a small bay tree bouncing around in the footwell of the passenger seat, changed into her uniform, the blue skirt, blue jacket, watched all the others turning up for their long service medals. They seemed so much older than she felt.

Brix came and nagged about the OPA job.

'I need you here,' he said. The tall boss of homicide eyed her up and down with his stern and craggy face. 'You don't look right dressed like that.'

'How I dress is my business. Will you give you me a good

4

reference?' She was anxious about this. 'I know there are things in the past they won't like. You don't need to dwell on them.'

'OPA's where people go to retire. To give up. You never—'

'Yes. I know.'

He muttered something she couldn't hear. Then, 'Your tie's not straight.'

Lund juggled with it. Brix was immaculate in his best suit, fresh pressed shirt, everything perfect. The more he stared, the worse the tie got.

'Here,' he said and did it for her finally. 'I'll talk to them. You're making a mistake. You know that?'

The forbidding red-brick castle called Drekar was once a small hunting lodge owned by minor royalty. Then Robert Zeuthen's grandfather bought it, enlarged the place, named his creation after the dragon-headed longships of the Vikings. A man intent on founding a dynasty, he loved the fortress in the woods. Its exaggerated battlements, the sprawling, manicured grounds running down to wild woodland and the sea. And the ornate extended gargoyle he built at the seaward end, fashioned in the fantastic shape of a triumphant dragon, symbol of the company he created.

The ocean was never far away from the thoughts of the man who built Zeeland. Starting in the 1900s Zeuthen had transformed a small-time family cargo firm into an international enterprise with a shipping fleet running to thousands of vessels. Zeuthen's own father, Hans, had carried on the expansion when he inherited the company. Finance and IT subsidiaries, consulting arms, hotels and travel firms, even a domestic retailing chain came to bear the Zeeland logo: three waves beneath the Drekar dragon.

By the time Hans Zeuthen died, not long before Troels Hartmann became Prime Minister, his clan was a fixture on the nation's social, economic and political landscape. And then the company fell into the nominal hands of his son as managing owner, heading a corporate board.

Robert, third generation, was cut from different cloth. A quiet, introspective man of forty he was at that moment wandering round the forest outside the family home looking for his nine-year-old daughter Emilie.

Thick woodland, bare in winter. Zeuthen marched through the trees, across the carpet of bronze autumn leaves, calling her name. Loudly but with affection. His ascent to the throne of Zeeland had come at a cost. Eighteen months before his wife Maja had left him. Soon the divorce would come through. She was now living with a doctor from the main city hospital while Zeuthen played the part of single father, looking after Emilie and her six-year-old brother, Carl, as much as he was allowed under the separation agreement, and through the ceaseless pressures of work.

Hans Zeuthen had lived through a time of growth and prosperity. His son was experiencing none of this. Recession and business failures had hit Zeeland hard. The company had been laying off workers for four years and there was still no real sign of any recovery. Several subsidiaries had been sold off, others closed for good. The board was getting anxious. Investors were openly worrying whether the enterprise was best left in the hands of the family.

Robert Zeuthen wondered what else they expected. Blood? The crisis had cost him his marriage. The precious bond of family. There was nothing left to give.

'Emilie?' he cried again into the bare trees.

'Dad.' Carl had walked up behind in silence, dragging his toy dinosaur. 'Why won't Dino talk any more?'

Zeuthen folded his arms and gazed down at his son.

'Perhaps because you launched him out of your bedroom window? To see if he could fly?'

'Dino can't,' Carl said innocently.

He tousled the boy's hair and agreed with that. Then called for his daughter again. Another day and it would be time for the kids to stay with their mother. For the best part of him to leave again. And that meant Maja too.

A figure came racing out of the trees. Blue coat, pink wellies, legs flying, blonde hair too. Emilie Zeuthen dashed towards him, launched herself at his chest, arms wide, pretty face all mischief.

The same old challenge. The one she'd made almost as soon as she could talk.

It said . . . *catch me, Dad. Catch me.*

So he did.

When he'd stopped laughing Zeuthen kissed her cold cheek and said, 'One day I'll miss you, girlie. One day you're going to fall.'

'No you won't.'

She had such a bright, incisive voice. A smart kid. Old for her years. Emilie led Carl a merry dance. Did that for the staff in Drekar too, not that they loved her any the less for it.

'No you won't, Dad,' Carl repeated and got the dinosaur to give him a playful bite on the leg.

'When can I have a cat?' Emilie asked, arms round his neck, blue eyes firmly on his.

'Where were you?'

'Walking. You promised.'

'I said you could have a pet. Anything but a cat. I've got to talk to Mum about it. Between us . . .'

Her face fell. So did Carl's. Zeuthen had never imagined he'd lose Maja, lose them a little too. He'd no idea what to say by way of comfort, no access to the easy words he was supposed to offer.

Instead he took them by the hand, Carl to his left, Emilie to the right, and together they walked slowly home.

Niels Reinhardt was in the drive with his black Mercedes. Another of his late father's bequests. Reinhardt was the family's personal assistant, liaison man between the Zeuthens and the board, a fixer and social arranger who'd been doing this ever since Robert was a child himself. Now sixty-four, a tall and genial man, always in suit and tie, he looked ready to go on for ever.

The newspaper was in Reinhardt's hands. Zeuthen had seen the story already. An exclusive claiming that Zeeland was about to renege on its promises to Hartmann's government and abandon Denmark as its headquarters.

'Where do they get these lies?' Zeuthen asked.

'I don't know,' Reinhardt replied. 'I've told the board you want to convene a meeting immediately. Hartmann's people are going crazy. He's getting questions from the press of course.'

Maja was on the steps of the house, green anorak and jeans. They'd met as students. Falling in love had seemed so easy, so natural. She didn't know who he was at the time, didn't much care when she did find out. He was the stiff, shy, plain-looking rich boy. She was the beautiful, fair-haired daughter of charming hippie parents who ran an organic farm on Fyn. They'd scarcely known a cross word until his father died and circumstances forced him to take the reins of Zeeland. After that . . .

She marched down the steps, the face he'd come to love wreathed once more in anger and resentment. Reinhardt, always a man wise to the moment, took the children by the hand, said something about finding dry shoes and led them into the house.

'What's this?' she said and pulled a piece of paper out of her jacket.

Pictures of a tiny tabby kitten. Small hands stroking the creature's fur. In one photo Emilie was clutching the little creature to her tummy, beaming at the camera.

Zeuthen shook his head.

'I've been to the school, Robert! She was funny with me last week. Wouldn't talk. As if she had some kind of secret.'

'She seems fine.'

'How would you know? How much time do you spend with her when she's here?'

'As much as I can,' he said and it wasn't a lie. 'I told her she couldn't have a cat . . .'

'Then where did she get it? She's allergic to them.'

'The kids are under supervision every hour they spend with me, whether I'm there or not. You know that, Maja. Why not ask your mother? You didn't need to come out here for this. You could have called.'

'I came here to take them with me.'

'No,' Zeuthen said immediately. 'It's on the schedule. You get them tomorrow. I can deal with this.'

Reinhardt and the children were back at the door. He looked as if he needed to talk. Zeuthen went over, listened. Hartmann's staff were demanding a statement. The board would convene within the hour.

'A body's been found at the docks, near our facility,' he added.

'One of our men?'

'There's no sign of that, Robert.'

It happened so quickly there was nothing Zeuthen could do. Maja pushed past him, walked up to Emilie, took her hands.

'I want to know about the cat,' she insisted.

The girl tried to pull back.

'Emilie!' Maja shrieked. 'This is important!'

Zeuthen bent down, said gently, 'Mum needs to know. So do I. Whose cat is it? Please?'

The years fell off her. An uncertain, shifty child again. Emilie said nothing. She struggled as Maja pulled up the sleeves of her blue coat.

Red skin, puffy and swollen.

She lifted the girl's jumper. Her stomach was covered with the same livid marks.

'There's a cat here,' Maja barked. 'What the hell have you been playing at? I'm taking her to hospital now.'

He'd never seen her temper until their marriage began to falter. Here it was again, loud and vicious.

Carl put his hands over his ears. Emilie stood stiff and silent and guilty. Reinhardt said something Zeuthen barely heard about postponing the board meeting.

Responsibilities. They never went away.

Zeuthen crouched down, looked his daughter in the eye.

'Where was the cat, Emilie?' he asked. 'Please—'

'It doesn't matter now, does it?' Maja screamed. 'I'll deal with that later. She's going to hospital . . .'

Emilie Zeuthen began to cry.

Troels Hartmann liked being on the stump. Especially when his opponent was a left-wing windbag like Anders Ussing. The world of Danish politics was a seething stew of small parties fighting for the right to make peace with their enemies and seize a little power for themselves. In the current climate only Hartmann's liberals and Ussing's socialists stood a chance of winning sufficient votes to hold the Prime Minister's chair.

The polls were close. One slip-up on either side could tip them easily. But that, he felt sure, was more likely to come from a loudmouth like Ussing than any of his own, carefully shepherded supporters. Morten Weber, the wily campaign organizer who'd won him the mayor's seat in Copenhagen, had followed into the Christiansborg Palace. He'd recruited Karen Nebel, a slick and telegenic media adviser who'd worked as a political hack for one of the state TV stations. It was as good a team as Hartmann had ever possessed. And he had a few tricks of his own up his sleeve too, though listening to Ussing try to wind up the audience in the run-down Zeeland docks terminal he wondered whether he'd need them.

It was a typical turnout for an industrial gathering: women from offices, a handful of burly stevedores in hard hats, some seamen, few of them interested in politics but glad of a break from work. The platform was on a pickup truck set by a pair of shiny barrel-like containers in an open building beneath a corrugated roof. The TV crews had been positioned at the front, the news reporters corralled into the seats behind.

Ussing was trotting out the same lines he'd been spouting up and down Denmark since the election campaign began.

'This government is starving the ordinary citizens of Denmark to fill the pockets of the rich who bankroll them.'

Hartmann stared straight at the TV cameras, smiled and shook his head.

'And today!' Ussing roared, like the trade union boss he once was, 'we see what Hartmann's weakness has won us.'

He held up that morning's paper, with the headline about Zeeland abandoning the country for a new low-tax base in the Far East.

'One of our biggest employers is joining the exodus now. While he sticks us with the bill they ship their jobs to Asia.'

A murmur of approval, white hats shaking. Hartmann picked up the mike.

'A sound industrial policy works for everyone, Anders. If we can keep Zeeland happy they'll employ more Danes in return . . .'

'Not any more!' Ussing yelled, slapping the paper. 'You've turned a blind eye to their monopolies. You've sucked up to them with your tax cuts and oil subsidies . . .'

The rabble-rousing was starting to work. He was getting a few cheers and the odd round of applause.

'The only sucking up that's going on here's from you,' Hartmann broke in. 'Easy words. Irresponsible ones. You'd have us believe you can wish this crisis away with a few sweet words while quietly dipping into the pockets of ordinary Danes and relieving them of what money they have.'

Hartmann scanned the crowd. They were quiet. They were listening.

'I know it's hard. For too long we've been reading about layoffs and bankruptcies. About private savings disappearing into thin air.' A long pause. They were waiting. 'If I had a magic wand do you think I wouldn't use it? This is the world we have. Not just in

Denmark. Everywhere. The choice you face is a simple one. Do we deal with these problems now? Or pass this mess on to our children?'

He gestured to the stocky, ginger-haired man next to him.

'If you want to duck your responsibilities, vote for Anders Ussing. If you've got the guts to face them, choose me.'

They liked that. Ussing took the mike.

'So when Zeeland bleat to the papers about moving you'll give them more of our money, Troels? Is that how it works? Another bribe for your friends . . .'

'If we make the climate good for business, the jobs will stay here,' Hartmann insisted. 'Our industrial policy looks for growth. But there are limits. We're in this together. Everyone contributes, just as everyone's affected. That means Zeeland too.' Hand to his heart, he said it again. 'That means Zeeland too.'

They were clapping as he left. Karen Nebel still wasn't happy as they headed for the car.

'I specifically asked you to steer clear of Zeeland.'

'What was I supposed to do? He had me on the spot. I can't ignore a question like that. Zeeland have to go public and deny the article.'

She was a tall woman with swept-back fair hair and a tense, lined face bordering on hard. Scheming at times but he could handle that.

'They will deny it, won't they, Karen?'

'I keep leaving messages everywhere. No one gets back to me. I think something's up.'

'Get it out of them,' Hartmann ordered. 'I've just about got a deal with Rosa Lebech's people sewn up. I don't want anything to get in the way of that.'

She scowled at the mention of the woman who ran the Centre Party.

'There's a homeless camp next door,' she said. 'I scheduled a stop there.'

'If I can talk to people, fine. I'm not just doing photo-ops.'

They got to the car. She held the door open for him.

'Troels. They're homeless. Pictures are the only reason we're here.'

Hartmann's phone rang. He saw the number, walked away from the car for some privacy.

'I just saw you on TV, honey. If I wasn't leading another party you'd get my vote.'

'I still want it,' Hartmann said. 'We've got to close this deal, Rosa. And after that I need to see you. Somewhere quiet.' He looked round, saw he was alone. 'With a big brass bed.'

'Oh my God. And your Dylan records too.'

'The deal first.'

'We'll back you as Prime Minister. So long as we know you're on top of Zeeland.'

He laughed.

'You don't believe Ussing, do you? Or that stupid rag this morning?'

'Let's talk about this later,' Rosa Lebech said.

Then she was gone.

Before he could think straight Karen Nebel was over, calling off the visit to the homeless camp. One of the security people was with her. He said they'd found a dead body round the corner.

'PET think there might be some kind of threat. The security systems have been compromised or something. They think—'

'I'm not giving Ussing more ammunition,' Hartmann said. 'Schedule it for later in the day. Unless PET come up with something concrete.'

'Who was the call from?'

He thought for a moment.

'My dentist. I forgot an appointment.' A shrug, the charming Hartmann smile. 'Elections. They do get in the way.'

The tie was uncomfortable. The shirt had seen better days. Brix had organized the ceremony and for some reason brought in the police brass band. They stood in the corner huffing and puffing at trumpets and euphoniums, making a noise that sounded like a party of drunken elephants.

She was trying to be polite listening to war stories told by an old officer from the sticks, waiting for the ceremony to begin, when her phone rang.

Lund walked away to take it.

'It's Juncker here. I'm still at the docks.'

'Hi, Asbjørn.'

A long pause then he said, 'Forensics have been taking a look at our bits and pieces. They're sure it's homicide. He was dead when the crane grabbed him. He'd been whacked about with a claw hammer. Looks like he got away from a ship and the bloke caught up with him at the yard. Chucked him in the car. We've talked to the bums here. They're clueless. Zeeland don't know of anyone missing.'

'That's it?'

'Someone saw a speedboat hanging round. They thought it was chasing a seal.'

'Why would someone chase a seal?' she asked, walking to the window, taking a long look at the weather outside.

'The coastguard said they got an interrupted call around two thirty in the morning. They don't know who from. The speedboat was cruising round near the junkyard not long after.'

Lund asked the obvious question. Had any nearby vessels reported a missing sailor? Juncker said no.

'It's probably left the harbour,' she said. 'You need to get all the local movements.'

'What movements? Zeeland have pretty much mothballed this part of the docks. Also . . .' He stopped for a moment as if trying to find somewhere quiet. 'There's all these PET guys here sniffing round. What's it to do with them?'

'It's OK, Asbjørn. They're human too.'

'You're never going to call me Juncker, are you?'

'Talk to Madsen. Do as he says. I'm busy—'

'The PET bloke wants a word. Man called Borch. Got the impression he knows you already. He's on his way.'

Lund didn't say anything.

'Hello?' Juncker asked down the line. 'Anyone there?'

'Talk to Madsen,' Lund said again, finished the call, looked down the long corridor, wondered how many more ghosts were going to come creeping out of the shadows.

She'd no idea what Mathias Borch did any more. Something important she guessed. He was bright, had shown that when they first met more than twenty years before at police academy. Now he looked a little broken and worn. Still had all his hair though, uncombed as usual, and the wrinkled face of a boxer pup.

Puppy.

She used to call him that. The memory must have been why she was blushing when Borch strode up, didn't smile, didn't even look her in the eye much and said, 'Sarah. We've got to talk. This body down the docks. Your kid there said—'

'Stop,' Lund ordered, hand up. Then she pointed to the door. Brix had started giving his speech. She could hear him talking about the strength of the corps, year after year, and how its integrity was the basis for justice and security in Copenhagen.

'Heard it all a million times,' Borch grunted. 'This is important . . .'

Lund muttered a low curse and took him in the kitchen.

'I'm sorry to disturb your day,' he said. 'I mean . . . congratulations and all that.'

'Don't overdo it.'

'You look good,' he said. 'Really. Are you?'

'What do you want?'

'I'm involved in this case. I need to know what you've got.'

'Nothing. We've got nothing at all.'

'So you've searched the docks? And the ships there?'

'We're looking. There's only one ship. Juncker got in touch with them by radio. They haven't seen a thing.'

He frowned. The puppy looked his age then.

'I expected more than that . . .'

'Listen! I haven't spoken to you in years. Then you turn up here, just when I'm about to pick up my long service medal, and start throwing questions at me. I'm going back in there . . .'

'I'm in PET. Didn't you know?'

'Why should I?'

'We think there's more to it. Two weeks ago there was a break-in down at the docks. It looked like the usual burglary. A computer gone, some loose change. Details of Zeeland's security system . . .'

'Isn't that their problem?'

He stared at her. It was a stupid remark. Zeeland was a huge international conglomerate. It carried clout, in government and beyond.

'What's this got to do with our man in bits?' she asked.

'There's no CCTV footage from last night. Two minutes after that failed emergency call to the coastguard every last camera got turned off somehow. He hacked into the system, froze it on old footage, then switched it back on before dawn.'

Borch grabbed a sandwich from a platter prepared for the get-together and took a bite.

'Burglars are rarely that smart,' he said, spitting a few crumbs down his front.

Brix had stopped speaking. Soon the medals and the diplomas would be handed out.

'Leave me your number,' she said. 'We'll keep in touch.'

He stopped her as she tried to walk off.

'Someone's taken down one of the most sophisticated security systems in the country. There's a dead man in the harbour when it comes back online. On the very day the Prime Minister's due to spend some time around there. The financial crisis. Afghanistan . . .' He laughed. 'Irate husbands. Hartmann's got as many people who hate him as love him.'

'I'll pass that on.'

'I don't want you to pass it on. I want you on the case. Brix has already agreed . . .'

'I bet he has.'

'You're better than OPA.'

'Listen! There's no one reported missing. The chances are he was a foreign sailor from a foreign ship and it's out of our waters.'

'I still want you on the case. And so does Brix.'

Applause from the next room, laughter too. The presentations had started. She couldn't just blunder in now.

'You do look good,' he said, and seemed a little embarrassed. 'Me . . .' A shrug, and she could picture him back in the academy, with all his grim humour and bad jokes. 'I just got old.'

She wanted to shout at him. To scream something.

Instead Lund said, 'I'm not getting this uniform dirty. I'm supposed to have an interview later.'

The Zeeland headquarters sat on the waterfront near the harbour. A modern black glass monolith with the company dragon stencilled across the top six floors, it was now surrounded by little more than construction sites turning the dockside into cheap housing. One of the few commodities that still sold.

Robert Zeuthen parked his shiny new Range Rover outside. Reinhardt was waiting in the lobby with news about the body in the docks. It was now a murder case but there were no indications Zeeland were involved. PET were working on it alongside the police. Troels Hartmann's presence in the area made their interest inevitable.

'Where did that cat come from?' Zeuthen asked.

'Not the house,' Reinhardt insisted. 'I'm still checking. This incident at the docks looks bad. It seems the security system was breached somehow. We've got a team looking into it. PET want to talk to them.' He frowned. 'Hartmann's more concerned about the newspaper report. He's waiting to hear us deny it.'

'I want you there when PET talk to our security people,' Zeuthen said. 'If there's a breach maybe it's not the only one.'

'I should be with you for the board,' Reinhardt said.

Zeuthen went to the lift, shook his head.

'I can handle that. Find out what's going on with PET. Keep looking for Emilie's cat. Maja's going to kill me for that. We both knew Emilie has that allergy.'

'Robert.' Reinhardt's hand was on his arm. 'I've reason to believe the board could be difficult. You may need me there.'

Zeuthen smiled.

'Not this time, old friend.'

Back in Christiansborg Karen Nebel was worried.

'People are starting to talk,' she said as they sat down in his office. 'They don't understand why Zeeland haven't denied the newspaper report.' Her phone rang. 'Maybe this is it . . .'

Hartmann watched her go out into the corridor to take the call then muttered, 'Are we supposed to jump up and down every time the press publish a lie?'

Morten Weber folded his arms, leaned back in the chair by the window.

'Sometimes.'

Weber had been there throughout Hartmann's career. A diminutive, modest, somewhat shabby man with wayward curly black hair, he'd steered Hartmann into the mayor's chair against all the odds. Then seized the chance to do the same with the Prime Minister's office when the opportunity arose. His knowledge of the Danish political landscape was unrivalled, and at times underpinned by a quiet, frank ruthlessness. No one dared speak to Hartmann the way Weber did. Even then there were explosions.

'We're dealing with Zeeland,' Hartmann said. 'Karen's on to it.'

'Good. I've cancelled this insane visit to the docks. PET aren't happy with what's going on there. And they don't want us to talk about it either.'

'Uncancel it,' Hartmann ordered. 'Ussing will say I don't care about the homeless.'

'Screw Ussing.'

'We're on the back foot here, Morten! Ussing's using Zeeland to say I'm stealing from the poor to give to the rich.'

'Troels—'

'I'm going,' Hartmann said. 'Even if I have to catch a bus. OK?'

Nebel walked back in, clutching her phone.

'We're not going to get that denial.'

Weber pushed his heavy glasses up his nose.

'You mean the story's true?'

'The board would like it to be. They're trying to work round Robert Zeuthen. They think he's weak. Ordinary—'

'Listen,' Hartmann interrupted. 'Zeuthen's father promised he wouldn't move any more of the company abroad if we helped them out. Robert said he'd abide by that. If they renege on the deal now I'll crucify them . . .'

'No you won't,' Weber said. 'You won't be in a position to.'

Hartmann fought to keep a rein on his temper. It was at times like this that Weber was at his most valuable, and infuriating.

'So what happens?'

'If you give in and offer Zeeland more sweeteners Rosa Lebech won't climb under your sheets. If you don't our own people will start smuggling the daggers in here.' Weber wrinkled his fleshy nose. 'My guess is Birgit Eggert. She thinks the Ministry of Finance is beneath her.'

'If Zeuthen's ousted we've got to give them something,' Nebel said. 'I'll talk to the Treasury. It doesn't need to be much.'

'Christ!' Weber yelled. 'Why not hand Ussing the keys to the office now? Can't you see the posters? If you're rich vote for Hartmann. If you're not—'

'We do nothing until we know where Rosa Lebech stands,'

Hartmann said. 'I can bring her round. Tell PET I'm going to the homeless camp whatever they say. And . . .' He walked to the cabinets, pulled out a clean shirt and a new suit. 'That's it.'

Nebel glowered at Weber when Hartmann strode off to the bathroom to change.

'I don't like losing, Morten.'

'Who does?'

'Why won't he listen?'

The little man laughed.

'Because he's a politician. Troels only feels truly happy when he's living on a knife edge. He likes the rush. The thrill. The danger.' He got up, winked at her. 'Don't we all?'

Brix was on the phone the moment she got back to the docks. He wanted to know what PET were up to.

'They seem to think there could be trouble for Hartmann's visit. It wasn't my fault I missed the ceremony. You told Borch I was on the case.'

'True.'

'So will you explain to the OPA people why I wasn't around?'

'When I see them. Go along with whatever PET want.'

That makes a change, she thought, and ended the call.

Borch and Asbjørn Juncker were marching round with clipboards.

'We need every vessel in the vicinity searched,' the PET man said.

'There's only one off this dock,' Juncker replied. 'It's been done.'

He had a folder of pictures. Lund always relished photographs. She took them off him and started to flick through the set one by one. Stocky dead man. Middle-aged. One of the tattoos had a woman's name, east European forensic thought. Another on his right arm was indecipherable. What looked like a knife wound had taken out the middle letters.

A black Mercedes drew up and a tall, straight-backed man got out, balding with neatly trimmed grey hair. He introduced himself as Niels Reinhardt, Zeeland's link man for the case.

'Robert Zeuthen's taken a personal interest,' the newcomer insisted in a quiet, polite voice. 'He wants you to know we'll help all we can.'

'Is the security system back in place?' Borch asked.

'We think so.' Reinhardt looked uncertain. 'One of our IT subsidiaries runs it. They cover everything from office surveillance to some private properties.'

Lund ran through the obvious questions. Reinhardt said there were no labour problems since the last layoffs. No unusual ship movements.

'They must have been around here before they took down the security,' Juncker said.

'No. We would have seen any intruders,' Reinhardt insisted. He looked down the dockside, towards an abandoned area at the end. 'Unless they came in through the old Stubben facility. That's been dead for years.'

'I have to go back . . .' Lund began, but Borch was pointing to his car already.

It was a few minutes away, a desolate wasteland, rubble and abandoned containers by the grimy waterfront.

'We were going to build a hotel here,' Reinhardt said as he joined them. 'No money for it now . . .'

'Who comes here?' Borch asked as Lund wandered round the gravel lane, hands in pockets, tie to one side, kicking at pebbles and rubbish on the ground.

'Fishermen,' Reinhardt said. 'Birdwatchers.' A pause. 'Lovey-dovey couples sometimes I guess.'

'You said there were no ships.' Juncker was scanning the grey horizon. An ancient rusting hulk sat there looking as if it hadn't moved in years.

The Zeeland man scowled.

'No working ships. That's *Medea*. One of our old freighters. She's mothballed for scrap. We sold her to a Latvian broker but he went bankrupt.'

Borch took Juncker's binoculars. The vessel was a good half a kilometre offshore. He scanned it, offered the glasses to Lund. She shook her head.

'Is there anyone on there?' she asked.

'It's the law,' Reinhardt said straight away. 'Even an old hulk like that needs a minimum three-man crew. We talked to them last night. And this morning too. They said they didn't see anything.'

He looked round at the empty ground, the sluggish Øresund.

'They wouldn't here, would they?'

19

Lund stepped towards the water's edge, swore as her best boots went into a muddy puddle. A single cigarette butt lay in the dirt. Fresh. Unmarked by rain.

Borch was on the phone.

'If you want to go out there,' Reinhardt said, 'I can call a boat.'

Asbjørn Juncker couldn't wait. Borch came off the call.

'According to the coastguard a Russian coaster sailed along here last night. It's going to St Petersburg. We're talking to the authorities there.'

'Thanks for the offer,' she said to the Zeeland man. 'We don't need it.'

Juncker started squawking. She walked to the car. Borch and the young cop followed.

'We've got to go and look at that freighter,' Borch said.

'You can if you want.'

'I don't have time! Hartmann's coming here. We've got security—'

'I don't need this,' she cut in. 'Asbjørn . . . will you get in the car? We're off.'

He hesitated for a second or two then did as he was told.

Borch crouched down next to the driver's window. Didn't look much like a puppy at all then.

'I hope the job's worth it,' he said.

Robert Zeuthen had inherited the men who ran Zeeland. Hand-picked by his father. Loyal, as long as the old boss was around.

Kornerup, a portly, unsmiling sixty-year-old with keen eyes behind owlish glasses, had been chief executive officer of Zeeland for almost twenty years. He began the meeting with a new version of the presentation he'd been making ever since Robert Zeuthen took over the presidency of the group.

'Moving the shipyard east will reduce costs by forty per cent or more. We can play the exchange rates to finance the move. If we start planning today we should be able to start shifting operations within a year. For the bottom line . . .'

'This is old news,' Zeuthen broke in. 'We know the arguments. We agreed that ten or fifteen years from now it might be appropriate.'

Eleven men around the table, one woman. Zeuthen was the biggest shareholder. But he didn't have an outright majority.

'The world's moving faster than we thought,' Kornerup replied. 'This is a decision for the board. If Hartmann loses the election we've got a red Prime Minister who hates us, and a red cabinet behind him. They'll bleed us dry.'

'Which is why we support Hartmann,' Zeuthen said. 'Why it's against our interests to undermine him.'

'If he caves in and agrees some new deal, fine.' The faces around the table nodded in agreement with Kornerup. 'But let's not fool ourselves. We're just postponing the day. The world won't wait for us to wake up. I know this is hard. This is the company your father created. But if he were here today . . .'

'He'd defend every last Danish job,' Zeuthen said.

'Perhaps we knew him differently,' Kornerup said and smiled. 'Perhaps—'

'No,' Zeuthen said. 'Enough.'

Kornerup scowled.

'There's much more to discuss, Robert.'

'Not with you.' Zeuthen nodded to his PA, got her to walk round the table with the documents he'd prepared. 'Kornerup has spent a lot of time researching how to abandon Denmark. Not much on how best to betray this company.'

A murmur round the board. Zeuthen looked at each of them.

'What our CEO appears to have forgotten is that the newspaper which ran this drivel is thirty per cent owned by my family trust. Also . . .' A quick smile. 'The managing editor went to university with me. So it really wasn't hard to get the emails you sent to their business editor.'

Kornerup for once seemed lost for words.

'You planted these lies in order to bounce the board into this position,' Zeuthen added. 'Whatever the merits of the case for a move to the Far East – and I'm happy to discuss them at a suitable stage in the future – this is an individual act of disloyalty that can't be tolerated. You're in breach of contract, Kornerup, as you surely know. We may wish to pursue legal action.'

He nodded at the PA. She opened the door. Two security staff there in uniform.

'These gentlemen will see you off the premises now. We will send on any personal belongings once we've examined your files here to see what else you've been up to.'

He glanced round the table again.

'Unless the board feels it wishes to ignore the leaking of confidential documents to the media. And God knows what else.'

Silence. He waved at the door.

'What I did,' Kornerup said, getting to his feet, 'I did for the benefit of Zeeland. This company stands on the precipice, Robert. You'll drive it over and won't even notice until they come to shutter this place.'

In silence they watched him walk out. Zeuthen shuffled his papers, put them in his briefcase.

'I'm sorry. My daughter's been taken to hospital. I have to go.' A pause. 'Unless there's any other business?'

He waited. Nothing.

'Good,' Zeuthen said and left.

Hartmann got his driver to take him to the school in Frederiksberg where Rosa Lebech was setting up her election meeting. She was six years younger than him. A lawyer turned politician. Still dressed for her old profession: cream shirt, dark trousers, black hair tidy and neat. A striking woman, beautiful and businesslike at the same time. He'd first met her when he was mayor and begging for coalition votes.

She was married then.

Nebel waited by the door until she got the message. Then she left the two of them, with just a PET security guard to watch.

'We must stop meeting like this,' Hartmann joked.

'Like what?'

'Like politicians.'

'You think we should find a mattress and a couple of candles? You can get your security man to guard the door.'

Hartmann nodded.

'I like that idea.'

'You're an arrogant bastard. Why am I going through all this?'

Hartmann turned and nodded at the bodyguard. He took the hint and walked down the corridor.

'That's the kind of thing I mean. Troels . . .'

He grabbed her waist, kissed her hard, wriggled his fingers inside her shirt until he found flesh.

Lebech broke away, giggling.

'Rough sex with the Prime Minister of Denmark. It's not as if I've got anything better to do.'

His fingers grappled inside her blouse.

'That was a joke!' she cried. 'Cut it out.'

He stopped then, looked like a little boy robbed of his favourite toy.

Hartmann sighed.

'What is it?' she asked.

'It looks like the Zeeland rumours are true. Robert Zeuthen's with us. The rest of his board aren't.' A short, wry frown. 'I may have to throw something their way.'

She sat down. Politician again.

'How much of a something?'

'Big enough to make them think twice. Small enough to make sure you climb in bed with me.' The big, cheeky smile. 'Metaphorically speaking. I know I don't have to worry about the literal side of things.'

She didn't laugh.

'Don't push me too far. You think I can sell my people on the idea everyone pays except Zeeland? I'm the party leader. I don't own them. I won't even ask the question. No point. I already know the answer.'

'Maybe they'd listen if they knew you were headed for high office. A ministerial post. Something you'd like.'

'Prime Minister?' Lebech said. 'I'd love that job.'

He folded his arms, looked at her, waited.

'My hands are tied, Troels. I can't push my people any further than I have. Some of them think Ussing's a better bet. If Zeeland are packing up they're going to go. However hard you try to bribe them . . .'

She stopped. Karen Nebel had marched in tapping her watch.

'Think about it,' Hartmann pleaded.

'I have. Sorry.' Her hand crept to his knee. 'But this is politics. That's all. Remember.'

Hartmann tapped his nose, squeezed her fingers discreetly, and nodded.

Then got to his feet and for the benefit of the audience of one shook her hand, wished her well with the campaign.

'We'll keep talking, Rosa,' he promised.

Carsten Lassen, Maja's boyfriend, was a doctor in the university hospital. Zeuthen guessed it was inevitable she'd take Emilie there. Inevitable too that Lassen would be waiting for him in the car park with Maja and the kids inside their VW.

'What is it?' Zeuthen asked.

'It's an allergic reaction to the cat she should never have touched,' Lassen snapped. He had on his white doctor's coat and the surly expression he wore whenever Zeuthen was around. 'It'll be gone in a few days if she keeps using the medication. And keeps away from cats.'

Carl started growling through his dinosaur the moment Zeuthen arrived. Emilie smiled and waved. Zeuthen opened the back door and told them to get inside his Range Rover.

'No,' Maja said, closed the door again. 'We need to talk.'

It was a while since they'd had the argument about where the kids were going to live. Zeuthen didn't want a replay.

'If you think this is going to get you custody of them—'

'She's got a rash all over! What the hell's been going on?'

'I don't know. Do you?'

'Either you're lying or you're not taking care of her.'

'No.' He was struggling to keep calm. The kids were watching and these rows upset them. 'I know what they do when they're with me. We don't have a cat anywhere near the house. It's not like this is fatal . . .'

Lassen heard that and barged in.

'It could be serious,' he said. 'If you leave an allergic reaction unattended—'

'This isn't your business,' Zeuthen pointed out. 'They're not your kids.'

A white van pulled in close to them. For a moment Zeuthen thought Emilie had waved at someone. But that seemed impossible. If there was a smile it hadn't stayed. Carl and Emilie looked worn and miserable as the argument grew and grew.

'There's a legal agreement,' Zeuthen pointed out. 'You can't just take my children from me when you feel like it.'

'The law!' Maja shrieked. 'That's what you're threatening me with now? Are you going to bring down the whole of Zeeland on us? Will that make you feel like a man?'

The door of the little VW opened. Emilie walked over, stood between them, gave each an accusing look. Lassen retreated to the hospital entrance.

'I saw the cat when I played at Ida's. That's all.' She looked at her mother. 'I don't want to live with you and Carsten. Carl doesn't either. We want to be with Dad.'

Emilie walked to the Range Rover. Carl was there already. Maja ran after the two of them, voice breaking and that was a sight that tore at Zeuthen's heart.

The kids climbed in the back, were doing up their seat belts.

'Look,' he said to Maja, as calmly as he could. 'We shouldn't be arguing like this. Not in front of them. I've got something to do. You can go to Drekar with them. Stay there till I get home.' He shrugged. 'I don't know when I'll be back. I can phone you from the car if you like. So you know when to leave.'

Lund's home for the last six months had been a two-bedroom wooden chalet in the suburbs. It lay on a narrow hilly road overlooking the city, behind a small, bare garden she was trying to revive.

She listened to the radio while she washed up some plates for Mark and his guest. Hartmann was back in the headlines, expected to make a statement about Zeeland when he visited the homeless camp PET had specifically warned against. He always did what he felt like. Never worked with the police if he didn't want to, even when he was trying to win an election.

Not that this one was looking good. Ussing was whipping up his troops, warning of fresh concessions to the rich. The Centre Party, whose support would probably decide the outcome, was wavering.

Lund looked in the oven, realized she hadn't taken the film off the supermarket lasagne, grabbed it, took a pair of scissors to the brown plastic then put the thing back inside and wiped her hands on her jeans.

The phone rang. Mark said, 'Hi, Mum . . .'

'It's not easy to find. You need to turn left at the yellow house at the end of the—'

'We can't come. Eva's sick. Another time . . .'

She looked at the table. The bottle of good chianti. The new wine glasses she'd bought. The candles.

Brix had sent round her long service diploma and a bottle of champagne. There was an envelope from OPA.

'Is it bad?'

'No. Just a cold. See you some other time.'

He couldn't wait to go. She could hear that in his voice.

'Mark,' she said, suddenly desperate.

'What?'

'I know . . . I know I haven't been around the way I should. I was never good at . . .' Saying these things, she thought. 'I'm sorting myself out. You've got every right to be mad at me.'

Silence.

'Mark?'

'Yes?'

'I just want to see you once in a while.'

'Things are really busy.'

'How about tomorrow?'

'Tomorrow's not good.'

She sat down. Juncker's photos were on the table. A severed head. A dead mouth set in a grimace. An arm with tattoos. A woman's name probably. Something else, a short word, the middle letters removed by a bloody wound.

'The day after then. You tell me when.'

'I don't know . . .'

The first letter on the obscured tattoo was a capital 'M' in a gothic script.

'It'll have to be another day,' Mark said.

The last letter was a lower case 'a'. Probably five or six letters in the word, that was all.

'Mum? Hello?'

She picked up a pen, hovered over the photo.

'Another day, Mum. Are you there?'

'Yes. Another day. That's fine. Just let me know.'

Then he was gone and she traced in the missing letters. Spelled out the word.

She called Brix.

'Hi, Lund. Did you get the champagne and the note from OPA? They want you to start next week. No need for an interview. Congratulations I guess.'

'Do we still have people at the dock?'

'You called them off. Remember?'

'Well call them back. There's a ship there. *Medea*. I want to see it.'

'You said it was nothing.'

'And send a team out to Stubben. I'm on my way.'

She enjoyed an excuse to drive fast, didn't bother with the light on the roof. A boat team was waiting by the dock. So was Mathias Borch. He said Hartmann and his team were half a kilometre away at the homeless camp.

'Tell him to get out of there,' Lund ordered.

'I tried. How sure are you?'

She passed him the photo, the name 'Medea' outlined in ink.

'When the dock office contacted the ship this morning it wasn't the crew they talked to. I asked them to try again just now. No reply.'

Borch glared at her.

'If I'd known this I could have stopped Hartmann!'

Lund shrugged, climbed into the inflatable with Juncker and the two-man boat team.

'So stop him now,' she said, and the dinghy lurched off into the harbour.

Troels Hartmann was handing out plates of stew to quiet, scruffy men seated at camp tables in makeshift tents. The place stank of cheap food and open drains. Newspaper reporters mingled with camera crews, following him from serving to serving, asking questions he didn't answer.

As soon as a camera came close he smiled. Karen Nebel watched and didn't. She wanted him back in Slotsholmen for a press conference.

Then Morten Weber led in a couple of men bearing crates of beer. A cheer rang out. A couple of the hobos grabbed bottles, stood up and toasted Hartmann.

He grinned, walked out.

Was still smiling when he turned to Weber and said, 'Handing out booze to alcoholics, Morten. Very clever.'

Weber laughed.

'You astonish me, Troels. Such a stiff-backed puritan in many ways. And yet . . .'

He waited for an answer, didn't get one.

'PET want us out of here right now. They think there's an immediate threat.'

'We need to get back for the press conference anyway,' Nebel added.

Hartmann shook his head.

'All the hacks are here. Why put them to the trouble?'

He marched to the car, sat on the bonnet, beamed for the cameras, waved them on. Even the reporters were taken aback.

Men in heavy coats were gathering round. They had earpieces with curly leads winding down their necks and looked worried.

'So,' Hartmann said cheerily. 'Let's not waste time, shall we? You've got questions? Ask me now.'

'Shit,' Karen Nebel muttered, and listened as they kicked into gear.

Weber was talking to the noisiest of the PET officers, a man who'd introduced himself as Mathias Borch. She went over, listened. The conversation was getting heated.

'I told you to get him out of here,' Borch insisted. 'Will you just do it?'

'Troels is Prime Minister of Denmark,' Weber said with a shrug. 'Do you want to try?'

'Just a couple of minutes more,' Karen Nebel added, trying to calm things down.

'We had a dead body round the corner this morning,' Borch replied, grim-faced.

He took out his phone. Called out a name over and over.

Lund.

Sarah.

No answer. But Karen Nebel saw the look on Morten Weber's face and it was one she'd never witnessed before. White, shocked. Afraid.

'We'll help everyone we can,' Hartmann said loudly from the impromptu press conference. 'But we can only do that if we all contribute. That means Zeeland too. They get no special privileges. You hear that. No more favours.'

She didn't like ships. There'd been one in the Birk Larsen case. A dead man strung up on a rope. One more wrong swerve in the dark.

The two men from the boat team were looking round the deck of the *Medea*. Juncker had followed her inside. It was like a vast, dead iron cathedral and stank just like the other boat. Of age and oil. Freezing cold in the long metal corridors. No sign of a thing until they got closer to the bridge. Then Lund put out a hand and stopped him going any further, pointed ahead.

A long smear on the floor. Blood. The same on the wall. Someone badly injured had lunged along here.

Trying to escape, she thought. The old trick – seeing these things in her head – was coming back however much she fought it.

A man had been hurt in this place. Somehow he'd worked his way free. Jumped into the freezing water and tried to swim for his life.

Must have been terrified for that.

A cacophonous racket cut through the darkness. She almost leapt out of her skin. Asbjørn Juncker was fumbling with his phone, bad rock guitar passing as a ringtone. Lund snatched the thing from him, turned it to silent like hers. Someone had been trying to reach her ever since they got on the *Medea*. She could feel the handset trembling in her jacket. That could wait.

Torch out, high in her right hand, they went down a set of stairs. Storage tanks. Blood smeared on the side. In the corner a dead man, naked except for a pair of grubby underpants, knife wounds all over his torso. Wire binding his arms to chest, his ankles.

'Lund,' Juncker whispered, walking round, torch and gun in his hands, pointing all the time.

She looked. Another corpse. Same condition. Knife wounds. Wire. They'd been tortured.

'You don't need a weapon, Asbjørn.'

'The docks office told us there were three.'

'Yes. The other one we found in pieces this morning. Whoever did this is gone. Too smart to stick around.'

On the bridge the only light came from the screens still alive on the control desks. There was a laptop near the wheel. She looked at it. A document was open. It seemed to be about Zeeland's computer systems.

Lund checked for a signal, told Juncker to call Brix and bring in a full team. Then phoned Borch.

'I don't know what's going on here,' she said, and told him about the bodies and the breach in Zeeland's security.

He listened, said nothing. Mathias Borch was a star at police academy. Smart and dedicated. But never a fast thinker.

'Hartmann's not there any more, is he?'

'He's throwing an impromptu press conference. Why don't you answer your phone?'

'I've been in the hold of this bloody ship. Whoever they were they're from here.'

She started walking around in the dark, torch in hand, looking.

On the wall at the back there were photographs. Lots and lots plastered on the painted metal.

She stopped. Politicians and industrialists. A face next to a news clipping: Aldo Moro. Former Prime Minister of Italy kidnapped by the Red Brigades, held captive for fifty-five days then shot and dumped in a car in the street. Next to him a news story about Thomas Niedermayer, a German industrialist seized by the Pro-visional IRA, pistol-whipped, murdered then buried beneath a junkyard outside Belfast. That story was more recent and Lund couldn't stop reading. Niedermayer's widow had returned to Ireland ten years after his death and walked into the ocean to die. Then both their daughters committed suicide. One constant stream of misery from a single brutal act . . .

'I'm looking at pictures of kidnapped politicians here,' Lund said and didn't even know if Borch was still listening. 'Dead ones. You've got to get Hartmann out of there right now.'

The PET people barged into the crowd of hacks, almost picked Hartmann off the bonnet of the car then threw him into a security van alongside Weber and Karen Nebel.

Flashing lights. Sirens. The three of them sat together on a bench seat, two armed officers opposite as the vehicle lurched out of the docks back towards the city.

'They can't treat me like this,' Hartmann complained. 'I won't allow it.'

'The police found two dead men in a ship offshore,' Weber said. 'Another this morning. Some photos of kidnapped politicians. They can.'

He got a vicious, spiteful glare in return.

'Lund's handling the case,' Weber added.

Silence between the two men.

'Who's Lund?' Nebel asked.

'There's history,' Hartmann said. Then to Weber. 'Talk to the Politigården. Not Brix. Go over his head. I don't want her near.'

'Is someone going to tell me?' Nebel asked.

'She made a big mistake once before,' Weber said. 'Nearly cost us an election. It's not happening again.'

His phone rang. The van bounced over rough ground, finally found some decent road.

Nebel turned on Hartmann.

'You should never have made those promises, Troels. You can't invent policy on the hoof. You don't know what Zeeland's response might be. You need to let me handle that side of things. I wasn't hired to watch you scoring own goals.'

He looked amused by that.

'Is that what I've done?'

'I can't work in the dark. I know you and Morten go back years. I don't. Keep me in the picture.'

Hartmann pretended to be puzzled.

'What exactly do you want to know?'

'Are you screwing Rosa Lebech?'

He rolled back on the seat, didn't look at her.

Morten Weber came off the phone.

'Zeeland have just put out a statement denying the article. It looks as if their CEO will be suspended. Robert Zeuthen is going on the record to say he personally, and Zeeland as a corporation, support the government's recovery plan all the way.'

Lights outside. They were entering the heart of the city. Slotshol-men. Soon they would be back in the warm offices of the Christians-borg Palace.

Hartmann laughed. Grinned. Weber wouldn't look at her.

'You both knew that was coming, didn't you?' she asked.

'Morten's got friends everywhere,' Hartmann told her. 'Maybe a little bird told him the paper were going to dump on Kornerup.' He slapped Weber's knee. 'Not that I want to know.'

The van pulled into the courtyard in front of the palace. Two officers came and opened the doors. Hartmann didn't move.

'We need a press release, Karen. You phrase them so carefully. So beautifully. I wish I had that kind of skill myself.'

A hint of a smile at that.

'But let me see it first, won't you?' he added. 'Then pop a copy in Ussing's pigeonhole with my warmest regards.'

She went ahead of them into the building. Weber stopped him on the steps, waited till the security men were out of earshot.

'Is she right? Are you popping something in Rosa Lebech's pigeonhole?'

Hartmann's face fell.

'I don't have time for this,' he said and started walking.

Weber's arm stopped him.

'I zipped up your flies once before with all that Birk Larsen nonsense, Troels. We were damned lucky to get out of that in one piece. Don't ask me to do it again.'

'I'm a single man. A widower. I work every hour God gives for this country. I've a right to a private life. A right to be loved.' Then, almost as an afterthought. 'I had nothing to do with that girl.'

'Oh,' Weber said, with a nod. 'It's love, is it?' He waited. No answer. 'In the middle of an election campaign? Which we may well lose anyway. With all this Zeeland crap, Lund hanging around . . . and you shagging the leader of the party we need to save our skin.'

Hartmann groaned.

'Show some faith, Morten. I'm on top of this. Rosa's bringing the Centre Party to the table. They'll back me as Prime Minister. Zeeland's fixed. And you're going to make sure Lund comes nowhere near.'

He put a hand to Weber's back and propelled him towards the palace.

'Aren't you?'

Maja Zeuthen had never liked Drekar. Before Robert's father died they lived in a former workman's cottage in the grounds, had the joy of bringing two beautiful children into the world in a small, tidy home meant for a lucky gardener.

There they'd loved one another deeply.

Then the weight of the company fell on his shoulders, and with it a growing sense of crisis. Not just Zeeland's. The world's. They moved into Drekar. Lived beneath the dragon. Got lost in its sprawling floors and cavernous, empty rooms.

Being the Zeuthen who ran Zeeland was a burden too heavy for him to share. She'd offered. Lost the battle. With that defeat love waned. The arguments began. As she drifted away he spent longer and longer in the black glass offices down at the harbour.

And when he was home they rowed. Two little faces watching from the door sometimes.

It was almost eight. The servants had put dinner on the table. She'd eaten with Emilie and Carl, trying to make small talk. Noticing the way they went quiet whenever she tried to introduce Carsten into the conversation.

He was younger. Struggling a little with his medical career. As Robert said they weren't his kids either and sometimes that showed in an uncharacteristic coldness and ill temper.

They cleared away the dishes themselves. Told Reinhardt to go home. He had a wife. Grown-up children. A house near the Zeeland offices by the waterside. But still he stayed around the mansion, watching, worrying. Robert almost saw him as an uncle, a fixture in the house when he was a boy.

Emilie and Carl went upstairs. To play. To watch TV. Mess with their gadgets.

She sat alone on the gigantic sofa, staring at the huge painting on the wall: a grey, miserable canvas of the ocean in a deadly gale. When they were splitting up Emilie said she hated it. The thing made her think of where grandpa had gone. Had Maja stayed it would have vanished before long.

Emilie came down, dressed in her blue raincoat, pink wellies and a small rucksack with childish pony designs on it.

'Where are you going?'

She didn't blink, looked straight at her mother.

'To feed the hedgehog.'

'The hedgehog? Now?'

'Dad says it's all right.'

'Dad's not here.'

'I won't be long.'

'I'll go and get Carl,' Maja said. 'He can come with us.'

Emilie sat down on the stairs. She was gone by the time Maja was back with her brother.

'Emilie!'

She tried not to sound too cross.

Then Robert phoned.

'Emilie's gone off somewhere. She said to feed a baby hedgehog.'

He laughed and she liked that sound.

'She's been doing that every night lately. We've got to work out what kind of pet to give her. I don't think she'll settle for a stick insect.'

'No.'

Did he realize he'd made her laugh too? Did she mind?

'Reinhardt found out about the cat,' she said. 'The gardener said he'd seen one outside the fence. Near a brook somewhere. Emilie was hanging around there one time.'

'Outside the fence?'

There was a brittle tension back in his voice then.

'That's what he thought. It's no big deal, Robert. Carsten said if we keep using the cream she'll be fine in a few days. I'm sorry I flew off the handle.'

'She shouldn't go out like that. We've got security for a reason.'

A short silence. Then he said, 'I'm coming home.'

Maja walked to the front door and wondered how long she'd have to wait this time. It was a tall, elegant reception area. The only ugly thing was the block of blue flashing lights and small TV screens for the security system that ran round the house and out into the grounds.

Eight monitors in all, mostly looking out onto trees moving in the winter wind, bare branches shifting restlessly.

As she watched one screen went blank except for a blue no-signal message. Then the next. Then, in a rush, the rest.

Photographs. Dozens. On the walls. On the floors.

Monochrome faces Lund didn't know. A Canon SLR camera with a telephoto lens. Documents on ship movements. What seemed to be a graphic description of the Zeeland security network, covering multiple locations. Industrial units, offices. Private premises too.

'I don't get it,' Juncker said, shining his beam on the camera. 'Why would someone hole up here, kill three sailors, all to take a pop at a politician?'

Lund was barely listening. On a desk in the corner she'd found a set of fresh colour prints, straight out of the inkjet there. Some were aerial shots off the web. Lawns and trees. A satellite view of what looked like a grand mansion.

An ordinary-looking man next to a shiny Range Rover. About forty, in a suit. He seemed deeply miserable.

'That's Robert Zeuthen,' Juncker said. 'The Zeeland bloke.'

She flipped over the print, looked at the next one. Zeuthen going to his car, two small shapes inside. There was a date stamp on the print. Four thirty that very afternoon.

'I don't get it . . .'

'So you said, Asbjørn.'

He went quiet after that.

Lund looked at the printer. A red light was flashing. Out of paper, mid-job. She picked some sheets off the desk and fed them into the tray.

The thing rattled and whirred. Then started printing again.

Out they came. Shot after shot.

Every one of them was a girl in blue jeans and denim jacket. Blonde hair. Not smiling much except when she saw her father and seemed to think he needed that.

Then the last one. Up close. This wasn't from a long lens. She was there, laughing for whoever held the camera. A kitten in her arms.

'This isn't about Hartmann at all,' Lund said, and got back on the phone.

Zeuthen slewed the big car on the gravel, left the door open as he ran into the house. The front door was open. Maja was there shivering in her green parka.

Wide-eyed, scared, hurt, she said, 'The police called. They said we had to stay inside. They were sending—'

'Where are the kids?'

'Carl's upstairs. Emilie . . .'

Her face said it all.

Zeuthen ran inside, got a torch, walked out into the grounds, flashing the beam around.

She came and joined him.

'How long?' he asked.

'She said she was going to feed the hedgehog. You'd told her it was all right.'

'How long?' he repeated.

'Forty minutes. An hour.'

Drekar was surrounded by a sprawling estate of ornate gardens, ponds, a lake, a tennis court, a croquet lawn, a picnic area. Then woods, stretching back to the coast.

A high security fence ran round everything, part of the extended surveillance network connected to the Zeeland offices by the docks.

A thought.

He marched back into the entrance hall, stared at the dead screens on the wall.

Then out to the drive. One of the garden staff was nearby, wondering what was going on. Zeuthen grabbed him, asked about the hole in the fence, near the brook. Which brook? There were several.

The man had no good answers. Zeuthen was getting desperate. A nine-year-old girl, lost in the vast gardens and forest around her home. It was like a fairy tale gone bad. Except most fairy tales went that way, for a while at least.

Blue lights down the long drive. Sirens. The two of them watched a car brake hard to stop by his Range Rover. There were more behind.

Two people got out. A young, tall skinny man with a scared face and an anxious demeanour. And a woman, plain, long dark hair tied back behind her head. Sad, shining eyes that seemed to be looking everywhere as she walked towards them.

She pulled out an ID card. A white car with *Politi* on the side swung to a halt nearby, then another. He could hear the relentless slash of an unseen helicopter, its blades tearing the night to pieces.

'Police. Sarah Lund,' she said. 'Where's your daughter?'

Robert Zeuthen turned towards the dense forest, trying to find the words.

That was where she always went of late, for no good reason. He should have noticed.

Through the dark wood where the dead trees gave no shelter Lund walked on and on. She'd set a sweeping path of officers to spread out into the dense, dark areas round the mansion. Left Juncker there to liaise with the rest of the crews arriving from the Politigården. The Zeuthens were no ordinary family. A threat to them was a challenge to the state itself.

She'd tried to tell Robert Zeuthen what to do. It was no use. The man was beyond her, ranting and running, dashing his torch beam everywhere.

Lund followed, dragged Zeuthen out of a low ditch he called the brook when he stumbled into it. Trying to talk. To reason. To see.

After a while they reached a tall, heavy fence. Open rough ground on the far side. There was a hole cut at the base, big enough for a child to crawl through.

He jerked at the wire, made the gap bigger.

'What is this, Robert?' she asked. 'You need to tell me.'

'She did whatever she wanted.'

'I need to know!'

It came out then. How someone had seen her here feeding a cat. How the surveillance system had gone down, not that it would have caught a hole like this in the first place.

Then he was on his hands and knees, scrambling through the gap, muddy suit, filthy smart office shoes, grubby hands.

Lund followed. Somewhere behind she could hear a familiar deep voice calling on her to stop, to wait.

Beyond the wire lay a saucer in the long grass next to a carton of milk.

She didn't bother trying to talk to Zeuthen any more. The bare trees, the cold dark night. The empty, indifferent countryside. None of this was new.

After a while he stopped, let out a shriek of shock and pain. Catching up she saw what was in his hands: a single pink wellington boot, the kind a young girl would wear.

'Please,' Lund said. 'Put it down. Don't touch anything.'

She didn't need to ask the obvious question: was this Emilie's?

More lights now. Brix still barking at her to stop, to wait.

Watching Zeuthen blunder on she wondered how often she'd heard that. How many times to come.

'You have to let us do this,' Lund said.

It's our job, she thought. It's all we do.

The helicopter was close above. She glanced back. A long line of officers, torches out, coming towards them. A tall figure that could only be Brix in front, bellowing.

Then she bumped into something, was confused for a moment.

It was Zeuthen. He'd stopped in front of a low thorn bush, torch on the naked branches. A child's rucksack, ponies patterned on the side, sat in the branches. He reached for it.

Enough. She ordered him to get back, elbowed him out of the way when he didn't, pulled on a pair of latex gloves, reached out and extracted the thing from the branches.

That took a while. It had been thrown there, deliberately. By the time she got it out Brix was with them.

'Do you have any idea where the girl is?' he asked.

Zeuthen couldn't talk. His wife turned up breathless, struggling to speak.

Then Juncker. He said they'd found tyre tracks down a rough lane a short way across the field.

'And this . . .' He held out an evidence bag, shone his torch on the contents. A small silver bracelet. 'It's got her name on it.'

Maja Zeuthen said nothing. Her husband could only stare at the tiny object in the young cop's hands.

A dog barked.

Brix went to the Zeuthens.

'I've got the army joining the search teams. We've got a helicopter in the area.'

'I can hear it,' Lund muttered, struggling with the zip on the rucksack.

'We're doing everything we can . . .'

The woman started sobbing. Zeuthen reached out for her. She pulled away.

Finally Lund got the rucksack open. Looked inside. Nothing but a cheap smartphone. Gingerly she took it out.

The screen came alive straight away. It was set up for a video call she guessed. All she could see was what looked like a van interior:

pale plain walls. Then a figure came in from the left and she knew he was looking at her. Black hood. Slits for eyes.

'I want to speak to whoever's in charge of the investigation,' he said in a cultured, measured voice.

They crowded round, looking, listening.

'Who is this?' Lund asked.

'Your name and rank, please.'

'Sarah Lund. *Vicekriminalkommisær*.'

'The girl's OK.'

'I want to see her.'

The screen went blank. He'd put the phone to his ear.

'I regret that's not possible.'

'What do you want?'

'Nothing unreasonable. I know these are tough times. But debts are debts. I'd like to collect what I'm owed.'

'A debt?' Maja Zeuthen shrieked. 'What the hell's he talking about?'

The voice laughed then.

'I hear we have an audience. Good. Let's all be friends. The question you need to answer's a simple one. How much is a girl's life worth? What exactly will you give to get her back?'

'Tell us what you want,' Lund repeated.

A long pause. Then, 'I just said, didn't I? Are you listening? I'll call tomorrow afternoon. On this number. I talk to you and you only, Lund. I look forward to your offer.'

'Yes, yes,' she said quickly. 'It's important you let me speak to Emilie. We need—'

One click. That was all. She looked at the phone. He was gone.

A bitter wind was winding through the dead trees, scattering its chill breath across the bare land.

Maja Zeuthen, eyes bright with fear and fury, standing, shaking, tipped back her long blonde hair, began to howl.

Two

Morning in the red-brick castle called Drekar. Robert Zeuthen woke on the sofa, still in his filthy suit and shoes.

For a long minute he was convinced this was a dream. A stupid, unbelievable nightmare. Then he looked round. At the painting she hated. The marks of a million muddy boots on the carpet, now being quietly cleaned by one of the staff. Knew this was real.

Knew too that he was on his own. Maja was gone, back to Carsten Lassen's little flat, a different life with a different man.

He got up, went to Emilie's room for no good reason. Looked at the empty bed. Picked up the doll she loved. Gazed at the animal posters on the wall. Stood by the window. Shook for a while. Cried looking out at the lawns covered in tyre tracks. Wiped his eyes on his grubby sleeve.

Reinhardt stood at the foot of the stairs, presentable as always in a black suit, dark tie, white shirt. He briefed Zeuthen on what the police had told him. It wasn't much.

'Does Maja know all this?' Zeuthen asked.

'She's been calling them all night I gather.'

'We need to talk to security and finance about the ransom. Fix a meeting.'

'That's happening already, Robert. PET are involved. We have to follow their lead.' He hesitated, then added, 'Whenever we've had cases like this in the past Kornerup handled them. He's very . . . adept.'

Zeuthen didn't understand.

'What do you mean . . . cases like this?'

'There was an incident in Somalia. Not long before your father died. Kornerup kept it out of the papers.' A wry expression on Reinhardt's long, bloodless face. 'He always knew how to manipulate them I suppose. If we could—'

'I fired Kornerup. We deal with this ourselves. The men that were killed . . .'

'Latvian. Our people are offering their families support.'

Zeuthen was looking at his clothes. Realizing he needed to change. To do something.

'If I'd known about the cat this would all have been different . . .'

Reinhardt put a supportive hand to his shoulder.

'Let's just get Emilie home, Robert. That's what matters now.'

Morning in the white stone fortress that was the Politigården. Lund had snatched a couple of hours sleep in a bunk then found time to go home briefly, get some fresh clothes. Prepare for the long day ahead.

The cheap smartphone stayed with her all the time. In the shower. When she pulled on the case clothes from before: a pair of jeans, heavy boots, a sweatshirt and one of the patterned wool jumpers she'd started to buy a lifetime ago when she took a young Mark to the Faroe Islands on holiday, to try to make amends for the divorce.

That worked.

Plugged into a charger, the handset sat on the desk in homicide while she watched Borch and Juncker going through photos from the *Medea*, the kidnapper's, the police's own. Brix stood over them silent, brooding. Dissatisfied.

The call had been made through the Internet and was untraceable. A stolen white van had been recovered near the docks. Emilie's other pink wellington boot was in there and her prints, no one else's. There was no new significant evidence from the ship. Every sign the kidnapping was the work of a lone operator who had prepared the abduction thoroughly in advance.

Around eleven the previous night she'd left Robert and Maja Zeuthen bickering and snarling at each other. Lund doubted either had slept. When she looked at the phone log she knew it. Constant calls, to Brix, to his superior Ruth Hedeby. To the Ministry of Justice and the Prime Minister's office too. Hartmann had issued a state-ment of sympathy along with a declaration of gratitude to Zeuthen for supporting the government. Then turned his terriers on the police demanding a quick solution.

As if we'd be looking for a slow one, Lund thought as Hedeby passed on the news.

When Nanna Birk Larsen went missing her parents, an ordinary working-class couple from Vesterbro, had no one to turn to. The Zeuthens seemed spoiled for choice. Not that it helped.

One slim piece of evidence: tyre tracks near the abandoned van suggested the kidnapper had moved Emilie into a larger vehicle.

'He could be three hundred kilometres away by now,' Juncker grumbled.

'It's a kidnapping, Asbjørn,' Lund said patiently. 'He's asking for money. Even if the girl's dead he'll still want to collect.'

Brix asked, 'What do we know about the van he left?'

'It belongs to a bunch of Serbian crooks,' Lund said. 'They run a prostitution ring. We pulled in the ones we could find. And some of their girls.'

He looked interested.

'It's not them,' she added. 'There's no trace of her anywhere near their brothel. They say the van was stolen three nights ago. They never reported it of course but . . . they wouldn't.'

They had four Serbs in custody and a line of trafficked women being steadily interviewed a few doors down. Lund had spent half an hour with the men already.

'The pimp kept a set of keys in the van,' she said. 'Places he used to house women when he brought them into the country. We're going through them.'

She'd been reading some background material on the Zeuthens. Divorce about to come through. Plenty of bitterness between the two of them. They had fifty-fifty custody of the children. She was living with a doctor from the university hospital, Carsten Lassen. No one else involved in the break-up. The cause seemed to lie principally with Robert Zeuthen's workload at Zeeland.

'No love lost between Zeuthen and his wife, is there?' she noted. 'Did you hear what she was screaming at him when we left?'

If you'd let her come home with me like I asked.

'People blame each other sometimes,' Borch said. 'It's a way of not blaming yourself. Fools no one.'

Lund closed her eyes for a second, wishing they could see this the way she did.

'It was an organized kidnapping. If he hadn't taken Emilie last night . . .'

Brix gave her a caustic glance.

'You should have checked out that ship when you first saw it.'

'That was my decision too,' Borch lied.

She wasn't listening. Just staring at the school photograph of Emilie Zeuthen on the desk, the one that seemed to be everywhere now – in the papers, on TV. Blonde-haired, smiling, staring straight at the camera with an intelligent, studied candour. Next to the picture were forensic shots of the men on the boat. Half-naked, like the victim found in pieces at the dock.

'Why did he torture these men?' she asked. 'What did he want from them?'

No one answered.

Borch threw some more photos on the table. Shots of a kitten. Emilie holding the creature in her arms, smiling for the camera.

'He must have groomed her well. Sarah . . .'

Lund barely heard. The tortured men bothered her.

'Sarah! You've got to keep that phone charged and with you all the time. We don't know when he'll call. Just agree with whatever he says. Keep him talking. We can trace—'

'We already know he's using the Internet,' she pointed out. 'He was smart enough to take down the entire Zeeland security network. Do you think he's going to give himself away with a phone call?'

'Better hope so,' Juncker grumbled. 'We've got bugger all otherwise.'

Sometimes she wanted to scream.

'Think about what he said. He never used the word ransom. He wanted an offer. A debt paid. What's he talking about? Who do Zeeland owe money?'

Borch seemed to take the point.

'They've got a turnover of three hundred billion kroner. Maybe they're arguing the toss over a heating bill somewhere. How are we supposed to—?'

'If it's just about money why doesn't he say how much he wants?'

'Ask him when he calls,' Brix suggested. 'Here . . .'

He passed over an email from Reinhardt at Zeeland.

'You wanted to know what the crew had been up to. According to the company the only one who'd been ashore in the last week was the mate. He asked for permission to leave because he'd been called as a witness in a court case. These places you're checking—'

'What court case?'

'I don't know. He was the one you found in bits in the junkyard. These lock-ups . . .'

Brix took a call. Held up a hand to be quiet. Finished it.

'Robert and Maja Zeuthen are here,' he said. 'We've got to brief them.'

'I'll deal with it.'

When she got to the door Borch came and stopped her.

'Sarah?'

He had Emilie's phone in his hand.

'Thanks,' Lund said and took it.

Morning on the island that was Slotsholmen, the seat of government power in Denmark. Breakfast in a quiet room near the Parliament building. Hartmann, Rosa Lebech, Anders Ussing. Coffee and pastries. One item on the agenda: a truce over Zeeland and Zeuthen.

'We need to keep them out of the election,' Hartmann said. 'For their sake, for the sake of the investigation, I don't want this to become part of the debate.'

Ussing, a gruff, coarse man who could always find the populist thread, shook his head.

'You're telling me I can't mention Zeeland? Are you mad? This is a major political and economic issue.'

'There's a family involved, Anders,' Lebech broke in. 'We must condemn the act and show them our support.'

Ussing was bull-necked, with a ruddy face and a sarcastic grin. Once a docker himself.

'I can see why you want to sweep it under the carpet. Zeuthen's kid gets snatched while PET spend the whole day nannying you around.'

'This is irrelevant,' Hartmann insisted.

'Prove it. I want a report from PET and the police on what happened yesterday at the dock. Give me that and I'll keep quiet about Zeeland. For now.'

Hartmann tried to keep a hold on his temper.

'You don't have any right to a report—'

'Maybe not. I still want it. Some justification for this truce.' A quick, ironic smile. 'After all we wouldn't want people thinking Rosa and I were simply dazzled by your handsome looks and irresistible charm.'

He got up, nodded at them.

'I'd like that report before the debate tonight,' Ussing added then left.

Rosa Lebech wouldn't look Hartmann in the eye.

'He's just trying to get between us,' he said, trying to take her hand across the table.

She pulled her fingers away.

'We're going to have to postpone the announcement. I can't get my people on side if Ussing's going to entangle you in this case. It happened once before—'

'The Birk Larsen girl was nothing to do with me! Nothing.'

'I know,' she said quietly. 'You washed off that mud. But new mud sticks. It's never the deed that kills you, Troels. It's the lie.'

'What lie?'

'You're going to have to work to distance yourself from this. I heard that policewoman Lund's on the case. Ussing knows that too. Give him his report. Shut him up. Then we can announce our support.'

Back in the office he broke the news to Karen Nebel. She didn't seem surprised.

'The press have been calling already. They've got wind of something. They want to know if the deal's off.'

'Stall,' Hartmann said. 'Just tell them . . .'

There was a newspaper on the desk. Tabloid. Most of the front page was taken up by a school photograph of Emilie Zeuthen. Nine years old. Long blonde hair. Beautiful.

Nanna Birk Larsen was a decade older. Same colour hair. Lovely too. Her picture haunted Hartmann every day for nearly three weeks when he was fighting for control of Copenhagen.

'Troels,' Nebel said and came and touched his arm. 'Don't let this get to you.'

'It won't,' he promised.

Maja Zeuthen came first, walking wide-eyed through the east European prostitutes the team had brought in for questioning, her estranged husband not far behind. An interesting couple, Lund thought. She had the damaged beauty of an out-of-work actress, wore casual clothes, not cheap but not smart. Zeuthen looked as if the first thing he put on each morning was a freshly pressed white shirt and tie then a clean, expensive suit. Not a man to turn heads. Not a man to run one of the country's biggest corporations if the role hadn't fallen to him by birth.

She took them to an interview room where they sat next to each other by the barred window in the wan morning light. Separated or not they were Emilie's parents. It was important they approached this problem together.

The phone was on the table. She made sure they knew that.

Then Lund took them through as much as she could. Told them about the van. How the evidence on the *Medea* suggested the kidnapper acted alone and was well prepared.

Zeuthen asked to see pictures of the vehicle. Lund hesitated.

'I don't want to have to call your superiors,' he said.

Brix had made it clear. These two got special treatment. So she pushed across the photos and asked, 'I don't suppose you've seen it before?'

To her surprise Zeuthen nodded.

'There was one like it in the car park at the hospital yesterday. I saw Emilie. I thought she waved at someone.'

Lund got a time, called in Juncker, told him to go and check it.

Then she showed them photos of the clothes they'd found in the van. The boot. A pair of jeans. A pink sweater. Maja Zeuthen blinked back tears and nodded.

'These are definitely Emilie's?'

'Of course they are,' Zeuthen replied. 'So he made her—'

'You can't read anything into it,' Lund interrupted. 'A kidnapper usually changes the appearance of anyone they abduct.'

She remembered the way Maja Zeuthen had looked at the women outside.

'There's no sign anything happened in the van. Nothing violent. Anything else.'

Zeuthen pulled himself together.

'I need to know the names of these men you've arrested. Where they live.'

'They're Serbs. They run a prostitution ring. The van was stolen from them. They're probably not connected.'

The mother got up and stood by the window, biting at her knuckles.

'I need to know . . .' Zeuthen started.

'He said he'd return Emilie in exchange for a ransom,' Lund cut in. 'These people aren't in that kind of business. They're . . . unpleasant. But legal.'

'So what are you doing?' Maja Zeuthen came and sat down again, stared across the table, at the phone. 'Just sitting around waiting for him to call?'

Zeuthen reached for her hand. She pulled away.

'Maja—'

'Stay out of this, Robert! If Emilie had come home with me!'

Lund let the silence fall between them. Then she said, 'This man had been planning to kidnap Emilie for some time. If it wasn't yesterday . . .'

She turned to Zeuthen.

'When he calls it's important you have an offer for him. Something. It wouldn't be wise to try to stall him.'

'I'm talking to PET,' Zeuthen said. 'To my own people.'

'*We're* talking to them, Robert,' Maja Zeuthen snapped. 'It may be your money but she's my daughter too.'

That hurt and she didn't even notice. Zeuthen got up, said thanks, shook Lund's hand with the diffident grace of a bank manager.

'The moment I know something we'll be in touch,' she said.

He nodded. The mother stared at the ceiling, mouthed a silent curse.

'This . . . debt he talked about,' Lund added. 'Do you have any idea what he might mean?'

'No,' Zeuthen said. 'Do you?'

They walked out through the ranks of waiting hookers. One of the day team came in and said there was no indication the *Medea*'s mate had testified in any court case recently. And Lund's mother had been on the phone, asking her to ring back. Something important.

Thirty minutes later she still hadn't returned the call. Juncker had got CCTV from the hospital car park. It was the kidnapper's van, watching the Zeuthens. No clear picture of who was at the wheel.

Mathias Borch came out of interviewing the Serbs and their women, sat down at the facing desk, looked to make sure the phone was next to her. It was almost eleven.

'Anything?' Lund asked.

'Some tips on sex toys. Not much use to me. This isn't a leap year, is it?'

He was married, two kids. Hadn't talked about his family much. Didn't look happy the one time she asked.

'You?'

'I talked to the courthouse. The mate didn't testify that day. He had a meeting with one of the deputy prosecutors. I've been leaving messages. He hasn't got back to me. So . . .'

She got up, grabbed her bag and coat.

'What if our man calls?'

The phone was on the desk.

'He said this afternoon,' she answered, picking up the handset. 'I won't be long.'

A voice from the back of the room cried, 'Hi, honey!'

Lund closed her eyes for a moment. Turned, saw her mother marching towards them.

'Honey?' Lund asked, then realized. Vibeke was heading for a beaming Borch who'd stood up, nodding and saying all the nice things he used to say, then planting kisses on both cheeks.

'You never told me Mathias was here! I haven't seen him in years. Not since . . .'

Juncker was watching this avidly.

'Not since you two . . .' Vibeke added. 'How long ago was that?'

'A while,' Borch said and made the kind of genteel small talk that had always infuriated Lund since it came so easily and with such obvious sincerity.

It was Vibeke who cut it short. She took Lund to one corner.

'I'm sorry to barge in like this.'

'This isn't a good time, Mum.'

'Here.' She pulled something out of her bag. 'I bought you a book on gardening. You don't exactly have green fingers. That little place of yours could use some flowers.'

Borch was eavesdropping. He looked amused. Lund dragged her further away.

Her mother couldn't take her eyes off him.

'I always thought Mathias was the one,' she whispered. 'Not that stuck-up creature you married.'

Lund pulled on her coat, ready to go.

'We need to talk about Mark,' Vibeke said quickly.

'What do you mean?'

'I don't want things to get worse between the two of you.'

'Things are fine. I invited him and his new girlfriend to dinner. They couldn't make it. That's all.'

Vibeke put a hand to Lund's shoulder, came close.

'He was really young when you two divorced. It was never easy afterwards. That horrible case. The one with the young girl . . .'

You're only interested in dead people.

A twelve-year-old Mark had spat those words at her during the Birk Larsen case and they haunted her still.

'You've been so busy with work, Sarah . . .'

'Why are you here?' Lund demanded and the whole office heard that.

Vibeke rarely shrank from speaking her mind. But she looked reluctant then.

'Mark asked me to say . . . he wants you to leave him alone. No phone calls. No contact.'

Lund felt cold. Stupid. Alone.

'He'll come to you when he's ready,' Vibeke added. 'Give him time. I'll talk to him.' She kissed Lund's cheek, smiled at Borch, looked at the door. 'It'll work out. Just not now.'

Then she left.

Borch came over and said, 'We could pop round the corner for a coffee if you like. I wouldn't mind a break from—'

'I'm going to the courthouse,' Lund said and that was that.

Hartmann finished the first morning event, an address to an office group near Kastrup airport, then headed for his blue and white campaign coach. Karen Nebel said the press were getting more aggressive over the story of the alliance with Rosa Lebech.

'We can't leave this festering all day. She's got to stop sitting on the fence.'

'She will,' he said, getting sick of this conversation. 'Give it time. Make sure Ussing gets some kind of report from PET. Anything. Write it yourself if you like.'

'Little busy for that, Troels. Birgit Eggert wants to talk.'

Eggert was the Finance Minister. A busy, scheming woman who'd coveted the party leadership for years.

'I can do without that, thanks.'

'Too late,' Nebel replied.

Eggert was by the coach dressed in a long blue wool coat, a campaign badge bearing Hartmann's photo on her lapel. Tall, grey hair cut short, a mannish, domineering face, she was in her mid-fifties, ten years older than Hartmann. But the ambition still burned.

She marched over, congratulated him on the campaign. Whispered in his ear, 'We need to talk. Alone.'

On the way back into the city the coach pulled in where she asked. By a green field next to the road. The two of them got out and walked across the skimpy grass.

'You remember this place, Troels?'

'Not exactly.'

'This was our business park. The one we set down in the manifesto for growth.' She laughed. 'I suppose that's one of the positive things about recessions. You don't look back so much. Just a bunch of bright hopes and memories. No one holds us to our past promises any more, do they?'

'They should,' he said. 'We're going to make things better.'

'And you're the man for the job. You've resurrected the party. People love you.' The smile. 'Most of them anyway.'

'I'm really busy, Birgit. What's this about?'

'We need to make sure we have Zeeland on board. Without them our economic strategy's in ruins.'

He shook his head.

'You read Zeuthen's statement, didn't you? The story was rubbish. Kornerup's gone . . .'

'Robert Zeuthen doesn't own Zeeland. He can't call all the shots. Kornerup didn't hold down a job like that under Zeuthen's father without having the stomach for a fight. You've told Rosa Lebech we'll drop cuts in social security . . .'

Eggert had opposed that from the start – and lost. He was surprised she wanted to bring up the subject and said so.

'The point is, Troels, you've given her all these concessions and she's still playing hard to get.' A pause. 'Politically anyway.'

Hartman thought about Morten Weber's warning: if a coup was to come from inside the palace it would, he said, be led by this woman.

'Ussing's tricks are putting her under pressure from her own party. She'll deal with it. Today.'

Eggert looked at the barren land, not at him.

'Rumour has it you're listening to more than Rosa's policies. Is that true?'

Hartmann glowered at her.

'Did you interrupt our election campaign to ask about my love life?'

'I don't give a damn about your love life,' Eggert snapped. 'I don't want to see everything we've built destroyed for no good reason. Ussing's not playing tricks. He's offered Lebech a deal. Full partnership in government if he wins. A senior ministerial post for her in return.'

No response.

'So she didn't tell you?' Eggert asked with a smile. Hartmann was ostentatiously checking his watch. 'Do you know the reason politics and love don't mix, Troels?'

'I'm sure you're about to tell me.'

'Sooner or later you find yourself having to choose. One above the other. Which will it be?'

Hartmann laughed.

'If you have to ask that you really don't know me at all. How's the economy, Birgit?'

'It's shit.'

'Best go and do something about that, don't you think?'

The courthouse was in Nytorv square, a grand building fronted by six Ionic columns supporting a classical portico. There was an inscription about justice on the facade and a flagpole jutting out of the top. As a cadet she'd walked up the staircase behind to see the view from the roof. Of late she'd spent more time in the adjoining jail, reached by a couple of sealed passageways across a line of grand arches.

Before she left the Politigården she'd gone through the Ministry of Justice staff database and looked at the deputy prosecutor's records and ID photograph. Peter Schultz was a middle-ranking official who'd worked for the ministry for ten years. He was forty, a thin, ascetic man with an artist's beard.

Lund rarely got on well with lawyers. They only wanted to talk to the police on their own terms. She had no reason to think Schultz would be any different.

As luck would have it he was on the courthouse steps, beneath the portico, when she arrived, saying goodbye to another member of the legal team. Lund interrupted, explained that she was the one who'd been leaving messages for him.

'Busy day,' Schultz said and eyed his colleague with an amused look. The other man walked into court, tapping his watch.

'Me too. Like I said I need to talk to you about a mate from a Zeeland ship. The *Medea*. He was the one killed down by the docks . . .'

'I got your message.' He gestured at the building. 'But I'm due in here and judges don't wait.'

'This is to do with the kidnapping of Emilie Zeuthen and three murders. I think the judge will understand.'

'You don't know him.'

She went and stood in front of the entrance to stop him.

'You met the mate?'

'Briefly.' He looked a little nervous. 'I don't know why. He showed up and demanded to talk to me. He couldn't speak Danish. His English wasn't good. He claimed he was owed money for a court appearance a while back. He was going home and he wanted it.'

Schultz waved to someone going inside, promised he wouldn't be long.

'The case in question never came to court. So there was no money.'

'That wasn't the reason he gave Zeeland. He wasn't going home either.'

Schultz's slight shoulders twitched for a moment.

'That's what he told me.'

The lawyer dodged round her and headed for the doors.

'What case?' she asked.

'Can't we do this later?'

'You want me to tell the Zeuthen family that?'

'A young girl had run away from home in Jutland somewhere. She committed suicide. The mate and a couple of others found the body in the sea near the dock. They were interviewed by the local police.'

'When was this?'

'I have to go. Call me tomorrow.'

'I need the names of the other men. Maybe they were the ones on the *Medea*. Schultz. *Schultz!*'

By then he was pushing at the green wooden doors, going into the building. One short smile and he was inside.

Lund's phone rang, her own, not Emilie's still safe in her pocket.

'I think we've got something,' Asbjørn Juncker said. 'One of the hookers says she thought she heard a child crying in a block near where she was staying. Industrial unit in Vasbygade.'

Her car was around the corner. The place was ten minutes away.

'I'll meet you there,' she said.

Reinhardt had spoken to PET and Zeeland's security people. Now he was briefing Robert and Maja Zeuthen in the executive offices.

'They both want you to hold back on the money. Whatever you offer he'll probably reject it. You need room to manoeuvre upwards.'

Maja scowled.

'It's not about money. It's about getting Emilie back.'

Zeuthen, shirtsleeves, tie still firmly at his neck, nodded.

'PET know that too,' Reinhardt insisted. 'They're not trying to talk you out of offering a ransom.' He looked at both of them. 'I said that would be pointless. They're trying to keep the negotiation process as brief as possible. For that you need to make him think he's won.'

'How much?' Zeuthen asked.

'As little as possible. He wants you to make the offer. It's just tactics. Go in low—'

'It's money that caused all this!' Maja Zeuthen cried. 'Don't be so cheap with my daughter's life.'

'It's money that's going to get her out too,' Zeuthen said.

'The man asked for an offer. He wants to know what Emilie's worth to us,' she went on. 'So tell me, Robert. How much?'

He went to the window, looked out at the docks and the city beyond.

'I want her home,' Maja insisted. 'I don't care how much it costs you.'

Zeuthen waited for her to say more. Then, when she stayed silent, said to Reinhardt, 'Give him what we discussed. If it's not enough then I'll raise it. Use my personal funds. This affects no one else.'

He got his jacket.

'Tell PET and the police,' he added. 'And the bank.'

He walked out through the offices, aware that every eye was on him. Went to the lift, apologized as he brushed into someone on the way. Stood alone watching the lights flick over from floor to floor. Got out in the car park.

Sat in his shiny Range Rover. Looked at himself in the mirror. An ordinary man, trapped inside a business suit, imprisoned by a pressed shirt, a staid tie, a set of values that had been impressed upon him since birth.

All he wanted was family. A loving wife. Happy children. Not wealth, not power. And now he was on the brink of losing it all.

In the deserted underground car park, in the rank stink of petrol fumes, the bland, emotionless face in the mirror mocked him.

Something foreign rose in Zeuthen's throat. Fury and temper. Sealed inside the vast car he ranted and screamed, hammered his fists on the leather wheel, stamped his handmade shoes in the footwell.

Let all the anger out, ripped his tie from his neck. Became for one brief moment a different man.

But it didn't last. And the world hadn't changed when the sudden fury receded. He rolled back his head. Knotted his tie in place after a while. Then slowly, carefully, edged the Range Rover out into the traffic and headed for the Politigården.

Lund was at the industrial unit in Amager when Brix called with the news of the Zeuthens' ransom offer: ten million kroner.

'What's that in euros?' she asked.

'I don't know. About one point four million or something?'

'It should have been in euros,' Lund said. 'He'll want to get abroad easily. Anyone's going to stick out a mile turning up in America or Italy or somewhere lugging ten million kroner.'

'Well that's what's on offer!' Brix barked. 'Sorry you weren't in the conversation. Borch said you were out chasing some old court case.'

'I'm in Vasbygade. Someone heard a child cry here last night.'

It was a grim place. She could scarcely believe even Serb traffickers would keep their slaves in a hovel like this. Bare industrial units, little more than concrete containers, set back from the busy road towards the airport. Easy access to fast exit routes everywhere. She could see why the kidnapper used it.

Juncker was scrabbling around at the back of the building. A couple of other officers were checking outside.

'Anything?' Brix asked.

'Not that I can see.'

'Zeuthen's coming in here to talk about the ransom. I want you there.'

'Fine.'

The young cop was on his hands and knees, looking at some marks on the floor. They were by a large filing cabinet. It looked as if it had been moved recently. She was starting to like Asbjørn Juncker. In spite of his boyish appearance he had a stubborn, awkward streak.

'What is it?' Lund asked.

He didn't answer. Got to his feet. Dragged on the drawer handles.

'There's something behind here,' he said and heaved the thing forwards.

It fell on the floor with a crash that echoed round the empty room. There was a narrow space behind. An iron grille over what looked like a low door.

'Get some tools,' Lund ordered.

The phone rang. She pulled it out. Looked at it. Dead screen.

Swore. Realized it was a different, more juvenile ringtone. Got Emilie's.

'Good day, Lund,' he said in the same flat, polite voice from the night before. 'I'd like your offer.'

'You're early.'

'And you're wasting time. You can't trace the call. I'm not an idiot.'

She walked outside, blinked in the unexpected hard winter sun breaking through the clouds.

'Zeuthen's willing to give you ten million kroner. Unmarked bills. Untraceable.'

Silence.

'How does that sound?'

Still he said nothing.

She moved away from the road and the traffic noise.

'We'll guarantee you safe passage. You tell us what to do. The family just want Emilie home. That's all. Well?'

'Well what?'

'Is it enough?'

He laughed.

'You're asking me whether this sum corresponds to the debt I'm collecting?'

Lund looked up and down the row of units. The place was decrepit. Most of the tenants probably bankrupt.

There was something about the way this man spoke. He sounded cultured, educated. And quite detached.

'Since I don't know what the debt is I can't ask that, can I?'

'What do you reckon the girl's worth?'

'I think you're pushing your luck. We're not stupid and if you hesitate we will find you. This is the best you can do. Take the offer. Give us the girl. Then get the hell out of Denmark.'

She thought he was laughing again. Then he said, 'OK.'

'So how do we do it? Where do we bring the money?'

'There's a train from Nørreport station at 5.23. Line A towards Hundige. I want you to deliver the money. If I see anyone else she dies.'

That was it.

Juncker came up and asked, 'Are we on?'

The campaign coach had been flitting from photo-op to photo-op around the city. Then Rosa Lebech called and asked for an urgent meeting somewhere discreet. Hartmann picked a quiet spot near the beach in Amager. On the way Karen Nebel took a call from Dyhring, the head of PET. Hartmann sat opposite, watched, listened to the tone of her voice.

'Good news?' he asked when she was done.

'PET say a handover's been fixed. Zeuthen's putting ten million kroner into the pot. The kidnapper said yes.'

'Let's hope it works.'

There was a beep from her iPad on the table. She looked at her email.

'Ussing says he's fine with the truce for now.'

'For now?' Hartmann asked.

'We don't expect any favours, do we?'

'I suppose not. When does the exchange take place?'

'Some time after five. You don't expect them to give me the details, do you?'

'I want to know the minute this is done.'

Nebel came round and took the seat next to him. Blue suit. Blonde hair tight behind her neck. Make-up perfect. She looked just like she had on the TV.

'A word of advice,' she said in a low voice so no one else could hear. 'Be careful with Rosa Lebech. She has her own agenda . . .'

'We all do. Has Birgit Eggert got to you too?'

'Rosa's got nothing to gain by coming out for you right now. If I was her I wouldn't.' She gazed at him, made sure he was looking, briefly touched the sleeve of his shirt. 'However I felt about you.'

Hartmann had wondered about Nebel a few times. She was attractive. Had a nervous hunger that made him think. Her marriage had fallen to pieces under the strain of government work. There'd been moments, late at night, when it so nearly happened. But she was staff. Like Rie Skovgaard when Hartmann was fighting to become mayor. And that hadn't worked out well at all. Office affairs were close, difficult to untangle. And Karen Nebel wasn't the type who'd take the inevitable gentle rejection easily. That last thought had finally stopped him. But only just.

'Why does she need another meeting?' Nebel asked.

The long, empty beach was approaching.

'Best I find out,' Hartmann said.

A couple of minutes later he was walking with Rosa Lebech, both wrapped up against the biting wind. In summer it was hard to find a space here. The hard November meant they were quite alone.

'If we keep meeting like this I need to buy one of those camper vans,' Hartmann said. 'Gas cooker and a pull-down bed. In fact that might not be a bad idea anyway.'

She wore a fashionable fawn coat, a red silk scarf round her neck. Looked tired, he thought. They probably all did.

'Ussing's fine with the truce.'

Lebech nodded. Perhaps knew this already.

'That's good news.'

'So when do you make the announcement?'

She looked at the beach. The sand whirling around in the wind.

'Tonight, during the TV debate would be good,' Hartmann added.

'We need to wait. Tonight's not good. It'll look better in the morning.'

'We can't keep on postponing this, Rosa.'

'There's only one story at the moment. The Zeuthen kidnapping. It's stealing the show.'

'Hopefully the show, as you call it, will soon be over,' he said, and tried not to sound too hard.

No answer.

'Has Ussing got to you?'

'Not me,' she said. 'To the deputy chairman. A few others. He's good at splitting people.'

'You can't seriously allow him to use a dreadful crime like this for his own ends.' He watched her closely. 'Can you?'

A moment then she said, 'You're right. I'll put my foot down. We'll throw our weight behind you after the debate tonight.'

'Thanks,' he said.

The campaign team were watching from the coach. He wondered whether to care. Then thought better of it. Placed a hand lightly on her waist, smiled. Left it that.

One hour to go. A team had assembled in the Politigården, ready for the handover. Borch was placing the money into a black holdall watched by Robert Zeuthen, his wife and Brix. Lund sat in the corner of the room, going through files on a computer.

'We could throw in a GPS,' Borch said. 'That way—'

'No!' Zeuthen insisted. 'Just do what he says. I don't care about the money.'

Lund sensed an argument brewing, came over to the table, looked at Borch. He got the message.

'How will he hand over Emilie?' Maja Zeuthen asked.

'We don't know,' Lund told her. 'He never said.'

Brix explained how the drop would be monitored from the Politigården, by radio, through access to nearby CCTV cameras.

'You're welcome to stay and watch,' he added.

'No,' Maja Zeuthen said. 'I want to come. It's my daughter. I can't just sit here, waiting.'

Her husband nodded.

'We won't get in the way.'

'You can be close by,' Lund said, looking at her phone. A glance across the table. 'If that's OK.'

Brix grunted then took the Zeuthens outside into the corridor. For a briefing Lund assumed.

'He didn't like that, Sarah,' Borch said.

'When this is over I'm warm and comfy in OPA. Should I care? That deputy prosecutor. Schultz. He knows more than he's letting on. And he still won't return my calls.'

'Maybe he's . . . busy?' Borch suggested.

'I'm telling you there's something wrong. This man wants a debt paid. We still don't know what that is.'

'Let's just get the girl out of there. Then take a look at Peter Schultz.'

She thought about that.

'Did I mention his first name?'

'Yes,' Borch said quickly. 'You did. Have you talked to your son?'

'Not now.'

She looked at the bag on the table. Ten million kroner. It was going to be heavy.

'You know what always brought me round when I had an argument with my folks? They used to bring me a pizza. And some beer. Always worked.'

'I remember,' Lund said.

In the TV studio, behind the stage for the coming debate, Anders Ussing was pacing among the monitors and crew. Yelling for

Hartmann. So loud Karen Nebel fetched him, left the two men alone.

'You need a tie, Anders,' Hartmann said. 'Some make-up too.'

'To hell with the make-up!' Ussing had a couple of sheets of paper in his hand. 'This nonsense you sent me . . .'

Hartmann picked up the papers. He hadn't seen the report on the previous day's incident at the docks but he knew what it contained. Not much.

'You said you wanted a report. I told them to get you one. And still you keep coming up with something . . .'

'You can forget your truce.'

Hartmann glared at him.

'Let's talk frankly. You're pissed off you tried to turn Rosa Lebech's head and failed. Don't bring the Zeuthen family into this.'

'Bullshit! I want a report that details everything. Not just the pieces that suit you.'

Hartmann screwed up his eyes and said, 'What?'

'There's a memo about this. Goes back a week. I know . . .'

'Listen.' He prodded the burly Socialist Party man in the chest. 'I don't have to give you a damned thing. You already know more than you should. Let's go and debate the real issues and leave this to the police.'

Ussing didn't move.

Then he grinned.

'The real issues? Yes, Troels. You're right. Let's do that.'

The station sat in the middle of a busy road: buses came and went either side. Long steps leading down to the underground Metro lines. Lund had the money on her back in a heavy rucksack. The place was busy. Commuters going home. People out for the night.

The train turned up on time. Lund got on board. Mathias Borch stepped in one door along. Glanced at his phone. They worked on the Metro. Wi-Fi too. They could stay in touch. So could the kidnapper.

One minute out of the station he called.

'Get off at Sjælør station and take line E north.'

'I need to talk to Emilie.'

But he was gone.

*

Brix had sent Robert and Maja Zeuthen to the central station, positioned them over the main hallway with three officers kept in constant touch by radio. Zeuthen knew this was a blind. They'd no reason to think the kidnapper would come to the busiest transport hub in the city. The Politigården wanted them out of the way, somewhere they didn't interfere with things. The rational side of him saw the logic. But Maja didn't. Nor, in his heart, did he. They both felt responsible, guilty over her disappearance. There was an urgent, pressing, stupid need to do something, even though in truth both knew there was nothing they could achieve beyond the obvious.

Find the money.

Give it to Lund.

Pray this would work.

Now they stood side-by-side watching the crowds move steadily through the station hall.

And all he could think about was the previous night. The chances he'd had to change things. To steer away from the unseen monster waiting outside in the wild ground beyond the bare trees and the failed high fence.

'Sometimes she'd come back and her shoes were wet,' he said, and hardly dared to look at her. 'I could have asked why. I should have known she'd been somewhere she shouldn't.'

Maja Zeuthen didn't look at him. Kept staring at the crowd below them. Ordinary people, bored, tired, disgruntled, heading home, knowing that nothing would happen to them that day.

'If I'd just let you take them with you . . .'

She sighed. Gave him a look he couldn't interpret.

Then she said, 'I'm sorry I didn't trust you, Robert. I know you did the best you could.'

'It wasn't enough, was it?'

'We'll find a way through this.' She was looking at him then, and for the first time in months he saw no hatred, no resentment in her eyes. 'We've got to. For Emilie's sake. For Carl's.' A pause. 'For ours.'

He looked into her clear blue eyes and wondered. She reached out and for one too-short moment touched his hand, squeezed it.

'We're rehearsing being divorced, aren't we?' she said. 'We need to get better at this.'

Zeuthen nodded. Felt more miserable than ever and was determined not to show it.

One of the officers with them was on the radio. He saw he was being watched. Ended the call. Shook his head: nothing.

The train rattled through the interior veins of Copenhagen, beneath the main station, rolling and grumbling.

Lund scanned every face. Focused on two in particular. A young man in black who sat down opposite, smiled, an obvious come-on. An older, shambling figure in an anorak one bench along, eyes on the floor.

Didn't look at Mathias Borch perched near the end of the carriage.

I thought he was the one.

Her mother had no right to think that. It wasn't her decision. But she did. And must have had a reason.

Pizza. Beer.

That wasn't such a bad idea either. A peace offering. A pathetic way to say: sorry for all these years of neglect.

The young man opposite kept smiling. Lund looked straight at him.

The phone rang.

'Get off at Vesterport,' the voice said. 'Go to the opposite platform.'

She looked at the red station indicator in the carriage.

'We're nearly there.'

'I know. The train leaves straight away. If you want to save this kid you'd better get a move on.'

Lund stood by the door. Waited. A shriek of brakes. She walked out onto the platform. On the other side the train was there already. Doors opening, beckoning. Borch was behind her. She looked down the platform. Didn't move.

Mark was there. Tall Mark. Eighteen pushing nineteen now though in her head he was still the lovely little boy she'd taken to the Faroe Islands once, tried to spoil, to convince he'd always be loved, the perfect, adored son, however much her parents loathed one another.

You're only interested in dead people.

That wasn't true. Or if it was the change came later, with the Birk Larsen case. Unwanted, unsought, or so she'd like to think.

He wore a scruffy parka. She wanted to buy him a new one the moment she saw it. But he was smiling, talking to a pretty young woman, fair hair, perky, happy face. Older than him. Lund saw that straight away.

Then she turned and Lund saw her huge belly. The way her hands curved round it, loving the child inside.

That was why he never came of late. Lund knew it in an instant. Understood too.

A voice from somewhere, now and long ago.

'Sarah! Hey!'

Borch was on the train, leaning back against the door to stop it closing.

Mark and his girlfriend got on. Puzzled, Borch stepped towards her.

The doors began to close. Lund leapt for them. Stabbed at the button. Watched as the train started to move, picked up speed. Saw Mark and his girlfriend flash past, eyes locked on one another.

Felt the ground start to slip beneath her feet.

Borch's hand stopped her falling.

'What happened?' he asked.

Head reeling.

'I'm sorry . . .'

A young girl. A kidnapper. Mark. The woman with him.

'What . . . ?'

'It was my son,' Lund said and was back with Borch then, trying to think this through. 'Shit . . .'

The phone rang.

Before he could speak she said, 'I missed the train.'

'Not very good are you, Lund?'

'Isn't that why you want me?'

Nothing.

'I've still got the money. We can do this.'

'I know. Talk to the people with you. Tell them to close down the Metro. Stop the trains. Cut the power. After that I want you to walk down the tunnel. The direction of the train.'

She looked at the black hole, the lights disappearing down its maw.

'I'm supposed to go down there?'

'You want Emilie back, don't you? Keep walking until you see a steel staircase on the right. Go up it. I'll be in touch then.'

'Listen—'

'You don't have time.'

Ussing went for the jugular two minutes into the debate. The subject was supposed to be economic policy.

'We need a broad-based coalition to get us through this crisis,' Hartmann said. 'A partnership based on trust and mutual respect.'

'What trust?' Ussing broke in. 'What respect? Your deal with the Centre Party's in tatters. They don't support you over Zeeland. They don't believe a word you say.'

'I'm not going to address Zeeland tonight for obvious reasons,' Hartmann responded. 'We can only guess at the pain the Zeuthen family are going through at the moment. I will not allow that to be the subject of political point-scoring. The Centre Party and I have a solid relationship . . .'

'That's over!' Ussing crowed. 'When Lebech finds out you've been deceiving us all.'

Hartmann shook his head and asked, 'About what?'

'About this!' Ussing raised the printed pages he'd brought. 'Your so-called report on the course of events leading up to Emilie Zeuthen's kidnapping.'

'This is not a subject for public debate . . .'

'It must be, Hartmann. While you doubled the protection around yourself this little girl was snatched from her parents. Even though your own Justice Minister met with Special Branch a week ago and discussed a specific threat to kidnap a member of the Zeuthen family. I've an internal memo from the Justice department that makes this crystal clear.'

Another wave of Hartmann's report.

'And there's not a word of that in here. A defenceless Emilie Zeuthen was seized while you strutted round Copenhagen begging for votes surrounded by the armed guards who should have been keeping her safe. How do you explain that?'

'I've already said,' Hartmann replied. 'I will not allow this family's pain to become an issue for public debate.'

The interviewer cut in.

'You don't want to comment at all on his accusation? Really?'

'I have complete confidence in PET and the police.'

Hartmann glanced at the edge of the studio. Rosa Lebech was supposed to be there, ready to make an announcement of the alliance the moment the debate was over. He could see her arguing with Karen Nebel. Shaking her head. Then walking away.

'That,' he added, 'is all I'm prepared to say.'

It took two minutes to shut off the power and the trains. Then Lund let herself down onto the track, took out her torch and walked into the cold, dank tunnel, past iron pillars, past old graffiti, keeping to the maintenance pathway on the right.

The line beyond the arches was still live. From time to time a train would lurch down it, all lights and noise, faces at the window. Lund had no idea how far she'd walked. Was beginning to wonder if she'd passed the point. Then the graffiti began again, a sign that this part of the tunnel was accessible to those in the know. On the right, rusty and old, a narrow ladder ran down from above.

She put her hands to the cold railings, placed her right boot on the first rung and began to climb.

After a minute she felt cold air, heard the noise of traffic above. The manhole cover was off already. Not much more and she was out. Maintenance cones and fencing surrounded her. She was in a cobbled square, yellow city buses running to one side.

The phone rang and he said, 'Can you see a fourteen bus?'

It was just coming to the stop. She ran towards the doors.

'You want me to get in?'

'No. Just throw the money inside.'

She stopped, looked at the crowd of people inside. Ordinary commuters. No easy way to follow. Then Lund took off the rucksack, walked to the entrance, pushed it onto the floor and watched as the doors closed. Straight away the bus pulled out into the street, the bag by the legs of strangers.

'Good,' he said.

Lund looked around. He saw every move.

'Where's the girl?'

Silence.

She knew where she was now. Nytorv square where she'd been that morning, badgering a reluctant Peter Schultz. Fast footsteps running. Mathias Borch coming towards her across the cobbles.

'Where's the girl?' Lund asked again.

'Look up, Lund,' the voice said in a bright, laughing tone. 'You should always look up. You need to learn that.'

The courthouse. The tallest building in the square.

Phone still to her ear she cricked back her neck, focused on the portico with its bold and visible inscription about justice. Saw nothing. Then at the peaked pinnacle, by the flagpole . . .

'What is this?' she whispered.

'Read what it says.'

She never took much notice of the words above the building. This was a place for business.

Med lov skal man land bygge.

With law shall the nation be built.

'Good joke, don't you think?'

Borch close by, scanning the square.

'I told you to come alone, Lund.' Severe and judgemental now, like a schoolmaster who'd come across mischief. 'Next time do as I say. Think twice about paying small change for the life of a little girl.'

The portico was illuminated by floodlights on the handsome building. Something drifted down from the summit. A handkerchief, floating like a giant snowflake in the winter night. Borch turned his torch on the portico. Lund's breath froze in her lungs.

High up, crouched at the summit of the pitched roof, was a man. She could just make him out, something just visible round his neck.

'Remember this,' the voice said, and then the figure on the building fell forward, a rope snaking behind him.

Tumbled down like a stone, shrieking, arms wheeling, legs flailing, stopped from crashing to the Nytorv cobbles by the noose round his neck and the long rope above.

A crack like a gunshot. A neck snapping.

Lund yelled something, saw the hanged man start to swing, a slow pendulum between the Ionic columns, the slight and bearded figure of Peter Schultz turning all the time.

In the street a woman screamed. Staff started coming out of the courthouse doors. Mathias Borch was running frantically round the arches, towards the adjoining alley, calling in backup.

A long time ago Lund had walked up onto the roof of the courthouse too. Any number of ways out of that place.

She was starting to get a picture of this man. Someone who could shut down a giant corporation's security system at will. Penetrate the underground tunnels of the city's transport system. Be one step ahead of them, always.

Gone already.

Thirty minutes later the square was swarming with police. A foul-tempered Brix. Borch desperately looking for leads. The sweep of the courthouse had produced nothing but a poor CCTV image of a man in a hood, entering through the west roof. The ransom money had been found untouched on the bus.

They'd got Schultz's body down from the rope. Now the front of the building was being sheeted off for forensic, and to keep out the cameramen and TV crews.

'He probably got in from the rooftops and left the same way,' Borch said.

'And there was no one on the bus?' Brix asked.

'There was never anyone on the bus,' Lund said. 'He didn't want the ransom.'

'You spoke to him . . .' Brix had listened in silence to her account of what happened at the station. 'Is he going to call again?'

'I guess. I need a car.'

'You guess?' His voice rose then, and that was unusual. 'What about Peter Schultz?'

'The mate from the Zeeland ship got in touch with him. He wanted money. Something to do with a court case. A suicide. Young girl. The mate and the other two crew members testified. We need to look into the case.'

Brix took a long, deep breath.

'Why didn't I know about this?'

'Because it only came out today,' Borch broke in. 'There wasn't time.'

'I need a car,' she said. 'I want another look at this place Juncker found.'

The homicide chief's long arm shot out.

'You're not going anywhere until I get that phone.'

'He said he'd only talk to me.'

'The phone!'

She muttered something and handed it over.

'Now you can go,' Brix added. He nodded at Borch. 'You too.'

On the way Lund took it out on the PET man. Gave him a hard time about the phone. They had no trace whatsoever except that he was using a mobile provider, routed through London.

'How the hell does he know all this stuff?' she barked. 'And why weren't you . . . more use?'

That made him mad.

'More use? Do you think I'd have spotted a man on the roof with a noose round his neck? Did you?'

They got to the car. She kicked the door for the hell of it.

'And,' Borch added, 'it wasn't me who stopped on the platform to say hi to someone either, was it?'

They got in, Lund in the driving seat.

'So,' Borch said. 'Mark's going to be a dad. Congratulations.'

There was a white police van blocking the way. Lund stamped on the horn.

'Why won't they move?'

'With a desk job at OPA, working nine to five, you'll have a lot more time to be a grandma too.'

She was minded to tell him to fuck off but when she looked she realized he meant it.

'Funny way to find out,' Borch said with a friendly shrug. 'He probably wants to keep it quiet until he's ready.'

'She looks nine months if she's a day!'

Another bang on the horn.

'Oh,' he said.

'It's probably down to her anyway. She looks older than him. Doesn't want me to know my eighteen-year-old son's about to become a father.'

Borch nodded.

'Couldn't be anything to do with you. Could it?'

Lund just stared at him.

'My advice,' he went on bravely. 'For what it's worth, which probably isn't very much . . . buy them a present. Something a bit better than pizza and beer. Go and congratulate them. Bring it out into the open. Try and—'

'You know nothing about me, Borch. Nothing about my life.'

That offended him.

'Really? I remember standing outside that little flat in the freezing cold, all my stuff in the street and not the first clue what I'd done wrong. Not a—'

'We were too young. We should never have moved in together.'

'Yeah, well . . . thanks for telling me now. I never thought that. My dad put down the deposit on that place.'

She banged her fist on the horn again.

'Do I still owe you money?'

'Technically, yes. I'll let it pass.'

'You're too kind.'

'No I'm not. Here's the truth. Anything emotional . . . you want to run away. Me, Mark, God knows what else . . .'

'Well at least that worked out for the best, didn't it? Now you're the happy family man. A wife. Two kids. Nirvana . . .'

Silence. She looked at him. Borch was staring out of the side window. He looked wretched.

Another slap of the horn and this time the van moved.

After the debate Hartmann summoned his Justice Minister Mogens Rank for an urgent meeting. PET found the nearest secure location: a government office in a bank building close by. There was frost on the ground by the time the campaign coach pulled up outside. Morten Weber was there already, anxious to brief Hartmann on the murder at the courthouse.

'What the hell has this got to do with Emilie Zeuthen?'

'The police don't know,' Weber said. 'The ransom wasn't picked up. They don't have a clue where the girl is.'

Karen Nebel came off the phone.

'Birgit Eggert's kicking up a stink. She wants a meeting. She's demanding we respond to Ussing's claims.'

'Is she?' Hartmann muttered.

Rank was waiting for them inside. A dapper man in his thirties with ginger hair and thick glasses he fiddled with constantly. Hartmann had appointed him out of gratitude for the help he'd provided during the last campaign. He was dry and nervy, but seemed a safe pair of hands.

'I can explain,' Rank said the moment Hartmann entered the small, secure room PET had found for them.

'Zeuthen's daughter's been kidnapped. A public prosecutor murdered. An explanation would be good, Mogens.'

He sat down at the table. Rank took the chair opposite. Weber and Karen Nebel joined them.

'I absolutely understand your anger, Troels. We're investigating where Ussing got this information. I expect answers—'

'I want to know if it's true! The inquest can come later.'

Rank squirmed on his chair.

'Well . . . if you'll give me the chance to explain . . . things have been very busy of late—'

Morten Weber banged the table.

'Did you know there was a threat to kidnap a member of the Zeuthen family? Yes or no?'

Rank didn't appreciate being shouted at.

'No,' he answered. 'Not in those specific terms. We received an anonymous email. I've asked Dyhring along. He's head of PET. His department received it.'

Then Rank called in a heavyset, middle-aged man in a civil servant's winter coat. He had close-cropped dark hair, a neatly trimmed beard. Sat down, handed round a set of bound reports.

'The sender was untraceable,' Rank continued. He tapped the documents. 'It calls itself an indictment.'

Weber snatched a copy, then Nebel and Hartmann. Thick type, page upon page.

'We get lunatic threats all the time,' Dyhring said. 'Nothing in this stood out. It's a diatribe against the state, against the government.'

'Left-wing rhetoric and doomsday nonsense,' Rank cut in. 'It's the work of a madman. How were we to know . . . ?'

Hartmann skimmed the first page, a rant about how the government was controlled by big business.

'It concludes by saying the guilty must be called to account,' Dyhring said.

'Is Emilie Zeuthen mentioned?' Hartmann asked.

'No,' Dyhring said firmly. 'Zeeland is several times. But the Zeuthen family . . . not once.'

Karen Nebel pressed a manicured finger on the report.

'And this didn't ring any bells?'

'We made a risk assessment,' Dyhring replied. 'There was no specific mention of the family. The threat came in right after you called the election.' He looked at Hartmann. 'It seemed to us to make more sense to focus on the safety of politicians.'

'Which is what he wanted you to think,' Weber suggested.

'That's possible,' the PET man agreed. 'We've no way of knowing.'

'You're paid to know!' Weber yelled. 'Jesus Christ if—'

'Morten.' One glance from Hartmann silenced him. 'Here's the position. We received no direct threat to the Zeuthen family. Had we known, PET would have acted. Ussing's pushing his luck.'

'I like that,' Nebel said and made some notes.

'It still doesn't explain how Ussing got to know of this before I did.'

Dyhring nodded.

'He claims the document was in his office mail at Parliament. We're looking into it.'

Hartmann picked up a copy of the evening newspaper. A new photo of Emilie on the front page.

'There is a link, is there?'

'Definitely,' Dyhring agreed. 'It was sent from the PC on the Zeeland ship. This is him.'

Weber threw the report back across the table.

'Is the girl still alive?'

Dyhring scowled.

'The policewoman screwed up with the handover.' He looked at Hartmann frankly. 'Lund. I think you know her.'

'Is the girl alive?' Hartmann demanded.

'We don't know. We don't even know if he'll call again. It's possible there's a connection with an old suicide in Jutland.'

'Mogens?' Hartmann asked. 'A suicide now? Is this news to you?'

'Very much so.'

'I want this material looked at again. I want to be able to state categorically that you had no reason to believe Emilie Zeuthen was in danger. Is that clear?'

Mogens Rank fiddled with the documents in front of him. Didn't look Hartmann in the eye.

'That . . . that won't be a problem, Troels. I guarantee it.'

Morten Weber sat hunched in a foul mood. He glared across the table at Dyhring.

'Whoever leaked that report's up to no good. I want you to find him. Give me a name.'

The PET man and Rank shuffled out of the room.

'Rosa Lebech's got a campaign meeting down the road,' Karen Nebel said. 'We can swing by and make sure she's on side.'

'She's not on side. I'm not going begging,' Hartmann grumbled.

Weber stayed quiet.

'Well?' Hartmann shot at him.

'I told you already, Troels. If you don't offer Rosa a sweetener she'll fall into bed with Ussing. If you do Birgit Eggert's going to start scampering round Slotsholmen with a dagger underneath her frock. Your choice.'

'They can both screw themselves . . .'

'Good thinking!' Weber cried, raising a plastic cup from the table in a sardonic toast. 'Let's go down with dignity. It's the only way.'

Robert and Maja Zeuthen sat at a table in the Politigården, furious with everyone. The kidnapper. Lund. The world. But mostly Madsen who'd been left alone in the room with them while Lund went through the place Juncker had found and Brix dealt with the commissioner's people upstairs.

'We gave him what he wanted,' Maja complained. 'Why didn't he take it?'

'Maybe it wasn't enough,' the detective suggested.

'And then he murdered this prosecutor,' Zeuthen said. 'Why?'

'We're not sure,' Madsen replied. 'It seems to be something to do with an old case.'

'What old case?' Maja demanded. 'What the hell's this got to do with me and my family?'

Madsen sighed.

'That's what we're trying to work out.'

'Will he call again?' Zeuthen asked. He seemed the quieter of the two. 'Do I need to come up with a better offer?'

'We're still looking into it. We've found the place he kept her.' He looked at them in turn. 'When we know more we'll be in touch.'

He got up, shook Zeuthen's hand. Offered his to Maja's. Got no response and left.

'I'm sure he's going to call.'

He tried to reach for her. She dragged herself away.

'Maja. He has a reason for this. He doesn't seem to be a madman.'

'He just strung up someone by the neck in the middle of Copenhagen!'

'I meant . . . there's a logic somewhere.'

'Meaning what? This old case, Robert. The prosecutor. Do you know what they're talking about?'

A sound at the door. Carsten Lassen was there. Donkey jacket and jeans. He nodded at Maja, didn't look at Zeuthen.

She got up, walked to him, took his arm, went down the corridor.

Alone.

He'd never felt that way much. Growing up in the midst of a happy, rich family, one of the new aristocrats, Robert Zeuthen had little time to himself. Life was always shared with others. On equal, decent terms usually.

He found the detective at a table in the adjoining office.

'Madsen, isn't it?'

The man looked exhausted. Disappointed. They took this personally too. Zeuthen could see that.

There were photos on the wall. Lots of Emilie, but men as well. The crew of the *Medea* he guessed. Alive and dead.

'Mr Zeuthen. I'm sorry. But you shouldn't be in here.'

Robert Zeuthen walked towards the corkboard, torn between the school photos and the pictures of slashed and tortured men. Madsen came and stood in front of him.

'You shouldn't see this.'

It was his daughter's photo he wanted to look at. That was all. A picture he knew by heart. Never thought about much.

'I tried to keep them safe,' Zeuthen said in a quiet, hurt voice. 'We had all the money in the world.' He looked at the downcast, sad-faced cop. 'It was worthless, wasn't it? I couldn't keep my marriage together. What right did I have to hold on to her? To Carl?'

Madsen sighed.

'You can't wrap your kids in cotton wool. No one can.'

'You're not me,' Robert Zeuthen said without thinking.

'No,' the detective agreed. 'For the last time . . . you have to leave this room now. Please . . .'

*

Gloves on, white bunny suit too, Lund walked round the tiny room in the Amager industrial unit where Emilie had been kept. There was a sleeping bag, empty noodle pots, water bottles and four short children's books next to where she'd been sleeping. A portable toilet in the corner, used.

Forensics were sifting and dusting.

'What about semen?' she asked. 'Fingerprints?'

Stickers on the wall. Numbers pointing to potential evidence. One more crime scene among many.

'Not that we've found,' the nearest forensic officer said.

They were setting up the lights to look for blood. Asbjørn Juncker followed every move. This was the first serious case he'd seen and it was starting to affect him. He was jumpy, upset, anxious.

'Why in God's name didn't he just take the money and let the girl go?'

Voice brittle and high too.

'Maybe he got scared we were too close to him,' she suggested.

There were shiny wrappers on the floor. And a can of Coke.

'He gave her sweets,' she said.

'That's what they do,' Juncker snapped. 'Isn't it?'

Borch came in. She didn't take much notice.

'She scratched her name with a plastic fork from the noodles,' Juncker said.

He was sitting on a box near the toilet.

'Asbjørn,' Lund said. 'Maybe you should go and get some fresh air.'

The name etched into the soft plasterwork was right next to him.

'What kind of a monster could do this to a kid?'

He got up, looked wild and so very young at that moment.

'The kind of monster who sits next to you on the bus and you never notice,' she said. 'Go outside. I don't want you in here like this.'

'The building opposite's got a CCTV feed. Take a look at it,' Borch suggested.

He scowled at her after Juncker had gone.

'You still don't do sympathy much, do you?'

'Sympathy won't bring Emilie Zeuthen back.' The room puzzled her. 'Unless I'm wrong he's really looking after this kid. It's as if he cares.'

He shook his head.

'He cares?'

A uniform man came in. He said Robert Zeuthen was at the door, refusing to leave until he spoke to her.

'You can't let him in here,' Borch said. 'Truly, Sarah. You can't.'

Zeuthen had already pushed his way into the adjoining room. Now he was shuffling his shiny leather shoes among the dust and cigarette butts, hands in the pockets of his smart business raincoat. Wide-eyed, shocked. Like a man who'd wandered into a world he knew existed but had never touched or truly seen before.

'There's a forensic process going on here,' she said calmly. 'I'll talk to you but you can't stay.'

Zeuthen gazed at her and for the first time she saw in him some evidence of power, of authority.

'You spoke to this man, Lund. You must know why he didn't take the money.'

'He said something about . . . small change.'

'Is she alive?' he asked and didn't take his eyes off her.

'I'm assuming so.'

The look in his face took her straight back to Birk Larsen's warm, ramshackle home in Vesterbro. They were like this whenever she gave them a hint of positive news: torn between relief and despair.

'This prosecutor, Peter Schultz . . . does the name mean anything to you?'

Zeuthen shook his head.

'I've been asked this already. I don't know anything about the man. Or some old case in Jutland. What happened to Emilie here?'

'Did you meet any of the dead sailors?'

'No.'

'Did you hear about them somehow?'

'No.'

'Did you—?'

'No, no, no!'

She waited. There was no point in pushing this man.

'Did he do anything to her?'

Lund drew herself up and tried to look convincing when she said, 'We've no reason to believe so.'

He nodded.

'I would like to see where my daughter was kept.'

Borch glanced at her. A look she could read. It said 'I warned you.'

She didn't speak.

'I'd like to see,' Zeuthen repeated.

'Walk where I tell you,' she said. 'Don't touch anything.'

They went into the tiny room. It was bright now with the neon lights of the forensic team. Soon the blue ones would come on. In the Birk Larsen case they'd revealed handprints, smears, all manner of stains around the walls. There was no such bloody evidence here. She could feel it.

Zeuthen stared at the sleeping bag, the spent food cartons, the empty bottles and cans. The numbers and arrows on the wall. The scratched name in the plaster.

'He gave her light and food,' she told him. 'This too.' There was a little electric heater next to the sleeping bag. 'It looks brand new. He must have bought it for her. He gave her books to read.'

Hunched inside his raincoat, the man said nothing.

'The fact she wrote her name . . . that's a positive sign,' she said.

'Emilie's like her mother. Strong-willed. Dogged. Doesn't . . .' He was straying and he knew it. 'Doesn't listen unless she wants to.'

Something caught his eye. Zeuthen bent down to pick it up.

'No!' Lund cried, there in an instant, hand out to stop him. 'Don't touch a thing!'

He couldn't stop looking at the books.

'She loves that one about the little monkey.' He turned to her. 'It's one of her favourites. How could he know that?'

'Maybe she asked for it?'

'And he just went out and found a copy? In the middle of all this?'

No, she thought. That was a stupid idea. He'd prepared for that too. He knew already.

Juncker was back at the door making noises about the CCTV from the building opposite.

'I need you to go now, Robert,' she said. 'We've work to do. I know you want to help. But you're in the way.'

Zeuthen didn't move.

'Does this touch you?' he asked.

'Yes,' she said. 'I'm sorry if you can't see that. It's just . . . me.'

He nodded. Went out to the shiny Range Rover in the mud

outside, brought the big car to life and edged it down the drab and dirty service road.

Juncker was good with technology. He had the CCTV on a laptop by the time Lund and Borch got there. The camera was aimed too far down the line of units to be of much use.

'No bloody good,' the young cop swore. 'All you can see is half of the building.'

A car moved through. Recent, clean. A woman at the wheel. Juncker stepped through the frames.

'Wait,' Borch said. He went back to the beginning.

Lund leaned in to look.

There was a circular mirror on the wall at the right of the frame, there to make reversing easier. A shape in it.

'What is it?' Juncker asked. 'A car?'

She got so close she was in their way.

'It's some kind of camper van,' Lund said. 'There's a number plate. If it's him it's going to be fake.'

Juncker zoomed in.

'This thing's ancient,' he said. 'Look at the lights. It's like something from the Eighties.'

Borch didn't like that.

'Old for a camper van,' Juncker added.

'Check it out,' she ordered. 'I need to talk to Brix.'

Carsten Lassen lived in a two-bedroom apartment near the Marble Church. A long way from the sprawling cold luxury of Drekar. Emilie and Carl had to share a room when they stayed. It was small, with a bunk bed. She always let her younger brother take the top because he thought that was fun.

Now he didn't know where to sleep at all. So Maja Zeuthen took the lower bed and read a book to him. After a while he climbed down, got under the sheets with her. Went to sleep.

She kept her arms around him. Remembered what it was like to hold Emilie. To hear her smart, sharp voice picking an argument over something or other.

Someone rapped on the door. She heard Carsten answer. Knew from the tone of his voice it was Robert.

Her hand brushed Carl's sleeping face. She never took much notice of the money. Before they split she'd been planning to take

77

a job, teaching in a primary school. Robert would have liked that. He didn't enjoy being kept any more than she did.

Then his father died and the world fell noisily to pieces.

'It's important. Where's Maja?'

She wanted to think he sounded like a stranger. That this new, hard tone in his voice made him hateful somehow. But that wasn't true. Circumstances affected them both. She'd never consciously wanted to leave him. Robert would have put up with anything, any row, any demand, to keep them together. The rift just happened, got slowly bigger every day. Then Carsten, kind, handsome, needy Carsten came along and filled the hole Robert had left. Some of it anyhow.

'Maja's got enough worries because of you.'

He had the flat, unemotional voice of a doctor. Could speak harsh words – ones she perhaps needed sometimes – without a second thought.

Through the door she heard him.

'Any business with Maja is business with me. So you say it to my face first.'

The argument was growing. Soon it would wake Carl.

She got up and shambled to the door, looked at the two of them. The only meaningful lovers she'd ever had. They sat at the table, the men on both sides, Maja Zeuthen at the end.

Talk about money and security advice. Options and plans.

'You went to this place he kept her?' she asked.

'They let me in. Lund didn't like that much but . . .' He shrugged. 'It was just a little room.'

'And they're sure she was there?'

'She scratched her name on the wall.'

He leaned closer in a way that, in another time, would have led to him holding her hand.

'They seem to think he knows her somehow. He'd bought her that book she likes. The one about the monkey. They want to know if we've noticed anything unusual. Among people we know. Some-one new getting close . . .'

'So you think it's me now?' Lassen asked, outraged.

Zeuthen looked at him and said, simply, 'No. I don't.'

Then after a while, 'They just want us to think about all the things we take for granted. Maybe see something we missed before.'

Lassen was still mad. He got up, found the custody schedule, threw it on the table.

'Here are all the rules. Your rules. The ones we follow point by point. You look at them.' He thumped his fist on the papers. 'You tell me where this bastard got close to her while she was with us.'

Maja had her hands to her face, crying. Lassen didn't even notice.

'You and your security people have harassed us from day one. We did our part. Now you've screwed up and you've got the cheek to blame Maja. How dare—?'

'Shut up! For Christ's sake, Carsten.' She was staring at the pair of them, tears running down her cheeks. 'Just stop it, will you?'

'No!' he yelled. 'You've wept buckets over this idiot and look where it got you. I'm not going to let him fuck up your life any more.'

'Please . . .' she begged.

He was in Zeuthen's face.

'Listen to me, Robert. She's left your golden cage for good. No going back. You've punished her for that every day since. It's done.'

He pointed to the door.

'Get out.'

Zeuthen didn't move. Then he saw her face. The sorrow. The embarrassment. The grief.

That made him leave. Nothing else.

Thirty minutes later he was back home. Reinhardt was on the phone as he walked in. A tall, genteel figure, patiently fielding phone calls with the police, with Zeeland's own security team.

When he finished he picked up his coat and brought Zeuthen up to date.

Little that was new. Zeeland's security advisers were taking advice from some specialists they'd worked with on the ransom case in Somalia.

'I never knew about any hijacking,' Zeuthen said.

'Your father handled it. Not long before he passed away. We had some people held by the pirates there. It took a while. Wasn't easy. But we got them out. For less money than they wanted. Without publicity too. Maybe they've got some ideas—'

'Have I treated Maja badly?' Zeuthen interrupted. 'Was I unreasonable?'

Reinhardt looked shocked by the question.

'No. Why do you ask?'

'Because she hates me. And I wonder if I deserve it.'

The older man shook his head.

'I don't believe she hates you, Robert. A divorce is never easy. I think you've been very understanding. She's the one who refused any financial support. I don't know what else you could have done.' He hesitated, then added, 'She never really liked the business I'm afraid. I think she had what she felt were . . . principles.'

By the time they got back to the Politigården Brix had a call out to stop and check all camper vans going through border controls. A team was working on registration records. The number plate was false. They had, at last, a lead.

'It's either a VW or a Fiat,' Borch said, throwing some photos on the desk. 'What they call an alcove van. Hard to tell which. These things all look the same.'

Lund pored over the prints. Brix came and joined them.

'I want checks on campsites,' he said. 'Lots of them are open during the winter now. People who've lost their homes.'

He glowered at the PET man.

'And there's this,' Brix added, throwing a heavy document straight in front of Borch. 'The kidnapper sent a kind of manifesto to the Ministry of Justice a week ago. PET knew all about it.' He leaned down, looked in Borch's face. 'Didn't you?'

'Sure. But we didn't know it was from him until tonight.'

He shoved the document to one side.

'Give,' Lund said and snatched it.

'There's no mention of an old case in Jutland, Sarah. It's just crazy left-wing nonsense—'

'You ignored a direct threat to Zeeland,' Brix cut in. 'Now I've got management on my back wanting to know why we were never told.'

Borch muttered something about talking to Dyhring.

'You're here. He isn't,' Brix said. 'Next time speak up a little sooner. I don't want . . .'

Madsen came in and said, 'We've just interviewed Peter Schultz's secretary. Schultz told you the mate was there asking for compensation, right?'

Lund nodded.

'Well, she talked to the man before he went in. He didn't mention that at all. He said he wanted to change his testimony in a case, one Schultz handled. Something about . . . his conscience getting to him. Also . . .'

He didn't look keen to go on.

'Also what?' Brix snapped.

'The girl's phone rang. We answered. He hung up.'

Brix closed his eyes.

'He didn't say a word?'

'Not exactly. He said he'd only talk to Lund.'

A female officer was standing behind him, Emilie's phone in her hand. She looked upset.

Then it rang. Brix nodded. Lund took the handset and answered.

The voice didn't sound so calm or genteel any more.

'If you give the phone to anybody else I'll take that as a sign you don't give a shit about this kid, Lund. Do we understand each other?'

'We had a deal. You broke it. They took me off the case.'

That laugh again.

'Is that why you're still in the Politigården?'

'What do you want?'

'A new offer. Think about it overnight. I'll call tomorrow. Maybe by then you'll grasp the seriousness of the situation.'

'Why did you kill Schultz?'

'Because I was owed. You can't fob me off with Zeeland's petty cash.'

'Why him? Why the three sailors?'

Silence. She thought she'd lost him.

'Do you have children, Lund?'

She couldn't answer straight away.

'Simple question. I asked if you had children.'

'Yes.'

'Boy or girl? How many?'

'A son.'

'Then you know what a child's worth, don't you? I'll call tomorrow.'

'Wait! How do I know the girl's still alive?'

Silence. Then a beep and a photo popped into the inbox. Lund opened it. Emilie Zeuthen in a dark coat, a woollen hat. Next to her that afternoon's paper with the school photo on the front page.

Lund put the phone to her ear. He was gone.

'You keep that thing with you all the time now, Lund,' Brix demanded. 'Charged. Ready. Understood?'

She nodded.

'Now go home. Get some sleep. We've got a night shift coming on. I want you all fresh for tomorrow.'

She didn't do as Brix suggested. Lund picked up pizza, some beer, and a box of chocolates then headed for the back street of Vesterbro where Mark lived.

Three months he'd been here and never once invited her round. A couple of streets from where the Birk Larsens still lived. Perhaps that was why she never pushed it.

It was one of the up-and-coming districts. Part old Vesterbro, grimy, dark with graffiti and some shady characters in doorways. Part new, with signs of building and renovation.

She almost walked past the door. It was next to a charity shop, the window full of pictures of cats and dogs up for adoption. Lund stood outside with the pizza, the beer, the chocolates, and just remembered to take off the price stickers before she rang the bell.

No sound so she knocked instead and a young, high female voice cried, 'Come in. It's open.'

A bare hallway, the smell of renovation. She walked into the first room. The woman she'd seen at the station stood in front of a wall trying to scrape off paint. There was building material everywhere, tools, sacks, pots. Not much furniture. Just a small table, a sofa, and a low double bed.

Lund stayed at the doorway, didn't know what to say.

The young woman marched up smiling, shook her hand.

'You must be from upstairs. I'm sorry about the noise. I'm almost done here.' She patted her belly. 'Don't want to take on too much. I'm Eva.'

'No . . . I came for Mark. Is he in?'

She put the pizza, the chocolates and the beer on the small table. There wasn't much room.

'No.' She had fair hair, a smiling, pretty face, long hair swept back from her forehead and large staring eyes. 'He went to drop off some rubbish.' Her jumper looked threadbare. It was covered with paint stains. Everything about the place spoke of penury. 'So much work to do here.'

'It doesn't matter.'

'Don't go. Are you Mark's mother?'

Lund didn't know whether she was glad to hear that or not.

'Yes. Sorry.' She shook Eva's hand again. 'Sarah. I brought . . .' A glance at the table. 'Just a couple of things. When will he be back?'

'I don't know. You can stay and wait if you like. Can I get you a coffee or something?'

Lund couldn't stop looking at the place and she knew that was bad. Just a ground-floor flat, one main room, a kitchen with a bath-room beyond. None of it finished.

'It's a dump,' Eva said, 'but we're doing it up. We got the place cheap because the people before went bankrupt. They wanted someone in who could see . . . possibilities.'

Enthusiasm. Lund never felt comfortable with that. Eva was maybe two years older than Mark, in late pregnancy, living in a freezing dump. And still she looked content.

'It's really nice you came round. Mark doesn't talk about some things much. You're a bit of a mystery. Not . . . not that he said anything bad. I wanted to meet you.' She patted her stomach. 'So you could see this. But he said we had a lot on our plates right now.'

There was a noise at the door. A voice, calling her.

Mark walked in. Happy, animated, a long piece of timber in his hands.

'Take a look what I found at the dump.' The wood was broken. But maybe there was something to be done with it. 'Someone just left it. Just . . .'

The smile disappeared the moment he saw her.

'Hi,' Lund said.

'Has something happened?'

'No. I was just in the area and I thought . . .'

She picked up the chocolates, pointed at the pizza and the beer.

'What do you want?' he asked and it wasn't a friendly tone.

'Nothing. It's just so long since we saw each other.'

Eva tried to keep smiling. Like a schoolgirl trapped in the midst of an unwanted argument.

He kept quiet.

'This is a big job you've taken on,' Lund said. 'If I can help somehow . . .'

'We'll manage. Did you speak to Grandma?'

'She didn't tell me you were having a baby. I saw you at the station . . .'

Eva sat down, looked at him.

'I wanted to say congratulations, Mark. I'd like to help . . .'

'We're fine.'

'We could use a place to sleep for a few days until the ceiling's done,' Eva said in a fragile, hopeful tone.

'Sure,' Lund agreed. 'Any time. There's a key right by the front door. It's underneath a plant pot. Just let yourself in. Call me if you—'

'Mum?' he said loudly. 'Can you listen for once? We're fine.'

A noise from somewhere. It didn't register at all.

'Your phone's ringing. You'd best go outside and answer it. Can you do that now?'

In the cold, dark street she took out the handset. Her phone. Not Emilie's. Lund looked at the number: Asbjørn Juncker. Maybe five years older than Mark. A smart young man, trying to shape the life ahead of him.

'Not making any progress with the camper van,' he said. 'Sorry.'

She could hear the sound of the Politigården behind him. It was a family of a kind, thrown together by circumstance, riven by argument and division at times, at others bound by mutual need and a sense of respect and decency.

'You'll get there, Juncker,' she said.

'So I'm not Asbjørn any more?'

'I guess not.'

'Progress then! I've got some papers on that case Peter Schultz was handling. The mate and those other two found that girl in West Jutland. Thirteen years old. An orphan. She'd been in a children's home for a while. Then foster care. They say she ran away. The Zeeland crew found her dead in the harbour.'

'Who handled the case?'

'Local police. They reckoned it was suicide. Peter Schultz signed off the papers. Hang on. Borch wants to talk to you.'

Lund crossed the road, moved back into the street lights. Heard the phone change hands.

'What about an autopsy?' she asked.

An older voice, worn and weary, answered.

'There's no mention of violence. Foaming round the nose and mouth. Liquid in the lungs. The pathologist was called Lis Vissenbjerg. She said it was death by drowning. Do you know her?'

'I don't spend my entire life around the dead, Borch.'

A long pause. Then he said carefully, 'I'm aware of that.'

'Where was the autopsy carried out?'

'Copenhagen. Department of Forensic Science in the university hospital. Want to see her tomorrow?'

'Fix it.'

'Did you find Mark?' he asked. 'Are things OK?'

She got to the car, took out her keys. Wondered whether she really wanted to talk about this with a man she'd loved and then abandoned twenty years before.

'I'll see you in the morning,' Lund said. 'Goodnight.'

Three

The Department of Forensic Medicine was in the west wing of the university hospital. She met Borch in the same car park the Zeuthens had used when they were watched by the kidnapper from his stolen van.

'Is it a boy or girl?' he asked as they walked up the winding white-tile staircase to the first-floor rooms where the autopsies took place. 'Or don't they want to know?'

Lund had the file on Schultz in front of her. Barely heard the question.

'Why would a deputy prosecutor lie about something like this? And the ship's mate? Why change his testimony two years on?'

They got to the top of the steps. A couple of attendants wheeled a gurney past. Beneath a plain hospital sheet a familiar shape.

'Had breakfast?' Borch asked.

'Yes.'

The downcast, boxer-puppy look.

'I haven't. I sort of left in a hurry.'

He wanted her to ask about his marriage. Something there wasn't good.

'We didn't have the chance to talk about the baby,' she said instead.

'It's a perfectly natural question, you know. Pretty obvious.'

Lund asked at a desk for Lis Vissenbjerg, showed her ID. They were waved through. This was the business end. Corpses on silver

86

tables, silent figures working round them. Blood and organs. The smell of chemicals and flesh.

'If I was about to become a grandad . . .' he began.

She turned, put a finger to her lips. Then found the room, pushed open the doors. It was tall and bright, with a semicircular rank of silver seats running round the back. An autopsy theatre. A stage for the last act of a life.

No audience now. Just a woman in a pale-blue smock and mask bending over a naked male corpse on a flat metal surgical table, a bored-looking attendant watching, hand to his chin.

'Lis Vissenbjerg?' Lund asked.

The masked face looked up. Told the attendant they were done for the moment and asked him to wheel the body away.

Then, as the fans whirred trying to clear the room of the smell, they sat down on the lowest bench seat and showed her the papers: an autopsy report on Louise Hjelby, a thirteen-year-old girl, Vissenbjerg's signature at the bottom.

'You must remember it,' Borch said.

'Why?' She was a tall, stick-thin woman in her forties, hair the colour of straw pulled back from a high forehead, a narrow, unsmiling face. 'Do you have any idea how many of these things I sign each year? Let me read it . . .'

She took the report. Six pages. Skimmed through them. Didn't speak.

'Why was the autopsy carried out here?' Lund asked. 'Not in Jutland.'

'I don't know,' Vissenbjerg said. 'I just deal with what they send.'

'Who?' Lund persisted. 'Peter Schultz?'

The name made her look up.

'I read about that in the paper. It was terrible. Is this connected?'

'Maybe,' Lund replied. 'Did he send the autopsy here?'

The pathologist shrugged.

'I can't remember. You'd have to go back through the files. If it's still there . . .'

'We think this case is connected with the Zeuthen kidnapping somehow,' Borch said.

Lund looked straight at her.

'It's possible the people he's killed were involved in covering up this girl's death. Maybe the kidnapper thinks it wasn't suicide.'

'I didn't cover up anything,' the pathologist said straight away.

'Did you speak to Schultz?' Borch asked.

'No. Why should I?'

Lund waited. Nothing more. Then she tapped a finger on the report.

'There are a lot of injuries to the body.'

'Yes,' Vissenbjerg agreed. 'They happened after she died. The girl had been in the harbour for a while. She probably got washed into rocks. Maybe hit by a boat prop or something.' The woman looked at both of them in turn. 'I didn't see a hint of anything criminal. If I had I'd have said so.'

Borch nodded.

'And no one argued with you? You never heard about the case again?'

'No. It was routine. If I remember correctly she was an orphan. She'd been fostered several times. No relatives.'

'Did anyone ask the three sailors who found her to give DNA samples?'

'Not as far as I know. They weren't suspects. No one was. Like I said, there were no signs of crime. Nothing to—'

'It says here she'd had sex,' Lund pointed out.

'Sometime. I don't know when. She was thirteen. Do you think that's unusual?'

Borch's phone rang. He walked to the door to take the call.

'You said there were no suspicious injuries.' Lund pulled out two photos of the girl's wrists. Covered in cut marks. 'What do you call that?'

'I call that self-harm. Good indication of her mental state. From what I remember the police said she was disturbed too. All the indications . . .'

Borch came back, apologized for the interruption.

'Asbjørn's found a campsite,' he said. 'We need to go.'

Lund scooped up the pictures and the report, stuffed them into her bag. Lis Vissenbjerg watched.

'Do you have a card?' she asked.

Lund gave her one and said to call any time.

'You really think this man's murdering people over this?'

'Looks that way,' Lund agreed.

The pathologist waved the card.

'If I think of anything I'll get in touch.'

Without being asked Reinhardt had brought an external security consultancy team into the Zeeland boardroom that morning. Zeuthen listened to them. A torrent of jargon. Wave after wave of impenetrable buzzwords.

One message, a lesson he'd already learned. The man wanted more money.

They spent forty-five minutes saying little more than this then he thanked them, told them he'd handle the matter himself.

Reinhardt watched them go.

'I hope you don't think I went over your head, Robert. We used these people in that situation in Somalia. They were very good.'

'This isn't Somalia.'

But in truth he didn't know what it was. Nor did the dispassionate, serious men he'd just sent packing.

On the way out they passed Maja, talking to the PA at reception. Zeuthen walked over, tried to smile, suggested they sit down together, talk this through.

By the window. The grey sea outside, underneath a sullen sky. They sat at the table.

'We need to keep down the amount,' Reinhardt cautioned. 'Leave headroom if he comes back for more.'

The morning paper was on her lap. A photo of Emilie next to the dead prosecutor.

'That's the lesson from kidnappings like this,' he added.

'This isn't a business deal,' Maja said in a faint, hurt voice.

'I know,' Reinhardt agreed. 'All the same you need to be practical.'

'How's Carl?' Zeuthen asked.

She looked up. Glad of that question.

'He asks about her,' Maja said. 'About you.'

'If you offer too much he may stall and ask for more,' Reinhardt said.

She shot him a hard stare.

'We can't risk angering him again!'

Zeuthen walked to the window, looked at the harbour, said nothing.

'That's why we need to come up with a figure,' Reinhardt replied. 'Before he calls. Before—'

'I'll pay whatever he wants,' Zeuthen interrupted. 'However much. Emilie's more . . .'

Maja was staring at him and for all their years together he couldn't read her expression.

'She's worth more than anything I can give,' he finished.

Reinhardt took a deep breath.

'PET don't want you to offer a huge sum, Robert. There are practical problems. It needs to be portable. We have to find it somewhere. Our own banks don't carry much in cash.'

'I can raise the money privately through Frankfurt. Send the plane there . . .'

Reinhardt shook his head.

'No one will insure you for this. We'll be taking the risk.'

'I don't care about the risk!' Zeuthen was close to losing his temper. 'Just organize this, please.'

Reinhardt looked taken aback.

'May I know what amount you have in mind?'

She was still wearing the old green parka. It had mud on it from two nights before.

'I'd give him this place if I could,' Robert Zeuthen murmured. 'Gladly if only . . .'

Out on the cold Øresund a ship's horn boomed over the flat indifferent sea.

The debate was planned for the Black Diamond, the gleaming glass library by the waterfront. Ussing, Rosa Lebech and Hartmann were there for a sound check. Karen Nebel had a preliminary report from Mogens Rank about PET's response to the dossier they'd been sent from the *Medea*.

'As you can see,' Hartmann told them, 'there was no direct threat to the Zeuthens. No one was involved in these decisions from the political side. It was PET's call entirely. Your accusation that I somehow dodged my responsibilities is false and misleading. Next time you find something stuck in your pigeonhole think twice before making a fool of yourself.'

Ussing flicked through the report.

'Your people still screwed up. Mogens Rank doesn't really believe he can crawl out from under this catastrophe by blaming PET, does he?'

Rosa Lebech kept quiet, looked uncomfortable to be there.

Hartmann held out his hand.

'Unless you've got more questions we should bury the hatchet. Let the police do their job. And we can do ours.' He nodded at the stage. 'When we get up there tonight.'

'I agree,' Rosa Lebech said finally. 'There's no need for a public argument in these circumstances.'

Ussing shook his head. That big, sarcastic laugh.

'So that's it? The Justice Minister investigates himself for thirty minutes and . . . surprise, surprise! You're all blameless.'

'This is too much . . .' Hartmann muttered.

'There's no mention in here of an old police case in Jutland. Why not?'

'More anonymous messages in your pigeonhole?'

'You've got too many skeletons in your cupboard, Troels. They go back years. I'm going to start rattling them.'

'Listen!' Hartmann yelled. 'I've given you every detail from the beginning.'

'Not everything,' Rosa Lebech said carefully.

He stared at her.

'Fine! If you're so unhappy with the government, cut a deal with him.'

He left them there, walked down the corridor back towards the campaign coach, Karen Nebel clucking like a worried hen behind him.

'Enough,' Hartmann ordered. 'I don't have to listen to Ussing's crap.'

Morten Weber was on a seat outside, looking at his messages. He got up and joined them.

'Went well in there, did it?' he asked.

'To hell with them. What's happening with the Zeuthens?'

'He's going to offer a fortune. They're not sure they can get the money together in time. We could offer to help. Maybe with a cash loan.'

Hartmann just looked at him.

Fast footsteps behind. Rosa Lebech ran up, stopped him with an outstretched arm.

'I've got appointments,' he said.

'You're not the only one with something at stake here, Troels. If you can't find the time to close the gaps . . . ?'

'What gaps? We've talked this through a million times.'

Karen Nebel intervened.

'We can find the time. The Ministry of Justice will answer any questions you have. We've nothing to hide here. Ussing knows that. He's just playing games. So . . .' She smiled. 'If you've got questions, put them to me. I'll deal with them personally.'

A long pause then Rosa Lebech said, 'OK.'

They watched her walk slowly back to the hall.

'How the hell did Ussing know about that Jutland case?' Hartmann wondered.

'You're sailing a leaky ship,' Weber said and left it at that.

The campsite was on waste ground thirty minutes outside the city. Decrepit caravans and motorhomes everywhere. More than two hundred Juncker said. Curious, scared faces watched their arrival from behind small, dusty windows.

Brix called as she got out of the car. The Zeuthens had come up with a ransom. The sum was breathtaking.

'Did you get anywhere with the old Jutland case?' she asked.

'Just focus on the campsite. And keep that phone turned on.'

Juncker had been there for an hour. A camper van that looked like the kidnapper's had checked in the previous night then left first thing that morning.

Lund looked at her watch. It was eleven thirty already.

'Why didn't I know earlier?'

'This place is a dump,' the young detective told her. 'The guy who runs it's downright weird. He doesn't turn up to work till ten.'

'Sarah!' Borch was coming off the phone. 'We've got something back from the Internet phone people. The call last night came through the site's Wi-Fi router here. We don't have a number. But . . .'

He looked round at the field full of caravans. The air smelled of woodsmoke and bad drains.

'Has to be him.'

She nodded. Juncker too. He looked happier than the night before. As if he was settling into the investigation.

'Has Zeuthen made an offer?' Borch asked.

'A hundred,' she said.

'A hundred million kroner?'

'There's got to be payment records. Names and addresses.' She looked at Juncker. 'Or am I missing something?'

'Let's go meet king troll,' Juncker said. 'You tell me.'

He was a man of about seventy with a crooked face, stroke probably, a flat cap, an old blue nylon jacket. He sat in a chair by the one building on the site: a low brick garage with a rotting car inside.

'I don't spy on people,' the site manager said. 'We're almost full. All two hundred and sixteen plots. Camper vans. Caravans. We've put up four cabins too. Got permission for them. Don't get pushy with me.'

The sign behind him read 'Tip Top Camping'. There was a picture of a children's playground. He saw her looking.

'We took the rides away to make space. People are more interested in getting somewhere to live. Don't get so many kids these days.' He scowled at them. 'If the social people find they're here too long they come sniffing. Take them away sometimes.'

'Easier to make money if you don't ask questions,' Borch noted.

'We used to have families come for holidays. Now they've lost their homes. They've got the banks on their backs. The credit card people. You want me to give them a hard time too?'

Borch was getting cross.

'This is about murder. The kidnap of a young girl. You saw him . . .'

'No I didn't.' The old man reached into his pocket and pulled out a receipt. 'He booked one night over the Internet. Left the voucher in the mailbox with the money. I didn't see a thing.'

Lund looked at the voucher. He'd used Peter Schultz's credit card. The lot he had been given was number sixty-four.

Borch held out a photograph of Emilie Zeuthen.

'Have you seen this girl?'

'Are you deaf? Didn't see him come. Didn't see him go. Leave people be. That's my motto. Don't get involved in their business.'

'You're a lot of help,' Juncker grumbled.

'I do what I can,' the manager said.

A noise. Something was vibrating in Lund's pocket. She pulled out Emilie's phone and walked round the corner.

The voice was calm again.

'What have you got for me now?'

She stood next to the nearest caravan. A woman, dark-faced, foreign, watched from behind the grubby curtain.

'The family's willing to pay a hundred million kroner. They just want Emilie back.'

In the silence that followed she tried to picture the man behind the voice. He was about her age. Educated. Intelligent. Experienced in ways she could only guess at.

'I want it in five hundred euro notes. It has to fit into five bags. No GPS. No ink cartridges. Don't play games this time. I won't give you another chance.'

'Understood,' she said. 'How do I know I can trust you?'

The laugh.

'What can I say? You have my word. Get the money. Be on the E47 with it. The bridge by exit sixteen at four p.m. on the dot.'

He was leaving them little more than four hours to prepare.

'That's a lot of cash to put together. I'm not sure they can do it that quickly.'

'They're Zeeland. They can do anything they want.'

'But—'

'Four o'clock. Don't screw up this time.'

She tried to argue. But it was too late. Lund walked back to Borch and Juncker, still trying to get something out of the site man. Told them the offer was on.

Brix checked in. Borch called PET headquarters. They walked to the car.

'Sarah.'

Borch had stopped, phone to his ear.

'They traced him. That's not Skype. He's using an ordinary mobile. He's somewhere in a ten-kilometre radius of here.'

The big grin. She hadn't seen that in twenty years.

'He's dropped the ball.' Borch clasped her shoulders, let out a little whoop. 'We're going to get this bastard.'

*

Between campaign events the Hartmann coach stopped at a temporary events office in a hotel in the suburbs. Karen Nebel was working on Rosa Lebech. The Centre Party was still holding out. The police had briefed Weber on the coming ransom exchange.

'Let's hope to God it works this time,' Hartmann said. 'Is Zeuthen fine with the money?'

'He's shipping it in from Frankfurt. Seems there's no problem.'

'Good . . .'

Weber winced and said, 'Can we have a quick word?'

Nebel didn't like that much but Hartmann agreed. They went next door into one of the unused bedrooms.

'Doesn't help if you make Karen feel she's outside the team, Morten.'

'Yes, well.' Weber looked awkward, worried. That was unusual. 'I just want to be careful until I know exactly where we stand.'

Hartmann grabbed a bottle of water from the bed, swigged at it.

'What are you talking about?'

'Ussing's just put out a new statement.'

'Oh for Christ's sake . . .'

'He's demanding an official inquiry right after the election whoever wins.'

'There's a nine-year-old girl somewhere out there! Does he even think about that?'

'Fine,' Weber said. 'Righteous anger. We all love it. But here's the thing. I talked to the Ministry of Justice. There's a lawyer I know there . . .'

'Don't have time for this.'

'You do, Troels. She thought she'd seen this old case in Jutland – the girl's suicide – before. She wasn't sure but when I mentioned the Zeeland sailors—'

'The case never went through them,' Hartmann interrupted. 'You were there when Mogens told us that last night.'

Karen Nebel appeared at the door. Weber glared at her.

'I just got through to Rosa. If we throw some low-level ministerial job the way of her troops she's fine with announcing the alliance tonight. I told her yes.'

'Good news!' Hartmann cried.

'We need to get moving if we want to make the announcement

before the debate,' Nebel added. 'So can you two deal with your argument later?'

'No need,' Hartmann said. 'We're done.'

The E47 crossed countries, starting in Germany at Lübeck, by ferry link to Denmark, passing through Copenhagen and running into Sweden where it ended at Helsingør. Brix had teams ready to block the route going both ways.

The busy motorway junction was by a bridge above what looked like a miniature version of the campsite Juncker had found. Only more mean this time. Little more than a rough encampment by a small lake.

Juncker had been talking to some of the locals. He had a pair of binoculars trained on the dismal hovels below.

'Apparently they call it the Mudhole. There's forty or fifty illegals down there.'

Lund took the field glasses, looked for herself. It wasn't just caravans. There was a wrecked van, a man in a tent, a couple of children playing with an old football.

'Every time we send them home they come back,' Juncker added.

Borch had spent most of the time on the phone back to PET headquarters. When he came off Lund said, 'I don't believe for one moment he's just going to walk onto this bridge and pick up the money.'

'No.' He pointed to the trailers and vans below. 'He's down there. We've traced the signal from his phone.' He pointed to a white vehicle parked at the edge of the camp, as if newly arrived. 'That's the motorhome. I'd put my life on it.'

Juncker rubbed his hands.

'So let's go in . . .'

'Brix said to wait for the call,' Lund told him.

He didn't like that.

'She's down there! Let's go.'

Borch put out a hand to stop him.

'Brix is right. We can't risk her getting hurt. We've got him cornered . . .'

Lund took another look through the binoculars. The camper van looked the right kind.

'Why's he suddenly started using a phone we can trace?'

Juncker rolled his eyes and retrieved his binoculars.

'Maybe because he can't get a data connection?'

Borch told her to get on the bridge.

'Why here?' Lund demanded. 'He's so exposed. This man lives off computers. He knew what was going on when he was on that ship. How the trains were running yesterday. And now . . .'

His phone rang again.

'It's time,' Borch told her. 'The Zeuthens are in the underpass on the other side of the bridge. Brix is with them. And the money. Will you kindly move?'

'This makes no sense.'

'When he calls do whatever he wants. We'll take him when he moves to pick up the money. Come on. Chop, chop.'

Juncker giggled at that and went back to scanning the campsite with the binoculars. It was getting dark. Lund drove round to the area Borch had indicated.

Three cars. Brix wearing a dark winter coat. Robert Zeuthen in the perpetual suit. His wife in a new blue parka.

A couple of uniform men unloaded five bags from the back of Zeuthen's Range Rover. Thirteen and a half million euros, all in the largest denomination note available.

Brix gave Lund some black body armour and told her to put it on. A woman officer led the Zeuthens to one side.

'I'm going to keep them out of the way,' he said. 'We can't be close by but we'll be listening in.'

'What's happened with the Jutland case?'

He didn't like the question.

'I talked to the local police chief in Jutland. He confirmed what the pathologist told you. It was suicide. That's a dead end.'

They put the money in the boot of her plain black Ford Focus.

'Good luck, Lund.'

'This Jutland thing . . .'

'Forget about Jutland! Take good care of the money. Yourself too.'

She drove onto the bridge. Dusk fell. Dusk turned to night. Two wheels up on the pavement she waited.

Twenty past five and nothing. Borch, Juncker, and the observation team shivered in the wood above the Mudhole, watching the white camper van below. The curtains were closed. Darkness inside. Borch's people thought the phone was in there. Another snatch team had assembled on a slip road beneath the bridge, led by Brix. The same level as the camp. Ready to enter instantly.

The Zeuthens were silent, anxious, listening to the rumble of cars above them.

Finally Maja strode over and tackled Brix.

'What's going on?'

'Please,' the homicide chief insisted. 'I'd much rather the two of you waited in the car.'

'He's more than an hour late,' Zeuthen said.

'We're doing what he wanted,' Brix pointed out. 'Lund's in position. She's got the money. It's his call now.'

A brief gap in the traffic. The noise from the bridge receded. In its place, briefly, what sounded like a phone.

It looked as if it would be the biggest debate of the campaign. Crowds swarming into the vast hall by the water. The news networks were running a planted story from Karen Nebel. They were saying the election was as good as over. Rosa Lebech was going to throw the Centre Party's weight behind Troels Hartmann for Prime Minister that evening. On the current polls nothing the Socialists could do would generate sufficient votes to give them power.

Hartmann walked through the campaign workers' room to the side of the hall, smiling, waving. Nebel by his side.

'I've got some of the papers accusing Ussing of exploiting the Zeuthen case tomorrow,' she said quietly as they made their way through the happy tables. 'That should give us more breathing space.'

Anders Ussing stood next to the exit, beckoning.

'He looks apologetic,' Hartmann noted.

'He should,' she said. 'Be gentle.'

'I always am.'

It was a short conversation. Ussing looked nervous, talked about only doing his job.

'Well it's over and done with now, Anders. Who goes first tonight?'

'You do, Troels. You've got rank on me.'

Hartmann gave him the politician's smile.

'I just want you to know,' Ussing added, 'that when you lose office over this . . . it's not personal. In any way.'

That made Hartmann laugh. Ussing was in a donkey jacket. No tie. Hair dishevelled. He didn't look ready for anything, least of all a debate.

'I'll tell you what,' Hartmann said. 'You worry about your campaign. I'll deal with mine.'

Karen Nebel sensed something from across the room. She flitted to Hartmann's side. Ussing nodded at her, grinned.

'It's not the first time Mogens Rank's led you up the garden path.' He beamed. 'Probably the last though. Good luck with the, um . . .' A hearty laugh. 'The alliance.'

'What the hell was that about?' Hartmann asked when Ussing wandered off. 'Rosa's with us, isn't she?'

'Yes. She told me . . .'

Morten Weber was marching across the room, tie to one side, papers in his hand, face like thunder.

Lund stared at Emilie's phone. It was quiet. Reached into her pocket, took out the police handset, said, 'Lund?'

'It's Lis Vissenbjerg. We spoke this morning. Can we meet?'

'This isn't a good time. Let me call you back.'

'You said this man killed Schultz over that case.'

A sudden rush of traffic. Cold night air in her face.

'It looks that way.'

Long pause.

'The thing is . . . that autopsy you got hold of . . .'

A truck roared past. Lund went and leaned over the bridge, looked down at the grubby little camp and the white camper van at the perimeter.

'What about it?'

'I should have told you this morning. I had concerns about the cause of death. I thought the girl could have been murdered. But when I wanted to run more tests . . .'

'What?'

'Schultz said he was under pressure from people above him. I'd be out of a job if I didn't do what he wanted. I've still got the original draft. You need to see it.'

Getting on for five thirty. No call.

'Hello? Are you still there, Lund?'

'Where are you?'

'At work. They . . . they put Peter Schultz on my schedule for today. I told them I couldn't possibly . . .'

'Bear with me,' Lund said.

She phoned Borch.

'The pathologist we saw this morning just called. She says Louise Hjelby's autopsy was changed. She's scared. She wants to show us something.'

'Later.'

Lund took a deep breath.

'There's nothing happening here. We're wasting time. He's done this for a reason . . .'

'I'm hanging up now. You stay where you are until Brix says otherwise. Bye.'

Alone on the bridge, shivering, dark hair swept back in a clumsy ponytail. Sick of the heavy body armour.

Lund checked her watch. Gone five thirty.

He wasn't coming. It was never going to happen.

She threw off the padded jacket, went to the boot, got the bags out, lined them up on the pavement. Sent Borch a short text telling him to collect them. Then climbed in the car, turned the key, pulled out into the steady night traffic.

'Private time!' Morten Weber demanded.

They went outside into the corridor. Weber slapped some pages on Hartmann's chest.

'Mogens Rank knew all about that old case. I've got the documents out of the Ministry to prove it. The investigation went by his desk.'

Hartmann swore.

'Can't this wait a while?'

Weber's beady eyes lit up with fury.

'Wait? There's a time bomb ticking beneath us. Can you really not hear it? Look!'

He pointed to the top page.

'Mogens signed the papers himself. It's there in black and white. Yet he said nothing when the sailors were killed. Nothing when Peter Schultz was strung up by the neck in front of the courthouse.

And PET say the kidnapper's indictment went straight to his government email address in the Ministry. Which isn't public by the way. Might have mentioned that too.'

'What does he say?' Nebel asked.

'Won't return my calls.'

'This has to wait,' she insisted. 'We've got a thousand people turning up for this debate. Let's deal—'

'I haven't finished,' Weber went on. 'PET think they know who's been leaking information to Ussing. They've found an official in Rank's ministry with a motive.' He looked at Hartmann. 'His name's Jens Lebech. Rosa's ex-husband.'

'Ex,' Hartmann said straight out. 'I never went near Rosa when she was married. They can't prove that.'

Weber slapped his forehead.

'Just for once can you try to think with something other than your cock? We need to start managing this right now. You've got to go back to Christiansborg and reel Mogens in.'

'The debate, Morten,' Nebel pointed out. 'People here. The media.'

'I'll handle this meeting,' Hartmann said. 'Cancel everything after that. And find him for me.'

Under the bridge they heard the sound of Lund's car banging on the road as she pulled off the pavement.

'What the hell's happening?' Brix asked.

Borch's phone buzzed. One text message.

'She says she'll answer Emilie's phone if it rings. She left the money where the car was . . .'

A furious Brix turned on Madsen.

'Get a woman officer up on the bridge. Find out what the hell Lund's doing.'

The Zeuthens saw all this from their car. Got out.

'Has he called?' Maja Zeuthen asked Brix.

'Not yet. I have to go up on the bridge. Can you please . . .' He pointed to the Range Rover. 'Stay out of this?'

The snatch team was in the woods. Madsen got on the phone to them saying Lund had left for some reason. They were to wait for the ambush and get ready to pick up the girl.

Robert Zeuthen stood by him, listening to every word.

He grabbed Madsen as he walked away.

'What's that about an ambush?'

'Not now . . .' Madsen said brusquely.

Zeuthen was a quiet man but stockily built. One quick move and he had the cop by the arm, dragged him round.

'I want to know.'

Madsen looked up to the observation team. Waved. Kept quiet.

Zeuthen walked off to his car.

In the trees above the camp Borch kept trying to raise Lund, got nothing but voicemail. A noise behind. He turned, saw Zeuthen's Range Rover lurching up the muddy lane.

'I don't believe this,' he murmured and watched Zeuthen and his wife get out and clamber through the ridged tracks towards them.

'This wasn't part of the deal,' Borch said, standing to block their way. 'You're putting your daughter at risk.'

Zeuthen walked to the edge of the clearing, looked down at the caravans and trailers. Juncker had his glasses trained on one, was pointing it out to a colleague.

'Is she down there?' Zeuthen asked. 'Is that the van?'

Borch came to his side.

'We can't be sure. Even if she is there we don't know he'll give her up willingly. He hasn't called. The money's still—'

'Something's coming,' Juncker cried. 'It's headed for the mobile home.'

Zeuthen and his wife tried to get closer, to see.

'I want you to go back to your car,' Borch insisted.

He told two of the officers to keep them away. Got his glasses to his face. Scanned the camp.

It was an old Fiat estate. A figure in heavy clothes at the wheel. The car pulled up outside the motorhome. The driver went to the door, unlocked it. Walked in. A flicker of gas lights inside.

It was the end of the day in the Department of Forensic Medicine. Most people were going home. Lund found herself walking down line upon line of deserted white-tiled corridors looking for the Vissenbjerg woman.

She didn't want to think about what was happening at the

bridge. Brix would stick it out until the bitter end. That was his nature. Unimaginative.

But there was no ransom handover. It was never in the plan.

Her phone rang. She looked at the screen. *Borch.*

'Before you start yelling at me understand this: it's nothing to do with money. This is about the old case. The girl, Louise Hjelby. The pathologist knows something. I'm more use here—'

'We can have that discussion later,' he cut in. 'Just now we need to know you'll answer the phone.'

'Of course I will! If it rings . . .'

'Someone's just entered the camper van, Sarah. It's happening.'

'You're in the wrong place. He sent you there for a reason. Listen . . .'

A noise. Movement in her jacket pocket.

Emilie's phone.

'I've got the call,' she said.

'Get him to talk for as long as possible,' Borch ordered. 'If we see it's coming from here we're going in.'

She left him. Answered.

'I'm sorry I'm late. Are you ready?'

'Yes,' she said, trying not to sound nervous. 'The money's all here.'

Hesitation.

'I can't hear any traffic, Lund. And that's a busy place.'

'We didn't know what was happening. I had to talk to my boss. I can be back really soon.'

'Forget it. I've changed my mind.'

'What do you mean you've changed your mind? I've got all this money—'

'The deal's off. I can get more out of him than this.'

'Meaning what?'

Lund looked round. She was close to the lecture theatre where they'd found Vissenbjerg neatly slicing a dead man apart that morning.

The line was dead.

She called Borch. He was trying to locate the source of the call, make sure it was from the motorhome.

'Well?' she asked.

'We're working on it.'

'Doing what exactly?'

No answer. He wasn't listening. Borch was shouting, shrieking. Something about Robert Zeuthen, one word over and over: *stop, stop, stop.*

Down the hill he ran, business shoes slipping in the mud, tumbling through thorn bushes, falling face first into the filthy ground, hands scrabbling, desperate.

Robert Zeuthen was a calm man with an ordered mind. But it had retreated then, couldn't take Maja's accusing glances in the car. And so a sudden mindless fury sent him racing towards the grubby white van the police were watching, no idea what to do when he got there. None at all.

He dragged himself to his feet. Bleeding, aching, hurting, he careered into the clearing, raced to the door, jerked it open.

Flashing lights coming down the hill. Voices and bellowed orders behind him.

Zeuthen ignored them, climbed inside. The stink of cigarettes and booze, of sweat and stark humanity. A figure in cheap dark clothes rising from a seat, shouting something in a foreign tongue.

They wrestled, fought, fell back through the door, lunged and punched and yelled and shrieked, tumbled to the grubby earth.

Fists flying. No words.

Then the creature found new strength, fought back. Caught Zeuthen hard on the chin with a bony fist, jumped on his chest, began to pummel.

Lights. More blows, not hard but painful.

Barrels gleaming in the dark.

They stood around in a circle. Heaved the shape off him.

Not so heavy, Zeuthen thought. Dark-blue jacket and a black wool hat. Two assault rifles poked their short barrels towards them. Arms back and raised.

Borch walked up, pulled off the hat.

Long blonde hair fell down. A mannish face. But not a man.

Zeuthen limped into the caravan. Borch followed. There was a phone on the table. Pizza boxes all around.

That was all.

The PET man walked outside, picked up the woman they'd found. Held her against the white camper van wall. Made her talk.

Then got a call himself. Listened. Finished it. Before he could do anything the phone rang again.

Looked at the name on the screen.

'Sarah . . .'

'Have you got the girl?'

'No. It was the right camper van. The phone he used earlier. He gave it away to an immigrant woman at a petrol station four hours ago. She didn't ask any questions. Why would she?'

'I tried to tell you . . .'

'Here's the thing. I just got a message back from the tracing team. That last call you received from him . . .'

Back in the city Lund stared down the gloomy corridor. The place smelled the way it did that morning. Of chemicals with the faint tang of blood beneath.

'Yes?'

'It came from a landline in the hospital. They think it was the forensic wing.'

Silence.

'If you're still in the building I want you out of there now.'

Borch waved frantically for a car.

'Sarah? Can you hear me?'

Lund didn't leave. She walked down the empty tiled corridor, boots clacking on the floor. Didn't know where to look. Could only follow her instincts and they led one place only: back to the lecture theatre where the silver table was the stage.

She found it down a dark corridor. Pushed open the double doors, fumbled for a light switch. Couldn't find one so she walked forward, reached for the torch in her pocket, turned it on.

Empty semicircular ranks of seats ahead. Borch's voice echoing in her head, going on about the baby and Mark.

But there was no one here and gradually as her eyes acclimatized to the dark she knew it. Just a pile of papers on the desk by the side of the table where Lis Vissenbjerg had been working.

She turned the beam on the wall. Located the bank of light switches and brought the theatre to life. Went back to the table and the desk, looked at the documents there. Notes for another autopsy report, one that was never delivered.

A brief read through the pages. Work to do here.

One of the fluorescent tubes flickered noisily above her head. It left half of the benches in darkness.

Lund glanced up at the thing. Cursed. Was about to go back to the autopsy report when it came to life and flooded the left side of the seats with a bright cold light.

A scream. She couldn't help it.

Lis Vissenbjerg was there at the end of the row, still in her white gown, slumped back against the pale wood. Blood round her throat. Blood down her front. Blood leaking onto the steps, dripping slowly down towards the silver table. Arms by her side. Eyes wide open. Dead as the man she'd been working on that morning.

Fingers shaking Lund scrabbled for her phone. Fumbled it. Saw the thing tumble slowly to the floor, bounce and clatter towards the woman's blood.

Heard something else too. Footsteps outside, hard, determined, diminishing.

She had her gun. The body armour was gone.

Lund retrieved her phone, went to the door and walked out into the long and gloomy passageway.

She tried to picture the place. First floor for business. Ground floor for offices. Basement . . .

Lund had been there once. Couldn't remember.

She was working along the passageway next to the lecture theatre. Empty clinical rooms, bare tables. Cabinets for bodies. Gun out, standard stance, she edged out working on the dim ambient lighting, afraid to turn on the main tubes in the ceiling for fear of revealing herself.

The footsteps were gone. Maybe he was too. She could hear her own breathing. The gentle workings of the air conditioning. Traffic outside. Sirens after a while, getting closer.

Thinking back she realized he'd read the same initial autopsy notes too. That was another reason why he came.

In the last room, next to what looked like a table waiting to be washed down, the phone rang, hers.

'We're outside,' Borch said anxiously. 'Where are you?'

'Going through the rooms.'

'Jesus Christ! Do you listen to a word I say?'

'He's killed the pathologist. I've got what she wanted to show us. There's a draft autopsy report here. Not the one we saw. She never submitted it. Schultz stopped her and . . .'

A sound behind.

A white-coated figure caught in the mirror of a shiny cabinet, dashing down the hall.

'Sarah?' Borch said. 'Hello?'

Gun out again she went to the door. Heard fading footsteps. A man fleeing.

'He's still here,' Lund said quietly. 'Going down to the ground floor. Maybe the basement.'

Didn't wait for an answer. Pocketed the phone and began to run.

Down the narrow stairs, in her head Borch's voice still asking about babies.

Down to the basement. A long corridor, ninety degrees either side. Just caught sight of a figure turning round the right-hand corner. Flying white doctor's coat. Back of head, dark hair.

Black shoes.

Lund kept on, past vast heating pipes, past electrical installations.

Another corner. A figure in white. Her gun went up. A woman started shrieking. The lift opened. Two porters there. A body on a gurney. They stared at her. At the weapon.

Lund looked down at their feet. All white hospital slip-ons.

No time to explain, no time to ask.

There was one way only he could go and so she followed, getting breathless, getting lost.

The smell of washing. Detergent and steam. She pushed open the door, found herself in a vast, empty laundry. Lines of gowns on racks, like skins shed for the night. Machines gently gurgling at the side.

A noise. Gun out, revolving round.

A face. She was aiming straight at Mathias Borch, black clothes, black hat, waving at her.

Two of them in a long, wide dimly lit room, filled with clothes and racks and storage cupboards. Plenty of places to hide.

Lund pointed to the right. Knew he'd understand. They'd worked together once. Had a feeling for it.

Now they moved slowly down the length of the laundry, Lund to one side, Borch the other. Nine-mill Heckler & Koch Compact pistols tight in hand, looking, hunting, listening.

Halfway along a sound. The ventilation rattling. The plumbing. Anything. Lund was next to pile upon pile of neatly ironed white sheets. Eyes scanning the floor, looking for a pair of black shoes. Wishing there was some way she could tell Borch.

Three more steps. A white gown thrown to the ground. He'd been here. Changing again.

'Borch?' she said.

And then a sound. One brief cry of pain. The thud of what sounded like a weapon on flesh.

'Mathias!'

She crossed the room and saw them. A figure in a heavy jacket, a three-hole ski mask obscuring his face. Borch in his arms. Pistol to the neck.

Lund lifted her weapon, aimed it. Kind of.

'Drop the gun, please,' the voice said and it was as calm and flat and intelligent as he sounded on the phone.

The hooded head was clear. But mostly she could only see Mathias Borch.

'I'm not fond of repeating myself. Drop it.'

'Shoot the bastard, Sarah!' Borch struggled in his arms. 'Just do it.'

Then he yelped with a sudden pain. She couldn't see but she could guess. A punch to the kidneys.

'Drop the gun or I kill him. And then you.'

'Sarah,' Borch pleaded, the pistol hard into his cheek.

She took a step closer.

'Do it!' Borch yelled.

'Three . . .'

Slowly so he saw, Lund held the gun, side on, pointed the barrel at the ceiling. Then crouched down to the ground, placed the weapon on the floor, slid it over.

Borch looked mad at her.

'I'll give you one final chance, Lund,' the man said. 'Bring me an interesting offer this time. Turn my head. Expect a call tomorrow.'

Then he retreated into the darkness near one of the rumbling laundry machines, dragging Borch with him.

She looked at her weapon on the floor. Heard a shriek of pain. Picked up the Heckler & Koch. Saw the open door. Borch on the ground in front of it.

Stepped over him, looked at the staircase rising up to street level.

Gone again. He knew this escape route too and she'd no idea which way to go after him.

Too many memories at that moment. Jan Meyer bloody in the dark, another partner lost.

'Mathias?'

She knelt down, touched his forehead. A cut there, bruise growing around it.

'Are you OK?' she whispered and put a hand to his cold, damp cheek.

Borch came to. Saw something in her eyes. Looked at the open door. Muttered a low curse.

Back in the autopsy theatre they were working on the corpse of Lis Vissenbjerg. Three men from forensic had started the painstaking job of detailing her death. No secrets about the method. They took one look and came up with an answer: he'd cut her throat, let her bleed to death on the spot.

'How's Borch?' Brix asked.

'Knocked about a bit. Pissed off. With me probably.' She looked at him. 'Not the only one.'

'You left a king's ransom by the side of the road without telling me. I'd no idea what was going on. The Zeuthens are going crazy.'

Lund waved away that last remark.

'He was never going to pick that money up. I told Borch to come and get it, didn't I?'

She took him over to the desk, jabbed a finger at the preliminary report.

'Vissenbjerg called me while I was on the bridge. She wanted me to see these papers. I think she was getting worried. If he went after Schultz he might come after her.'

Brix took the notes.

'That's the original report. She didn't think the girl committed suicide at all. Schultz told her to take that out of the autopsy or she'd get fired. He said he was being leaned on by someone.'

'Who?'

'She didn't get round to telling me. We need to pull in whoever investigated the original case in Jutland.'

Brix shook his head.

'Why are people getting killed because of this? Where's the connection with the Zeuthens?'

'There must be one. I ought to check on Borch. He was never good with cuts and bruises. What did you get out of the campsite?'

'Nothing. He just handed that camper van and the phone to some impoverished foreigner he saw at a petrol station and said if she waited for him by the gravel pit there might be something else. It's a woman from Estonia. She thought . . .'

He went quiet.

'Thought what?'

'She thought he seemed kind. He told her he felt sorry for someone in trouble. It was all down to big business and the government. Ruth Hedeby's going to haul me over the coals when I get back. I don't have a damned thing to tell her, do I?'

Lund tried to think of something to say. Then Borch walked in, holding a piece of surgical gauze to his neck.

'Are you OK?'

'They said I nearly needed stitches.'

Her eyes widened.

'Nearly?'

A caustic glance then, 'Do we have witnesses here? Anything?'

'What do you think?' Brix grumbled.

'He arranged that motorway stunt as a diversion,' Lund told them. 'He wanted space to get to Vissenbjerg. He's chasing this old case. So . . .' At least they were listening. 'We need to work out where he's going to look next.'

'Why the hell didn't you shoot when you could?' Borch demanded.

Brix wasn't interested. They'd taken the camper van into the forensic garage in the Politigården. He wanted them to check it out. Find something he could pass off as a lead.

Borch stood in front of her, waiting for an answer.

'You could have taken him.'

She walked back towards the exit.

He followed, asked, 'Why . . . ?'

'How would we have found Emilie Zeuthen if I'd shot him?'

'You could have wounded him in the arm or leg or something. You're a good shot—'

'No I'm not! You know nothing about me. If you hadn't interfered . . .'

He threw up his arms.

'Oh it's my fault now! You were wandering round in the dark when I turned up. You could have shot him and—'

'You were standing there!' she yelled. 'In the way.' Then, without a thought until the word had emerged, 'Again.'

He latched on to that.

'Again?'

'I just couldn't. OK?' Lund said and wished she could go somewhere quiet, sit alone for a while, not think about him or Emilie Zeuthen. Or any of the old ghosts either.

That shut him up for some reason. So she walked out to the car.

Borch wasn't the only one hurting. Robert Zeuthen had cut himself on the hand in the pointless fight at the campsite. Sore, miserable, aching, Zeuthen was driving his Range Rover, Reinhardt in the passenger seat, Maja in the back.

Then the old man broke the news of another murder. A pathologist.

'The police are asking if we know anything about this,' he added. 'I told them it was a mystery to us. The prosecutor. The woman. Some case in Jutland. We've dealt with none of these people. They seem to think the kidnapper wasn't after the ransom.'

'Why not?' Maja asked, the first words she'd spoken since they got in the car. 'What in God's name does he want?

'They don't know. He's told them he'll call again tomorrow with a new demand. The last one. Though of course he said that before.'

'Did he mention Emilie?' Zeuthen wondered.

'That's all he said.'

Maja's voice was getting louder, angrier.

'There must be more than that. Did he say why he didn't want the money?'

'No. I've arranged for it to go into the National Bank, Robert. After that . . .'

Zeuthen looked at his wife. Asked if she was OK. She looked pale, worn out.

'Stop,' she ordered. 'I want to get out.'

They were on the outskirts of the city. Lights. People in the street.

'I'll take you to Carsten's,' Zeuthen said.

'Stop the car!'

He drove on. She started shrieking. Zeuthen pulled in by the side of the road. She was out in an instant, dashing into the bushes. He leapt after her.

'Maja . . .'

Maybe she wanted to be sick and couldn't. Maybe she couldn't stand the sight of him, the big car, the talk about money. Sobbing, close to hysterical, she walked out of the bushes, started marching aimlessly down the pavement.

'Talk to me,' he begged. 'Please.'

She turned, furious, eyes shiny with tears.

'Emilie's not coming back, Robert. Can't you see it?'

He caught up with her. She kept walking.

'I'll get him what he wants. Whatever it is . . .'

'Maybe she's dead already.'

That made him mad.

'No. She isn't. Emilie wrote her name on that wall. For us. She knows we're coming for her. She knows . . .'

His leg hurt. Must have bruised that too somewhere. He was limping, pathetic in the freezing night, their breath misting up around them.

She stopped by the railings. He tried to hold her slender shoulders.

'If you'd just let her come home with me,' she cried. 'Where she belonged. Just . . .'

No words. Nothing to do but put his arms around her. Tears against his cheek. His against hers.

Maja sobbed at his neck, fought for a while. Gave up. Her arms drifted round his waist. Clutched him. It was like the old closeness. The love that had vanished.

Mouth to her ear, he whispered the words, meant every one of them.

'I'll bring her back. I promise. Nothing else matters. Nothing . . .'

She didn't speak. Just cried.

'I promise,' Robert Zeuthen said again. 'I'll make this better.'

There was an election poster on the fence. Troels Hartmann,

beaming out at the world. Prime Minister. A good man they all said. Someone on your side.

Hartmann had the radio on as the car pulled onto the cobbles of the Christiansborg courtyard. The murder in the university hospital and its probable connection to the Zeuthen case made the lead item. But Anders Ussing came a close second, accusing Hartmann's government of negligence over the abduction of Emilie.

Reporters and TV crews crowded round the car. The news bulletin carried a brief report of the failed ransom, and the suggestion that the kidnapper's motive might not be money at all.

'There's been no statement from Hartmann, the police or PET,' the report continued. 'Ussing claims both the kidnapping and the murders could have been avoided if the Justice Minister had heeded the warnings he received.'

'As if he'd know,' Hartmann grunted then got out, smiled for the cameras, let the bodyguards push through the mob, get him into the building.

He went straight to his office. Mogens Rank was waiting there fiddling nervously with a pencil.

Hartmann sat down, Weber and Nebel at his side. Opened his hands, stared at the smartly dressed man opposite, waited.

'I'm sorry I didn't get back to any of you on the phone,' Rank said, smoothing down his jacket. 'I was looking into what's happened here. It seems we did know about this girl, Hjelby. It was just after we came into office. I was overwhelmed with work. I didn't—'

'Tell us about it, Mogens,' Hartmann demanded.

'It was nothing. A thirteen-year-old girl was found dead in a harbour in West Jutland. Three Zeeland sailors came across the body.' A shrug. 'Which meant, of course, the case had to go by my desk.'

'Why?' Morten Weber asked.

Rank looked at him, surprised.

'Zeeland were behind us during the campaign. It only seemed right to take an interest.'

He looked at Nebel, as if for support. Got none.

'All the evidence said it was suicide,' Rank added. 'So I assumed the case was closed.'

'Last night you said you knew nothing about this,' Weber pointed out.

'Yes,' Rank agreed. 'I apologize. I was busy. It was a few pages that crossed my desk and required no action. I forgot.' He looked at Hartmann. 'I'm sorry, Troels. I know I've embarrassed you. But really, however much Ussing wants to make of this, that's all there is to it.'

Morten Weber groaned and let his head fall briefly on his arms.

'You forgot, Mogens?'

'Yes. Don't you believe me? Why would I lie?'

'And when these same three sailors are murdered?' Weber yelled. His hand twirled at his ear. 'Still no bells ring up here?'

No answer.

'When the deputy prosecutor involved in the case got strung up from the courthouse? And now the pathologist's dead too?'

'No bells. Sorry.'

Weber got up, walked to the wall, kicked it hard.

'We were looking for Emilie Zeuthen,' Rank barked at him. 'I didn't have that old case in my mind. It seemed of no importance . . .'

Hartmann sighed, stared at him.

'But it was, Mogens. Tell me truthfully. Have you interfered in any of this? Acted in a partial manner?'

'What do you mean?'

'He means,' Weber cut in, 'did you do anyone a favour? Zeeland for example?'

'Of course not! Why would I? As far as I could see the case was solved.'

Hartmann slammed his fist on the table.

'But it wasn't. Was it?'

A long silence.

Then he said more quietly, 'Emilie Zeuthen's life hangs in the balance. She could be dead over those . . . pieces of paper you ignored. The bastard behind this has told the police they've one final chance to get her home. We don't even know how . . .'

Rank pulled himself up, shook his head.

'The very suggestion I intervened is absurd. Outrageous. I resent it deeply.'

Another roll of his head.

'And it's not my fault Ussing's been given all this material. Rosa Lebech's husband's got it in for you, not me.' He jabbed a finger across the table. 'I won't take the blame for your peccadilloes.'

Weber came back to the table, looked at Karen Nebel.

Then, before Hartmann could speak, said, 'Don't talk to the media until this thing's over, Mogens. When I call, you answer.'

Rank nodded, looked relieved to be allowed to go.

'I should throw him out of the fucking window,' Hartmann grumbled when he'd left.

'You can't,' Weber said straight away. 'You may be facing a revolt inside the party very soon. Like it or not Mogens Rank's on your side. In principle anyway.'

Hartmann swore again.

'I don't trust him. We need to check his story.'

A knock at the door. Weber opened it. One of the attendants with some bags of food.

'We need to eat first,' he said, opening them up, putting plastic boxes on the table. 'I got sushi. Hope that's OK.'

'To hell with food!' Hartmann yelled. 'I want to know what happened. From the moment that report came into Rank's ministry and the second he decided to dump it.'

Weber laughed.

'What's funny?' Hartmann asked.

'The only people I can get to investigate Mogens are the ones he appointed himself. Who investigates the investigators?'

'I want—'

'I know what you want,' Weber cut in. 'I'll talk to Dyhring. See if we can prise him away from his master.'

Hartmann seemed mollified by that.

'I should warn you,' Weber added. 'Jens Lebech's in custody. This is starting to get close. We've been here before. I know you're worried about Emilie Zeuthen. We all are. But you're the Prime Minister. We're fighting an election. For everyone's sake you need to keep your distance.'

He got a foul look back for that.

'We haven't been here before,' Hartmann insisted. 'Don't say that. What happened back then . . . was nothing to do with me.'

Morten Weber smiled, didn't say another word.

*

Back in the Politigården forensic garage they were going over the recovered camper van. Plenty of evidence Emilie had been inside. Nothing to suggest where she'd gone. Juncker was getting tired and grumpy, like the night before. At times he reminded her of a young Mark, when he was funny, charming and just a touch troubled. It was her fault she never noticed the fragility until it was too late. Looking at Asbjørn Juncker going over the van, big eyes staring at the evidence, she saw her own failures so clearly.

'What's he after if it's not the money?' Juncker asked.

The contents of the van had been set out on tables in front of the vehicle.

'Does he just want to kill people? Is that it? He's a lunatic.'

Lund stared at the objects in front of her.

'This man's not a lunatic. Tell me what you have.'

He took a deep breath and started to point.

'Got blonde hair and bits of food from the back of the cabin. He probably put her in front of the TV so he could watch her in the driver's mirror. The van was stolen four days ago from a dealership. The plates were changed.'

The curtains were taped up. There was no way the girl could see out.

Madsen came in and said the Zeuthens had arrived, demanding to speak to someone.

'They're very persistent,' he added.

'Get Borch to deal with it.'

He looked surprised.

'Borch's gone to Jutland. I thought you knew. PET wanted to look into the cold case.'

Juncker was chuntering again. Something about how she should have shot the man when she had the chance.

'Fine,' Lund retorted, then took a few of the things in plastic evidence bags and left.

Back in the office she began to spread them out in front of Robert and Maja Zeuthen. The couple looked different. They didn't seem to be at war any longer. Brix sat in, listening mostly.

'He gave her toys and things to read,' Lund said, spreading out a series of jigsaws, puzzles, books and magazines. 'Do these things mean anything to you?'

The mother pored over them.

'The books ... this magazine ... they're her favourites. How could he have known that?'

'Maybe he asked her?' Brix suggested. 'He's trying to make her feel secure. As if she's a part of this. Not a prisoner.'

'That's true up to a point,' Lund agreed. 'But it's more likely he knew about these things before. He got close to Emilie somehow. Do you have any idea—?'

'No!' Zeuthen interrupted. 'How can you be sure he doesn't want money? You didn't do what he asked. You left the bridge.'

Brix came to her rescue.

'He went nowhere near the ransom. Not today. Not yesterday. He didn't have Emilie with him either. It's not possible. He's just playing. Trying to draw us away from what he really wants to do.'

'What's that?' Maja asked.

'To get to the bottom of this old police case,' Lund said. 'A thirteen-year-old girl was found dead in a harbour in West Jutland. Not far from some Zeeland facilities. Those three dead sailors of yours came upon the body. He wants—'

Zeuthen slammed his hand on the table.

'I've told you. I know nothing about this.'

'It looks as if the girl was murdered,' Lund added. 'Someone covered it up.'

Maja Zeuthen turned to him.

'How are you involved, Robert?'

'I'm not. I've never heard of it until now.'

'It doesn't mean you personally,' Brix said. 'You're symbolic. Maybe to him you are Zeeland. Someone else in the company could know about the case . . .'

'I've asked Reinhardt to get our security people to check the records. Talk to him. What else are you doing?'

Lund hesitated before answering.

'We're still trying to track some things—'

'You've no idea, have you?' Maja Zeuthen interrupted. 'After two days . . . not a clue.'

No answer.

Zeuthen said, 'When he calls again tell him I'll pay anything. There's no ceiling. Whatever he wants.'

'He's not looking for money . . .' Lund started.

'Just tell him!' he shouted. 'And this time do as he says.'

117

He got up, marched out. The mother stayed.

'Emilie scratched her name on that wall,' she said. 'Maybe she left something else . . .'

'We searched the camper van.' Lund got to her feet. 'I'm sorry. We didn't find anything of much use.'

'Her room at home . . .'

'We searched that too,' Brix said.

She glared at them.

'I'm her mother. I see things you don't.'

With that she left. Lund thought about what she'd said. Returned to the garage downstairs. Juncker was still grumbling like a tired toddler. She told him to go home and get some sleep. He didn't move.

Inside the caravan she sat where Emilie might have been. Juncker watched, kept quiet for once.

'He could see her all the time,' Lund said, eyeing her own reflection in the driver's mirror. 'Except for the corners and there's nothing there.'

She got up and walked into the tiny toilet. The window was taped up with black plastic so Emilie couldn't look out. But she couldn't be seen either.

'I've been through the toilet roll,' Juncker said. 'There's nothing there.'

The tape had been pulled back on one corner. The glass was opaque underneath. Lund slowly removed the plastic and breathed on the surface.

Finger marks.

'We need something dusted here,' she said.

Juncker sat outside and watched. Guilty but fascinated. One of the forensic officers came over, got out a brush and powder and went to work.

Gradually the letters emerged.

Top C. 03. KPS.

'She left a message and I never saw it,' Juncker whispered. 'I'm rubbish at this.'

'No you're not,' Lund said and gently punched his arm. 'I told you. Learn to look.'

'What does it mean?'

'Emilie's a clever kid. She's telling us where she's been. Top

Camping. 03 is the ring road. That's the route out from the camp-site.'

'And KPS?'

She moved closer, stared at the letters.

'Somewhere else he's been keeping her. If we're lucky . . . where she is now.'

Around eight Karen Nebel came into Hartmann's office and said he had an unexpected visitor: Rosa Lebech demanding a private meeting.

He took his head out of a speech for the following day then told her to bring Lebech in. She looked angry, hungry for something.

'I'm not passing judgment on the Justice Minister just yet,' he told her. 'I want to get to the bottom of it. Just like you . . .'

'I don't give a shit about Mogens Rank. What are you and PET doing with Jens?'

Hartmann thrust his hands into his trouser pockets, kept quiet.

'He was picked up at home. In front of the kids for pity's sake.'

'We don't tell PET what to do, Rosa. We're not that kind of government. They're investigating a leak of confidential informa-tion. That's their business. Not mine.'

She came close.

'You knew they were going to arrest him, didn't you?'

'No. I knew they suspected him.'

'Because of us! Because he knows!'

'I wasn't aware he did,' Hartmann said carefully.

'I told him a couple of weeks ago. I didn't want him or the kids to hear from someone else.'

Hartmann nodded, smiled. Took her hand. She didn't recoil.

Soft voice. Understanding.

'You did the right thing. This is awkward for all of us. I had nothing to do with it. If Jens is innocent they'll let him go. I can't get involved. And even if I did know . . . do you think I could have told you?'

She pulled away at that.

'Yes. You could. You're too much trouble. I have to defend you to my party. Now I've got to do it to my family. Enough's enough . . .'

She was getting loud. The doors were open. There were civil servants still around. Hartmann got up and closed them.

'If Jens leaked those files he got us into this mess. Blame him. Not me.'

'He's innocent. I want him released.'

'If he's innocent he will be. Love . . .'

Again he reached down and squeezed her fingers. Then touched her cheek.

'I wish to God we were just a couple of ordinary people. That we didn't have to jump through these hoops. We've talked about this. For now we do.' His fingers rose and brushed her short dark hair. 'Let's meet later. Put the politics to one side.' He cocked his head to one side, grinned. 'Let's just be us.'

Rosa Lebech retreated from him, folded her arms.

'If you want a meeting call my campaigns officer. She keeps the diary.'

Weber was walking past as she marched out.

'Not a happy woman,' he noted. 'I wonder at your choices sometimes. Couldn't you have picked someone a little less perilous? Say . . . an actress. With a drug problem. And tattoos.'

Hartmann seemed amused by that.

'It's the heart, Morten. If you had one you'd understand. Rosa's pissed off PET have brought in her husband.'

'Yes, well. They won't be holding him. Insufficient evidence at the moment.'

'That's good,' Hartmann said.

'Is it?' Weber scratched his head. 'If so it's the only thing that is.'

'Don't play games, please.'

'Why not? Everyone else is. I had a long talk with Dyhring. Our PET man.'

'And?'

Weber picked up a calendar printout, and a list of names.

'In the middle of that Jutland case Mogens Rank attended a business association dinner out there. So did Peter Schultz.'

'What does Rank say?'

A shrug.

'He says he doesn't remember ever meeting Schultz. For a government minister his memory truly is shocking at times.'

'Do you believe him?' Hartmann asked, half in hope.

'I'd like to, Troels. Honestly.'

*

Back at the Politigården Juncker wouldn't go home. So she sent him out looking for the camper van's tracks while she went upstairs to view the traffic CCTV they'd recovered. They had the van leaving the motorway at an industrial area exit, number fourteen, then rejoining the road on the way to the petrol station where he handed over the keys and the phone to the first person who'd take them. They'd no idea where he went after that, but Lund thought it a good bet he'd taken the exit to leave Emilie somewhere close by.

Someone called Eva Lauersen kept calling. Mark's girlfriend she said. But before Lund could phone back Brix brought in a tubby, silver-haired man with a broad Jutland accent. Nicolaj Overgaard. Local police station chief when Louise Hjelby's death was investigated.

He looked . . . sleepy. None too bright.

Lund parked him opposite her. Brix sat on the corner of the desk. She asked who might have been upset by the suicide verdict: family, boyfriends, someone close?

'Nobody I can think of,' Overgaard said. 'The girl was in a foster home. Hadn't been there long. They moved her around a lot. No one really knew her much.'

His clothes seemed too light for winter. A pink checked shirt. A jacket made for warmer weather. Lund scribbled a note and gave it to Madsen.

'The original autopsy report's turned up,' Brix said. 'Different to the one that got filed here. It says the girl was murdered.'

The old cop lifted his head. He had a nervous tic. Right eye, flickering.

'It seems clear Louise was attacked and injured before she went into the water,' Lund added.

'Can I see this report?'

Brix handed it over. Overgaard flicked through it, too quickly.

'You're saying you never saw that?' Lund asked.

'News to me.'

'How's that possible? The pathologist said Peter Schultz pressed her to write a false report. If Schultz leaned on her he must have leaned on you.'

Overgaard just stared at her, didn't speak.

'And they're both dead now,' she added. 'Think about it.'

'No . . . no one put pressure on me.'

121

'So there was nothing irregular in the investigation?' she asked. 'You found a girl who'd been murdered and dumped in the water. Then you signed off a report saying it was suicide.'

He didn't like that.

'We did everything by the book. Those sailors said they found the kid in the harbour. The autopsy I got back from Copenhagen said it was suicide. I don't know where you got this new one . . .'

'The pathologist wanted us to see it,' Brix broke in. 'We found it next to her body. He'd cut her throat. Schultz . . .'

'I read about that,' Overgaard said in a voice close to a whisper.

'He appears to be interested in those familiar with the case.' Brix's mouth made an approximation of a smile. 'Like you.'

Madsen came back with the answer to Lund's query scribbled on a pad.

'If you feel vulnerable,' Lund said, 'we could offer you protection. A little help would be appreciated in return.'

A nervous laugh. Overgaard got up.

'No. I'm going down to the Police Association to cheat at cards. No one's interested in me.'

'Sit down,' Lund said.

He looked scared.

'Sit down,' she repeated.

The sudden, false good humour was gone.

'What is it now?'

She showed him the note. A flight number.

'Why are you in such a hurry to leave Denmark? You booked a flight to Bangkok today. It leaves just before midnight. You're not going to the Police Association to play cards. You're running away.' Lund put her arms on the desk. 'Why is that? Who are you afraid of?'

'Did somebody make it illegal to travel?' Overgaard demanded.

'Straight after the Hjelby case was closed you retired and moved to Copenhagen. You live on your own. You don't know anyone here.'

Something in his eyes then. Resignation. Naked fear.

'Stress. They gave me a pension. I wanted to be in the city. That's all there is to it. Shit! I came here voluntarily. I told you all I could. I'm going . . .'

He didn't move. He was an old cop. He knew.

Brix nodded to one of the night team.

'Reserve a cell for our colleague here. Remind him of his rights.'

'What the . . . ?' Overgaard began.

'We've reason to suspect you're withholding important information,' Brix went on. 'I've a nine-year-old girl out there who could be dead tomorrow. If you know anything—'

'I don't!' the old cop screamed. 'Nothing. I've got a plane to catch. Let . . . me . . . go!'

Madsen came in with a couple more men and took him away.

'Go home, Lund,' Brix ordered. 'Get some sleep. Keep the phone close by.'

She'd been thinking, dreaming for a moment.

'This man goes where he likes. Does what he likes. Knows what's coming next.'

'True,' he agreed.

'Borch thought he was wearing body armour when he was at the hospital. He's got a handle on computers. Security systems. Weapons for all we know . . .'

'Lund. Go home.'

She didn't move.

'He's winning, Brix. He knows where he's going next. And we don't have a clue.'

He picked up Emilie's phone from the desk. Then her car keys. Held the things until she took them.

Maja Zeuthen still hated the Zeuthen family home. Too easy to get lost. Too cold in places. Too many dark corners, hidden passages, rooms a family of four could never use.

But Emilie and Carl adored Drekar. They knew it better than she did. Loved playing hide and seek in the upper floors, burying themselves in dusty attics and storerooms, emerging filthy, laughing, full of mischief. Once she found them climbing to the very top, saying they wanted to find grandad's dragon and see through the creature's eyes. After that she'd put the upper storey out of bounds.

Still, it was the place they grew up. Part of their childhood. It was never going to be easy to drag them away to Carsten's tiny bachelor flat in the city, make them happy there. It wasn't the size. Or even, mostly, that it was his place, not theirs. Something was missing. The love that initially joined them, mother and father, sister and brother. Tied to one another by the magic that was family.

She sat in the downstairs playroom going through their things, Carsten next to her, trying to help as best he could. Next door they could hear Robert and Reinhardt talking quietly about the investigation. They were doing what they could. Robert had set him looking for any information Zeeland possessed about the Jutland case. There seemed little of note. The sailors' papers were in order. They were witnesses, never suspects.

Carsten sat muttering under his breath as she ran through some of Emilie's scrapbooks, her photos, some poems.

Then Robert said, too loudly, 'Check with the directors too. I want to make sure we're not hiding anything.'

'That's it,' Carsten snapped, got up and went to the door.

She didn't follow. There'd been enough arguments. But she heard.

'What are you hiding?' Carsten yelled. 'Is this all down to you and Zeeland?'

She could picture it now. Robert looking resentful. Reinhardt being the servant he was, walking to close the door.

'Maja's going crazy trying to find the smallest thing that could bring Emilie back. Is she looking in the wrong place, Robert?'

'Carsten,' she whispered. 'For the love of God shut up . . .'

Loud footsteps. He'd walked into the room.

'What's happening? What have you done? It's your stinking money that's brought this down on our heads, isn't it? Well? Will someone answer me?'

The door closed. Maybe Reinhardt had pushed him out. Carsten started hammering on it. He wasn't an angry man by nature. If he was she would never have fallen lazily into his bed when the marriage crumbled. But he sensed something now.

Maja looked at the hand-drawn page in front of her and thought: perhaps he's got his reasons.

A photo of her and Robert looking younger and so happy, her head on his shoulder. Both smiling. Emilie had cut it into the shape of a heart. Drawn flowers and birds as a border. On the opposite page four silhouettes. Mother, father, two children, hand in hand walking through a field full of childish, exaggerated daisies, a woodland, their own, behind.

A line of text above: *The Best.*
A line of text below: *The Zeuthens – that is US!*
Carsten was still ranting outside.

Her hand went to her mouth. She started to sob, to choke, to feel the tears run slowly down her cheeks.

Emilie was lost in the dark world beyond the meadow, past the giant flowers, through the bare forest. They all were.

Lund's home was in a backstreet of Herlev, a suburb nine kilometres north of the city. Nothing special. The giant shape of the huge local hospital close by. A street of low bungalows, none alike. Then her simple red wooden cottage. She'd moved in six months before, had yet to finish furnishing and decorating the place. The tiny garden was full of sickly plants in pots green with algae. The wheelbarrow she'd picked up for pennies at the junkyard was still parked near the front door, now brimming over with rainwater.

Life would come back to the little garden somehow. Once there was the time.

She parked her car in the road as usual. Couldn't stop thinking about what she'd said to Brix. This man was special. The way he knew things. His detailed preparation. He was no ordinary sailor out for revenge.

Then she thought about Mathias Borch. There was a good professional reason to call him.

Before he could say much she cut in.

'Did you hear we picked up the old police chief from there? Nicolaj Overgaard?'

He laughed. Sounded nicer now he was distant. Younger too.

'Yeah. I went to the local police station here. They were really impressed by that. He was quite a popular guy.'

'He knows something. I'm sure. I'll give him a hard time tomorrow.'

A sudden noise. She wondered what it was. Then realized: a ship's horn blaring down the line.

'Where are you?'

'Down the harbour. I wanted to see where they found the body. Do you think KPS could be a company that's closed or something?'

'Could be,' she agreed.

He went quiet. She thought she'd lost him.

'Sarah? Are you OK?'

'Long day. I didn't do too well, did I?'

'None of us did. It went the way he planned. We weren't to know. You were good.'

'Don't be ridiculous.'

He paused again. Then said, 'I've got to go now. I just wanted to say . . . I understand why you didn't shoot.'

'Good. Maybe I didn't use the right words. I can't find them sometimes. You should know that.'

She was sure he giggled then.

'Should I? Remember when we went to the beach and you left me there? Just drove off and abandoned me. You found the words you wanted then.'

Lund didn't answer. There was a light on in the house and suddenly she wasn't thinking about Borch at all. Just a man smart enough to take body armour with him when he needed it, and stay ten steps ahead of everyone chasing him.

'Sarah? Hello?'

She put the phone in her jacket. Reached into the glove compartment. Took out the nine-mill pistol.

Walked slowly, warily to the front door.

Pushed at it. Open. The sound of someone moving inside.

One living room. Two bedrooms off. A tiny kitchen. A bathroom so small it might have been in one of the camper vans they'd been looking at.

Gun down by her side Lund walked into her home, saw the shape come out of the shadows. Lifted the weapon, finger tight on trigger.

Looked.

Long fair hair. Mouth wide open. Shrieking.

Screaming.

'Oh,' Lund said and dropped the gun.

Eva Lauersen stood holding on to the nearest chair, the shabbiest, clutching at her bulging stomach.

'Sorry,' Lund said.

'Owwww . . .'

She was doubled over as far as the bump would let her. Lund started praying . . . *not now, not now, please God . . . not now.*

'Sit down, Eva.'

Lund placed the handgun on the small dining table, came over and helped her into the chair.

'Deep breaths,' she urged. 'All the way down to the stomach.'

Eva looked younger even than Mark then. She wore a long-sleeved grey jumper flecked with paint stains. A tatty old sweatshirt underneath.

'I tried to call,' she whimpered, giving Lund a scared look. 'You said we could just turn up. You told us where the key was.'

'I said I'm sorry.'

'You had a gun!'

Lund nodded.

'Where's Mark?'

She was getting her breath back. Older than her son. But younger in some ways too. Nice, charming. Maybe not so bright.

'I think it must be the hormones,' Eva said. 'Just . . .' Her arms waved. 'Pumping through my body. I go a bit mad at times.'

'Wait,' Lund ordered and put on the kettle.

'No let me!'

Eva jumped up, found the pot. Some teabags. Looked more at home in the kitchen than Lund would ever be.

'We had a row. I shouted at him. I think he's having second thoughts. I got upset. I couldn't . . .' She grimaced. 'My mum and dad split up. They don't live here any more. I couldn't think of anywhere else to go.'

Lund made her sit down and took over. She could at least make tea.

'Does Mark know where you are?'

Hands on belly, eyes on the threadbare carpet.

'I left a message but he hasn't called.'

'That doesn't mean he's having second thoughts, Eva.'

'The flat's a dump. We've got no money. This is all so stupid . . .'

Lund got the tea though she really wanted a beer.

'Things will work out. When Mark finishes his apprenticeship he'll earn more money.'

Eva's big round eyes stared at her.

'The company laid off all the apprentices three months ago. He's driving a cab. All hours. He only touches my tummy if I ask him. He never . . .'

Lund had to ask.

'The baby wasn't planned?'

Eva looked at her as if that was the stupidest question she'd ever heard.

'Mark was happy when it happened,' she said quickly. 'He said he wanted a real family more than anything. Because he'd never had one. He didn't want to end up alone. Like . . . like . . .'

The big blue eyes closed.

'Oh crap. I'm sorry. I shouldn't have said that. I'm just stupid . . .'

'No you're not,' Lund insisted.

'Should I leave?'

'You're staying here.'

Lund's phone rang. Eva was staring at the gun.

'Don't touch,' Lund said, and answered.

Borch again.

'Are you OK? You just went.'

'I'm fine. That bang on your head.'

'It really hurts.'

'Take some paracetamol.'

'I did. It's still bad. I think I've got whiplash.'

'Whiplash?'

'They say it can last for months. Maybe I need one of those neck collars . . .'

'Oh poor Mathias. The pain. Think yourself lucky. At least you get spared childbirth.'

Eva was watching her, wide-eyed again, hand to her mouth.

'You've got the reports I sent up from Jutland?' he asked primly.

'I took them home with me. Didn't I say that?'

'No. I put crosses against some passages. You might want to raise them with Nicolaj Overgaard in the morning.'

'OK.'

'I'm going to sleep now. If I can. Goodnight.'

And he was gone.

She fetched the reports from the car. When she got back Eva was still sitting upright in her chair like a schoolgirl waiting to be told what to do.

'You look wiped out,' Lund said. 'Help yourself to some food. Anything. Take my bed. It's all right. You're welcome to stay as long as you want.'

For a moment she was worried Eva expected a kiss. But then she shrugged, said she wasn't hungry and took herself off.

Lund weighed up Borch's reports. Lots to go through. Hours.

She went to the sink, poured away the mug of tea. Got a bottle of beer out of the fridge and drank it while frying a couple of eggs.

Then she took another beer, the eggs, some bread and a couple of slices of ham to the table. Sat down and started to read.

Four

Saturday 12th November

Just after nine Lund was back in the Politigården checking a report from the night team and some fresh information from Borch in Jutland. Juncker had gone out on the road to chase potential locations.

'We haven't got anything that looks like KPS,' he said when he called in. 'Maybe he was trying to pull some trick with the camper van. We don't know for sure she was in it when we caught the thing on CCTV.'

He sounded fresh. He was young. She wasn't and had slept badly on the hard single bed in the tiny spare room, wondering about Eva and Mark, what kind of future their child might have.

'Take a look round the harbour,' she suggested.

A pause, then, 'May I ask why? Nothing we've got—'

'This man's got something to do with ships. He keeps coming back to the docks. To Zeeland. I'm just guessing but I think this is his world. Where he feels comfortable. Where he retreats when things turn bad.'

Another long moment.

'That makes sense,' the young cop said.

'Thank you, Asbjørn.'

'I thought I was Juncker.'

'Today's a new day. The harbour. Start looking.'

When she came off the call Brix was there anxiously asking if she still had Emilie's phone with her. Lund rolled her eyes and showed him.

'Did we get anything else out of our friend from Jutland?'

He shook his head.

'Ten hours we've had him in here and all he can do is whine about going to Bangkok to see his girlfriends.'

'Let me at him,' she said and grabbed a notepad and pen.

'He is a colleague!' Brix pointed out. 'I'd like a bit more to go on than a ticket to Thailand.'

She stomped off to the holding cell, Brix behind her, and got one of the guards to let them in.

The first thing Overgaard did was moan about the quality of the breakfast.

'I'm not here to talk about food,' Lund said, sitting down. 'Or your teenage hookers in Bangkok. There's a young girl out there. I'm trying to keep her alive. Either you come up with something that helps—'

'Or what?' Overgaard snapped. He was trying to look cocky. Didn't work. He was a nervous, frightened man.

'Or I kick you out of here and let you fend for yourself. Maybe you can get a ticket out to love land tomorrow. Will that be time enough do you think?'

He was staring at her, mouth open, terrified.

'Think about it,' Lund went on. 'Peter Schultz covered up Louise Hjelby's death and he got strung up from the courthouse. I know. I watched. Lis Vissenbjerg wrote a fake autopsy. So he cut her throat and sat her upright in a lecture theatre in the hospital, bleeding to death. He has a certain kind of style, don't you think?'

She wondered if the old man was going to cry. Instead he asked, 'Do you like seeing dead people?'

'It's my job.'

'It wasn't mine. I was a police chief in the back end of nowhere. We pulled up drunk drivers. Threw the odd burglar into a cell. We never had the kind of shit you deal with . . .'

Brix bridled at that.

'You were a police officer. You were supposed to cope with whatever came your way.'

Lund slapped the original police report on the bed.

'According to this pile of crap you believed Louise Hjelby ran away from her foster home and drowned herself five days later. Five days . . .'

'So what?'

'Didn't it seem the least bit odd no one saw her? Didn't you want to know where she might have been?'

Overgaard waved a dismissive hand.

'The kid was an orphan. She'd been in God knows how many different homes. She used to wander away on her own.'

'I hope you're right. We've got officers down there going through every single line of your report,' Lund promised. 'She was thirteen. She'd had sex not long before she died.'

He frowned, shrugged.

'Didn't that strike you as curious?' Lund asked. 'Given that as far as you knew she never even had a boyfriend?'

'Do you think she was going to advertise the fact? Who says this pathologist got it right anyway?'

Lund smiled at him.

'Good question. We're checking that too. She's coming up sweeter than you.' Another rap of the fingers on his report. 'You were very happy to conclude that the kid didn't just throw herself into the water. She tied herself to a concrete block too.'

Another wave.

'I don't remember the details . . .'

She threw a photo on the table. A lump of cement, the remains of a heavy rope tied through a ring.

'We've recovered the block from your forensic store. It weighs forty-six kilos. She was a short, slight, thirteen-year-old girl. I doubt she could even have moved that thing on her own. Certainly not carried it to the dockside and thrown it in.'

'Maybe it was already on the pier. She just pushed it over—'

'Maybe?' Brix cried. 'You should have called in a homicide team the moment you saw this. Even a hick police chief—'

'You knew this girl had been seized,' Lund interrupted. 'You knew full well she was kept somewhere, raped there, then murdered and thrown into the dock. You're an accessory . . .'

His grey head was going from side to side.

'I'm putting all this in front of a judge,' Lund promised. 'If you're lucky he indicts you. If you're not you can walk out of here on your own and wait and see what happens. We won't be covering your back.'

Overgaard's heavy chin was on his chest. He didn't say a word.

'Thanks to you we're dealing with a kidnapping and a bunch of murders,' Brix told him. 'I want a name. I want to know who was leaning on you to bury this thing. How a man in your position—'

'I was doing my job!' Overgaard yelled. 'That's all.'

They waited. The old cop looked lost and desperate.

'I was just a nobody. Happy that way. Nothing ever happened there. Then this kid turns up. We thought the Zeeland sailors had something to do with it. They'd been in port.'

'It wasn't them . . .' Lund cut in. 'If they'd killed her why would they report the death?'

'I didn't do . . . murder. I sent it off to Copenhagen for an autopsy. Next thing that deputy prosecutor turns up, breathing down my neck. He says . . . it's suicide. End of story. Argue with me and you'll be out of a job. No prospects. No pension.'

'So you rolled over?' Brix said.

'No! I tried to argue . . . he was from here. One of you. Schultz talked to the crew as well and they shut up after that.' Overgaard looked away. 'He seemed to know all kinds of people.'

'What sort of people?' Lund asked.

'Maybe a month afterwards this man turned up. He didn't think it was a suicide. He wanted the case reopened.'

'Give us a name.'

'He never said who he was. Danish. Forties. I thought maybe he was family but they said she didn't have any.'

'This man . . .'

'He said he'd been away at sea for a long time. Probably for Zeeland by the sound of it.' He looked up at them. 'That's all I know, honest. I was just trying to do my job. Schultz came along and got heavy. I never liked it. I had a breakdown after that. Stress they said.'

'You're breaking my heart,' Lund told him.

'Schultz was leaning on me! What was I supposed to do?'

Brix looked him in the eye.

'You were supposed to say no.'

'What sort of people?' Lund asked again.

Nothing. Then Overgaard said, 'I've told you all I can. What happens now?'

'We put you in front of a judge,' Brix said. 'We get you remanded. No chance of bail. Not with that ticket to Bangkok in the file.'

Nicolaj Overgaard put his grey head in his hands and groaned.

A face in the corridor, anxious at the glass. Mark.

Brix noticed. Seemed to know she had family difficulties.

'I'll get someone to deal with this one,' he said, nodding across the table. 'Keep it short.'

Lund found Mark waiting on a bench seat near the office. She sat down next to him, asked if he'd talked to Eva. A shake of the head.

'She slept at my place last night. It's OK. You can use it if you want.'

'No thanks. I can cope.'

The juvenile petulant tone was there already.

'She thinks you've got doubts about the whole thing. You don't want the baby.'

He looked as if he hadn't slept.

'I told her to calm down. That she could trust you. If it's about money I can help . . .'

'What if I do have doubts?'

This wasn't the place to talk. Too many people. She asked him into an unused cubicle. To her surprise he followed, sat down opposite her.

'Of course you've got doubts,' Lund said. 'Eva must have too. It's only natural. I did. Just like your father.'

'And look what happened there.'

He'd thrown these accusations at her constantly when he was angry. With some justification. That didn't make them any the less tiresome in the end.

'I never regretted having you,' she said. 'Just that I made such a crappy mother.'

'And I'm supposed to play happy families now? What if I'm just as fucked up as you? At least you and Dad had decent jobs. Some money. Me . . .' He pulled a few notes out of his pocket. 'That's a night's work. I can't keep Eva and a kid.'

So many things she'd wanted to say over the years and never quite found the moment.

'Mark . . .'

The phone rang. Emilie's. She snatched it out of her pocket, looked at him, wagged a finger and said, 'This is important. Stay here. We need to talk.'

She went out into the corridor. Answered on the fifth ring.

'I thought you'd gone walkabout, Lund. You're not playing games again, are you?'

Calm, rational, intelligent. In control. He didn't change.

'Sorry. I was talking . . .'

'Shame you got that Overgaard creature. I had a big surprise waiting for him at the airport.'

Lund closed her eyes and said automatically, 'Are you keeping tabs on us all?'

'What do you think?'

'Listen. If he's guilty, and I think he is, he's going to court. We'll do that. Give yourself up. Bring Emilie in. I know what you want. We're looking into Louise Hjelby's case . . .'

'I don't have much faith in the courts. Or you. Unless you can tell me who killed her.'

'I need time,' she said.

'You've had two years.'

'No. I've had less than two days. I can't unravel a riddle like this in an instant. How did you know this girl? How did you find out?'

A crowd was gathering round. Brix was watching her.

'You've had all the time in the world, Lund. Spin me a story if you like.'

'It's not a story! I can see a mistake was made—'

'A mistake?' His voice got louder at that and she could just detect a note of anger in it. 'Did you really say that?'

'I didn't mean—'

'Is it a mistake when a whole society turns its back on a young girl's murder? Is that all it takes? A flash of some money?'

'No. Please. Listen—'

'I'm past listening. Your stinking world's falling down. You should be tugging at the walls, not trying to keep them standing. What's Zeuthen offering now?'

One of the tech team was at the back, shaking his head. Another call over the web. Untraceable.

'Whatever you want.'

'Does he think he's rich enough to get his life back? How much? Two hundred million? Five hundred?'

'I told you. There's no limit.'

He laughed at that.

'The idiot hasn't learned a thing, has he?'

'Tell me—'

'This is the final demand. I mean it this time. No negotiation.'

'What . . . ?'

A long, deliberate pause.

'Oh come on, Lund. We're getting to know each other here, aren't we?' The laugh had a finality to it that chilled her. 'You've worked it out. Surely you have.'

First thing that morning, ready for another day of campaigning, Hartmann told Karen he needed to stop by his old family house in Svanemøllevej, near the embassies in northern Østerbro. The place had been on the market for almost a year. The estate agent thought there might finally be a buyer. But there was a problem with damp. Money to be spent or knocked off the price. No one else to make the decision.

She sat next to him as the black Mercedes made its way down the street. The weather had taken a turn for the worse. Constant sleety rain, a low dark sky.

On the way Morten Weber took some calls. PET had come to the conclusion that Mogens Rank never spoke with the deputy prosecutor at the meeting Weber had uncovered.

'Are they sure about that?' Hartmann asked.

'They say so,' Weber replied. 'Mogens made his presentation and left.'

'Good.'

'Maybe,' Weber said. 'There were some drinks at the Ministry afterwards. Lots of mingling. Mogens can't remember whether he talked to him there or not.'

'Does that man remember anything?' Hartmann grumbled.

Nebel was going through the morning papers. They were casting doubts about Rank's future. Ussing was still making hay out of the failures in the kidnapping.

'I want a meeting with Robert Zeuthen. I want to talk to him in person.'

Weber's hands shot up in protest.

'Stay away from Zeuthen. There's a wounded bear in the road here. No point in kicking it.'

Hartmann turned to Nebel and said, 'Fix it.'

The car stopped at a large house. No lights. No sign of recent life. Hartmann gazed at it through the window, went quiet.

'Let's get this over and done with,' he said.

Weber stayed in the car, on the phone again. Hartmann walked up to the front door, let himself in. Karen Nebel followed. He'd left Svanemøllevej eighteen months before, moved into a smaller bachelor flat near Christiansborg. The place still had memories. Back when he was nothing more than a city councillor, dreaming that one day he might become mayor of the city, he'd bought the house with his wife, a lawyer. Two years before he became mayor she'd died, pregnant, of cancer. That pain still lingered within these walls. The younger Hartmann had wanted nothing more than to rise through the Danish political aristocracy with her by his side. When she was gone a different side of him emerged. A relentless womanizer, unable to settle.

Not long before he became Prime Minister a brief period of stability had arrived in the form of Benjamin his kid brother, almost twenty years his junior, newly kicked out of college in America. Lost for a way back into the world, Benjamin had been a lively, infuriating feature in Hartmann's bachelor life for a while, flirting with left-wing journalism and campaigning, arguing constantly. Usually in good humour.

For a year things had stabilized. Hartmann had fallen into a loving, faithful relationship with a beautiful schoolteacher working in a poor area of Nørrebro.

Then the pressures of office seemed to intensify. He spent more time in Slotsholmen than he did at home. One day, a few weeks after Hartmann became Prime Minister, he lost Benjamin. The beautiful schoolteacher not long after. Hartmann was single again. Unencumbered. All the old ways returned.

He stopped in the kitchen. Once he'd sat here, being cunningly interrogated by Sarah Lund. Wondering about her too. She'd seemed an interesting, attractive woman. He was too intrigued to notice she was simply trying to snare him. The Birk Larsen case almost ended his political career, even though he had nothing to do with the girl's murder.

It's never the deed that kills you. It's the lie.

What Rosa Lebech said was true. And it so nearly finished him then.

He walked upstairs. Karen Nebel followed.

'It's a beautiful house, Troels. You should just pay to have the damp fixed and make them stick to the asking price.'

He went to the window, looked at the overgrown garden. Brambles had almost covered the summerhouse where his wife had liked to sit during those last difficult months. The roses needed pruning. The fruit trees too.

'I used to chop wood out there,' he said with a smile. 'Nothing better when you want to think about something. No phones ringing. No emails. Nothing but . . . the people you want close. And this.'

He rapped on the wooden doors.

'I hung those myself. I was pretty good at DIY.'

She laughed.

'You?'

'Why not?'

Nebel hesitated.

'I never really thought of you that way.'

'What? As a family man?'

He walked across the landing and pushed open the door there. A small room with a window out to the front.

'This was going to be the nursery. I put up the wallpaper, every last bit.'

Cartoon cars running up and down the wall, grinning, racing, flying.

'We knew it was going to be a boy. Thought so anyway.' His fingers touched the paper. Damp. 'When Benjamin came back he went for this room straight away. Twenty-six years old. Always a kid.'

'I only met him once. He was bright. Funny.'

'Crazy,' Hartmann added. 'Maddening.' A smile. 'Had an opinion on every subject under the sun, and it was always the right one. I loved him.' He cocked his head to one side. 'Sort of envied him really.'

He went to the cupboard, opened it. CDs and computer games. Left-wing posters and a baseball bat.

'Mum always called him the happy accident. I was at university when he was born. Never lived at home when he was growing up. I guess . . .' Hartmann picked up a cap. Boston Red Sox. 'I guess I was more the serious uncle than a big brother really. By the time they kicked him out of Harvard I was all he had left.'

He put on the cap. Nebel sniggered, came and removed it.

'Not the image.'

'Suppose not.'

He looked out of the window.

'I loved having him here. He drove me nuts. Then . . .'

She smiled. Struggled for something to say.

Morten Weber came up the stairs, popped his head round the corner.

'I talked to Zeuthen's man Reinhardt. He'd be happy to give you an audience later. If you want it.' Weber didn't seem too comfortable. He knew this house of old too. 'This place has seen happier days. You should sell it to someone who'll bring some life back to it.'

'Yes,' Hartmann agreed. 'Any news on the girl?'

'There's a new demand.' Weber looked downcast. 'I'm afraid it doesn't look good.'

The phone calls were being captured automatically. Robert Zeuthen sat in Drekar's downstairs office listening to the playback from a Politigården voice recorder.

'*Oh come on, Lund. We're getting to know each other here, aren't we? You've worked it out. Surely you have.*'

'*No I haven't. Tell me.*'

'*Zeuthen says he'll pay anything?*'

'*Yes.*'

'*Then by all means let him.*'

'*Robert Zeuthen had nothing to do with the death of Louise Hjelby. If you give me time I'll get to the bottom of that. I can't . . .*'

'*A life for a life. Don't you think that's reasonable?*'

Zeuthen sat rigid, no emotion on his face.

'*You get the girl. I get him. A loving father would do anything for his daughter. He should be grateful for the chance to prove it.*'

'*Grateful? No one can agree to that. Ask for something reasonable.*'

A long break. Lund looked at the recorder, wondered if something had gone wrong. So did Zeuthen. His right-hand man Reinhardt sat bloodless, shocked, shaking his head.

'*I'm the most reasonable man in Denmark. That's my final offer. I'll call back this afternoon. Make sure you have a car ready. I want you and Robert Zeuthen in it.*'

Brix reached forward and shut off the little machine.

'Let me say immediately,' he told them, 'this is a preposterous demand. One we cannot agree to.'

Zeuthen's eyes narrowed, turned on him.

'When did I give you ownership of my life?' he asked in a quiet, calm voice.

'The solution lies in the Hjelby case,' Brix replied. 'He's convinced someone inside Zeeland pressurized Peter Schultz to shut it down. If you can find us a lead inside your organization . . .'

Zeuthen wasn't looking at him. His eyes were on a painting on the wall: a wild grey ocean, a ship tossed by the violent waves, the Zeeland dragon on the side.

'If there's anything that can help us find your daughter,' Brix added.

'How many times do you have to ask this? Wouldn't I tell you?'

Reinhardt intervened.

'We've been through all the records. Checked everything. There's nothing to add. I'm sorry. Can't you trace the call? Why's this man still free?'

'Because he's clever,' Lund said. 'And knows things we don't.'

Brix caught Zeuthen's eye.

'I'm going to arrange bodyguards for you until this is over.'

Reinhardt didn't like that.

'We have our own security. There are people who might think it's more efficient than yours.'

'It's for me,' Zeuthen said with a grim smile. 'To make sure I don't wander.'

'Robert . . .' Lund started.

'No need,' he interrupted. 'I've got the message. You must excuse me now. We have important visitors. Niels will show you out.'

Back in the cold, airy hall three people stood in quiet conversation. Lund was almost on them before she realized.

Hartmann. The little adviser Weber who'd given him an alibi he'd never needed in the Birk Larsen case. Karen Nebel, the TV journalist turned spin doctor.

'Hi,' Lund said and looked into Hartmann's face.

He didn't look much older. Still handsome. Might have been more so if he smiled.

'You,' he said. 'Long time.'

'It is.'

Brix was coughing into his fist.

'Could have been longer,' Weber growled.

Hartman slapped him down for that. Started on a lecture. Fine words, beautifully delivered. About how he wanted everything done to bring the case to a satisfactory conclusion.

Lund's phone rang. She went away to take the call. Asbjørn Juncker sounding excited.

When she got back the speech was finished. Probably for her benefit anyway. Instead Weber leaned over and said, 'I gather PET have pulled in Jens Lebech again. What's going on there?'

'Who?'

'Jens Lebech . . .'

'Leave it,' Hartmann ordered. 'Any news on the girl?'

'Not that I can talk about,' Lund replied.

To her surprise he didn't push it.

With muted goodbyes they went outside.

Brix muttered something under his breath.

'I couldn't ignore him,' Lund complained.

'Is there any news?' he asked.

'Juncker thinks he may have narrowed down the area Emilie's being kept.'

He brightened at that.

'Where?'

'Near the docks.' She glanced back at the red-brick castle. A grand, imposing palace. Looked up at the dragon on the roof, like the prow of a Viking ship. 'There's a surprise.'

The three of them watched the tall figure of Niels Reinhardt walk steadily towards them. Amanuensis, butler, personal assistant. The man had been at the right hand of Hans Zeuthen for decades and now did much the same for his son.

'I'll handle this on my own,' Hartmann said then gave Reinhardt a serious smile, shook his hand, walked into the private office of the Zeuthen empire.

Model ships everywhere. Paintings of the sea. Robert Zeuthen got up from a massive walnut desk to greet him. The two men sat next to one another on a sofa in front of the marble fireplace.

Nothing in the hearth. This vast palace seemed cold, deprived of life.

'The police are doing everything they can,' Hartmann said. 'I want you to know that the government and I are absolutely behind them in this. We're praying for a solution that gets Emilie back home.' He watched Zeuthen nod. The man looked as if he hadn't slept in days. 'I'm confident you have the very best people in the police, in PET on your side.'

Zeuthen scarcely seemed to be listening.

'Anders Ussing is trying to take advantage. He's spreading shameful rumours. I've given him all the information I can to disprove them but still . . .' Hartmann scowled. 'It's politics I'm afraid.'

'Politics?' Zeuthen asked in a weary, suspicious tone.

'Not for me,' Hartmann insisted. 'I'm sorry this has become part of the election campaign, Robert. It's quite indecent. If there's anything . . .'

Zeuthen got up from the sofa, walked to the window.

'So there's no truth in what the press are saying?' he asked.

Hartmann joined him. The rain had stopped. Reinhardt was on the lawn in front of a tiny set of goalposts. Laughing as a young boy tried to kick a ball past him. Zeuthen's wife stood there and watched them both, her face the very picture of misery. Beyond the rise of the garden was the distant dull line of the sea.

'No uncertainty or doubt about the handling of the case?' Zeuthen added.

'I'm looking into these stories. If anything improper has occurred I'll deal with it.'

He made sure Zeuthen saw him then.

'I assure you we're doing everything we can. I hope . . . I hope this doesn't affect your support for our campaign. It's much appreciated. If you were able to reaffirm that at some stage. Say later today . . .'

Hartmann couldn't interpret the look on the man's face at that moment.

A knock on the door. Reinhardt came in. He'd changed into an incongruous pair of red slippers but his trousers still dripped water onto the carpet.

'I'm sorry to interrupt. I had a call from Brix. He said they found the place they thought Emilie was last being kept. There's no sign of her I'm afraid.'

'They found out where she was?' Hartmann said, offended. 'I talked to Lund outside. She never mentioned this.'

Reinhardt ignored him.

'They have to make some preparations for the exchange, Robert.'

'What exchange?' Hartmann demanded. 'I'd like to know . . .'

Zeuthen stared at him, said nothing, walked out of the room.

A deep breath. Hartmann sat down. Wished he'd handled this better. Weber and Karen Nebel wandered in.

'Some good news anyway,' Weber announced. 'Mogens wasn't at that Ministry drinks party. He never met Schultz there. PET didn't come up with anything on him either.'

Hartmann walked to the window. The boy was kicking the ball again. Maja Zeuthen looked just as wretched as before. Zeuthen came out, said something that made Carl laugh.

'He doesn't know,' Hartmann whispered. And wondered: how do you tell a child such a thing? Zeuthen was a man, and the words failed Hartmann when he tried to speak with him. He hadn't been trying to beg a fresh reaffirmation of Zeeland's support. Not really. But struggling for something to say.

'The police have been searching a factory near the docks,' Weber went on. 'They thought she might have been kept there. Nothing so far.'

'There's some kind of exchange being planned,' Hartmann said. 'Did the police mention that?'

He shook his head.

'Then how do you know they're telling you the truth now?'

No answer. He looked out of the window.

The boy ran to his father, hugged him round the waist. Then the mother came close too. At that moment they looked ordinary. Just another couple with a kid. But the Zeuthens couldn't be that way. They weren't born to it. Any more than he was.

'That's one more reason we should back off,' Karen Nebel said quietly.

The factory was just a kilometre away from the scrapyard where the Zeeland mate's body had been found. Decrepit, empty buildings. The letters 'KPS' written in old-fashioned script on the tallest.

Madsen had set a dog team to work. Asbjørn Juncker was going frantic looking for leads.

'She's got to be here somewhere,' he said, pointing at the line of derelict buildings. 'There's a million places to hide.'

'That doesn't mean a thing,' Lund told him.

Brix leaned against the wall, talking intermittently with Ruth Hedeby, his immediate boss in the Politigården. Someone was stirring it back there. Hartmann probably, Lund thought. He needed to have Robert Zeuthen on his side. They'd kept the latest demand from the politicians. Only the closest team and Zeuthen knew. Brix had been hoping for a lead that meant it would never need to be considered. That was looking a slim possibility now.

'She could have seen the name when they were driving past,' Brix said mournfully.

'No,' Lund insisted. 'Emilie's a bright girl. She wouldn't have written down just anything.'

The place was so big. Madsen must have had fifty officers running from the water's edge to the decrepit warehouses. An old-fashioned nautical time ball stood on a squat brick tower at the end that led towards the homeless camp where Hartmann spoke the previous Wednesday.

She called the Politigården, got someone to run a check. Knew the answer before the operator gave it.

'This was a Zeeland subsidiary,' Lund said to no one in particular. 'They'd been running it down for years. Closed it finally eighteen months ago.'

Brix said nothing.

'He's one of theirs,' she added. 'Why can't they come up with a single name?'

'We've looked everywhere,' Juncker insisted.

'He knows every last piece of Zeeland's security system,' Lund said, voice rising. 'What's the betting he's got a map of this place? He can hide wherever the hell he likes.'

Brix took a call. As she watched he barked out a curse and fetched a hard kick against some corrugated iron fencing, started yelling something she couldn't hear.

'Keep looking,' she said quietly.

He came off the phone. She walked over.

'We need to get names and photos out of Zeeland,' Lund insisted.

'We need to show them to Overgaard. He's the only witness we've got who's met this man.'

Huddled against the cold in his long black winter coat Brix stayed silent.

'OK,' Lund added. 'I'll do it.'

'No point,' he mumbled. 'Overgaard's dead.'

She blinked. Shivered on the windy, abandoned dockside.

'How?'

'He managed to tear off the sleeve of his shirt and hang himself. He was gone when the guard looked in.'

Brix put a pale hand to his chin, thought for a moment.

'We're going to have to go through with this somehow. You need to find me an officer Zeuthen's build and age for a stand-in. I don't want him anywhere near. Hear that?'

Yes, she thought. But would he?

By three thirty the city was swamped in rain. Night was starting to fall. The wind howled outside the Ministry of Justice window. Mogens Rank was watching the TV. It was meant to be a debate about the economy. Instead it turned into a heated argument about the Zeuthen case.

Ussing repeated the refrain he was chanting everywhere: Rank had been given the opportunity to take action to prevent Emilie's kidnapping and ignored it. Hartmann fought back with accusations of his own. Ussing was using a criminal case for his own political ends. The investigation was being handled effectively. He went on record to defend Rank's actions, and deny that he'd done anything improper.

Mogens Rank smiled at that, gave the words a round of quiet applause. Then he made his way through the internal corridors that linked his building to the rest of Slotsholmen, wandering the passageways once used by his predecessor Thomas Buch until he stood in the Christiansborg Palace itself, the quarters of the Prime Minister.

Hartmann's door was open. He was talking to Karen Nebel and Weber.

Rank knocked, smiled, asked for a word.

The chair swivelled round, Hartmann looked him up and down and asked, 'The police are being cagey, Mogens. What's going on?'

'They're trying to arrange an exchange. An officer's taking the place of Robert Zeuthen, I believe.'

Nebel and Weber stopped what they were doing and began to take notice.

Rank outlined the kidnapper's latest demand.

'It would have been useful if I'd known that when I saw Zeuthen earlier,' Hartmann muttered.

'I only found out after your meeting. These are police matters, Troels. Keeping us informed isn't in their nature. Or their priorities.'

'When I ask it is.'

Rank sighed.

'I just wanted to say how deeply I regret all the trouble I've caused. How much I appreciate your words on the TV just now.'

Hartmann sat silent, expressionless. The other two stood and watched.

'You've handled a series of very difficult events admirably,' Rank added. 'I'm sure that will be reflected when it comes to the vote.'

There were some documents on the desk. Hartmann picked them up, began to read.

'I'm aware there've been failings in my ministry. Things need to be tightened up. I'm on it already.'

'Are you?'

'Yes. Well.' A bright, optimistic smile. 'I'll leave you to it.'

'Just one thing,' Hartmann said, looking up from the papers.

'Yes?'

'When I spoke on TV it was for the benefit of the cameras. I didn't have much choice.'

'Troels . . .' Weber muttered, only for Hartmann to wave at him to be silent.

'I won't excuse your forgetfulness, Mogens. If that's what it turns out to be. People have died. A young girl's missing. And you've done nothing but squirm and lie and duck your responsibilities from the outset.'

Head to one side, arms behind his back, Rank glared at Hartmann.

'From now on you'll have nothing to do with this case. The police and PET will report directly to me.'

'You can't do that,' Rank said with an easy laugh. 'It's unthinkable.'

'Go home. Stay away from the office. Keep out of the media. Step out of line and I will drop you from the high heavens. I promise.'

Rank was about to say something, thought better of it.

'If by some chance we survive this shitstorm you've brought down on us,' Hartmann added, 'and by some miracle win the election . . . don't expect a call from me. Any questions?'

Nothing. Mogens Rank walked briskly from the room.

Weber came to the desk.

'Don't start,' Hartmann warned him.

'You can't sack him! He's one of the most loyal ministers you've got. If Birgit Eggert comes running—'

'He's gone. Live with it.'

Nebel sat down.

'You've just made sure we get all the blame if the girl turns up dead,' she said. 'Even if Mogens does keep his trap shut. Which I doubt.'

'I know what I'm doing.'

'Doesn't look like it.'

Hartmann ignored that and turned to Nebel.

'Find out what's happening with the police. I'm not going to let Sarah Lund keep me in the dark.'

She reached for her phone.

'Outside, please.'

The two men watched her leave.

'Why do I do this?' Weber asked. 'What's the point when you ignore everything . . . ?'

'You do it because you've got nothing else. Just like me.'

'It's unwise to piss off your friends. You never know when you'll need them.'

'If you'd rather go and wait this out with Mogens . . .'

Weber shook his head. He rarely lost his temper but the moment was close now.

'I saved you! Without me you wouldn't even have a seat on the council let alone . . .' His hand swept the grand office. '. . . this.'

Hartmann leaned forward, looked him in the eye.

'I know what I'm doing.'

'You can keep saying it. Won't make it true. You've got Rosa Lebech's old husband coming at you. Birgit too. Next to her Mogens Rank's little shitstorm's going to be a breeze.'

Zeuthen and his wife were in the family room. The two of them were agreed. They'd stay at Drekar, be briefed by the police during the operation. They didn't want to be in the Politigården. To know the details.

Carl came running in, looking for his toy car.

'Maybe you left it in the garden when you were playing with Mum,' Zeuthen said.

'I think Emilie took it when she went on holiday. She's always stealing my toys.'

Zeuthen smiled at him, patted his head, told him to take another look outside.

Maja watched Reinhardt and Carl leave. Soon she heard their voices, one low and gruff and friendly, the other high and bright, beyond the window.

'I'm sorry about Carsten,' she said. 'He'd no right to throw all those things at you.'

'He's upset. We all are.'

She was in jeans and an old T-shirt. He wore another dark business suit. Zeuthen never quite knew what brought them together. What she saw in him. It wasn't the money or the position. In truth she hated those.

'He shouldn't have spoken to you like that. I know you'd never do anything to harm the children. You've always been . . . a good father.'

That seemed to hurt him and she never wanted to do that. Not when she was thinking straight anyway.

'So they're sending some officers here?' she asked, trying to change the subject. 'We wait with them this time?'

A brief smile. Carl came running in, Reinhardt behind him. He'd found the car and wanted to tell the world.

It was his father he ran to first, anxious to show him.

'Emilie didn't have it!' Carl cried.

'No,' Zeuthen agreed and tousled his hair, held him, too tightly for a moment.

The boy pulled away and looked at him, puzzled.

'You all right, Dad?'

The doorbell.

'Do you think it's the police?' Maja asked.

Robert Zeuthen took a good look round the room. For a moment she thought he was going to come over and embrace her. She wondered what she'd do if that happened.

Instead he said, 'I'll go and see.'

Carl brought her the car then, chattered happily. Reinhardt stood there, wouldn't look her in the eye.

The front door slammed and somehow she knew he was gone.

'What's happening?' she asked. 'What's Robert doing?'

Another snatch squad in place. Another armed team waiting for instructions. The latest photographs from Zeeland had arrived. Lund was getting them checked. A stocky man from uniform was putting on body armour. He was around the same size as Robert Zeuthen. Similar hair. It might work in the dark but not for long.

The stand-in started buttoning up his white shirt over the armoured vest. Lund was talking to Juncker who was still down at the abandoned factory.

She took one look at the man who'd just walked into the room and cut the call.

Zeuthen came straight up to her.

'I've thought about this. Emilie's my daughter. My responsibility. I want to go.'

Brix was out of his office in an instant, shaking his head.

'You may not know who this man is,' Zeuthen added. 'But it's pretty obvious he's not stupid. He'll know if it isn't me. He told you this is the last chance. If—'

'We've a plan already in motion,' Brix cut in. 'More people looking for her than ever. I can't abandon that now.'

Zeuthen didn't budge.

'You know she's dead as soon as he sees it's not me. I'm the only chance we've got to save her. The only chance you have to take him.'

Brix shook his head.

'I can't take that risk.'

'You don't have to.'

149

Zeuthen walked over to the stand-in, looked at the body armour.
'That should fit,' he said.

Asbjørn Juncker was still at the abandoned factory. They'd searched every building. Looked inside basements, storage tanks. Found no trace of the girl.

Reluctant to leave he'd climbed to the top of the tallest block. Emilie wrote down those letters because she saw them somehow. Perhaps the van had simply passed this place. Or she glimpsed them from another location nearby.

Night had fallen. No stars, only low cloud spitting rain. The distant lights of the nearest occupied buildings glittered like Christmas decorations come early.

Twenty-three, all of his career spent in the sticks or the suburbs, the most serious case he'd seen until now was a burglary with violence. Those things happened. The abduction of a child by a determined, organized man willing to kill without a second thought was beyond imagination. And that worked at him. Kept him awake.

Alone on the roof of the tallest building, buffeted by the winter winds, Juncker took out his binoculars.

'Emilie . . .'

His whisper caught on the blustery night air.

It was the name of his sister too. She was thirteen, an ordinary, happy girl in Vesterbro. He told himself that didn't matter. It was his job anyway.

'Emilie,' he sighed and started to count off the grimy broken windows in the block opposite, one by one.

Zeuthen came prepared. A lawyer by his side. A set of indemnity documents he'd drawn up and was ready to sign with witnesses, absolving the police of any responsibility in the event of his death.

Brix phoned the commissioner.

He was out at a meeting.

Phoned Ruth Hedeby.

No answer.

Lund listened to his moans.

'They don't want to make the decision,' she said. 'They daren't. It's up to us.'

'That makes a change,' Brix grumbled.

'They're right, aren't they? We're the ones who've got to deal with this.'

'And the consequences. I don't want Zeuthen anywhere near this man. He'll kill him. Maybe Juncker will come up with something . . .'

'He hasn't.' She took Emilie's phone out of her pocket. 'What am I supposed to say if he calls and asks to speak to Zeuthen? He'll know if it's someone else.'

'Maybe we can work round that.'

'This is the last chance! He told us that. If we don't follow what he says she's dead. Then what happens? At least if Zeuthen goes he'll be out there with me. If we can't protect him there we're screwed anyway.'

Her phone went. Juncker. Nothing to report. She told Brix.

He glanced back at the room, Zeuthen and his lawyer.

'Get him ready,' he said.

Marked police cars gathered round the bottom of the building. Juncker looked over the edge. Blue lights flashing.

Someone shouted up, 'Hey, kid! Are we going or what?'

He could see everything from up here. The Zeeland offices across the water. The scrapyard where the case began. The homeless camp.

In the distance the bright lights of the city. Church spires. Slotsholmen and the tall tower of City Hall.

'Juncker!' came a voice from below. 'We need to go.'

One last turn. Three hundred and sixty degrees on his heels. He'd seen Lund do this when everyone else wanted to give up.

You have to learn to look.

That's what she said and for all her awkwardness and unpredictability she was the most interesting and incisive detective he'd ever seen.

Somewhere around two hundred and seventy degrees the binoculars caught a window on the top floor of what looked like an abandoned office block maybe half a kilometre away.

A light was flashing on and off. Not flickering as if it was failing. But regularly as if someone kept throwing a switch.

He scanned the rest of the building. Not a sign of life.

Went back to the window. Felt his breath catch as the light stayed on and a figure came close to the glass.

Young girl in a dark coat. Pale, pretty face. Blonde hair tucked back beneath a black beanie.

'Emilie,' he murmured.

As he watched, the glasses trembling in his hands, she moved away from the window. Looked scared. A figure briefly crossed his vision. Burly, dressed in a nondescript dark jacket. A ski mask on his face, two holes for the eyes, one for the mouth.

Then the light went out and it didn't come back.

Lund had body armour on. Waited in the Politigården car park, Zeuthen by her side.

The phone rang.

'Are you ready, Lund?'

He sounded calm but his voice was breathy. As if he was walking somewhere.

'Yes.'

'Both of you?'

'That's what you wanted, isn't it?'

'Take the motorway south. I'll call you back in a little while.'

They'd got a large unmarked saloon, GPS tracking live on the dashboard.

'Last chance, Lund. Remember.'

She drove. Zeuthen was in the passenger seat. As they came out of the station there was a figure by the side of the road.

Slight, pretty but with a sad, frightened face.

Maja Zeuthen watched, open-mouthed. Saw her husband.

Started to yell as Lund put her foot down and surged into the open road ahead.

No time to explain, Asbjørn Juncker barked at the men with him to follow, raced round the corner, back towards the office block.

Arms flying, legs pumping. No breath to make a phone call. Barely room to think.

He was faster than them. On his own by the time he got close to the building. A noise came to him, like the growl of an angry animal. It got louder and louder and still he didn't stop.

One last corner. Asbjørn Juncker raced round. Saw the lorry almost on him. Lights bright, full beam. Heavy haulage truck thundering down the road.

152

The sound became a rising scream.

Juncker stood there in the monster's path fumbling for his weapon. Couldn't find it. Couldn't move.

It was high above him, bearing down. A face behind the wheel. The ski mask. A pair of dark eyes.

Then something hit him hard. The young detective found himself flying to the side of the road, a heavy shoulder bringing him down to the hard ground.

Confused, short of breath, he rolled round just in time to see the truck lumber along the dingy lane towards the motorway.

Madsen was with him in the dirt, rubbing at his arm, calling Juncker all manner of names.

'He'd have mown you down, you idiot.'

'It's her,' Juncker said and pointed to the lorry disappearing round the corner. 'Emilie. It's her.'

The older cop got to his knees, pulled out his phone.

Juncker crawled to his feet. In his head he could still see her at the window. A scared little girl, snatched into the night.

The media pack was outside Christiansborg screaming for a statement. Hartmann stayed in his office brooding while Weber and Karen Nebel chased their contacts in the police and PET.

The only firm news they'd got was that Robert Zeuthen had agreed to the exchange. He was willing to offer his life in return for his daughter's.

'I should have been consulted,' Hartmann whined when Weber came in and told him.

'Why?' Weber asked.

'Because I should! If we lose Zeuthen and his daughter we're screwed. Those bastards out there will rip me to shreds.'

'That's probably not Brix's top priority right now. Before you make another public statement maybe we ought to talk about tone and wording.'

'I want that kid back!' Hartmann yelled. 'Do you think I don't?'

'Of course not,' Weber answered. 'You just have a kind of . . . unfortunate turn of speech on occasion.'

'I lost Benjamin.' His voice was soft and hurt. 'I know what it's like. You don't.'

The mood was all wrong. This campaign kept swinging back and forth. Hartmann was no stranger to that, knew the key was to make sure the final turn, in his favour, came on polling day. But it was hard to judge such delicate movements without knowing where he stood.

And Birgit Eggert kept nagging in the background, demanding a meeting, complaining about everything under the sun.

Weber thought he should see her. Face her down, kill any rebellion before it began. The little man had been right about one thing: Mogens Rank was one of their strongest supporters of old. To Hartmann that made it important to distance the man from Christiansborg. The accusation of meddling in the Zeuthen case seemed impossible to dispel.

A sound outside the window. Hartmann looked. Another TV van turning up. They sniffed blood.

'Don't they have better things to do?' Hartmann muttered. 'Why do they keep hanging around?'

The door opened. Karen Nebel came in, threw a set of photos on his desk. The two men came and looked.

'One of the papers has got them,' she said. 'They're going to run a story tomorrow morning.'

Morten Weber was on the phone first.

'Mogens,' he roared. 'Get your arse in here this minute.'

Borch got back to the Politigården as the operation began. Brix stood in the ops room, a headset on, giving out orders to the remote teams: no helicopter, plain pursuit cars at a distance, all communication on encrypted comms channels.

Caution all the way.

They had a registration number for the truck that had nearly killed Asbjørn Juncker. It was a fake. But the vehicle, a black lorry, had been briefly caught on traffic cameras entering the motorway. The team near the factory had established Emilie had been kept in the building Juncker had found.

'What about the phone he's using?' Brix asked. It was PET's job to monitor telecoms for the operation.

'No luck,' Borch said. 'He's changed the SIM or something. Must be using a different Internet company.'

'You've got to be able to track a phone!'

Borch cocked his head.

'You can't find a damned truck. Don't start. Are Lund and Zeuthen covered?'

Brix was bent over some maps.

'I've got armed teams close by.'

'He knows that. Is this the best . . . ?'

Brix looked up, nodded to a side room. Something in his face stopped the PET man.

Maja Zeuthen was there listening, wide-eyed, scruffy in an old jumper and jeans.

'Watch what you say,' Brix told him.

Out in the car. Rain and light evening traffic. What Lund thought were backup vehicles dogging them three hundred metres behind.

Zeuthen sat in the passenger seat, tie neat, dark expensive winter coat, hair tidy, face glum.

'What do you intend to do, Lund?'

'When we know the location, we get near, pull you out, grab Emilie. Brix is good. He's got people around. You just can't see them.'

Zeuthen glanced at the driver's mirror. A support car was always visible.

He didn't need to say it.

'What if he finds out we're not on our own?'

She reached into her jacket, pulled out some gum. Offered him a piece. Zeuthen shook his head. He didn't look like a gum person. Lund popped a chunk into her mouth anyway.

They were headed out of the city. No sign of a truck. He had to call soon.

'We can manage this,' she insisted. 'We work together. We follow instructions.'

He was watching her.

'And you've done this before?'

'Oh yes,' she said and wondered: did he know that was a lie?

Lund was almost glad Emilie's phone rang at that moment.

She put it on the car speaker.

'Is Robert Zeuthen there?'

'Yes. Do you want to talk to him?'

'Plenty of time for that later, Lund. Where are you?'

The car comms were hooked into the Politigården. Brix would be hearing every word, monitoring the vehicle each step of the way.

'Coming up to exit thirty-seven. Where are we going?'

'I only invited two to this party.'

'That's all you've got.'

The slip road was visible through the rain. They were well beyond the city, in flat farmland.

'Do I sound like an idiot?'

'I'm in a car with Robert Zeuthen. Like you asked. Tell us what to do.'

'Take exit thirty-eight.'

She was drifting into the slip road already. Came out, back into the motorway. Saw the backup car make the same manoeuvre.

'If at any stage I sense you're not alone this is the last you'll hear from me. You do understand that, don't you?'

'Got it.'

A sign for exit thirty-eight came up.

'I hope so,' he said.

They had a map of the area spread out in the ops room. Exit thirty-eight led to a narrow country road and then a network of smaller lanes. Farms. A few small industrial units. Lots of empty land.

'There's nothing there,' Brix said. 'This can't be right.'

Borch was next to him.

'He's taking her out into the open. If he's on that road he can see those cars you've got. From miles away.'

'OK,' Brix said and ordered Juncker and his people to fall back further.

'He's seen them already!' Borch cried. 'What's Lund supposed to do?'

'Follow his instructions. We've got her on the GPS. When she stops, we move.'

'This is a joke.' Borch got to his feet. Went for his jacket. 'I'm out of it.'

A voice on the radio. Asbjørn Juncker's.

'I think we've got him,' he said. 'Volvo FH16. Looks like the one we saw in town. It's got a shipping container on the back. The tail light's smashed.'

'A container?'

'Hang on,' Juncker said, voice breaking up over the radio. 'We're getting closer. We could stop him—'

'Keep back!' Borch yelled, grabbing for the mike.

'Keep back,' Brix repeated. 'Don't do anything.'

'We could pick him up for the broken light,' Juncker suggested.

'I said fall back and wait,' Brix barked. 'Just do it, will you?'

They were out in dark countryside, steady rain coming down.

Lund called in.

'I can still see your cars, Brix. Get them away. I'm about to hit the exit.'

'You're fine,' he came back. 'Asbjørn's got a visual on the truck. He's almost two kilometres behind you. He can't see a thing. We'll keep people on you. Another couple of cars are heading for the truck. Nothing within viewing distance.'

Zeuthen was listening to every word.

The slip road came up. She was half expecting another call telling her to go somewhere else. But it never came. Lund edged off the motorway, headed down the lane.

Maja Zeuthen wandered into the ops centre unnoticed. Brix was absorbed, talking into his headset. Carsten Lassen arrived from work. He put his arm round her shoulder, persuaded her to go back into the side room where she was supposed to wait.

'Carl's with your mum. She says he won't go to sleep.'

'He knows something's wrong. Of course he won't . . .'

Brix walked in.

'We've made visual contact with the truck. We think Emilie's inside. We plan to stop it . . .'

She folded her arms, closed her eyes for a moment.

'He said if you did anything . . .'

'You can't believe him, Mrs Zeuthen. Everything he's told us has been a lie. I can't go into the details but we're taking every precaution. Emilie's safety is our priority. Above all else.'

'Can I go?'

'Go where?'

'Can I be somewhere close? She's my daughter.' She put a hand to his arm. 'Please.'

He nodded, called an officer.

'We'll organize a car. You'll have to wait until the operation's over. Do what we say. OK?'

'OK,' she said and reached for her coat.

The road turned into a single track then, to her surprise, broadened. Brix had kept to his word. There were no more headlights on her tail. No lights anywhere. Just the rainy way ahead.

Borch called.

'The truck's approaching an exit. We're going to stage an accident and stop him. We've got a SWAT team and some marksmen from the Army.'

Zeuthen swore and shook his head in the passenger seat.

'I'll just keep driving,' Lund said.

'Do that. One more thing. Maybe this was nothing to do with Zeuthen. Or Zeeland.'

'What do you mean?'

'When I was in Jutland I checked the papers. Schultz and Overgaard cooked the reports. They said she disappeared on a Friday. Not true. I checked with the foster family. Louise went missing the day before. Thursday.'

'So?' Lund asked.

'Those men from the *Medea* only came into harbour on the Friday.' A pause. 'Do you understand what I'm saying?'

She thought about it, said yes. Then finished the call.

'They're going to shoot him?' Zeuthen asked. 'With Emilie there?'

'They know what they're doing. Trust—'

Emilie's phone rang.

'Have you reached the woods yet, Lund?'

She glanced outside the window.

'No. Just fields.'

'You'll see a line of trees soon. A track up to the right. There's a disused workshop. Wait for me there.'

Juncker was in the passenger seat, Madsen behind the wheel. Still a good way behind the turn-off Lund took. Suddenly the gap between them and the truck widened.

'He just put his foot down,' Juncker told Brix in ops. 'I mean *really* put his foot down. Are the accident team ready?'

A short pause then Brix said they were.

The traffic had picked up too. It was hard to keep in contact without being conspicuous.

'Keep your distance,' Brix said. 'You've got twelve hundred metres to run to the accident. They're blocking the road now.'

The problem changed. The truck was slowing down now.

'I don't know what he's playing at,' Juncker muttered.

A double row of lights. Had to be a junction. Maybe a kilometre to go.

Then the lorry swerved abruptly to the right. Juncker swore. Madsen braked too hard, skidded on the wet road, fought to bring the car under control.

The truck had turned from the slow lane onto the slip road.

'He's leaving the motorway,' Juncker told them. 'Going early.'

Brix came back straight away.

'You're sure?'

'Exit thirty-seven. He's on the lane now. What do we do?'

'This can't be right.' The voice in Juncker's handset sounded oddly lost for a moment. 'Lund went out on thirty-eight.'

The police saloon had slowed, was back under control. Juncker looked at Madsen, nodded.

'Yeah well. We're following him.'

'Keep back!' Brix shouted.

One giant truck lumbering down the side road. A single car behind it.

A line of derelict buildings separated by a potholed muddy road. Lund was starting to recognize his signature. He liked these dark and damaged places. Something about them matched his mood.

She drew up at the first door. The place seemed deserted. In spite of this a line of ancient dim electric bulbs was strung between the abandoned warehouses, casting a yellow light on the wet cracked concrete, the broken windows, the shattered timberwork of what must once have been a rural industrial unit.

To Let signs on both sides. Broken and dusty.

Brix's voice came out of the dashboard.

'Asbjørn has a visual,' he said. 'We're keeping in contact with him. Borch's on the way too.'

Nothing made sense.

'Where is he?' Zeuthen asked from the passenger seat.

Brix must have heard.

'He's a long way from you. Stay where you are. It's safe.'

Lund got out. There was an abandoned fridge next to the car. A couple of discarded barrels.

'How far?' she asked into her phone, so Zeuthen couldn't hear.

'Too far,' Brix said. 'There could be more people than we thought.'

Zeuthen joined her, shivered in the freezing night, asked what was going on.

'They're following him,' Lund said. 'Best stay in the car.'

He didn't move.

The lights bothered her.

'Has he seen your people? Lund?'

She walked up the narrow path between the units.

'Lund!'

'I don't think so.'

No one came here any more. It was a miracle the power still worked. There was no good reason for the lights to be on at all.

Then a noise.

Lund took out her torch and her gun.

It sounded like a bird. But it wasn't. A phone was ringing somewhere.

Close to the last unit on the right.

'Stay behind me,' she ordered and the two of them walked towards the sound.

Water butts overflowing in the steady drizzle. An old, abandoned bike. A rat scuttled in front of them. From somewhere she heard the flap of wings. Something big. A crow or an owl.

The ringing got louder. On a stack of tyres, she saw the phone flashing.

Old Nokia. Lund answered.

'You took your time. Say cheese.'

'What?'

'A joke. Don't you get it? In your vehicle, please.'

She nodded at Zeuthen. Walked back to the police saloon.

'No, Lund,' he said and he was laughing. 'Not your car. I laid on more suitable transport for you.'

'I'm not much in the mood for jokes.'

'Are you ever? Look up. Like I said, say cheese.'

Turned on her heels. Scanned the units in the dim light, helped out with her torch.

'Look up!'

Attached to the broken drainpipe of the nearest unit was what looked like a webcam. A blue light flashed steadily from the bracket.

'Leave your phones where I can see them,' he ordered. 'Tell Zeuthen I'm flattered he wore a tie.'

Lund put her own phone on the ground. Got Zeuthen to do the same.

'Good. Now look ahead. See the van?'

Another trademark. A rusty old commercial heap, sitting by the road beyond the buildings.

'It's a present for you. Keys in the ignition. Ready to go.'

She didn't move.

'I'm waiting, Sarah,' he said. 'Hurry up. We've got a date.'

Juncker and Madsen had followed the truck into deep countryside. They were keeping back as much as they could. But on deserted narrow lanes it was hard to believe they weren't seen. And another three cars were behind them, crewed by the armed team waiting to pounce.

'I don't like this,' Juncker told Brix. 'It's getting too obvious.'

A long pause then the chief came back.

'OK. Four hundred metres ahead you go under a railway bridge. After that the road splits. Let the SWAT team past once you're through. They can take the route he doesn't use, cut back and intercept him ahead.'

Madsen sniffed at that and looked at him.

'They're going to need to hurry,' Juncker warned.

The bridge came up. A narrow underpass, barely wide enough for the truck.

Madsen braked hard. Juncker's hands flew to the dashboard, saved himself from hitting the glass.

Brix heard. Started yapping down the line.

The lorry was stationary, all lights on. So wide nothing else could get past.

'Juncker? What's happening? We don't see you moving on the GPS.'

'He's stopped under the bridge. Maybe he's looking at the map or something.'

It was hard to see in the dark. The cab was hidden.

'Is the engine running?' Brix asked.

The tailpipe was moving. Grimy smoke puffing out into the night air.

They could just make out the sound of a door slamming.

'Shit!' Madsen barked and was out before him.

Guns up, torches, scared, short of breath, they took one side each. Went down past the container. Got to the cab. The front.

The backlights of a car were just vanishing in the distance as a train roared over the bridge above them covering Juncker's curses.

When it was gone he picked up his radio.

'We've lost him. He's blocked the bridge. We can't get past. He's left the container but . . .'

Everything here was planned.

'Do we have anybody on the other side?' Juncker asked.

Silence gave him the answer.

The radio channel was open. The men by the bridge and the abandoned truck could hear Brix calling.

'Lund. We have a problem here. Lund? Come in . . .'

A long silence then a familiar voice.

'It's Borch. I'm at the workshops. Their car's abandoned. I just picked up her phone from the ground. Brix?'

Nothing.

Half a kilometre away the PET man looked down the dismal line of abandoned buildings and wondered where she was.

It was an old Ford van that smelled of animals: dogs probably. He phoned when they set off from the workshops. Told them to look in the glove compartment. There was a cheap satnav there, a route preprogrammed into it. A robotic voice gave directions.

Winding rural lanes. Circuitous turns. Then, finally, a bigger, broader road, one that seemed strangely empty.

'Do you have any idea where we are?' Zeuthen asked.

'Do you?' she replied and didn't mean it unkindly.

Wherever it was this was a place the likes of Robert Zeuthen probably never visited.

The road grew wider. Still no more traffic. Then there was a sign: construction work ahead. Dead end.

Lund kept following the voice in the satnav. Finally they found themselves heading to a bridge over a broad river. Couldn't be far from the harbour. She could smell the salt of the Øresund on the air.

Traffic cones and flashing yellow lights. The construction crew had gone home for the day. The lanes worked down to one. Ahead of them a red and white warning barrier blocked the way, what looked fresh asphalt beyond it.

Lund slowed to a crawl then a halt.

The satnav announced, 'You have reached your destination.'

Brix didn't have any teams near. She felt sure of that. The man had got what he wanted: the two of them alone.

She left the headlights on full beam, got out. So did Zeuthen. The bridge superstructure was lit. Some of the street lamps leading to it.

Across the bridge stood a big truck, lights on, name sign too, parked up. Nothing visible in the cab.

Zeuthen started to walk for it, hands in pockets, coat blowing in the wind.

'Stay here,' Lund told him. He didn't stop. 'Robert! We don't know what he wants.'

He looked back at her, resentful. But shuffled to a halt.

The new phone rang.

'Send Zeuthen over. When I've got him the girl walks.'

Lund looked behind her then ahead. Saw nothing anywhere.

'This isn't going to work,' she said. 'We've been tracked here. The place is all tied up. You can't get away. Let's talk . . .'

The laugh.

'You don't give up, do you? If your people were here I wouldn't have time to make this call. I'd be dead already. Please. I wish you no harm. Send him over now. I won't ask again.'

Zeuthen must have read her face.

'I'm going,' he said and started across the bridge, towards the lights of the truck.

'Robert! Stay here. If you're dead he's got no reason to let her go. Listen!'

She stepped in front of him, put a hand to his chest.

'We'll have officers here soon. We can negotiate. If he's got you he can do what he likes.'

He was still ready to go.

'I'll do this,' Lund said and started walking.

Hartmann had Rank in his office again, determined this would be the last time.

'Did you or did you not have a meeting with Peter Schultz?'

Birgit Eggert was in the meeting. It seemed wise.

'This is becoming tedious,' Rank said, a little tetchily. 'I've told you before. Not that I recall.'

'And these?'

Karen Nebel had got the photos from a press contact. Hartmann slapped them on the desk.

'The Ministry of Justice CCTV system. Two years ago. One week after the girl died in Jutland.'

Rank went through them slowly, one by one.

'What did you talk about?' Hartmann asked.

'I don't remember.' He looked up. 'If you met a casual acquaintance in a corridor would you recall what you said? Two years on?'

'Is that going to be your answer when these appear in the papers? They have them. Will you just stand up and say . . . hell, I don't remember? Really—'

'Enough!' Rank shouted. 'I've been a loyal minister of yours, Troels. An admirer. I supported you . . .' He glanced at Eggert. 'When others thought you too . . . perilous a proposition.'

'We're past that,' Hartmann said. 'I need the truth.'

Ten steps, gun out, low down in her right hand, phone up to her left ear. It rang again.

'Lund. What are you waiting for?'

'I'm coming for Emilie. I want to see her.'

'I told you to send Zeuthen over.'

He sounded mad and that was a first.

'Robert will come when he knows his daughter's safe. That's a fair bargain. You wanted a deal. That's it.'

'What is this?' he yelled. 'What do you care for these people? Why risk your life for the likes of them?'

'Because they're innocent. Like Louise Hjelby. Zeuthen did nothing to harm her. He's gone out of his way to try to help us find out what happened.'

Closer. She could smell diesel on the briny marine air.

'Don't give me this shit—'

'It's the truth. What happened was terrible. We're working to fix it. But Robert Zeuthen wasn't to blame.'

She still couldn't see anything, work out where he was.

'You're lying. Zeeland had the case closed. Zeuthen's responsible and you know it.'

'Get serious,' Lund cried. 'Do you think a man like Zeuthen would go to all this trouble to save three foreign sailors? You believe that? I thought you were smart.'

She heard him curse.

'Ask Zeuthen,' he said.

Her finger gripped the trigger. Still no sign of him anywhere.

'I don't need to. I know he had nothing to do with it. Overgaard and Peter Schultz changed the evidence reports. Louise disappeared the day before they said. The *Medea* wasn't even in port then.'

A low, incomprehensible grunt.

'Did you hear me? Those sailors weren't in the country when she went missing. You've been chasing the wrong people all along.'

Too many things to think about. She was walking. Seeing nothing. And something told her he was in the same position.

'You murdered three innocent men. All those sailors did was find her. Schultz made them change their evidence so it looked like suicide. That's what they told you, didn't they?'

The truck engine was running. No one behind the wheel.

'Did Schultz tell you it was Zeuthen?'

No answer.

'Thought not,' Lund said. 'Whoever he was shielding it wasn't Zeeland.'

The headlights were so bright she had to bring her gun hand up to shield her eyes.

Lund raised it higher, said, 'I'm going to lose my weapon now. I don't have anything else.'

She crouched down, placed the gun on the road, kicked it away.

'When Emilie's safe we can talk. I want to get to the bottom of this just as much as you.'

Walking forward at a snail's pace Lund moved round to the driver's side of the cab. The door was ajar. Lund climbed up.

Empty. A curtain marking off the space behind. She opened that, shone her torch down the length of the truck.

Nothing.

'All fine words, Lund. But too late. The man deserves to suffer as I have.'

Worried, getting desperate, she half fell from the cab, looked back across the bridge.

'He's got nothing to do with this!'

A sudden blast of cold wind caught her. Zeuthen was walking down the bridge alone, looking puzzled.

Then they both heard it. A lone, high cry on the breeze.

'Dad! Can you hear me? *Dad!*'

Zeuthen looked around. So did Lund.

No sign of the girl anywhere.

Then her cry came again and they knew.

He was by the edge of the bridge before she got there, hands on the rail, trying to see something in the darkness below. A new sound. The low steady rumble of a marine engine. Just visible in its own lights on the water a small craft was headed towards the bridge.

'Dad!'

She was there and all Zeuthen could do was answer her frantic call like a wounded animal hunting a lost cub.

Lund retrieved her gun. The girl's cries turned to shrieks and then screams.

Back by the rail the picture was clearer. A speedboat, long nose, light at the rear.

Deck mostly in darkness. Lund pointed her weapon over the water anyway.

Then they saw. A man in black. A small shape struggling in the stern. As Lund and Zeuthen watched he drew what looked like a blue tarpaulin bag over the girl's head.

She tried to aim. Didn't trust herself. The boat vanished beneath the bridge. The girl's cries grew muffled.

Zeuthen was running to the other side already, yelling.

A car screamed up behind the white van. Borch leapt out.

Lund had the phone to her ear. Was offering anything he wanted. Running to join the two men on the far side.

No more cries from below when she got there. Borch was trying to train his weapon on the water. Zeuthen hung over the rail.

From below only the steady murmur of the engine.

The boat emerged. The sound grew louder. A single muffled cry then nothing.

Lund looked. Lights by the water's edge, red and green. Lights on the bridge. Lights, small and ineffective, on the craft below.

Looking was all she had mostly. There was something about her lucid, all-seeing eyes that stopped her blinking when others couldn't help it.

This was something to witness and remember.

The boat.

Robert Zeuthen screaming.

Lund gave up on the phone. Got her gun over the edge.

The man with the ski mask had a blue bundle in his arms. A weapon in his right hand.

Hand moved back. One shot to the head and something jerked inside.

Robert Zeuthen shrieked, 'No!'

The black arm came up. A second bullet into the chest and the tarpaulin leapt with the shock.

Borch loosed off wildly with his gun. A couple of spurts of water leapt up from near the stern.

Then the man there heaved the dead shape to the side. Something orange was attached to it by a coil of rope.

Lund remembered the photos they'd shown Overgaard: a block of cement used to weigh down the dead Louise Hjelby.

A cruel and deliberate resonance. The heavy weight went over first. The blue bundle followed.

The water swallowed her.

More shots. Borch again. Lund too.

The lights went out on the little boat. The sound of its engine grew to a roar. They could just make out the sharp nose as it bucked up under the sudden burst of power.

They were emptying their weapons into nothing and knew it.

No words.

Lund looked at Robert Zeuthen. The coat was on the ground along with his jacket and body armour. In his tie and waistcoat he was climbing over the rail, ready to leap.

She put out a hand, stopped Borch firing. He leapt for the man but too late.

Down Robert Zeuthen went, down to the black water. Feet first, arms waving, a single thought in his head.

Crying a single word as he fell.

Emilie.

Emilie.

Emilie.

For fifteen minutes they pressed Mogens Rank. Hartmann. Birgit Eggert.

Like the lawyer he was he stonewalled them every inch of the way.

Finally Hartmann's patience ran out.

'Tell me the truth or I'm going to PET. Dyhring isn't with you any more. Your time's up.'

Through his thick glasses Rank gazed back at him. Thought for a moment.

'You have a strange sense of gratitude, Troels. They told me that when I backed you and so many others didn't. I suppose I should have listened.'

'Just throw him to the wolves,' Eggert butted in. 'No point in wasting time.'

He smiled at her.

'Then Troels next? The truth is I simply wanted to make sure everything was done properly. Zeeland were mentioned. We were . . . we are very close to them. What I did was in the interests of the party—'

'Is that why the press are crucifying me now?' Hartmann screamed. 'You put a lid on a murder investigation. Now Robert Zeuthen's paying for it. And so are we.'

'I did no such thing. Nothing that was against the law. I wouldn't do that, for Zeeland or for you. Trust me. This is not somewhere you wish to go . . .'

'You shelved the case! You withheld information . . .'

The door opened. Karen Nebel, Weber behind her. Rank was shaking his head, staring at the table.

'Dammit!' Hartmann yelled. 'Look at me when I'm talking to you. What the hell were you thinking?'

'They say he shot her,' Nebel cut in. 'Emilie Zeuthen's dead.'

Rank took off his glasses, closed his eyes. Birgit muttered a low and bitter curse.

Hartmann opened his mouth to speak. But there were no words.

Thirty minutes later the bridge was lit up on all sides. Police and recovery vehicles parked sideways across the road. Lund stood on her own at the water's edge below, Borch not far away, too shocked for words.

Brix left them alone.

Asbjørn Juncker had been working with the diving crew. A helicopter had been brought in to survey the river leading back to the city harbour. In the dark, looking for a small boat without lights . . . no one held out much hope.

'Any sign of the girl?' Brix asked.

'The river's tidal here,' Juncker said. 'The current's strong. She could be anywhere. They say . . .' He brushed his bleary eyes with the sleeve of his jacket. 'They think they ought to be able to pick her up in a couple of hours.'

The sound of another car arriving. So many now no one took any notice. Then a soft, worried female voice came crying her name.

'Where is she?' Maja Zeuthen asked, walking up to Brix as he stood by the water, towering above the men around him.

Lund looked, was about to say something. This was her call. Her responsibility. Then the woman saw another figure down the bank. Robert Zeuthen, shivering in a blanket Borch had found when he fished him out of the river.

Zeuthen's tie was gone. His hair a wet mess. Trousers soaking. But it was his eyes that had changed most of all. Scared. Marked by a sight he could never have imagined.

'Robert?' his wife asked.

He trembled in the blanket, said nothing. She came to a halt in front of him, didn't reach out with a comforting hand.

Shook her head and, voice breaking, said, 'Can't be. Can't be . . . Robert . . . no.'

A team of divers in orange suits rolled their rubber inflatable to the riverside, gently pushed it off its trailer into the black water.

Maja Zeuthen was crying, had that hysterical exhaustion that accompanied a sudden, violent death. Nothing new. Lund had seen this so many times. Felt impotent on every occasion.

'Sarah . . .'

Borch came close, tried to put a hand to Lund's shoulder. His voice hadn't altered with the years. It was still tender when he willed it. Kind, comforting. Eager to ease away the pain with affection. Love even.

But what if the pain was deserved? What if, in that agony, lay knowledge?

'We did all we could,' he said and touched her hand. 'Everything.'

'Not now,' Lund said and shrank away into the darkness beyond the floodlights and the busy shapes that milled around them.

Five

She didn't sleep. A picture kept running round her head. A burly figure dragging a blue tarpaulin bag over the child's head, the boat about to disappear beneath the bridge.

They vanish. An engine rumbles and echoes beneath the arch. The small craft emerges on the other side.

Two shots. The heavy fabric recoils. A small bundle roughly dumped over the stern, weighed down by an orange block.

Another memory. Troels Hartmann's black campaign car hauled out of the canal near the Pinseskoven forest. Water pouring from the doors. A sad body crammed in the boot. An eel that writhes down a girl's naked limb. Nanna Birk Larsen, nineteen when she died. One more innocent lost in the dark.

Lund sat shivering on a rickety chair in the garden of her little bungalow looking at the dead shrubs and wilted flowers.

She wasn't sick but she longed to be cured. She wasn't depressed but she wondered what it would be like to be happy.

Little movies playing over and over in her head dispelled those dreams. Always would until she managed to lay their cause in the ground.

'Sarah?'

Eva didn't watch TV or read papers. Mark's girlfriend lived outside the world that absorbed Lund and her peers. Nothing much mattered except the immediate life around her, and the one growing in her belly.

'I made some tea. Some of my own.'

She wore a dressing gown over jeans and a nightshirt. Pulled up a second rickety chair and handed over the mug.

Lund tasted it without thinking. The tea reminded her of bath salts.

'Herbal,' Eva said, raising hers in a toast. 'Good for you.'

Lund tried to smile.

'I hope I can stay another night. I haven't slept that well in ages. It's so quiet here.'

She seemed cheery in a brittle, frightened way. Didn't know a thing about the story that would surely be gripping the whole of Denmark.

'I've got some backache but your bed's good. Then when the baby kicks . . . ooph!' She beamed at Lund. 'Did you get that too?'

Didn't wait for an answer. She was babbling, nervous.

'I got some cushions from the sofa. Now it's OK.'

Lund put the tea to one side.

'Did you get to talk to him?' Eva asked.

She shook her head and asked blankly, 'Who?'

'Mark.' Her voice had a simple brightness that could become annoying. 'You were right. It was just a little argument.'

'I tried to,' Lund told her. 'Something came up. I'll get hold of him again.'

'Don't worry. We can manage. There's a scan today. He'll show up for that.'

Lund got up, picked a pair of rusty clippers out of a nearby plant pot, removed some twigs off the shrub in front of her. Tried to fool herself this counted as pruning.

Eva watched.

'It's just routine, I think. Hospitals still scare me. You hear so many stories. BOPA called.'

'OPA,' Lund corrected her.

'Yeah. Well. They said they'd call back. You don't need to do that. Sarah?'

Puzzled, Lund looked at her.

'Taking things off that tree,' Eva added. 'It's dead. You can't bring it back to life.' She tapped the trunk. 'The roots are gone. If you lift it out . . .'

Lund grabbed the thing with both hands and pulled. The base came out of the pot in one dried lump.

'This could be a really nice little place if you plant the right things,' Eva added. 'I used to work in a garden centre.'

Lund couldn't take the force of her wide, innocent smile. Something on her face must have told Eva that.

'Well,' she said. 'I'm going to have a bath if that's OK.' She took Lund's mug. 'I'll make you normal tea next time. Sorry.'

Lund watched her go back inside. Threw the spent shrub into the hedge. Went to work.

Thirty minutes later, back in a sullen ops room in the Politigården, she was listening to Madsen update the team. The speedboat had been found abandoned in the harbour close to the Zeeland terminal. Juncker was collating ship movements through the Øresund. Brix believed the kidnapper could have got himself on the crew of a departing vessel and fled the country.

Lund looked at Juncker's growing list. The harbour was busy. Departures for Russia, Sweden, Norway, Britain, further afield.

'If he's on one of those . . .' Madsen said and left it at that.

'Where's Brix?' she asked.

Madsen grimaced.

'Hedeby called him in for a meeting with the charmers upstairs. There's an inquest going on.'

'What do you expect?' Asbjørn Juncker moaned. 'We screwed up big time.'

She skimmed through the ship movements.

'If he's on one of these there's nothing much we can do anyway.'

Juncker glared at her.

'So we just give up!'

'I didn't say that, did I?' Lund retorted, her voice too high, too loud. 'We did what we could. I don't know what else—'

'You could have waited for us,' the young cop threw at her.

'No, Asbjørn. We couldn't. You weren't there. You didn't see—'

'You could have shot him at the hospital.'

Enough.

'For a wet-behind-the-ears kid you've got a lot to say for yourself.'

'Maybe it needs saying, Lund! You did everything he asked. You let her die in front of her father—'

'Juncker!' Madsen intervened. 'Shut up. Take a break. You're talking shit.'

'Really?'

He did get up though. Lund saw he was still covered in mud from the previous night. Hadn't been home at all.

'The lad doesn't mean it,' Madsen said when he'd left the office.

Lund kept looking through the papers.

'There's nothing here about the body.'

'They think they've found the concrete block. They can't get it free from some wreckage down there. Maybe she's in the mud beneath.'

'Tell the parents I'll brief them when they're ready.'

Madsen nodded.

'Juncker's wiped out. First case like this. It's got to him.'

'He meant it,' she said. 'Maybe he's right. Call the Zeuthens. Let's see what they think. Oh. And tell PET they need to deal with Interpol. That's their call.'

Madsen nodded at the next-door office.

'Borch's here. He hasn't been home all night either. You can tell him yourself if you like.'

In Drekar Robert Zeuthen came to on the office floor, half-dressed, his mouth tasting of stale brandy, his head between the waking world and that of vile recurring dreams.

Opened his eyes. The painting was there. The grey sea, threatening waves, the bucking Zeeland dragon. The canvas Emilie always hated.

Miserable, she said. Scary.

At some point he could barely remember Zeuthen had thrown a bottle of booze at the thing. Brown stains dripped down the frozen sea, leaked onto the fine carpet beneath.

He crouched there for a while, wishing the nightmare away. Then, when he realized it wouldn't leave, went upstairs, showered, put on new woollen suit trousers, a clean white shirt, a tie. Combed his hair. Cleaned his teeth. Shaved. Became the man he was meant to be.

When he got downstairs Niels Reinhardt was in the office shuffling a couple of morning papers into the waste bin. Emilie's photo on the front.

Zeuthen walked to the window. Looked out at a day that was

bright and ordinary for November. Stared at the grass and the ocean beyond.

'I don't know what to say,' Reinhardt told him. 'We're all beyond shocked. If there's anything . . .'

Zeuthen was transfixed by nothing more than the expanse of flat grass. Here the family played in the heat of a bright summer. He could picture her now, kicking wildly at Carl's football, laughing as it flew away.

'There are many messages of condolence,' Reinhardt added. 'You don't need to do anything until you feel like it. I can handle all this. The media. A couple of reporters tried to get into the estate.'

Reinhardt came to the window.

'They won't be back.' He hesitated. 'I had a call from the police. They think they've found her. There are some problems but they believe they'll be able to recover Emilie soon.'

Zeuthen closed his eyes.

'They'll need to take her to the forensic department first I'm afraid. The police say that whenever you want they will offer you a full report on where matters stand. The timing's entirely up to you.'

Two years before, when Zeuthen's father passed away, Reinhardt had handled everything, proved a rock for the family in a time of grief.

'I'd like to leave the practicalities to you,' Zeuthen said, back to staring out of the window. 'Contact the priest. Tell Maja I'm happy with whatever arrangements she wants.'

'Carl's at his grandparents'. He knows nothing about this. It's up to you and Maja when you want to . . .'

Was it raining? Was that what streaked and ruined the day?

Zeuthen gazed out at the lifeless lawn, the sea beyond, and realized he was weeping.

'I'll leave you now,' Reinhardt said and walked slowly, quietly from the room.

Mathias Borch seemed to have commandeered the little office he'd found. There were photos on the wall. Emilie. The bodies of the sailors. Schultz and Lis Vissenbjerg. He looked busy when she walked in, was working the photocopier, churning out page after page.

'Brix seems to think he's fled the country,' Borch said when she came in. 'On what grounds—'

'Why don't you just go home, Mathias. You've got a family . . .'

She didn't like the look on his face then.

One of the junior PET men attached to the Politigården team stuck his head through the door and said Dyhring wanted an immediate report on the situation.

'Yeah, yeah, Kasper,' Borch answered then waved him away. 'Why did he take the speedboat all the way to the harbour? He could have abandoned it anywhere. Had a car waiting. I don't—'

'It's not our problem any more. Interpol are taking over. Madsen's sending them the material.'

He went to the wall, and the photos on the clipboard. Lund stayed where she was.

'This man knows what he's going to do every step of the way. He kidnaps Emilie Zeuthen. He murders those sailors. The prosecutor. The pathologist. Then he rejects shitloads of money all because he wants to avenge a forgotten crime out in Jutland.'

'Yes,' she said and took a seat.

'But when you tell him there's a chance he's wrong about Robert Zeuthen what does he do?' Borch made a gun shape with his right hand. 'He shoots the girl anyway. Why?'

'Does it matter?' she asked.

'Yes. It does. If there's one thing we know about him it's that he has some warped sense of justice. He doesn't think he's a criminal. He believes he's a righteous warrior out to avenge Louise Hjelby. If that's the way he sees himself how can he take Emilie's life as if it doesn't count?'

'But he did. Just go home will you? Let's leave this to Interpol . . .'

'I did go home.'

He didn't look at her when he said that. Just pulled a pack of cigarettes off the desk and lit one.

'I didn't know you smoked.'

'You do now.'

She reached out, took the cigarette, stubbed it out on the desk then threw it in the bin.

'Not allowed in here any more.'

'I sat outside in the car. Watching Marie make breakfast for the girls.' He picked up another cigarette, lit it. She did nothing. 'It all looked so nice. They were probably chatting about what to eat, when to go swimming.'

He looked up at her.

'I couldn't go in there.' He pointed at the photos on the wall. 'Not with this running round my head. We can find this man, Sarah. I don't think he's run away. He's not like that. We've overlooked something. It's like . . .' He patted his jeans pockets, looked crazy for a moment. 'Like I've lost my phone. Or my keys . . .'

Another knock. The PET man Kasper walked in.

'Dyhring's going crazy. He wants to talk to you now.'

The explosion was sudden and so unlike him. Borch kicked at the desk, sent it flying onto its side, papers on the floor, coffee mug, everything.

'Didn't I tell you already?'

Kasper stood there, hand on the door.

'Yes, Borch. You did. But he's still ringing—'

'I'll be there for fuck's sake! Give it a break.'

He grabbed his jacket, sucked on the cigarette. Stabbed a finger at her.

'We're missing something, Sarah. Think about it.'

Hartmann didn't show up in his office in Christiansborg that morning. Weber and Karen Nebel tried his apartment. Then security came back and said he was at his old house in Østerbro.

The two of them went there straight away, bickering about how to proceed. Nebel was full of positive phrases about support and help in making decisions. Weber listened as they walked up the path to the house and said, 'Maybe he just needs a bit of time to himself.'

'We're in the middle of an election. If he goes walkabout Birgit Eggert's going to start scheming again. He shouldn't be sitting in this old dump when half of Denmark's asking what's going on.'

Weber kept quiet.

'OK,' Nebel said, getting the idea. 'You've known him since for ever. And I'm just the new girl who doesn't understand a single thing.'

'I wouldn't put it quite as harshly as that. Troels is a strange animal. He's simple but complicated. Thick-skinned but sensitive at the same time.'

'Oh,' she cried. 'An enigma. That'll look good on the election posters.'

'They don't need to see that side of him. It's for the best. Believe me.'

The argument seemed about to go up a notch. Then they heard something. It took a moment for the sound to register.

Weber groaned.

'Oh God. He's back to chopping wood.'

She followed him into the garden behind the house. Hartmann was in a green country jacket swinging at logs with an axe.

'How's my little tree elf this morning?' Weber asked brightly. 'Building ourselves a new bunker to hide in, are we?'

Hartmann chuckled, looked happier than he'd been in days. A pile of neatly quartered logs ready for the fire stood by him.

'That's a good one, Morten. Have you used it before?' Hartmann pointed at the wood. 'These need to go inside. I'm lighting a fire. Give us a hand, will you?'

'I don't do manual labour,' Weber told him. 'Why do you think I came into politics?'

'I've decided I'm keeping the house,' Hartmann announced. 'It's too nice to give to someone else.'

He grabbed an armful of wood and walked through the open back door. They followed. Hartmann stacked the logs by the side of a large fireplace in the living room.

'The thing is,' he said, 'this place only seems cold and lost because no one's been paying it any attention. If I light the fire the damp will go. If I move back in . . .'

'Bit far from the office,' Nebel noted.

Weber took a deep breath, glanced at her, launched in.

'OK, Troels. An update. PET are going to take care of Rosa Lebech's loopy husband. There'll be no more leaks from him. In return he won't be going to court. I've got calls in with the police . . .'

'I've decided to resign as Prime Minister.'

They went quiet. He took off his gloves and laid them carefully on the logs.

'And as party leader of course. I should have listened to you both and backed off the Zeuthen case. It was stupid to get involved. I just couldn't help it. I'm—'

'Is this a joke?' Weber yelled at him. 'Are you taking the piss or what? We've worked our arses off—'

'This is Rank's doing,' Nebel cut in. 'Not yours. He's going to have to bear the blame.'

'No,' Hartmann insisted. 'He was my minister. I'm responsible for him. I won't have this kind of scandal happening over Emilie Zeuthen's grave.'

'Oh please!' Weber kicked the pile of logs, sending a few scattering across the carpet. 'Leave your tender ego out of this for once. We'll hang Mogens if we need to and that's it.'

'I want you to set up a meeting with Birgit Eggert,' Hartmann continued. 'My mind's made up.'

Weber came and stood in front of him.

'Your mind's not yours to command. Haven't you worked that out yet? We're a team. This is not going to happen.'

'Set up a meeting with Eggert,' he said again.

Karen Nebel shook her head.

'You don't have the right to give up. We've got a campaign behind us. Hundreds of people who've put their faith in you.'

Hartmann nodded.

'Maybe they shouldn't have done. Just call Eggert, will you? I'd like to pay my condolences to Robert Zeuthen in person when he's ready. Make a call on that too.' He looked at his grubby hands. 'I need to change.'

Then he went back outside.

'I don't believe this,' Nebel muttered.

'I do,' Morten Weber said. 'Unfortunately. When you speak to Eggert say he's minded to resign. *Minded*. That's all.'

The corridors were long and dark and winding. Sometimes even Lund felt lost in the interior maze of the angular grey building that was the Politigården.

November. Rain fell on the central circular courtyard that was supposed to have a roof, an eye above it like the Pantheon.

Lights on everywhere. People she didn't know shuffling from department to department, floor to floor.

OPA worked in a different modern building. An ordinary block near the station. A place of safe boredom and predictable hours. There'd be time to tend to the garden, maybe ask Eva's advice on what to plant.

It was only lately that she'd noticed how people sometimes looked at her. That beneath their puzzled, worried gaze she'd felt an ache to be like everyone else, to slide into the same unthinking contentment and eke out the day.

Now she had to face Maja and Robert Zeuthen to explain the inexplicable. Lund had never run from these difficult moments. It was her job to break the worst news of all. The Zeuthen case was different. More and more in her head it was starting to rank with the murder of Nanna Birk Larsen. Not simply a vicious, impenetrable crime. Just as much a mark of the times, a way the world was falling slowly, steadily into uncaring chaos.

Lund walked into reception. Three of them there. Zeuthen in another dark suit, black tie, blank face. His wife in the green parka, hair straggly, face drawn. Next to her the boyfriend.

Carsten Lassen stayed behind. Zeuthen and his wife went into an interview room and sat by the barred window while Lund took the seat opposite.

'We're doing everything we can to trace your daughter's murderer,' she began and realized her words were an echo of the ones she used with Pernille and Theis Birk Larsen six years before, probably at this same table.

She wondered what the two of them were doing now Theis was out of jail. Looking at the Zeuthens a thought came unbidden. Time healed nothing, but love eased the pain. The Birk Larsens' devotion was tested then confirmed with a terrible finality. Maja Zeuthen scarcely glanced at her husband, though he couldn't take his eyes off her. There seemed no such catharsis coming their way.

'We suspect he may have escaped on a ship out of the country,' she added. 'Interpol are handling that side of the investigation. They have a full schedule of ship movements . . .'

Her voice sounded detached, as if it belonged to someone else. Like a minister reciting an old prayer, never noticing the words.

'We still think he may be a former Zeeland employee with a grudge.'

Lund wished they'd say something. Acknowledge one another's presence.

'We can offer you counselling,' she added and thought again of a weary priest, reciting the same old refrain.

'Where is she now?' Maja asked in a tired, weak voice.

'There are some technical issues with the diving operation. I'm sorry. I can't be precise.'

'What was she wearing?'

Zeuthen was trying to catch his wife's eye and failing.

'You saw?' Maja persisted. 'You were there, Lund?'

'I don't really know. It was very dark—'

'She was wearing a dark coat,' Zeuthen interrupted.

'Was she afraid?'

Still the woman wouldn't look at him.

'She didn't see anything,' Lund told her. 'It was all very . . . very quick. The boat went under the bridge. I'm not sure . . .'

Borch's voice kept wanting to say something in her head.

'I don't know what I saw exactly. I don't think she could have understood what was happening. I didn't.'

Maja Zeuthen nodded.

'I want to see her.'

Lund just looked, wondering what to say.

'Did you hear me? I want to see her.'

'I'll pass that on. If there's anything else . . .'

Zeuthen moved, tried to take her hand, spoke her name.

'No!'

It was almost a shriek. She half-ran from the room. Through the door they could see Carsten Lassen open his arms, embrace her.

Zeuthen sat back hunched in the hard Politigården chair, biting his lip.

Then he stared at Lund and she knew that expression so well. Hatred. Blame.

'I'm really sorry,' she said. 'I still don't understand . . .'

The look didn't change. He got up and left without a word.

Lund sat there in the interview room, hearing the voices around her. Maja Zeuthen. Pernille Birk Larsen. So many and they all asked the same question . . . why?

Hair back in a ponytail, smarter than usual, black sweater, black trousers. Dressed for a funeral and she'd never even noticed. She bent over and just for a brief minute allowed herself to cry.

*

Hartmann wouldn't be deterred. By midday he was in Birgit Eggert's office with Weber by his side, discussing the practicalities. There was an obvious glint of opportunity in her face.

'If we act decisively,' Eggert said, 'and choose a new candidate now we can at least limit the damage. We've fat chance of leading a new coalition but we ought to be able to play a principal part in it.'

Hartmann nodded, went to the window, kept quiet.

'This is ridiculous,' Weber broke in. 'No serving Prime Minister's ever stepped down in the middle of an election campaign. We'll be a laughing stock.'

'And what will we be if Troels doesn't quit?' she cried. 'The Zeuthen girl's dead. We're getting the blame. This case could haunt us for years.'

'Emilie Zeuthen is nothing to do with Troels!' Weber yelled.

'Neither was the Birk Larsen girl,' Eggert retorted. 'But that damn near finished him.'

Weber smiled at that. Hartmann was listening.

'But it didn't, Birgit. We saw it through. We stuck to our guns. We won. And the people who kept faith are still with us now. In the group here—'

'You think?' she said with a quick laugh. 'I've been making calls.'

'Been doing that since this thing kicked off, haven't you?'

'Everyone's in agreement. Troels is hurting the party.'

'Bullshit!'

'Morten! You're no beginner here. He's always going to be the Prime Minister who lost Emilie Zeuthen. Who damaged our relationship with Zeeland. Nothing he can do can change that.'

Hartmann came away from the window, joined them.

'For God's sake say something,' she begged. 'We're looking for a way out.'

Hartmann nodded.

'You deserve one. Get Karen to call a press conference, Morten. Some time this afternoon that suits.'

'To hell with it,' Weber said and got his coat. 'Write your own death notice. I've got better things to do.'

Mark was born in the same hospital, a few doors along from the tiny room where Eva now lay, big belly exposed, jelly on her skin, waiting for the ultrasound to begin.

Lund watched, holding her coat. Still trying to push away the memories and images of the night before.

The radiologist, a smiling Indian woman, was gently moving the sensor around.

A picture on the monitor next to the bed. Not much for the uninitiated to see.

'The little one's feeling a bit quiet today, Eva.' She glanced at the visitor. 'Take a seat. I don't bite.'

Lund pulled up a chair.

'I'm really grateful you came,' Eva told her. 'Even if it's more for Mark than me.'

'The baby's turned round nicely,' the doctor said. 'Won't be long now. Here. Take a peek . . .'

All the details Lund remembered, wondering at the very idea there might be a new life inside her. A heart, a head, arms, legs.

Eva looked, smiled nervously, reached out and gripped Lund's hand.

'Nice little fingers,' the woman added, pointing at the screen.

'Mark should have seen this,' Eva said and sounded as if she was about to cry.

'Look away now if you don't want to know if it's a boy or girl!'

Eva did, said she could feel the baby moving.

Her head was turned to Lund's.

'Can you see what sex it is, Sarah?'

A blue tarpaulin being pulled over a young girl's blonde head. The bridge. Two shots. The fabric moving. A black car emerging from the canal near Pinseskoven, water falling everywhere.

Lund was silent. The doctor looked surprised, embarrassed.

'This all seems fine,' the woman said. 'No problems. Nothing you really need worry about.'

Eva gasped and said she'd felt a kick.

'I'll wait outside,' Lund murmured and left them.

There was an empty bench seat. She sat in the middle. People walked past. Pregnant young mothers. Fathers with their children. The elderly. The sick. The pathetic. The dying. The long and endless procession. Still all Lund could see was that small figure, the blue shroud falling over her.

Two shots. And then the black water.

She liked being alone. Could live for ever in the little red cottage on the edge of the city. Untouched by everything. Going to work in OPA. Coming back in the evening. Watching TV with a beer and something from the microwave.

Footsteps. They came close. Someone sat down. Lund looked.

Borch, clean-shaven, the smell of shampoo about him. Fresh clothes.

'Brix said you were here.'

One glance then she refused to look at him.

'I don't want to talk right now.'

'Tough. I do.'

'Borch—'

'Last night on the bridge you told him he'd got it wrong. Later we find his boat. He's gone out of his way to leave a trail for us. To make it look as if he's vanished.'

Lund brushed a strand of stray hair from her face.

'I don't have the time now.'

She got up to leave. He followed her down the long corridor.

'This morning there's a break-in at the Maritime Authority archives. Same pattern. Security goes down, just like Zeeland's. He's in.'

She walked more quickly. Borch kept up.

'Here are copies of the stolen papers.' A sheaf of documents in front of her. 'They're routes and port calls for the *Medea*. He was checking what you told him, Sarah!'

Lund turned round, desperate to lose him.

'I don't care. I'm finished—'

'No!'

Borch was loud. A passing doctor glared at them, put a finger to his lips.

She turned on him.

'What the matter with you?' Lund shrieked. 'She's dead.'

'He listened to you. You made him think twice. That means something. Maybe he planned to go abroad and changed his mind. I don't know but you made him stop and think about what he was doing.'

The tears were back. Lund put a finger to her head.

'But we saw. I can't stop . . .'

He was ready for that. Anxious for it.

'Saw what?

'Saw him shoot her.'

Mathias Borch folded his arms.

'Did you?' he asked.

Nebel was in her car by the sea in Dragør when Hartmann called. She made an excuse. A real one. She was about to talk to Mogens Rank. Didn't have the resources to fix anything just then.

It was a small place for a minister of the state. A bachelor's cottage at the end of a terrace. Gulls hung in the air. Waves crashed noisily on the shore. Winter had arrived: short days, long nights, cold and wet for months ahead.

Rank was a quiet, self-effacing man. If he had vices no one knew. He did his job, went home afterwards, was a polite, efficient servant of the party.

She wondered if he'd turn her back at the door. The way he'd been spoken to . . . perhaps she deserved that. But Mogens Rank simply smiled, asked her inside, made her a cup of good coffee, sat her down in a tidy living room that smelled of polish and a lively log fire.

'I'm sorry this case has hurt Troels,' he said before she could begin. 'It's not done a lot for me either.'

So many books on the wall. They looked read too. Rank didn't have a life outside politics. It was so obvious.

'I've taken the phone off the hook. Turned off my mobile. The press keep hounding me. I can't sleep.'

'Refer them to me,' she said.

A weak smile.

'But I'd have to answer if I did that, Karen.'

He wasn't wearing a tie. She couldn't remember seeing that before.

'It's best to come clean, Mogens. Everything's going to come out in the end. Admit you put pressure on Peter Schultz . . .'

'But I didn't,' he cried.

'So what did you do? All I want is a clear and incontrovertible statement that Troels knew nothing of this. That he's innocent—'

'Like me?' Rank cut in. 'All I did was ask Schultz what was going on. Whether it was something we needed to worry about. Oh God . . .'

He took off his glasses, rubbed his eyes.

'I've had enough of this. I feel dreadful. I'm sorry. I need to go to bed.'

'Was anyone else present? Can someone back this up?'

Rank took a deep breath and shook his head.

'It was a brief chat in the corridor at the end of a meeting about something entirely different. Of course there were no witnesses.'

Nebel pulled out her file.

'You have to cut out the lies, Mogens. If you don't do that I can't save you.'

Glasses back on he glared at her.

'What lies?'

She showed him the PET report.

'The security system shows he was in the ministry for two hours. You don't chat in the corridor all that time.'

Mogens Rank folded his arms.

'I accept I should have told you I met Schultz before. I'm no more happy with that than you. But I assure you all that happened was a brief conversation. I asked Schultz if we had anything to worry about over Zeeland in the case of that girl's death. He assured me we didn't. That was it.'

She passed him the papers.

'The guard has him coming into the building at 13.54. He left through the ministry exit at 16.10.'

'He could have gone anywhere,' Rank pointed out. 'He might have walked all the way to Christiansborg for all I know.'

'But he didn't! We'd have seen. It . . .' Her mind was racing. 'It would have been on the internal CCTV somewhere.'

'I'm not mistaken,' Rank insisted. 'Not this time.'

Outside Hartmann called again, asking her to start the arrangements for his resignation.

'Let's talk about this when I get back,' Nebel said.

Early evening in Drekar. A subtle, nagging sense of guilt had played on Maja Zeuthen, persuaded her to remain close to her husband as the search for Emilie's body continued. The grief was theirs to share however much Carsten Lassen hated the idea.

Yet the source of that nagging anguish took so long to arrive. At four Reinhardt drove to the Politigården to find out what was happening. At five he had no news. At six he was told the diving teams were still struggling with the current and had yet to free the concrete block from debris under the water.

Carl would stay with her for the foreseeable future. She'd demanded that, not knowing why, and Robert hadn't argued. Sick of waiting for another call she went upstairs, looked in Emilie's room, toys and books and clothes scattered everywhere. Tidied a few away for no good reason. Then went to Carl's room, looked for some familiar things to take to the little apartment in the city.

When she came down Zeuthen was in the study, dressed for work as always.

'I can't find Carl's bedtime book,' she said. 'The one with the car. I looked—'

'Maybe it's in his room.'

'I've already looked there, Robert!'

The sudden savage anger in her voice was unwanted, not aimed at him. Not really.

She went for the door.

'Her hair was under a black hat . . .' Zeuthen said and that stopped her.

She stayed at the door, looking at the grand entrance hall, the black and white tiles. This place seemed so empty without the children. Not hostile. Just dead.

'He must have bought the hat,' he said.

Maja turned, looked into his eyes.

'I keep . . .' He tapped his head, too hard, was shaking in front of her. 'Keep seeing her in here. She cried out to me and I shouted back. Except—'

'Robert . . .'

'When she first called out I couldn't see her. Then I realized she was looking up at me from the boat and . . .' Voice cracking, fighting to keep some semblance of control. 'I knew she was scared. I saw it. I so . . . so . . . wanted . . .' His head, the neat and serious hair, turned from side to side. 'There wasn't time. She was there and I couldn't save her.'

Maja Zeuthen picked up the bag with the few things of Carl's she'd chosen, walked away.

He followed, didn't come near her. As if he no longer dared.

'If you think it's my fault for God's sake say so. I can't bear to think . . .'

Tears. His. Hers.

'If you think there's something I could have done . . . somehow . . . please . . .'

Married eleven years. Lovers a brief ten months before. They'd shared a bed, two children. Lives once fused together in a happy union.

But when she looked at him then, mouth open, eyes damp, lines on his face that were never there before, she'd no idea what to say.

They might have been strangers. So like a stranger she walked out of the front door, went to her car, never said a word.

Karen Nebel wasn't answering her phone. In the end Hartmann ordered one of the junior media staff to assemble a press conference.

He was about to go to the meeting when Weber came back, tried one last time to talk him out of resigning.

'My mind's made up. I'll make sure you and Karen get employed by the new team.'

'Thanks a bundle,' Weber snapped. 'Do you honestly think I'd work for that old boot?'

'It's an open election,' Hartmann pointed out. 'There's no guarantee Birgit's the next leader.'

Weber closed his eyes, made a steeple with his fingers. A schoolmaster's gesture, deliberate too.

'In many ways you're a child, Troels. It's one of your redeeming qualities. Doesn't matter much usually. We're used to it. But you have to listen to me now. This is premature. You're making a terrible mistake.'

A knock on the door. Ussing was there. He looked hesitant for once.

'May I?'

Weber sat down and watched.

'I don't take any pleasure in this,' Ussing insisted, uncomfortable they weren't alone.

'You worked hard enough for it, Anders.'

A laugh. A shrug.

'That's the game, isn't it? Politics. It's not chess.'

'But it is,' Weber interrupted. 'And this is check. Not checkmate.'

An awkward smile then Ussing said, 'You did your best, Troels. I'm sure this is the right decision. It's never easy to hide skeletons in the cupboard.' He held out his hand. 'No hard feelings.'

Hartmann didn't move.

'Skeletons?' he asked.

'I don't want to push it.'

'I look forward to watching you do better.'

'Got to win the election first.' Ussing thrust his hands into his pockets. 'Rosa's asked for a meeting. So maybe it won't be so hard. I won't . . .'

He stopped for a moment, as if considering something.

'I won't pursue this when we're in power.' The hand came out again. 'This is a time to be magnanimous. Shake on it?'

'There's a door over there, Anders,' Weber said. 'Try walking through it.'

He withdrew the hand and said, 'If that's the way you want to play things.'

Then laughed, left them there.

Morten Weber raised his eyebrows, stared at Hartmann.

'Are you really going to roll over for a cock like that?'

'Shut it, Morten.'

'I guess Rosa didn't turn out to be such a faithful bed mate either . . .'

'I said . . .'

Karen Nebel hurried in, breathless, a laptop beneath her arm.

'I've been trying to reach you for hours,' Hartmann complained.

'Busy,' she said, and opened the computer, put it on the desk.

'I've got a press conference.'

She hit the keyboard, pulled up a video.

'Not before you see this.'

'It's about to start.'

'Morten. Close the doors.'

The little man wandered over, did as he was told, came back to the table.

'If this is one more pathetic trick to get me to stay . . .' Hartmann began.

The video came alive. CCTV footage. Familiar location. The lobby of the Ministry of Justice. Mogens Rank and the dead Peter Schultz.

'I got this from security,' Nebel said. 'Mogens met him out in the open. Where everyone could see.' A smile. 'Odd place to put together a conspiracy, don't you think?'

'Too late,' Hartmann muttered.

She fast-forwarded the footage.

'There you go. Seventeen minutes. Not two hours like we were told. Mogens heads off for another meeting. Schultz goes to the toilet.'

'Karen . . .'

'Schultz comes out and walks to the corridor for the Parliament building.'

Weber came closer, looked interested.

'So I got them to pull out the CCTV archives there.'

'I'm going,' Hartmann announced.

'If Karen thinks this is important,' Weber cut in, 'the least you can do is hear her out. We got you into this place . . .'

'This is pathetic . . .'

Nebel was trying to open another file.

'I've fixed it so you can both keep your jobs here. Will you kindly cut this out?'

Morten Weber let loose a howl of fury.

'We're not here for us. We're not here for you either. It's the party. You made it. You lead it. If you're gone and Eggert's in the chair we're screwed . . .'

'I never knew you were so high-minded,' Hartmann snarled.

'Oh go on then. Resign. Play the pitiful, self-righteous prig if you like. I won't watch—'

'I've heard enough from you for one day, Morten. Who do you think you are?'

Weber got to his feet.

'A man who serves a fool,' he said. 'Which makes me an even bigger fool.' He got his briefcase. 'Bye, Troels.' A smile, a wave to Nebel. 'Karen. Try to stop him making a complete idiot of himself when he goes through with this nonsense.'

Then he walked out, slamming the doors behind him.

'I'm sorry about that . . .'

But she wasn't listening. Nebel had found what she wanted. Hartmann grabbed his papers. She got up, stood in front of him, put a hand to his chest.

'Unless you want me to storm out of here too you will watch this till the end. After that go home and chop your bloody logs if you like . . .'

That stopped him.

The video was paused. Two men in suits on a staircase, backs to the camera.

'This is the entrance by the show grounds,' she said. 'Schultz saw someone else. They went into a meeting room. Stayed there for fifty-five minutes.'

'Karen . . .'

She moved the video forward. Hartmann watched then pulled up a chair.

Schultz smiling. The other man turned. Smiled too. Shook his hand.

Hartmann took Karen Nebel's hand, kissed it.

'What do I tell the press?' she asked.

'You tell them the Prime Minister's too busy to talk.'

Lund was back on the bridge. The construction signs had been cleared. The stolen truck was gone. On the bank downstream a diving team continued to labour, working under floodlights, struggling in the dark.

She walked on the white line down the centre. Stood where she had the night before. Went to the point where they first heard Emilie's voice. Thought about her memories. Then crossed the road, stopped close to the point where the boat emerged.

The mind filled in gaps to see what it expected. Tried to make sense of the impenetrable. And sometimes invented things. Borch had been right: she wasn't sure what she'd witnessed at all.

A voice from below. A vessel moving on the surface.

'We're bringing her up,' a man cried. 'Keep clear.'

Figures in red suits bent over the edge of a boat, looking at the frogmen's green lights rising from the river.

An orange shape emerged. The cement weight he'd tied to the tarpaulin. Then a severed rope.

Someone swore. Lund listened.

The blue bundle had disappeared. They'd have to go back to dragging again, a much wider area this time.

There'd be no body yet. Perhaps not tomorrow. Ever.

Lund got back in her car, drove to the Politigården, went straight to the forensic garage where Juncker and Madsen were looking again at the boat. Borch had been sniffing around. She listened, pulled on a pair of disposable gloves, told Juncker to come with her.

The speedboat looked smaller under the bright lights of the garage. Room for two people in the little cabin. Not much more.

A head bobbed up from the bows.

'You took your time,' Borch said with a grin.

'So he stole these papers this morning?' Lund asked as Juncker pulled some steps closer to allow her to get on the deck.

'Exactly.'

His head went down again. When she climbed on board she saw he was looking inside a storage hatch built into the bows. A sizeable one.

'Do you remember seeing him open this?'

'No,' Lund said. 'He was at the back. Nowhere near.'

She walked to the stern, looked round. Little here matched what she saw in her memory.

'So the thing is,' Borch said following her, 'he was in a hurry. Making it up as he went along and that wasn't like him.'

'It couldn't have been at the front,' she insisted. 'There wasn't enough time when he went under the bridge.'

Juncker put his hand in the air.

'What on earth are you two talking about? I thought you saw him shoot her. Then shove her overboard.'

'We saw something,' Borch agreed. 'Let's rewind this, Sarah. Where was she in the end? Where was he?'

Lund turned a circle on her heels.

There was a hatch. It ran the width of the boat at the stern. A single handle in the middle. Just by the point at which they'd seen the blue tarpaulin and the orange block go over the side.

She took out her torch, lifted the lid, looked inside.

Pulled out the thing she found there.

Black hat. Small. Wool. Blonde hairs around the edge.

They got a pool car for the drive to Gudbjerghavn, the little town in West Jutland where Louise Hjelby died. It was close to Esbjerg where Zeeland ran most of the port facilities. Lund took the wheel. Borch was fast asleep in the passenger seat, snoring more loudly than she remembered. Asbjørn Juncker had dozed off in the back. Before that he'd been remarkably chipper. Just the idea Emilie might be alive had cheered him so much that a little of his good humour had spread to her. Then, like a toddler, he curled up on the seat.

On the way Lund called the Politigården and got Madsen to talk to the sleepy police station where Nicolaj Overgaard had once been chief. Brix was being interviewed by an investigator from the Ministry of Justice. The first step in the disciplinary process. One that would reach her soon. She was glad the chief was out of things at that moment. It meant there was no need of explanations. Her and Borch's idea – hazy, insupportable probably – was that the kidnapper would return to Gudbjerghavn to hunt for new leads. She wanted the locals to check for strangers asking questions. And she was hungry for a look at the Hjelby case herself.

'Get Brix to call me as soon as he's out of the meeting,' she said. 'We'll be there soon.'

To her surprise the call didn't appear to wake the men. Lund looked at Borch. They'd set off in a hurry. His jacket lay on the floor by the side of the seat. The car's heating wasn't so great. She took a hand off the wheel, got the jacket up and spread it over him as best she could.

'When will we be there?' Juncker asked from the back seat.

'You made me jump. I thought you were sleeping.'

'Not sleeping now. May need a leak soon though. When will we be there?'

'Soon, Asbjørn,' she said in the best motherly tone she could manage. 'Try to hold on if you can.'

'What are we looking for exactly?'

A red van was stolen from Copenhagen harbour that morning not far from where the speedboat was abandoned. They had its number in Gudbjerghavn. A start.

'You really think she could be alive?'

'Until someone proves otherwise.'

'Where do you know Borch from?'

'Is that relevant?'

'Just being friendly.'

'We went to the academy together. He was in the year below.'

He uttered a long, knowing, 'Oh . . .'

'What does that mean?' she asked.

'It means . . . oh.' He laughed. 'You two were lovebirds. Come on. It stands out a mile. And I heard your mum . . .'

The talking woke Borch. He stretched, yawned, listened to her tell him about the stolen van.

'When you two were a couple did you argue like you argue now?' Juncker asked chirpily.

Borch stretched again, turned, stared at him and said, 'What?'

Anxious to change the conversation Lund asked about Gudbjerghavn. Feeder port for the Zeeland facilities in Esbjerg for decades. During the economic crisis the company had steadily run the place down. A couple of years before they pulled the plug completely. Two thousand residents. Most of them out of work.

'Why didn't you wake me up?' Borch asked.

'Have we got any crisps or something?' Juncker added. 'Also I really need to pee.' A pause. 'Unless someone's got a bottle.'

She pulled in at the next service station. Juncker bought some food. He and Borch went to the toilet. Then the two of them returned looking lively.

Back on the road Borch said, 'I hate falling asleep in cars. The last time I dozed off with you driving was in Norway. I woke up with a bad back in a lay-by somewhere.'

'It wasn't my driving that gave you a bad back.'

'Oh . . .' Juncker said slowly. 'What were you doing in Norway? Apart from the obvious . . .'

Borch stifled a snort. She went quiet. Not long after they pulled into Gudbjerghavn, found the police station. A low two-storey building with one car in front.

The officer in charge was by the bonnet, enjoying a smoke. He eyed her ID when she got out.

'We've been in touch with Copenhagen,' he said and threw his cigarette in the gutter. 'They didn't know what we were talking about.'

'I asked for a search.'

'Not a lot to look at here.'

Borch stayed back for some reason. Then changed his mind, walked up to the man, smiled, shook his hand and said, 'Good to see you again. It's about the Zeuthen case. Check with Zeeland if you like.'

Lund wondered at that. Still the uniformed officer wasn't impressed.

'According to Copenhagen the kidnapper killed the Zeuthen girl then hitched a ride on a ship out of the country. Nothing to do with us.'

'Red van,' Juncker broke in. 'You've got the registration. Let's get moving, shall we?'

'This place is dead, sonny. If it was here we'd have seen it.'

He pulled out another cigarette and lit it.

'Overgaard went out with my sister for a while. Bit of a moron. Didn't deserve to be chief here. But all the same . . .'

'Listen . . .' Borch began.

'There's a boarding house round the corner. Nothing swanky but it's all we have,' he said, heading for the car. 'Talk in the morning if you want.'

Lennart Brix had instigated plenty of disciplinary proceedings against others and dodged a good few himself. There was no avoiding this one, or the consequences. Ruth Hedeby had made that clear when she led him to an interview room and introduced the investigating officer from the prosecutor's department. His name was Tage Steiner, a lean man as tall as Brix, with a fixed stare behind rimless glasses.

Brix listened to Steiner reel off a list of one-sided questions, did his best to answer. There was a good response to most of them. Not that it mattered. Emilie Zeuthen was dead. And so, professionally, was he.

After the last pointed attack he got bored.

'Let's be candid, Steiner. You need a scapegoat and I fit the description.' He leaned back, looked at the man opposite, a lawyer, a civil servant, not a cop. 'Don't pretend this is about something it's not.'

Steiner sipped at his coffee and said, 'I'm just doing my job.'

'Me too. If you think you've got a case then make it. Don't waste my time right now. We're still—'

'Your handling of the investigation was deeply flawed,' Steiner cut in.

'Were you a police officer in another life? Do you feel qualified to judge?'

'I'm judging you, Brix. Like it or not.'

'We followed standard procedures. Made all the right decisions . . .'

'And the girl died. An honourable man would hand in his resignation without being asked.'

Brix checked his watch. Said nothing. The door opened and Ruth Hedeby came in, ignored Steiner when he told her to leave.

'I need you now,' she said and waited until Brix joined her.

'What the hell's happening, Lennart?' Hedeby asked in a whisper. 'I just heard Borch and Lund and Juncker are in Jutland. They're asking for extra manpower for a search.'

'For what?' he asked.

'I rather hoped you'd tell me.'

The prosecutor got up and walked over.

'I'm developing a very interesting impression of this whole department I must say. Perhaps the problem goes deeper than a single officer.'

Hedeby started clucking, trying to make him happy. Brix's phone went.

He looked at the name on the screen, strode back to the office.

'Even by your standards this requires some explaining, Lund.'

'Maybe he didn't kill her. He wants to get to the bottom of the Hjelby case. We think he stole a van from the harbour and brought her out here.'

'Why would he spare the girl?'

'I told him Zeeland weren't responsible for Louise Hjelby's death. Murdering Emilie balances out nothing. He wants to know who killed Louise.'

Through the window across the hall he could see Maja Zeuthen pacing up and down.

'Do you have the least bit of evidence to back this up?'

'He hid Emilie in the front hold of the boat. We found her woolly hat there.'

Brix took a deep breath.

'A woolly hat?'

'He's not going to stop until he knows what happened. Emilie's a sideshow for him now. We need more people out here.'

Ruth Hedeby walked in front of him.

'Get Lund back,' she ordered. 'Put a stop to this immediately.'

Madsen and the other men moved away, sensing the coming storm.

'Brix?' Lund asked.

'I'll make sure there's support from the surrounding districts. Get Borch to do what he can.'

Hedeby pulled out her phone and said, 'If you won't do it, I will.'

'Ruth.' Brix came over, put his hand on hers. 'I don't have time for this. The girl may still be alive. If you want to stop this investigation just when we might have a breakthrough feel free.' He nodded at Steiner. 'But you'll be talking to him next. Not me.'

The prosecutor was out again, demanding the meeting resume.

'I want some cooperation around here,' he added.

Brix was on him then.

'Cooperation? Why ask me? No one's playing that game. All they're doing is trying to cover their own backs.'

'I could get you out quietly with a pay-off,' Steiner said. 'Or noisily with half the media in Copenhagen watching. Just put your hands up . . .'

'Fuck you,' Brix roared. 'What are you going to tell your masters in the Ministry of Justice? We took the team apart just when it looked like we might find Emilie Zeuthen alive?'

That shut him up.

Hedeby came between them.

'We'll postpone until tomorrow. I'll take the responsibility for that decision.'

Steiner nodded, snatched at his briefcase.

'Damned right you will.'

She was still there when Brix went back to the call.

'Did you hear that, Lund?'

'A bit.'

'You'd better be right this time.'

He told Madsen to work on the local districts, get resources out to Jutland. The detective nodded at the waiting room.

Maja Zeuthen was there, wide-eyed, curious.

'I hate to tell you,' Madsen whispered. 'But I think she may have caught a bit of that.'

*

A small jetty running out into gentle waves. A dead ship listing a few hundred metres offshore. The smell of diesel, rotting seaweed, dank water.

Men and women were starting to arrive from the neighbouring districts, grumbling about the cold night, asking for overtime. Borch had sent them out to check all the local places where a visitor might stay. There was no sign yet of the red van.

Lund kicked at the ropes on the concrete, tried to picture what this might have been like.

'They found her here?'

Borch nodded.

'The Zeeland ship was moored opposite. The harbour was still working then. Can we go now?'

Lund didn't move. She was looking for new pictures in her head. Useful ones. Images that would replace the memory of Emilie and the boat from the previous night.

'Someone could have driven Louise down here and thrown her in the water. There doesn't need to be any connection with the docks at all.'

Borch sniffed the heavy air.

'Shall we concentrate on why we came? Finding the man . . .'

'Can't divide the two,' she said. 'If the foster family are right Louise disappeared a day before we thought.'

'True,' Juncker agreed. He was reading a map of the area, trying to locate some holiday homes they'd been told about.

'If Peter Schultz changed the date,' Lund went on, 'he must have had a reason. Something happened the day before. He was trying to distance her murder from that.'

'I've put out a call for the van,' Juncker said. 'Given details to the cab drivers.'

Borch took the map, placed it on the bonnet of their car, described a circle round the town with a gloved finger.

'Take a ten-kilometre radius. We'll start there.'

'Oh for God's sake!' Lund cried. 'He hasn't booked himself a room in the local bed and breakfast. We know what he's like. Look at scrapyards and caravan sites.'

'Fine,' Borch agreed. 'You can go with him.'

'No.' Lund waved the car keys. 'I want to talk to the foster family first.' She nodded at the local police. 'They can give you a car. They seem to prefer you to me anyway.'

When Brix went to talk to the Zeuthen woman he saw that the young doctor, her boyfriend, had turned up. A man who seemed permanently angry and wanted to take that out on the first person he could find.

Brix listened to him begin to whinge again then said, 'The salvage crew are doing what they can.'

The woman was peering at him, hugging herself in the green parka.

'Why's it taking so long?' the boyfriend demanded.

'The rope that attached the tarpaulin to the block snapped. The current's very strong. She could have gone a long way.'

He wasn't happy with any of that.

'But you started looking straight away? You didn't piss around like every other time?'

'We started straight away,' Brix agreed. 'If she's there hopefully we'll find her soon.'

Maja Zeuthen's head went up.

'If? I could hear you arguing in there. I thought . . .'

'I'm sorry you heard our discussion,' Brix said and passed over his card, a personal number on it. 'That's unfortunate. If you'll excuse me . . .'

He turned to go.

'Brix!' She had a high voice, determined when she wanted. 'What do you mean "if she's there"? I thought I heard . . .'

Put on the spot by the idiot lawyer. By Hedeby too. He could take that. But giving this woman hope . . .

'We're examining every aspect of last night,' he said.

'She could be alive?'

Her eyes were pink from crying, full of pain.

'Mrs Zeuthen. I don't—'

'It's a simple question.'

Brix looked at her. Couldn't bring himself to make the agony worse.

'No. I don't believe so. I'm sorry.'

*

Karen Nebel had called off the press conference. At nine she sat down with Hartmann to listen to the evening news. It could have been worse. Speculation that he was going to take the unprecedented step of standing down was still doing the rounds. So was a fresh rumour. There were new developments that could change the whole case. Hartmann might weather the storm, maybe even regain the initiative.

He smiled, patted her arm.

'I imagine that's down to you.'

'It's what you pay me for,' Nebel told him. 'I'm using up some credibility here, Troels. We need to deliver.'

'Any word from Morten?'

'Not a thing.'

He shrugged.

'He does this sometimes. We're like an old couple. You argue. You get back together.'

'Maybe you don't need him any more.'

The smile became more stiff. His hand came away.

'One day, perhaps. Not now. You've checked? They've started the meeting?'

She looked at her watch.

'Fifteen minutes in. They're probably about to get down to business.'

He clapped his hands, got his jacket, checked his shirt and tie. Walked across the courtyard to the Parliament building. A couple of photographers caught off guard realized he was there, began snapping, flashing.

Troels Hartmann beamed, the election look. Confident. Open. Honest.

Then he found the committee room and marched straight in.

Rosa Lebech, grey suit, TV-neat hair, serious face, was at one end of the table. Anders Ussing at the other. Both surrounded by their staff.

Ussing looked outraged.

'Haven't you quit yet?'

'Something came up,' Hartmann replied.

Rosa Lebech stared at the table, embarrassed.

'This is a private meeting,' Ussing complained. 'You can't just barge in here.'

He sat down. Told the advisers to get out. They looked at their leaders. Lebech nodded. Then Ussing. Soon it was just the three of them at the table.

'Cut a deal yet?' he asked her.

She didn't answer.

'You misled everyone,' Ussing said. 'You can't expect support after the way you handled the Zeuthen case.'

'The police and PET dealt with that. Not me. I will hold them to account though. Same for everyone involved. Rosa?'

'We can talk later, Troels.'

'True.' He nodded at the door. 'This isn't for your ears.'

She swore, snatched up her papers, marched out.

'I hope this is good,' Ussing said, laughing.

'It's wonderful. There you are trying to pillory me because my Justice Minister doesn't recollect every second of a seventeen-minute conversation with a deputy prosecutor two years ago.'

'More to it than that . . .'

'While at the same time you said nothing about your own involvement in the affair.' Hartmann threw a set of photos on the table. 'Mogens Rank. A few minutes in a corridor. Nothing said of importance. You . . .' He pushed forward the picture of Schultz and Ussing meeting in the Parliament building. 'Almost an hour with him alone in your office. Here you are going in.' One picture. 'Here you are shaking his hand when he leaves. Dated. Timed.'

Ussing said nothing.

'And you have the temerity to accuse Mogens Rank of twisting the facts?'

'Who gave you this?'

'Does it matter?'

'Is this official? If you think I've done something wrong you should set your friends in PET on me.'

'I intend to. After all . . .' A smile. 'You wouldn't want me to withhold relevant information, would you? You met Schultz while he was dealing with this old case.'

'And you think I pressured him somehow? Why would I do that?'

'What did you talk about?'

'It was private. Nothing to do with you. Nothing to do with Zeeland either, or that case. If it had been I'd have said so before. Even for you this is low . . .'

He patted Ussing on the shoulder.

'We'll let PET decide, shall we?'

Hartmann left him then. Back in his office he told Nebel what had happened.

'A private meeting?' she asked, incredulous. 'Right after Schultz met Mogens Rank?'

'Maybe that's all it is. Why would Ussing be involved? Doesn't matter. He's worried. So's Rosa. I need to sleep on this. Maybe I should call Birgit . . .'

Her hand was over the phone before he could get there.

'The police think Emilie could still be alive,' Nebel said. 'They're in West Jutland. It looks as if the kidnapper took her there, trying to find out about the case from before.'

Hartmann struggled to take that in.

'Here's what you do,' she went on. 'I fix a TV statement for half an hour. You look grief-stricken. Express sympathy for the family. You say you're investigating how the kidnapping was handled and want answers. You confirm there may be new information that will change the case. Then you say tomorrow you're going to call in the party leaders and ask them not to make the Zeuthens' private tragedy a sparring point in the election.'

She had a media brain. That never went away.

'Do I need to clear what I say with PET? With Brix?'

Nebel laughed.

'No, Troels. You need to clear it with me. I want you word perfect before we go on air. It's a statement, nothing more. You won't be taking questions.'

She picked up a notepad, began to scribble a few lines.

'If the girl's dead we can show we acted with compassion and dignity. If she's alive we'll take the credit and leave Anders Ussing in the gutter where he belongs.'

The foster parents lived in a small, plain bungalow on a hill overlooking the harbour. The man was a ship's engineer, unemployed. The woman seemed to do nothing and was away, staying with relatives. He was tall, unsmiling, suspicious. Perhaps Lund's own age. Louise Hjelby had moved in not long before her thirteenth birthday.

'What are you looking for?' he asked after Lund showed her ID and came in.

'I don't know really. Some friends. People she spent time with.'

'She didn't go out. She only had us. No one else. Louise had a tough upbringing. She was a shy kid. Why am I telling you all this? We've been through it before.'

There was a photo on the sideboard. She walked over and picked it up. A girl with a white bike. Long black hair. Unsmiling but not unhappy.

'Is that her?'

'Who else would it be?'

He wanted her out of there which meant Lund was more determined than ever to stay.

'How did she get placed with you?'

He took the photograph and put it back where it belonged. There was no dust anywhere here. No disorder. They were tidy, proper people.

'Louise lived with her mother in Copenhagen until she died of cancer. They put her in a children's home for a while. There were some cuts or something and the home closed.'

He sat down at an old-fashioned table, gestured for her to take the seat opposite.

'They told us she'd been with quite a few different families. It wasn't that she was difficult. She couldn't settle. Then three years ago she came to us.'

A long glance round the room.

'We couldn't have kids of our own. This place always seemed so empty.'

Lund took out her notebook.

'Did she mention her father?'

He shook his head.

'Not really. Her mother told her some fairy story. That he was a big hero who sailed the seven seas just like Pippi Longstocking's dad.'

'Did she ever say a name?'

'Louise was a clever kid. I don't think she believed in fairy stories. Not any more.'

'A name?'

'No. I suppose she hoped one day he'd come for her. But it never happened.'

This was hurting him. She could see that. One more shake of his head and then he turned to her.

'We tried to do everything we could. I thought we were getting somewhere. She seemed happy. We felt . . . I guess . . . we felt like a family.' A hard glance at the photograph. 'But I suppose we didn't really know what that was like. So one day . . .'

The place was no bigger than her own little cottage. Yet it felt like a home. Much more than she'd ever managed.

'If you thought she was happy she probably was. Louise didn't kill herself.'

'Sorry?'

'We think she was murdered.'

He didn't know what to say.

'If I could see her room . . . her things . . .'

Without a word he took her to the garage. Full of boxes. No space for a car. Photographs and scrapbooks. He ran through that final day. Louise rode to school on her bike, was due back in the early afternoon as usual. Always used the same route: past the harbour, along the water by the pier.

'She definitely went missing on a Thursday? Not Friday?'

The suspicious, hostile look returned.

'You don't forget things like that.'

'Who was the last person to see her?'

He had to think about the answer.

'The head teacher. She saw her pushing her bike towards the harbour. But then . . .'

'Then what?'

'A bit later someone told me they'd seen her up on the main road. Nowhere near the school. I told that policeman, Overgaard. He said he checked and it was someone else. All those politicians were in town for the election. I don't think the police had much time for Louise.'

Lund gave up on the girl's things.

'Did they ever find the bike?'

'If they did they never told us. They didn't tell us much anyway.' He closed his eyes for a moment. 'Murdered? Our Louise?'

'We think so.'

'She was a kid. Just getting her life back. Who'd do that? Why?'

The autopsy gave the answer to that. But she looked at this decent man, realized how much grief she'd raised from the ground already, and kept quiet.

On the way out Lund gave him her card. Went to the car. Breathed in the soiled maritime air.

Then she made some calls. The last one to Borch telling him she was going to the school.

Maja Zeuthen walked straight into Drekar, through the black and white tiled hall, into the office. He was there with Reinhardt. It looked as if the two men had been close to an argument, and that was unheard of. Robert was unshaven, hair adrift, tie gone. The place stank of brandy, not that he looked the least bit drunk.

Then she saw. Broken bottles. Broken glasses. Shattered lampshades. He'd taken down the vast grey painting of the ocean and the Zeeland freighter. Slashed at it. Maybe put a boot through the thing.

He looked more than distraught. Pathetic. She'd never seen that before, didn't know how to feel.

The argument resumed. She soon worked out the source. Robert had sent his own recovery crew out to the bridge to look for Emilie. The police had brusquely turned them back.

'You can't interfere,' Reinhardt insisted. 'Not like this.'

'If they can't find her I will.'

A maid came in and started to sweep up the broken glass. Reinhardt dismissed her. He glanced at Maja.

'Robert wants to talk about the funeral,' he said in a quiet voice then left.

She thought about sitting next to him. Stayed where she was.

'We need to discuss this with the church,' he began.

'Carl's staying with Grandma. I've got Carsten outside with the car. We're going to look for her. Are you coming?'

His head came up. Baffled. Offended.

'She might be standing by the road somewhere. Waiting for us.'

Robert Zeuthen's eyes grew wide with disbelief. She thought there might be tears coming.

'I heard them in the Politigården,' she added. 'They wouldn't talk to me. But I heard. Lund doesn't think she's dead.'

'Lund!' he cried. 'You believe her. What is this?'

She pulled a torch out of her green parka.

'This is me looking for our daughter. We're starting at the bridge. I thought you'd want to come. Maybe he put her on a boat somewhere. Maybe . . . they don't know what happened, Robert!'

'I know,' he whispered. 'I saw . . .'

Such agony in his eyes.

'He shot Emilie. Then he threw her in the water.'

'Lund saw too, didn't she? And she doesn't think she's dead. Are you coming? Or do you want to stay here and wreck the bloody place instead?'

He got to his feet and she knew what he was thinking.

'I'm not crazy,' she snapped. 'I asked you once if you could feel it. If she was dead. You said no. Do you feel it now?'

'I saw! Is this what we're going to tell Carl? That his big sister's coming back?' He hesitated, looked round the ruined room. 'That everything's going to be the way it was? When we were happy?'

No words by way of answer. Nothing in her head at all.

'I need your help with Carl. With the funeral,' he pleaded. 'Don't ask me to believe in something I can't.'

'Fine,' she said and left him.

The school was near the pier. Swings in the playground. An empty car park. A low single-storey building, peeling paint and windows with simple drawings in them.

Borch called and demanded to know where she was.

'Louise's school. Did you know this town was swarming with politicians when Louise Hjelby went missing?'

No answer straight away. Then he said, 'We searched all the holiday homes. Didn't find a damned thing.'

'Oh.'

'No need to rub it in.'

'I didn't!'

'Yeah, well. There's a pig farm we ought to look at. Want to come?'

Poor Borch. He wanted her company.

Lund went to the front door of the school. Tried the handle. It was open. She went in.

'What are you doing, Sarah?'

'There's a teacher I want to see. She said we could meet here. She was the last one to see Louise alive.'

The place seemed to be in darkness. Lund found the light switch. Blinked at the sudden brightness. The walls were covered with paintings and posters.

'I expect you to join us with the pigs,' he said, a hopeful note in his voice.

'You always knew how to sweet-talk me.'

'Is that a yes?'

Phone to her ear she walked on. A classroom, upturned chairs on desks, funny faces scrawled on paper covering the walls.

She walked to the long windows. Broken glass, shards on the inside.

'I think he's been here,' she said softly. 'Someone's broken in.'

'Coming,' he said straight off. 'Stay where you are. And do it this time.'

Lund put the phone away, took out her gun. She turned right into a dark passageway.

At the end a door, just ajar. The light on. It was an office, white walls, charts, timetables, family photos. A filing cabinet stood by the window, the top drawer pulled open. She was rifling through the papers inside, pupil records, when there were footsteps behind, back in the corridor.

Gun up, cold in her short raincoat, aware of the school smell, disinfectant and a sweaty gym somewhere nearby, she walked out, looking.

Two things, simultaneously.

Borch came flying through the entrance, pistol extended, waving side to side.

From a door opposite a woman in a long waistcoat, blonde hair, too long for her age, stepped out, stared at them, started to shriek.

Twenty minutes later, back in a temporary ops room set up in the boarding house, the teacher sipped nervously at a cup of coffee. Along from the bedrooms the place was bustling with locals and officers from neighbouring districts.

'Rushing round with your guns,' the woman complained. 'In a school. I've never seen anything like it.'

Lund mentioned the name Louise Hjelby. The teacher put down the coffee, didn't speak for a while.

'Maybe the wind broke the glass,' she said.

'He was there, looking through your files.'

'Someone could have left the drawer open. Nothing happens here,' the woman replied. 'Nothing. Ever.'

'Tell me about Louise,' Lund asked.

A brief smile.

'She was a lovely little kid. Bright. Polite.' She closed her eyes. 'I think she'd been hurt by something over the years. Losing her mother I guess. Being in a home.'

'Did you believe she killed herself?' Lund asked.

'Not really.' She nodded at the local cops. 'But they said so. Who am I to argue?'

'We think she was murdered.'

The woman regarded her the way she did before: as if they were lunatics.

'Murdered?'

'That's what I said. On the day Louise disappeared you noticed her pushing her bike towards home after school? Did anyone else see her?'

Another caustic glance at the local officers.

'One of her classmates said she did. Up on the main road. God knows what she was doing there. But they . . .' A hand waved across the room. 'They told her she was mad so that was it. I don't know why you keep asking me all these questions. I went through all this with that officer of yours when he called an hour or two ago.'

'Who called?' Lund asked.

'He said his name was Mathias Borch. He was very nice and polite I must say. Didn't sound like the kind of person who'd wave a gun in my face.'

At the end of the table Borch looked up at her.

'Shit,' he muttered and asked the woman for her phone number.

Ten minutes later. They'd let her go. Lund had sat alone, brooding mostly. Borch came back and said they couldn't trace the call.

'He's back on Skype again I guess.'

She looked at the desks, the busy officers. The search had thrown up nothing.

'He wanted something at the school,' Lund said.

Borch came over, stood and leaned on the desk by her side.

'Sarah. He probably wasn't even there. It was just a broken window. If you'd helped me search—'

'You didn't find anything.'

'Maybe if you'd been with me . . .'

She put a hand to her head. Long day. Memories of the night before, the blue tarpaulin, the shots, the figure pushing something over the side, kept creeping back in. Along with them a tiny shape on a hospital monitor, a life to come hidden inside Eva Lauersen's swelling belly.

He took a call. Something about it made him walk off towards the bedrooms.

She followed at a distance. He went into his own. The door was open so she stood outside and listened.

You could judge so much from the tone of a voice. He was talking to a superior. Probably Dyhring the taciturn boss of PET who seemed to nag him, pull his strings constantly.

'In that case,' Borch said, 'we've got a big problem. She's worked that out already.'

He was pulling on a fresh shirt in the mirror. Saw her there.

'We'll talk later,' he said and finished the call, came round and met her at the door.

'Anything?'

'Who were you talking to?'

'Headquarters.'

He buttoned up his shirt. She walked in.

'Your room's down the hall. It's nicer than mine. I think you've got more—'

'Cut the crap,' Lund snapped. 'What's going on here?'

His eyes closed. The puppy look.

'Huh?'

'How did he know to use your name?'

'Maybe he's psychic. Why ask me?'

She got closer.

'This place was dripping in politicians two years ago. PET looked after them. You must have had officers here when it happened. Were they involved in covering up the old case? Did you give them a hand?'

He thought about it, nodded as if he was taking the questions seriously, then said, 'No.'

'So why were you here two days ago?'

He seemed offended.

'I was trying to help. I wanted . . . I wanted to give you something.'

'Oh for God's sake. You expect me to believe—?'

'I had nothing to do with the old case, Sarah. Maybe he heard my name on the radio. Or perhaps he's . . .' A sarcastic tone entered his voice. 'He's programmed us to have this conversation. Either that or you're paranoid as hell as usual . . .'

Lund swore, turned to go. He was on her, strong arms dragging her back.

'Why the hell don't you believe me? Why's it so hard for you to trust someone?'

He was getting mad with her and she'd scarcely ever seen that, even before when she'd surely asked for it.

'You're talking crap.'

'No I'm not! You shut out everything the moment someone gets close to you. Us back then. Your son. Me now.'

Hands up, she stepped back.

'You now? Fat chance.'

'It's true! I loved you. I wanted you. And you threw me out of your life because that scared you . . .'

'No . . .'

'Yes!'

Borch stood there in his fresh shirt, unshaven.

'Yes,' he repeated more quietly. 'I could take being dumped because I bored you. Or you found someone else. But you . . .' He came and jabbed a finger in her face. 'You walked away because we were so damned right together. And that scared you. That . . .'

Lund turned on her heels and left him again.

Out by the bridge it was raining. Maja Zeuthen looked up and down the long empty road, stood by the rail, tried to imagine the scene in her head.

Gave up after a while. Talked to the salvage team. Still looking, they said.

Made Carsten Lassen drive down every track nearby. Didn't listen to him much. Couldn't lose the memory of Robert, distraught, lost, vulnerable.

There'd been that side to him when they first met. He was the solitary, diligent student, shunned by everyone. She was the beautiful party girl all the men wanted to court.

It wasn't opposites attracting. Nothing like that. As they got to know one another that distant summer they met somewhere in the middle, his shyness melting, her brief attraction to the wild life dissipating in awe at his quiet, loyal honesty.

Everything happened by degrees, accidentally. And yet was inevitable somehow.

Memories.

After an hour she was soaked, walking down another dim and narrow road. Torch out. Calling her daughter's name.

Back in the ops room. Still nothing. One of the team said Juncker was looking for her. Not now, Lund snapped. Went outside. Sat in her car. Wished she still smoked. Ran her fingers through her damp hair. Wondered whether she ought to drive all the way back to the city. Wake up the next morning and put on an office uniform: white blouse, grey skirt, sensible shoes. March to a desk in OPA. Look at the pile of paper clips. Start to count.

The door opened. She prayed to God it wasn't him.

Asbjørn Juncker fell into the passenger seat.

'I think I've got it,' he said cheerily.

'Got what?'

He looked at her.

'You've got a mood on. I've been asking around the local men. I think I've got an explanation. A journalist rang the nick this morning asking questions about the Hjelby case. The desk told him to call Borch in Copenhagen because he'd just been here.'

He pulled out his notebook.

'I phoned the paper. They didn't know anything about it. No one's been calling here. He's on the ball, isn't he? Got to say that for him.'

On the ball.

Computers. Maps. Weapons. Now a glib phone call to steal a

working officer's identity. Couldn't disagree. And she'd yelled at Borch for that. Brought something out of him she hadn't wanted to hear.

'Well!' Juncker waited for a response. Got none. 'That's me done.'

Climbed out of the car, back into the rain.

On a good day there was only one road ahead. Simple, clear, incontrovertible. That made life so much easier. Sparse, bare, lean. Lonely.

Lund put a hand to her mouth and checked her breath. Then sucked on a mint. Brushed down her coat for no good reason except prevarication.

Something else she loathed.

Got out. Walked through the busy ops room into the accommodation wing at the back.

Down the corridor. Room sixteen. Knocked on the door.

Borch was in shirt and jeans still. The bed was made. Double too.

'Asbjørn just told me he probably called here this morning and the locals gave him your name.'

He still wore the hurt and boyish look that always amused her. 'Did he?'

'So it looks like I must have . . . sort of misunderstood really.'

He listened, nodded.

'That's an apology?'

Lund marched in, kicked the door shut behind her, threw off her coat.

Put her arms round his neck.

'No. This is,' she said and kissed him.

An embrace that was long years coming.

Her hands ripped at his shirt.

His fingers lifted her coarse wool jumper.

Back in the dead flat land outside the city Maja Zeuthen stumbled on through the dark. Torch beam flashing. Voice rising. Seeing nothing.

Finally she stopped. Didn't know where she was. Carsten behind her. Sounding weary and cross.

The wrong voice.

She had to silence that weasel whisper. Too much pain to get here. The road back could only be worse.

'Maja. For God's sake . . . *Maja!*'

A handsome man and he knew it. So wanted to forget she had a life before.

He caught up. Stood in front of her. The rain came down. The icy wind began to howl. She could smell the river, the rank water, the marshy foetid land.

'This is crazy.' He took hold of her shoulders. Cold, insistent eyes in hers. 'We need to go home now. She's not here. You know that . . .'

He hugged her. Hard. As if he could squeeze the grief out of her with nothing but the strength of his arms.

Gentle. That was the word she'd always associated with Robert. Too placid to rule over Zeeland. Too kind and caring for that world.

'Maja . . .'

Another man's voice in her ear.

'Not now, Carsten,' she said then shrank from him, walked back to the car.

Six

The gentle wash of distant waves. Screams of bickering gulls. An unfamiliar bed. The insistent ringing of a phone.

Lund woke up naked beneath the cheap polyester sheets of the Gudbjerghavn boarding house. Alone. Not quite with it for a moment.

Clothes strewn across a too-bright orange carpet. The clock said eight thirty-one. It was her phone ringing in the bag by the bed.

She grabbed for it, grateful Borch was gone.

Brix shouted, 'Where are you?'

'I'm just . . .'

'There's been a break-in at the school. Borch's running the show. He's not mine. You are. Get there.'

The curtains were only half closed. She wondered who might have seen. Climbed out of bed, shut them completely. Scooped her clothes off the floor, went back to her own room. The quickest shower possible. Then through the temporary desks, past watchful interested eyes, and out to the car.

Not long after Lund set off for the school Hartmann parked himself on a seat in the little cafe Morten Weber liked to use every morning before coming to work. It was near his modest home not far from the central station. Weber had bought the place when he got his first job as a political researcher after university. They were in the same year together. Handsome, articulate, charming, Hartmann was the public face of the partnership, Weber the backroom brains.

Together they'd plotted and schemed, moving through the ranks of local politics, first into Copenhagen City Hall, then on to the ultimate prize: the premiership.

Mostly they saw eye-to-eye. But the tensions were always there and sometimes they erupted.

'You're late,' Hartmann said as he sat down and ordered a coffee. The ministerial car was outside, the bodyguards lounging in a brief patch of winter sun. Weber didn't look up. 'Can I buy you breakfast?'

'I can pay for my own breakfast. Piss off.'

'Makes a change from a cheery good morning. Coming into the office by any chance?'

'Hangings aren't much fun, thanks.'

Hartmann nodded.

'I didn't resign, you know.'

Weber's beady eyes turned on him.

'You're still thinking about it. We went through this six years ago. The last time Lund was hanging around. You'd have given up then if it wasn't for me.'

That was true. But he didn't need reminding.

'I thought we had Ussing,' Hartmann said. 'Could be wrong. Maybe those pictures Karen found were too good to be true. Turns out Schultz and him were old friends. Used to play squash together sometimes.'

'Never trust a man who plays squash.' Weber, a tubby man, was not given to exercise. 'It's unnatural.'

'They're still looking for Emilie Zeuthen. Brix is acting coy. I don't think he's a clue whether she's dead or . . . if Lund's on to something.'

Weber pushed away his coffee cup, looked at his watch, yawned.

'I need you today, Morten.'

'You always do.'

'So are you coming?'

'Going deaf?'

'By the end of the day either I'll be king of the castle or have Birgit Eggert standing over my cold, still corpse. Do you really want to miss this?'

Weber finished his coffee, lifted his cup, caught the eye of the pretty waitress behind the counter. Without a word she came over and filled it, beamed at Hartmann, got the smile back in return.

'Don't even think about it, Troels,' Weber hissed when she'd left. 'That kid's nineteen. Not a day more.'

'Just being friendly. People expect it. You always think the worst of me.'

'What do you think your chances are?'

'Good question,' Hartmann noted. 'If I can throw a little dirt Ussing's way and it sticks . . . good. Should God be kind and have Emilie Zeuthen turn up alive . . . who knows?'

Weber closed his eyes.

'You only worry about the things you can control. How many times do I have to say this?'

'I can't control anything if you're not there. Is this the usual routine? We argue. You quit. A few hours later you turn up in the office as if nothing's happened. We all applaud. Good old Morten. He comes back in the end.'

They'd played out that scene many times.

'Don't be presumptuous.'

'I'm not. I need you. Today more than ever. I'll give you anything you want.'

The little man thought about that.

'Well?' Hartmann asked.

'You don't quit. You only go if you're fired.'

'Agreed.'

'You listen to me more than Karen.'

He laughed.

'I do that anyway. Didn't you notice?'

Weber thought for a moment. Then said, 'Very well. If I can I'll get you back into office. Whatever it takes.'

Hartmann patted his hand.

'And after that you'll lean on the university. Tell them to throw a professorship my way. I want out of this. I've had enough.'

That was a shock.

'Let's talk about this later.'

'No!' Weber's voice had moved up a tone, got louder. People were looking. 'That's the deal. Take it or leave it.'

'I don't like ultimatums. You always told me to reject them.'

'I'm not God!' Weber yelled. 'I don't know everything. Jesus . . .'

'Later,' Hartmann insisted.

'You just don't see it, do you?' Morten Weber tapped his head. 'Somewhere in there you still think you're John F. Kennedy running the Copenhagen White House. And I'm your clever kid brother Robert, whispering wise words in the background.'

'I had a kid brother,' Hartmann said with a sad air of resignation. 'I loved him but he wasn't so clever.'

Weber closed his eyes and murmured, 'I didn't mean it that way.'

'Not a bad dream though, is it?'

'It's still just a dream. Want the truth? You're Don Quixote and I'm your pathetic little sidekick Sancho Panza. All we do is tilt at windmills. Even now. When we were young we thought we could make things better. Now we're old we're just struggling to stop them getting worse.'

There was despair in his face at that moment. Something Hartmann had never witnessed before.

'I didn't realize you'd come to feel that way. Is it me?'

'No! Any more than it's me. Or Karen. Or Ussing. Rosa Lebech. Or . . . anyone. Try to listen for once. It's the world. We've fucked it. Right, left and centre.'

The Prime Minister of Denmark had no words at that moment.

'There's the deal,' Weber said again.

'Whatever you want,' Hartmann agreed. He nodded at the car and the bodyguards outside. 'If you've finished I can give you a lift.'

The school looked different in daylight. Children ran around under the bright winter sun, filling the playground with happy voices. Lund walked straight in, found Juncker in the office she'd seen the night before.

Filing cabinets open. Papers scattered everywhere.

'Where the hell have you been?' he asked.

'What happened?'

'You never answer questions, do you?'

'What happened, Asbjørn?'

'The cleaners reported a break-in. Borch thinks that smashed window you saw was him trying it out. Maybe he hung around until you left.'

Borch was on the floor, cross-legged, sifting through papers. Didn't so much as look at her.

'I tried your room,' Juncker said. 'You weren't there. I was worried.'

'Big girl now,' Lund told him. 'You need a shave.'

He had the faintest of beards. It didn't look right.

'Did Borch find anything?' she asked.

Juncker pointed at the man on the floor.

'You mean . . . *that* Borch?'

He got to his feet, glanced at her, pointed to the school photos on the walls. Year after year. The procession of kids moving through the classes.

'As far as I can work out he was looking for pupil records.'

'So he was here last night?' she said.

He grimaced.

'Not when we were.'

'He was in the vicinity then?'

'The vicinity,' Borch agreed testily. 'Yes.'

Juncker looked at her, puzzled by his abruptness, and shrugged. A forensic officer was dusting for prints on the wall.

'He took a photo of Louise Hjelby's class,' Juncker cut in. 'I've asked for a copy from one of the other parents.'

She stared at him.

'Other parents?'

Juncker nodded.

'He's either her dad or her uncle or something, isn't he? Why else would he do all this? Mother left the bloke's name off the birth certificate. We don't even know if he came near the kid. Knew she was alive. Lund . . .' He touched his mouth. 'You've got toothpaste. There. Bit of a hurry I guess . . .'

She licked a finger and got rid of it. Juncker found the photo. Form 7B. Louise was the saddest-looking kid in class. Dressed in black. But she was holding the hand of the girl next to her.

Lund took the picture over to the teacher, asked who she was.

'Katja. The two of them always got on well. Sat next to each other.'

'Is she here?'

The outraged look they'd seen the night before.

'She said one of your men spoke to her yesterday. She's upset enough.'

'Yesterday?' Lund demanded.

Borch shook his head. So did Juncker.

'Where is she?'

The woman walked to the window. Pointed to a tall girl in jeans, a green wool hat, a cheap jacket.

'Come,' Lund ordered.

Outside with Juncker and Borch. Katja was reluctant to talk with the other pupils around. So they walked to some rough ground beyond the school. At four the previous day she'd been stopped on her bike outside town by a man who said he was a police officer.

Juncker got a precise location, went to check it out. Borch showed the girl a photo of Emilie Zeuthen.

'That's the girl in the papers.'

'Have you seen her?'

'No.'

'This man,' Lund said. 'What did he look like?'

She pointed at Borch.

'Like him. Ordinary. Dark hair. He wanted to know if I was the one who saw Louise after school the day she went missing.'

'And you did?'

'Yeah.' She pointed along the road. 'By the town sign on the way in from Esbjerg. I was going to feed my horse.'

Lund pulled out a map, checked the exact place.

'Why was she there? Didn't she usually go back along the waterfront?'

'She said there was something wrong with her bike. The gears I think. She was probably going to get it fixed. I think that's why she got a lift.'

'A lift?'

'A man in a black car. I thought Louise must have known him. He picked up her bike and put it in the boot for her.'

'What did he look like?' Borch asked.

'It was a long way. I didn't really see. They drove off before I got there . . .'

'What kind of car?'

'Black. Big. Fancy . . . I don't know.'

Lund was pushing for more. The girl started to cry. So she asked the same questions, again and again.

'Sarah,' Borch said finally. 'Please?'

She went quiet. He looked at the girl.

'Can you remember which way the car went?'

Too late. Too many tears.

'I don't know! I told Mr Overgaard. Louise didn't kill herself. We were friends. He just said I should shut up if I knew what was good for me.'

Borch asked, 'This man you met yesterday? You told him all this?'

Katja nodded.

'I need to make a call,' he said and walked away.

Robert Zeuthen was in the Politigården nagging Brix, demanding answers.

'I've got marine crews,' he said. 'They could help find her.'

'We've got the Navy. The Air Force. Our own people. We've enough resources.'

'And how long are we supposed to wait? Do you know what this is doing to Maja? She thinks Emilie's alive for God's sake.'

The police chief kept quiet.

'This is your doing. She heard you talking . . .'

'That's unfortunate,' Brix replied. 'I regret it happened. We have to examine every possibility . . .'

'And this farce in Jutland?' Zeuthen's voice was high and loud. On the edge. 'What's happening there?'

'We've found nothing to indicate your daughter's still alive.'

'Where is she?'

Brix shook his head.

'Emilie was thrown into a fast-flowing river. The rope that was attached to her broke. She could be anywhere. Sadly it's not unknown for these searches to last—'

'I've got to go and talk about a funeral. With a wife who doesn't believe she's dead.'

'I'm sorry . . .' Brix began.

'Sorry isn't good enough. If you haven't found my daughter by the end of today I'll take care of this myself.'

Zeuthen walked out into the corridor. Reinhardt had left a message. Maja was reluctant to join him at the church.

He called her. Got voicemail.

'I'm going whether you're there or not, Maja,' he said.

Across the city in Carsten Lassen's little flat, Carl by her side, she watched the message icon come on. Waited. Listened. Deleted the call.

The little boy was playing with his toys. He knew something. She was sure of that. It would have been strange if he didn't.

Maja Zeuthen put down her phone, closed her eyes. Felt two small arms come round her head, hold her.

'Mum?' he asked. 'Why are you crying?'

No answer.

'I'll take care of you,' Carl promised and kissed her hair.

On Weber's advice Hartmann's first line of attack was the Centre Party. Rosa Lebech wouldn't answer his calls so he ambushed her in one of the galleries of the Parliament building. She didn't smile. Didn't object when he asked her to join him in one of the quiet alcoves. Karen Nebel listened in. Weber was elsewhere, testing the water.

'We shouldn't be talking, Troels,' she said, glancing at Nebel. 'Not until matters are resolved.'

'I understand why you cosied up to Ussing. It's not a problem.'

'Then what do you want?'

'Your support. As we agreed.'

'Troels! Your Justice Minister could have contributed to the death of Emilie Zeuthen! You knew that and you never told me. You had Jens arrested—'

'Dyhring pulled him in. Not me.' He kept his eyes on her. 'I've asked them to go easy on him. There won't be charges. There could have been . . .'

'And I'm supposed to be grateful?'

Hartmann thought about his answer.

'I wouldn't expect you to be ungrateful. PET are looking at the Zeuthen case. And any link Ussing may have there.'

She scowled.

'Anders told me all about the Schultz man.'

'Told you what?'

'They were old friends. He's amazed you're trying to pull a stunt like this. It's insane—'

'Oh for God's sake, Rosa,' Nebel snapped. 'What's the point? We've begged and cajoled you a million times. Offered you cabinet posts. Cut our policies and replaced them with yours. And still you swallow Ussing's line whatever we do . . .'

'Maybe that's because he's more credible.' A sideways glance at Hartmann. 'And doesn't come with such . . . history.'

'Doesn't help with your ex-husband leaking papers everywhere! He could go to jail for that . . .'

'Karen!' Hartmann cut in. 'No one's going to jail.' He took Lebech's hand, made sure Nebel saw. 'Rosa and I just need some private time to talk about this. Before any leaders' meeting. We can—'

'I'm with Ussing,' Lebech said and snatched her fingers away. 'I'm sorry. In the circumstances you leave me with no choice.'

She walked off.

'Thanks for butting in about the husband,' Hartmann grumbled. 'That really helped.'

'The woman doesn't trust you any more. It's pointless . . .'

'She's a woman. It's never pointless.'

Weber was walking along the corridor. He looked shocked, put a finger to his lips.

'Temper, temper, people.'

'You're back then?' Nebel said.

Weber smiled.

'Pleased to see me?'

'Always.' She looked at Hartmann. 'Don't get excited. I haven't had much time to check this out. But I've someone you need to meet. One of Anders Ussing's former employees. He's got a tale to tell.'

Weber folded his arms.

'I hope it's a good one,' he said.

They stood by the main road outside the school, both on their phones. Borch to PET. Lund to Brix. Not looking at each other.

He was last off the call. Looked round.

'We've gone all the way along the coast and the main road. No sign of him.'

'I've double checked,' she said. 'There's no mention of a black car anywhere in Louise Hjelby's file. Overgaard interviewed the girl. He must have kept it out.'

'Maybe . . .'

'No! Not maybe. What other explanation is there? A big, black expensive car the girl said. Don't see many like that round here. A businessman's car.' She watched. 'Maybe a politician. There were plenty of them about.'

He took out a map, spread it on the roof of the car, holding down the corners against the brisk sea breeze.

'I don't think the car's important right now. Where's Asbjørn?'

Lund screwed up her eyes and looked at him.

'Not important? She was putting her bike in the back . . .'

'Yes! Two years ago. Right now we're looking for Emilie Zeuthen. And a red van.'

There was an odd mix of embarrassment and anger between them. Shame perhaps too.

'He wants to find out what happened,' Lund said.

'First things first. The Zeuthen girl . . .'

'Are you pissed off with me because of last night? Is that why you're being so objectionable?'

The accusation hurt.

'I wasn't being objectionable. Was I?'

'Very.'

'You keep going back to the old case, Sarah. We've got a new one here. A live one . . .'

'Can't we even discuss the black car? I mean . . . after . . .'

He screwed up the map.

'For the last time . . . it's not about last night.'

'Louise Hjelby was found dead after she got into a black, smart saloon. The driver put her bike in the back.'

A marked white car had pulled up behind. Juncker was climbing out.

'In case you can't see this,' she went on, 'right now our man's trying to find out where the black car went and who was driving it. Doing the job we're supposed to.'

'Fine! Look for the black car.'

Juncker walked up.

'I'm not interrupting any—'

'No, you're not,' she barked.

'Good,' he said with a cheery grin. 'Because while you two have been killing time yelling at each other I've found a bloke in a garage. Who saw something.' He tapped his chest. 'I did that.'

'What garage?' Borch asked straight off.

'Out of town. On the way to Esbjerg.' Juncker pointed to the white car. 'Just follow me.'

The place was as much a junkyard as a garage. Abandoned wrecks in front of a long white building. Inside a solitary man in greasy overalls worked on an ancient Lancia.

He barely looked up when Juncker said, 'I heard you kept a record of cars driving down the road.'

The mechanic shook his head.

'Do I look like I've got time for that?'

'I heard . . .' Juncker started.

'You heard wrong. My boy does. We've got all sorts of cars here.' He gestured to the rusting wrecks. 'French. Italian. Japanese. American. He likes lists.'

The man gestured towards a smashed-up Ford.

'For some reason he keeps his books in the glove compartment in that thing. Take a look if you want.'

Lund made sure she was there first. The windscreen was broken but the interior looked reasonably clean. Four notebooks inside. She started to flick through. Childish writing. Dates. Numbers.

'He's more crazy about number plates than he is about cars. If he sees a new one he writes it down.' The man put a mucky spanner on the bonnet. 'I think he's dreaming of getting out of this dump one day. Aren't we all?'

He laughed, waved.

'Here he is. Hi, Jakob!'

A fair-haired boy of around ten was riding his bike towards the house next to the garage.

'I'll talk to him,' Borch said. 'You take a look at the books.'

Juncker asked the mechanic how long the boy had been keeping numbers.

'Maybe three, four years,' the man said.

Borch was having a long talk with him. Friendly. Lund watched. Walked over. Butted in and asked about a red van.

Jakob held out his wrist. There was a number scrawled on it.

'Could it be this one?'

'It was red?' Lund asked.

'Yeah. It was out by the holiday homes.'

'When?'

'This morning. When I went to school.'

Juncker ran for the car.

'I want those books,' Lund told the father. 'I'll send someone later.'

By the water near the Little Mermaid Hartmann and Weber met the man Karen Nebel had tracked down. His name was Kristoffer Seifert, about forty, slick suit, slick hair, ready smile. Used to be one of Ussing's admin workers. He said he was there two years before when he met with Peter Schultz.

'I came in to get some papers signed. I saw them.'

Weber asked why he didn't work for Ussing any more. The fixed smile never cracked.

'There was a problem with the campaign budget. Nominally it fell under me.'

'What kind of problem?'

'Things didn't add up. It wasn't my fault. You want to hear my story or what?'

Hartmann told him to go on.

'Ussing asked to meet Schultz. They were talking. He'd moved a couple of appointments to fit him in.'

Weber was beginning to growl.

'They were friends, weren't they?' he wondered.

Seifert hesitated then said, 'I always wanted to work in government, not opposition. I've got a degree in political science. I'd like to put it to good use.'

'The story . . .' Weber sighed.

'Right, right. Well I would never eavesdrop of course. But Ussing asked me to stand outside the door. Which was odd frankly. Uncalled for. I couldn't help but hear.' He nodded. 'Really. It was impossible not to.'

'Hear . . . what?'

'Ussing was interested in a case Schultz was handling. About a dead girl in West Jutland. I don't think the prosecutor was keen to talk about it. Why would he? It was nothing to do with us.'

Hartmann stopped. A cyclist went past.

'Ussing insisted,' Seifert added. 'He wouldn't take no for an answer.'

Weber looked interested finally.

'Did he say why?'

'I got the impression there was something he didn't want to come out.' He retrieved an envelope from his pocket. 'I worked in Brussels for a couple of years. Lots of experience. It's all here.'

'What didn't Ussing want to come out?'

'Something to do with the girl. I didn't hear exactly. He was getting quite worked up.' A shrug. 'Then they came and closed the door.'

Hartmann and Weber exchanged glances.

'I'm freelancing at the moment. Any time you want me to start . . . I'm flexible.'

'You need to tell all this to PET,' Hartmann said.

He looked worried.

'PET? Why?' A nervous laugh. 'This is just politics . . .'

Weber's phone went.

'I really don't want to get involved with the police.'

'But you are,' Hartmann said then walked off towards Weber striding by the water, talking anxiously all the while.

He waited.

'What do you make of that?' he asked when Weber was off the call.

'It stinks. We need to go back to Christiansborg. Birgit's parking her tank on the lawn. It's a big one.'

Fifteen minutes later Hartmann met her in the Parliament building. She was breathless, looked busy.

'I think we may have some fresh information,' he began.

'No time for that now, Troels. A party committee meeting's been called. It starts in an hour.'

'I'm the Prime Minister, Birgit. I think I'd know if that had happened.'

'Well it has. There's only one item on the agenda.' She passed him a single sheet of paper. 'We want to do this decently. Without rancour. If you're willing to be persuaded to step down of your own accord we'll do what we can to bring you back in a government position at some stage.' A grim smile. 'Depending on the results of course.'

'And if not?'

'We'll collectively and publicly withdraw our support for your leadership of the party.'

Hartmann screwed up the paper, threw it down the stairs.

'You've really left us with no other option. I'm sorry.'

She checked her watch.

'One hour.'

There was only one place for a Zeuthen funeral: Frederik's Kirke, the Marble Church, the grand domed basilica that dominated the area west of the Amalienborg Palace. It was empty save for the three of them: Zeuthen, his wife, the woman minister.

'We want a private occasion,' he said. 'Only family and friends.'

'Have you thought about hymns?'

Maja Zeuthen's head went down. Despair and fury in her face.

Zeuthen in his dark raincoat, tie crooked, hair uncombed, said, 'There was something we sang at her christening. I think it was called . . .'

He shook his head.

'I can't remember.'

'"Teach Me, The Night Star",' Maja whispered.

The place was so dark. Even the brass and bronze of the candelabra seemed to be in mourning.

The minister made a note, said it was a beautiful choice.

'There's a point in the ceremony where I can say a few things about Emilie.' She looked at them in turn. 'If there's something in particular you'd like me to talk about. I don't know if her little brother will be joining us. But if he is I'd like to mention him.'

Silence between them. Their eyes didn't meet.

'We haven't decided whether Carl's coming yet,' Zeuthen told her.

The woman nodded.

227

'Sometimes it can be helpful for them. A way of saying goodbye. To walk forward. Place a flower on the casket. There's a certain beauty—'

'Beauty?' Maja Zeuthen cried. 'My daughter's dead. Murdered. How can that be beautiful?'

The minister stiffened.

'No one can take away your pain, Maja. But we mourn because we've loved. It's the love you must remember. The love that remains. For you. For Carl. Maybe it would be good for him to see you supporting each other . . .'

Head down, fighting back the tears, Maja Zeuthen got up, walked to the massive doors, shook them.

Tight shut.

'Maja?'

His footsteps coming nearer.

'Why's this bloody place locked?' she shrieked. 'Who did that? I want out of here. These stupid platitudes . . .'

He was there, eyes pleading, hands too.

'We need to arrange this. We need to make these decisions.'

'Let me out of here, Robert. You don't own me. The church doesn't either.' She turned, yelled for the minister. 'You hear that?'

He leaned against the pillar.

'We need to tell Carl. We should do that together . . .'

As dark as night in the alcove by the door. She stopped shouting, saw him starkly outlined in a single shaft of light from the bulb above.

The same face she'd fallen in love with. Never thinking that one day she'd witness such pain there.

'Let me out . . .' she whispered turning round and round.

Brix was tidying his things. Getting rid of a few papers he'd rather not share. Wondering when Ruth Hedeby would be back with Tage Steiner, preparing for another assault. The last one.

He'd called Lund in Gudbjerghavn. Heard nothing that made him think he could save himself. Stood by the window in his office wondering how much he'd miss this place.

Then Madsen came rushing in.

'If it's Hedeby tell her I'm busy.'

The detective looked puzzled at that.

'It's not Hedeby. The salvage crew have got the kid. They're bringing her in now.' He glanced at his watch. 'In ten minutes she'll be in forensic. I was wondering if . . .'

Before he could finish Brix was on his way.

One last drive round the town. Lund at the wheel. Borch sat tired and silent next to her.

'He's got to be here,' she insisted. 'Anything from Asbjørn?'

The rain was back. A steady, icy wind too.

'Nothing,' he said. 'Is this really worth it?'

The map was spread out on his lap.

'We've looked everywhere. It's a waste—'

'He's clever! Don't we know that? He's . . .' Lund had been thinking about this for a while. 'I worked with someone once. He'd been in the Army. Special forces. He said there were people there who could go anywhere. Make themselves invisible. Louise's mother told her he was a hero. Travelled a lot. Maybe . . .'

Maybe he's like Ulrik Strange, she thought. A decent man destroyed by history, by events.

Borch took a deep breath.

'About last night . . .'

'I know,' she cut in anxiously. 'It shouldn't have happened.'

A car came down the opposite lane. The headlights caught his face. Hurt. Frightened even. Eyes on her, nowhere else.

'No. It shouldn't,' Borch agreed.

Nothing more. She pulled into the side of the road, took the map from him.

'The problem is . . .'

'It's all right. You don't need to say anything.'

That got to him.

'Actually I do. The problem is . . . I don't regret it.'

Lund ran her finger down the map. Looked ahead. Tried not to listen.

'Not one bit,' he added. 'So . . .'

She kept silent for a long while then pointed ahead.

'That lane.' A stab of a finger on the map. 'Where does it go?'

The headlights had caught a line of construction tape, snapped by something as it crossed the track.

Borch sighed.

'There's a derelict boatbuilder's yard down there. The local men checked it out.'

'A boatyard?'

'OK. So he likes boats . . .'

'They would have put the tape back, wouldn't they?'

'Sarah . . .'

She put the car in gear, drove over the torn barrier.

Half a kilometre along the track came to an end. Lund got out, Borch behind her.

A hazy line of mist was drifting in from the nearby sea, carrying with it the low moan of a distant foghorn. At the entrance to what must once have been a busy industrial area was a security fence. Torches out. Borch walked in front. The gate was ajar, the padlock on it smashed.

They went through.

The place seemed to get bigger along the way. Workshops and storage units. Abandoned boats seemingly wrecked on the concrete. A couple of half-built hulls. Masts and rusting engines. One giant propeller.

They reached the water. A single light blinked at the end of a small jetty like a waking eye staring at the coming fog.

Everywhere they passed looked wrecked. Broken windows. Leaky timber walls. Decrepit but scarcely private.

The last building was different. Metal, no glass, no opening at all except for a single door.

A paint shop from the smell. Or somewhere they once worked on engines. Maybe both. She started to say something but Borch shushed her into silence.

Pointed at the door: ajar.

Inside. Paint. Oil. Grease. Chemicals. Shapes under plastic shrouds. Tools rusting in racks. Decay alongside labour. If he had a hallmark this was it.

They pushed past the engine area. Found themselves in an extension. Thick ropes hung like nooses from the ceiling. From below came the rhythmic sound of waves lapping against stanchions. They were over the sea, without windows, any frame of reference.

She found a light switch, flipped it. Moved on. After the ropes came chains and low sliding platforms for working under hulls, under engines.

Gun over the torch she walked on, forgot about Borch, was talking to herself.

He was here.

She knew that. Felt it. Could smell him.

Then, in a corner, the beam fell on a white shape and Lund understood she was finally closing on an answer.

They had bikes like this in Copenhagen. Not fashionable. Just cheap and serviceable. A little ungainly it leaned upright against a long grey plastic sheet.

Borch was behind her.

'That's hers,' she said. 'Louise's. I saw it in the photograph at the foster home.'

She bent down, took a pair of latex gloves from her pocket. The chain was off. A schoolkid's rucksack sat next to the back wheel.

'Sarah?'

Not now, she thought. I'm thinking. Or trying to.

'Sarah!'

Borch had shifted another set of plastic sheeting further along the wall. Something on his face, sad and young and shocked, told her to look.

Two beams in front of them. The grey curtain thrust aside.

On the floor a grimy fawn mattress. Bloodstains on the edge, on the floor by the side. A set of chains, like manacles.

'You had men check this place?' she asked.

'They said the gates were locked. He must have turned up this evening. Jesus . . .' Borch looked ready to scream. 'That bastard Overgaard didn't even bother to look here, did he?'

While he poked around the interior she stayed there, looking at the mattress, the bloodstains. The manacles. Trying to picture something.

Phone.

'Lund?' Juncker said.

He sounded down.

'Asbjørn—'

'Listen to me,' he cut in. 'I just had a call from that garage we went to. The one with the kid who kept the numbers.'

'Yeah. Fine. We're at the boatyard the locals were supposed to check earlier. I need people—'

'Listen to me! When I talked to him again he said Borch was out there before us first thing this morning. He spoke to that kid. Took one of his books before we ever got there.'

A mattress. An act of violence. A girl's life ended here and in some way she couldn't begin to comprehend the simple, brute cruelty of that act had been lost.

'What book?'

'From two years ago. He says they know Borch. He was out here when Louise Hjelby first went missing. He was around asking questions back then.'

It was dark. She didn't know where Borch had got to.

'You hear what I'm saying?' Juncker's voice was shrill and worried. 'Someone's screwing us around here and you don't need to be a genius to work out who.'

Footsteps. His torch. Lund put the phone away.

'I found the red van parked out the back,' Borch said. 'Let's get going. We can bring a team in here later.'

She didn't move.

'Sarah!'

Back to the new Borch. Bossy and efficient.

'Why's the book important?' she asked.

He was in the corner, somewhere she couldn't see.

'What book?'

She followed the line of his voice, turned the torch on him.

'The book you got from that boy this morning. Before we went out there.'

Nothing.

'It was you and PET who took that black car out of the equation, wasn't it? You just erased . . .'

Cocked head. The 'you're going crazy again' look.

'What are you talking about now?'

'Did Schultz order that? Or did you tell Schultz what to do?'

'Neither.'

'You didn't come out here to find something for me!' she yelled. 'You were covering your tracks. Trying to make sure we never found . . .' A glance back at the mattress and the bloody chains. 'Any of this.'

He looked outraged.

'I know you saw the boy this morning.'

'I can't talk about that right now.'

'Who's in the book? Who are you hiding?'

He folded his arms. Came closer.

'Here's the picture, Sarah. The boy was noting random registration numbers when the girl went missing. One in particular stood out. We checked it. That was our job. It came out clean. False lead. End of—'

'Why were you involved?'

His hands went up.

'Because . . .'

There was a sound from somewhere. Footsteps. Machinery. An old industrial engine kicking into life.

Then a loud crash. She flashed the torch. The heavy metal door at the end of the room slammed shut.

Borch ran, put his shoulder to the frame. Got nowhere.

Down from the ceiling it came, snaking and noxious, a blue-grey winding cloud.

Diesel smoke. Lots.

No windows. No ventilation she could see.

Just the picture in her mind, the one that always came unbidden: outside an ancient generator, a pipe from the exhaust to the single ventilation chimney in the roof.

Borch banging on the door, yelling, getting furious.

Lund kept her torch on the fumes curling towards them.

Breathe in. Breathe out. Breathe in.

No choice.

The first unwanted lungful. She started to choke.

Karen Nebel briefed Hartmann on the way into the party committee. The police thought they were getting somewhere in Jutland. They still didn't know whether Emilie was dead or not.

On the way a well-groomed figure raced after him on the staircase. Mogens Rank.

'Troels! Troels! Please stop. Don't be mad at me.'

Hartmann turned.

'I'm sorry it's come to this,' Rank told him. 'I want you to know. I have a vote. It's yours. It always will be. This has nothing to do with you.'

'We've tried to tell Birgit that,' Nebel pointed out. 'She doesn't seem keen to listen.'

Rank nodded.

'She has ambitions. It's just . . .' A shrug. 'Politics. I suggest when we start the meeting . . .'

'There isn't going to be one,' Hartmann said brusquely and walked on.

Into the committee room. Long table, chandeliers above. Papers being spread. Water jugs in place. Birgit Eggert stood on her own at the end. New black suit, hair perfect, ready for the cameras.

Hartmann walked straight up. Nebel and Rank stayed back, listened.

'This is very simple, Birgit. We're looking into new information about the Zeuthen case. I have every confidence it will clear the government of all suspicion.'

'Troels . . .'

'As a party member, as one of my ministers, you're answerable to me and me alone. This disloyalty does not go unnoticed.' He pointed at the table. 'Go and tell your acolytes you're sorry you wasted their time.'

A hint of a smile.

'And what information might that be?'

'We've a witness who saw Ussing putting pressure on the prosecutor. Someone who was on Ussing's staff. PET are investigating. For that reason I can't say more—'

'Please tell me you're not talking about that clown Kristoffer Seifert.'

Mogens Rank threw up his hands in despair.

'Oh for pity's sake, Birgit. Do you take us for complete idiots? Of course it's not Seifert.' He caught Hartmann's stare. 'I mean he nearly wound up in court for stealing from Ussing's campaign funds.'

'Mogens . . .' Nebel whispered.

'Not that this is relevant,' Rank added quickly. 'In the circumstances. All the evidence must be examined. And will be . . .'

'PET are looking into this,' Hartmann insisted.

'You had your chance.' Eggert picked up her papers. 'We're starting the meeting. Stay or go. Up to you.'

Two floors down. Forensic. A plain cold room. Men Brix knew standing round, waiting.

This was the act in the drama they both wanted and loathed. The end of one hunt. The start of another.

Dripping dank water the bag stood on the shining silver table, the size and shape of a child. Pale blue through the mud and weed. A name on the side. A picture of a sail.

Lund had said something. About how it was hard to separate the man they sought from the ocean. Saltwater seemed to follow him everywhere. Perhaps flowed in his veins, pumped through an unfeeling heart.

Yet something drove him too. Unfinished business.

The lead pathologist was there. So was the chief forensics officer. Both stood silent in white bunny suits, scalpels in hand.

One for a body. One for evidence. Which to choose?

'What is it?' Brix asked.

The forensic man answered.

'A tarpaulin bag for a sail from a small dinghy. Common type. You can find them everywhere in the harbour.'

The water smelled of salt and decay. Soon there would be worse. No shrinking from it.

'Well?' the pathologist asked, raising the sharp scalpel. He nodded at his colleague. 'Me or him? You choose.'

What had happened had happened. The present didn't shape the past. Only the other way round, much as one struggled to hope otherwise.

Brix turned to the forensics officer and said, 'You.'

Then stepped back, took a deep breath, reminded himself of the stench to come and watched as the man pulled up his mask.

A couple of officers walked out, couldn't take it. He envied them in a way. Soon, when the prosecutor and Ruth Hedeby had done their work, such ignorance would be a part of his daily life. He wondered what it felt like. Comforting or simply bleak.

'Cutting,' the forensics officer announced then placed the sharp scalpel at the head of the bag, near the ties, and moved slowly, carefully, making a shallow incision the length of the fabric.

A new smell. Brix couldn't place it.

The forensic man didn't turn.

A second cut, horizontal across the middle. Then some more.

This was happening too quickly. What lay beneath needed to be extracted carefully from the covering, like a butterfly pupa rescued from its cocoon.

Then another cut and Brix was on him, starting to shout.

Only to fall into silence.

The forensic officer pulled down his mask. Shrugged.

Brix looked, tried to place the smell.

Cloth and resin. Fresh. Unused.

Pristine, folded tightly, still white for the most part, it sat inside the blue bag.

A sail. Nothing more. A blackened bullet hole near the top. A second at the middle.

'Lund was right,' Madsen said behind him. 'She was . . .'

By then Brix was marching back into the corridor. A man renewed.

'Tell Hedeby the case is back on,' he ordered as the detective tried to keep up. 'Find every officer you can. I don't care if they're off duty. I want them in here.'

People to inform. An order to be decided.

'Tell the Zeuthens we need an urgent meeting,' he added. 'Get Lund on the line.'

Back in the ops room. There was a buzz there already. Juncker had been on from Jutland. They thought Lund had tracked him down finally. But it wasn't going well.

A paint shop. An engine works. One skylight high in the roof.

Outside the generator rattled and shook. They could feel its breath mingle with theirs. He'd been there all the time. Watching. Listening.

Borch did what men did. Tore at the walls, threw things, yelled.

Brick and metal everywhere. Sleeves to mouth, short breaths. Not that it did any good.

A sound. Unfamiliar yet one she knew.

Emilie's phone, ringing in her pocket.

Lund took it out, went to a corner, tried to find the air to speak.

'This is fun,' she said, half-gagging.

'I just want the book, Lund. Not you. Give me that and you can live.'

Borch was there. She told him. He grabbed the phone, barked,

'Listen! We don't have the book. There are men on the way here. Turn that thing off, will you?'

Nothing.

She looked up at the distant skylight in the roof. Borch got a bucket, told her to stand on it. She tried, couldn't even reach the first beam.

'I can't do this,' Lund said, fell back to the floor. 'You get out there. Kill the engine. Come back for me.'

Hesitation on his face. She yelled at him till he moved.

Fit man. One leap from the bucket, arms on the beam. Pulled himself up. Climbed along the joist then up to the roof. Gun through the glass. Old iron moving. The briefest scent of night air coming down among the fumes, like water in a drought.

She sniffed it. Closed her eyes. Tried to think.

When she opened them he was halfway through, legs disappearing.

Gone then. A body rolling down a corrugated iron roof.

She heard him fall.

Heard him groan.

Then another sound.

The sharp retort of a gun.

Borch tumbled from the workshop roof, landed on the muddy ground, turned twice, heard something. Rolled out of the way.

Looked up. A black figure. Ski mask. Gun in hand. Barrel pointed straight in the face.

'The book,' said a flat, cold voice and then the gun blazed, so close to his head the sound deafened him for a moment. The smell of cordite rose above the stink of the nearby generator wheezing and rattling, sending its poison to Lund inside.

Got his breath back. Tried to see something behind the mask.

'I don't have the book. I told—'

'If I have to kill you I will.'

'I don't—!'

A kick in the guts then. Another in the head. Borch yelped. Struggled to stand. Thought about fighting.

But the blows kept coming. After a while that was all there was.

*

237

Coughing, eyes hurting, lungs shrieking, Lund kicked the junk across the floor, looking, looking.

One thought in her head: she'd heard the sea beneath the timber floorboards. It was there, cold and bleak and uncaring. A way out. Had to be.

In the corner close to the door she found it. A couple of grimy hinges.

A handle, round, rusty. Stiff.

Three heaves and it shifted an inch. Three more in the grey haze working its way around her and she'd got it free.

The hatch came up. In the beam of her torch the water shone beneath, a good five metres. An iron ladder, at the foot a walkway that had to lead to the jetty at the front.

Lund went down, hand over hand. Got to the rickety iron grating. Made her way to the concrete pier. Climbed up. Looked along.

One upright figure, another on the ground. Then the man bent down, kicked Borch once more, started hunting through his pockets.

On she walked, gun out, quiet, trying to still her breath.

Something changed. As she watched he retrieved what looked like a plastic evidence bag from inside Borch's pocket, waved it at the stricken figure on the ground, cursed and yelled, 'What's this then, shithead?'

A book, she thought. The book. The one Borch said he never had.

Still walking.

The man in the ski mask stood back, took out his gun, pointed it straight in Borch's face.

Lund loosed a shot then, a wild one. She never could get this right.

'Put it down!' she yelled still walking straight at him.

He drew back and it was as if she could see an expression behind the mask: amusement.

'Put it—'

His gun came up so quickly a part of her she didn't recognize started to wake.

One shot.

His.

Missed her.

One shot.

Hers.

A yelp of pain. Black figure hurled into the darkness near the rumbling engine.

She didn't stop to think about it. Got to Borch, bent down. Blood on his mouth. Touched his cheek.

'Sarah . . . He's got the book. You need to . . .'

No hesitation, gun up she walked towards the generator.

Bare floorboards on the mud. A couple of footprints. Maybe some bloodstains. Nothing else.

Weapon out higher. Walked on.

Saw nothing.

In the distance the sound of sirens and a flicker of bright blue.

From the sea the low turn of a small boat engine.

Not a light on the water. Gone again.

Borch was with her then.

'I shot him,' she said. 'I saw him. I hit him.'

And God knows how, she thought.

Borch tapped his chest, winced at the pain.

'I told you before. He's wearing a jacket of some kind.' He patted himself down. Seemed halfway happy with what he felt. 'Still must have hurt though.'

'You're telling me,' Lund whispered.

Borch looked at her then, kept quiet.

'What kind of man is he?' she asked.

He thought about it.

'Unusual,' Borch said. 'Very.'

A phone flashed and rang. Hers this time.

Lund listened. Looked at Borch.

'She's alive,' Brix said from what sounded like a bustling ops room. 'Emilie's alive somewhere. We're back in business.'

The committee meeting was in full flow. Fifteen people round the table. Eggert in control.

'We're all fallible,' she said. 'But as politicians we will be held accountable for our mistakes. It's not as if we're talking about a single error here. Your relationship with Rosa Lebech alone—'

'A private matter,' Hartmann insisted. 'It's never interfered with my work or the policies I pursue.'

'I doubt her husband would agree there,' Eggert said with a

marked disdain. 'And your whole handling of the Zeuthen case . . . You ignored every warning you received. You allowed Mogens Rank to appear blameless when we now know that's not the case.'

'This is bullshit,' Rank intervened. 'My ministry was not—'

She thrust the evening newspaper in front of him.

'Read this, Mogens. The media make or break us. It's no use complaining they've been . . . unkind. The truth is what they make it. You dodged questions on the case. While Troels has become involved in a way quite unbefitting a Prime Minister. Our credibility as a party has been undermined and here we are days from an election. Ship rudderless, sinking in front of us. We owe it to the party, to the electorate, to the Zeuthens . . .'

Rank waved her into silence.

'It's not for the party to remove the Prime Minister. He represents the coalition . . .'

'You think they're behind him now? Even Rosa won't come near. If she's slipped out from under the sheets . . .'

Hartmann turned on her then.

'Am I hearing this? Is this what we've become? A bickering, gossiping, backstabbing bunch of chancers looking to hitch a ride to the next fast show in town?'

He looked round the table, at every face.

'I got you here. I made this work. Yes . . . our credibility, our future, our standing with the public, with Zeeland . . . all these are at stake. But we have a plan. Ditch me and you ditch that vision. You chose me for the same reason I chose you. Faith.' Hartmann slammed his fist on the table. 'I need that faith now. So do you. I demand it.'

Silence. Broken by Birgit Eggert's brief laughter.

'You speak so well, Troels. But words won't bring Emilie Zeuthen back to life. Either resign or we abandon you. A dignified exit or a bloody civil war. The choice is—'

Behind them the double doors opened. Karen Nebel marched in, looked at him. Hartmann got up. So did Mogens Rank. They listened in private.

Eggert was going on to practicalities. A meeting of the business committee. Rules and procedures.

'Troels!' she shrieked. 'Will you kindly come back to the table and deal with this?'

It was Mogens Rank who answered. He pushed back his glasses, looked at her amiably and said, 'You'll have to excuse me. We have news from the Politigården.'

'Good news,' Hartmann added. 'The police have recovered the bag they thought contained the body of Emilie Zeuthen. It was a ruse . . . There was nothing in it but a dinghy sail.'

Nebel threw some photos on the table. The blue muddy bag, two bullet holes, white material inside.

'They firmly believe Emilie's alive,' Rank added. 'I'd rather be dealing with that than spending time here discussing . . .' A wave of his hand. 'Whatever this was meant to be. Birgit?'

She wore the most fragile of smiles, said nothing.

Hartmann walked out. Nebel followed. Briefed him on what she knew. The police didn't believe Emilie had been taken to Jutland. She was more likely to be kept captive somewhere close to the city.

Back in the office the three of them sat down. Hartmann closed his eyes, looked thoughtful. Nebel was checking her messages. Weber went for the booze cabinet.

'Not now,' Hartmann said, suddenly coming awake.

Weber stopped, looked puzzled.

'You and Karen have had a long day,' Hartmann added. 'Go and have a drink on me somewhere.' He pulled out his wallet, threw some money on the table. 'With my gratitude.'

'What are you going to do?' Nebel asked, grabbing the cash.

He looked round the comfy room. The sofas. The paintings.

'I just want a little quiet time to myself. Go on.' He waved at them with the back of his hands. 'Shoo!'

They got up, puzzled.

'And order me some food on the way out. Lobster, salad. Enough for two. I'm starving.'

Weber sighed, gave her a knowing look and they left.

Hartmann went to the office fridge. Two bottles of champagne. Good quality. Nicely chilled.

Ought to work.

The boatyard was lit up like a fairground. Scene of crime officers. Local cops rubbernecking. Too many people. She tried to keep them back but Gudbjerghavn had never seen this before. It was a spectacle, not to be missed.

Brix was back on the line demanding to know how the man got away.

'He had a boat,' Lund told him. 'He always has a boat.'

'The girl—'

'We found where Louise Hjelby was murdered. I don't think anyone even looked. There was a black car. Borch had some numbers in a book . . .' And kept them, she thought. 'He heard us talking. He took it.'

Lund thought of the low mattress, the bloodstains, the manacles.

'Whoever killed Louise must have been so confident. He didn't even try to clean up. Or maybe . . .'

Perhaps that was someone else's job. And it was still going on.

'How come Borch got that book? Not you?'

He always knew the right question to ask.

'You need to ask him that. Or Dyhring. Someone from PET. I don't know.'

When she came off the phone she realized he was there, listening.

They went to a corner of the workshop, beyond the forensic officers, near the white bike. He had a bandage on his arm where the man beat him. Nothing broken.

'There was a reason,' Borch said. 'I want to tell you.'

'Do you?'

'Yes. You're owed. And . . .'

She got up, walked out into the night.

Juncker briefed her. They were searching the sand dunes. A couple of nearby caravan sites. There was no easy way to guess where he'd gone.

'He'll have a plan,' she said. 'All ready. All prepared. Just in case.'

The young detective nodded.

'I guess so . . .'

Borch came up, insistent at her side.

'I didn't stand in the way of anything, Sarah. Will you listen to me?'

Juncker glared at him.

'I think there was a bloodstain on the timber near the generator,' Lund said. 'I shot him. He was wearing body armour but he may have cut himself. Could be wounded anyway. I want forensic to take a sample and send it to the lab.'

The van had been found in the boatyard car park. No sign of Emilie. The dogs didn't react when they were led inside.

'She was never here,' Lund said. 'We're going back to Copenhagen. Whoever was in that black car—'

'I did what I could!' Borch cried.

She walked on, under the red and white tape, back towards the police cars.

'I was trying to help . . .'

Mad, she stopped and turned on him.

'So who were you covering for? Whose arse is PET protecting here?'

Juncker folded his arms, glared at Borch.

'Yeah. I'd like to know that too. I thought we were supposed to be a team.'

'You don't have clearance!' Borch's voice was strained. 'Until . . . until . . .'

It was Juncker who lost it, not her.

'That kid in there was raped and murdered. Emilie Zeuthen's still missing somewhere. And here you are . . . bleating on like some bloody jobsworth. You make me sick.'

'I'll drive,' Lund announced and held up her keys.

Juncker climbed into the passenger seat.

A face at the window.

'I need a lift,' Borch pleaded.

'We don't have clearance,' Lund said and drove off.

Brix had expected to show Robert and Maja Zeuthen a body. Instead it was a grubby blue bag with a folded bundle of fabric inside. Two gunshots. Firm proof it was the object Zeuthen saw from the bridge.

The bag had been moved to a small room in forensic. The Zeuthens stared at it, didn't say a word.

'I wish I could answer more of the questions this raises,' Brix added. 'It's clear he intended to fool us. But—'

'You think she's alive?' the mother asked.

Brix hated direct answers.

'He was traced to Jutland. There are no signs Emilie went with him. From what we can see she was taken in the speedboat to Copenhagen harbour. After that . . . We're searching the area, looking at ship movements. He certainly had access to a container.'

He looked at Zeuthen.

'He has some kind of maritime connection. Beyond that . . . I would caution against too much optimism. He's a violent, organized man. If . . .'

Robert Zeuthen turned on his heels and marched out of the room. His wife followed. Brix too. The man was on the phone already, calling in the head of Zeeland's security department and his team.

'Mr Zeuthen . . .' Brix began.

'We'll manage our own search of the harbour. It starts now. We know these places better than you. Frankly from what I've seen . . .'

Brix shook his head.

'I understand your frustration. I can't allow you to interfere in our operations.'

'You wasted forty-eight hours on this nonsense!' Zeuthen yelled.

'They weren't wasted. My officers—'

'We were about to tell our son his sister was dead. Can you imagine that? What are we supposed to say now?'

Brix didn't move.

'This is an unusual case. You'll only complicate matters if you try to interfere.'

Zeuthen walked off without another word. The woman stayed.

'This isn't the right way,' Brix said. 'Please . . .'

'He wants to do something! Can't you understand that? We both do.'

'Then look nearer to home. This man got close to you. Close to Emilie. He knows things about you, about Zeeland, he shouldn't. If we could understand that . . .'

'You've been all over my family, Brix. All over Zeeland . . .'

'It doesn't mean the answers aren't there. Just that we haven't found them. A different pair of eyes. A closer pair, perhaps . . .'

'I'll see what I can do,' she promised.

He watched her walk down the corridor, meet her husband outside. They seemed a little less distant than before.

Then he went back to the ops room. Saw the interest, the eagerness, the energy. The case was back from the dead.

Robert Zeuthen was in the office in Drekar with Reinhardt and a team from Zeeland's security section. Grey, serious, determined professionals, talking about places to look, shipping records, destinations.

Maja had heard a couple of the servants gossiping. Zeeland didn't run itself. There were board problems even before Emilie was kidnapped. Whispers about mutiny and how Robert wasn't his father.

And he wasn't. She'd never have married him otherwise. Listening to them talk, watching him try to guide their efforts, she felt powerless. As did he.

They had a big monitor by the table. Maps and shipping movements displayed there. He was asking where the police had been, what they were doing. It seemed comprehensive, to her anyway.

'They've checked all the ships in port,' Reinhardt said.

'What about the containers?'

'They're sealed. We can't just—'

'I want you to talk to the freight station people,' Zeuthen interrupted. 'Tell them we want every last one opened and checked. We'll cover the losses. We'll pay for any subsequent costs caused by the delays.'

The security officer shook his head.

'We don't have the right. They're cargo. The contents are private property. If—'

'Ask their price. Then pay it. I doubt they'll argue.'

'The board needs to meet,' Reinhardt added. 'It's important—'

'Not for me,' Zeuthen snapped.

A noise at the door. Carsten Lassen was there, looking at Maja. Carl was with him. He'd been crying.

She went to the boy. So did Zeuthen. Lassen looked shamefaced. He'd had the TV on. Carl had heard the news.

'I forgot. I'm . . .'

Maja had her arms round the boy, gave Lassen a look. He took the hint and left them.

They went to the family room, sat Carl between them, arms round him. The way it used to be.

'Mum and Dad are looking for her,' Zeuthen said. 'Everywhere. We'll find our Emilie. We both . . . we all miss her.'

'What if you don't?'

Her hand went to his hair. Zeuthen's followed.

'But we will,' Maja told him.

'When?'

'Soon.'

He rolled over on the settee, put his head on her lap, his legs on his father's.

'I went looking for her,' the boy said.

She wanted to cry but wouldn't allow that.

'Where?'

'I thought she was in the gap. But she wasn't.'

Maja Zeuthen closed her eyes. The old mansion was so big. The kids spent long hours exploring places she'd never even found.

'What gap, darling?'

He looked worried. She asked again.

'The place Emilie goes when she doesn't want to hear things.'

Zeuthen put his hand to Carl's cheek.

'Hear what?'

'You two. Fighting and stuff.'

They glanced at one another. A shared moment of grief, of guilt. Of something that hadn't yet died however hard they'd tried to kill it.

When she looked up Carsten Lassen was at the door, lost and miserable, a small case in his hand.

'Let's find a biscuit. And milk or something,' Zeuthen said and led his son away.

Lassen came in. Said, uncertainly, 'Maybe we should pack Carl some more of his things from here. So he feels at home with us.'

She didn't speak.

'Is there any news?'

Maja shook her head.

'Did Carl or Emilie ever mention a secret place they had? They called it "the gap"?'

He laughed, not kindly.

'You think they'd share secrets with me?'

Maja looked at the old, familiar room. Thought of the happy times in here. The break with Robert had hidden them somehow. Only the quarrels and the pain were visible then. They'd sent Emilie scuttling into the shadows, to a place she could only guess at. Perhaps somewhere she was taken from finally, never to return.

'We'll stay here tonight,' she said softly. 'It's best for him to be near his father right now.'

A nod, a bitter smile. She'd disappointed him once more.

He placed the bag on the floor.

'If that's how you feel.'

Maja scarcely noticed he was gone.

The gap.

A place they'd sent her.

The gap.

She had to know.

Near midnight Lund arrived home. Brix called as she walked through the door. On the way from Jutland she'd whinged about Borch and PET and the missing notebook. He'd raised it with them. Come up with next to nothing.

'They say it was a routine check, Lund. Nothing special.'

'Is that why Borch was there two years ago sweeping up everything he could lay his hands on?'

'He wasn't. If he had been he'd have found that boatyard, wouldn't he?'

'Borch got that book without telling me. He had a reason.'

A low curse down the line.

'They're PET. They do security for politicians. You know their games. Don't get paranoid.'

The house was in darkness and very cold.

'I'm not,' she insisted. 'They must have kept a copy of the car numbers they picked up before.'

'I've got Dyhring coming in here tomorrow first thing. You can come and watch me kick his arse from pillar to post. Did Borch give you anything?'

'No,' she said and left it at that.

'We got a preliminary result on the blood you found. Looks like he's Louise Hjelby's father.'

A sound behind. Eva wandered in wearing a nightdress, bleating at Lund not to turn on the heating. She was carrying a candle in a jam jar. There was a smell like incense. She walked round lighting more candles. Plant pots on the carpet, on the tables, everywhere.

'Everything that was still alive I brought in,' she said. 'If the room's too hot they'll think it's spring. Then they wake up and they die.'

Lund put down the phone. Wondered what to do.

Eva said very earnestly, 'The thing is . . . if we get a bit of winter without frost they can go out early so long as we keep an eye on them. If not . . .'

'I can't freeze all winter for the fucking plants,' Lund murmured.

Eva smiled, pretended to ignore that.

'I made some pumpkin soup. Very healthy. Want some?'

No answer. Lund walked to the fridge, looked at the beers.

'No!' Eva shrieked and rushed to shut the door. 'You didn't see!'

Photos on the front. Ultrasound images from the hospital.

'I'll get the soup going . . .'

'I'm not interested in soup, candles, plants or pictures of babies right now.'

One beer. Cold and beckoning. She took out a second for good measure.

'No need to get mad,' Eva complained. 'I'm only staying till tomorrow.'

Lund looked at her, felt for one brief moment a pang of guilt.

'Do you ever read papers, Eva? Or watch TV?'

'Not right now. It's all so miserable. What if the little one hears?'

The pang of guilt got bigger.

'Have you talked to Mark?' Lund asked.

She had a naive and pretty face, one that advertised its pain so freely.

'He said he didn't know what to do. About me. About . . .'

She patted her belly and Lund so wished she hadn't.

'I need to think about myself. About the baby. I can move in with a friend I think. You don't need to worry.'

It wasn't too late to fry an egg, even if the plants might scream.

'You can't live like that with a baby. There's always the flat.'

A shrug, one that said: defeated.

'The ceiling's got asbestos. They've closed the whole block. Going to come down.' A brief laugh, not bitter. She probably couldn't manage that if she tried. 'Probably why we got it on the cheap.'

Lund knocked back more beer. Wondered if she'd hit three.

'I guess it's not so weird being a single mum,' Eva said. 'You managed it.'

'No, I didn't,' Lund said without thinking. 'I thought I could. I wanted to. So much. But . . .'

'But what?'

'Things didn't work out with Mark's dad. I thought I didn't need him. Didn't need anyone.'

Bright eyes shining in the candlelight Eva asked, 'Why didn't it work?'

'Maybe I would like some soup.'

A glimmer of recognition.

'Were you pregnant too? Is that why you got married?'

Lund laughed. Nodded.

'And you didn't love him?'

Too close but those eyes wouldn't leave her.

'No. I loved someone else. Before. But I was scared. So I chased him away. It seemed easier . . .'

A noise. Her phone was ringing.

'You can stay here as long as you like,' she said. 'I'll be proud to have a picture of your baby on the fridge. Any time . . .'

Lund pulled herself together, picked up her phone, said, 'What's up?'

'Why did you stop me, Lund? What was that bastard to you?'

The voice from Emilie's handset. Cold. Intelligent. Cultured.

Her head was spinning.

'How did you get my number?'

'I can get anything I want. Your friend from PET deserved to die. You heard what he was covering up. So did I.'

'Where's Emilie? What have you done with her?'

'There's still a trade to be made here. I need your help.'

She walked across the room. Something in her tone sent Eva scuttling to the cooker.

'We know you didn't take her to Jutland. Is she alive?'

'The book lists twelve black cars. I need names and social security numbers for the drivers. I'll manage the rest.'

'Don't be ridiculous. Come in. Give me Emilie. I'll find who killed your daughter.'

Silence then.

'We've got your blood. I know you're Louise's father. She told her friends you were a good man. A hero. Is that what heroes do? Steal children in the night?'

'Someone stole mine.'

'This can't go on. You're hurt. I shot you.'

'Had worse. I'll call tomorrow. This phone from now on. I want names and social security numbers. I want . . .'

Eva was back with a bowl of soup and a puzzled smile.

'Not a chance,' Lund told him. 'Do you want your daughter's case solved or not? Give me Emilie and I'll find who murdered your kid. Play these games and he's going to walk free.'

She didn't know if he was still there.

'We're pulling in PET tomorrow. If they kept a copy of those car numbers we start there. First thing. OK?'

A long wait.

'OK,' he said finally. 'Don't disappoint me. That has consequences.'

'Emilie . . .'

'You don't have to wait till morning. There's a copy by your front door.'

A car engine started in the road.

He was gone by the time she got there. Nothing but two distant red lights disappearing down the hill to the city.

A white envelope on the mat.

One page, a photocopy. The childish handwriting of a young boy in Jutland. Numbers. Letters. Nothing more.

Seven

The Politigården was alive with activity when Lund turned up. She went straight into the meeting with Brix, Borch and the PET boss. Before anyone could speak Dyrhing began with an update. The car the kidnapper used had been found abandoned in a backstreet near Nyhavn. There was blood on the passenger seat. Not much.

'We'll put your house under surveillance,' he added. 'Maybe he'll return.'

'Thanks but I'd place more faith in the local kindergarten,' she shot back. 'We can handle it.'

The faintest of smiles on Brix's face. Borch was in a dark suit and tie, clean-shaven. Tired. He looked like a salesman nervously waiting for a job interview.

'Our brief isn't your brief,' Dyhring said carefully. 'You may look at what you see and interpret events . . . mistakenly. Two years ago we had to make sure Hartmann wasn't unfairly tarnished.' He gazed directly at Lund. 'We all know he suffered that once before. As Prime Minister he didn't deserve to go through the same ordeal again.'

'From me?' Lund asked. 'Hartmann made himself a suspect in the Birk Larsen case. If he'd told the truth from the outset we wouldn't have dragged him in here thinking he killed the girl. He could have helped us get to the bottom of that long before—'

'The Birk Larsen case is dead,' Brix broke in. 'We're not going back there.'

'How do you know Hartmann wasn't involved in Jutland?' Lund demanded.

Brix rolled his eyes.

'Fair question, isn't it?' she added.

'We looked at transport records for the day. GPS locations,' Dyhring said. 'He was in the car with his chauffeur and staff all the time. That was all we needed. No one from PET talked to Peter Schultz. Whoever put pressure on the man . . . it wasn't us.'

Borch kept quiet.

'Schultz's behaviour took us by surprise,' the PET chief went on. 'We've been straight with you throughout.'

Brix snorted.

'Except Borch stole the book. An important piece of evidence. Right from under our noses. And you'd never even have mentioned it if we hadn't . . .'

Dyhring didn't blink.

'I was going to tell you all about it this morning. We had to take a look first and work out what it meant. As I said before, our brief is not your brief. We have other responsibilities.'

'Covering politicians' backs?' Lund asked.

'No need to get smart with us. You of all people ought to know we need to watch our step.'

She snatched a piece of paper from the table, a copy of the page the kidnapper had left her, brandished it at them.

'Which one of these twelve cars is it?'

Silence.

'Peter Schultz changed the date of the crime to cover for one of these vehicles. Which one . . . ?'

'If we knew that,' Borch said, 'we would have told you.'

'So have you got a tongue?' She tapped the paper. 'Is Ussing's car there?'

'Yes,' Dyhring agreed. 'We're looking into the suggestion he knew Louise Hjelby. This so-called witness sounds a touch dubious . . .'

She looked at Brix and said they needed to interview the man.

'Parliament's our call . . .' the PET chief began.

'Your brief's not our brief. The Hjelby girl was raped and murdered then dumped in the harbour as if she didn't even matter. Rape. Murder. They're ours. And if all the kidnapper wants in exchange for Emilie Zeuthen is the truth I'll give it him.'

'Unless you have any other suggestions?' Brix asked.

'There are protocols here,' Dyhring insisted. 'Matters of security to do with the government. With Hartmann.'

'Are you telling me the Prime Minister doesn't want the police to go near a murder case?' Brix asked. 'After we exonerated him over the Birk Larsen girl?' He shrugged. 'I find that hard to believe.'

'You can't just march in here,' Dyhring snapped. 'You search the harbour. We'll assemble the investigative team. Once—'

'Screw that,' Lund said. 'We've had men down the harbour all night. This is ours now.' She nodded at Borch. 'We'll keep him in case he remembers something else along the way. I'll let you know if I need more.'

Brix broke into a broad smile.

'Unless you want to go bleating to the Justice Minister,' he added. 'Though from what I hear I doubt he's going to stick his head above the parapet. So . . .' He clapped his hands. 'Let's get on with it, shall we?'

Juncker had been at the harbour since seven, didn't feel tired. Just angry. With PET. With the kidnapper. With himself. Walking round the port, hard hat on, he wondered if they'd ever find her.

The night team had established the car the man had used was stolen from one of the piers. That was all they had.

Then Lund called.

'Don't give me a hard time,' he pleaded. 'Plenty of places he could have hidden Emilie here. I bet only a quarter of the warehouses are busy right now.'

'Go through every one,' she ordered. 'Check the boats. Look at the cameras. Someone must have seen something.'

'Is that like . . . a law? Lund's law?'

A pause. He was sure he made her laugh sometimes.

'Yes, Asbjørn. It is.'

'Speaking of laws . . . what should I do about Zeuthen's people? They're everywhere.'

Three suited men wearing grey helmets were watching him as he spoke.

'Are they supposed to be with us or something?' Juncker asked.

'No. They're not. Don't take any crap from them. And don't let them tell you where you can and can't go. I'll have a word here . . .'

He had to ask.

'What about Borch?'

'What about him?'

'Are you two OK? I know he was screwing us around. But he's a nice guy. I mean . . . he got us back on track when we thought Emilie was dead. Can't be all bad.'

A long silence.

'I've got to talk to some people in Christiansborg,' she said. 'Call me when you find something.'

Hartmann's first stop of the day was a debate with the other party leaders at a commercial garden nursery west of the city. He sat in the black saloon with Karen Nebel going through the suburbs. As they drew up at their destination she leaned over and adjusted his tie.

Licked a tissue. Dabbed at something on his collar.

He recoiled, like a child with a fussy mother.

'I can't have you photographed with lipstick on your shirt,' she said briskly. 'Sit still.'

He did. Looked a little guilty.

'Need I ask?' she wondered.

'Tell me about this place.'

Familiar story. Almost a hundred employees. Heavily in debt. Running on bank credit. Facing imminent closure.

'You might get a rough ride,' she warned.

'From you or them?'

Nebel picked up her briefcase.

'What you do in your free time is none of my business.'

'It isn't.'

'Theoretically,' Nebel added. 'If there's a political dimension . . .'

'Then I'll mention it.' He hesitated. 'But it's personal. Honest.' His hand strayed to hers. She blinked very slowly. 'I really appreciate what you've done.'

'You should. I'd rather you didn't hump Rosa Lebech in the office though. People may notice.'

'People?'

She tapped her chest.

'Like me.'

They got out.

'Rosa won't be siding with Ussing,' he said as they went for the door. 'Something changed her mind.'

'Must have been a policy decision,' Nebel commented. 'He hasn't gone public on that. Nor has she.'

Hartmann tapped the side of his nose and winked. She couldn't stop herself laughing.

'You're a dreadful human being.'

'Oh, come on! No one wants a saint running the country. Not if they've any sense. A scoundrel with a streak of integrity's so much more reliable . . .'

She reached up and got the last of the scarlet stain from his collar.

'Let's just focus on the integrity, shall we?'

A busy crowd of people in overalls. In the midst of the photographers and reporters Anders Ussing was answering questions. Rosa Lebech stood to one side looking . . . tired.

Nebel put on her best smile, strode over, gave her a sheet of paper.

'Slept well? No, no need for an answer. The organizers wanted to ask a few extra questions. If it's OK . . .'

'Fine with me,' Ussing announced.

Lebech muttered something about talking to her political adviser and walked off.

Ussing came and stood close to Hartmann.

'Even for you this is a dirty game, Troels. Do you really think you can steal the election with gossip from a fool like Seifert?' A laugh, not much confidence or humour in it. 'You must be desperate.'

Hartmann was unmoved.

'I thought you wanted me to get to the bottom of the Zeuthen case. PET seem to think you can help. Are you asking me to stop them?'

'One word, you shit . . . one wrong word and I'll bury you in a libel suit. I promise . . .'

An aide came up, whispered in his ear. Ussing's face froze. He strode off to take a call.

'Anders has to return to Christiansborg,' the man explained. 'The police want to talk to him.'

'That's a shame,' Hartmann said. 'Couldn't they wait?'

'Apparently not.'

Ussing pushed his way through the press mob, ignoring the shouted questions. Camera flashes. A face like thunder.

Hartmann wandered over to where Lebech was standing.

'Well,' he observed with a wink, 'looks like it's just you and me.'

It was cold in the office. She went to the lockers in the cloakroom, got out a patterned wool sweater, pulled it over her shirt. When her head popped through she realized Borch was watching from the door. Smart suit, ironed shirt, dark tie.

'Why are you dressed like that? You look like you're selling insurance.'

A sarcastic smile in return. Then he came over.

'I work for PET, Sarah. You know there are things I can't tell you. Don't be like this. I don't deserve it. I did what I could.'

Her hands tugged at the jumper. She remembered him doing that in the shabby little bedroom in Gudbjerghavn.

'Why did you come here? Why couldn't you have stayed—?'

'I wanted to see you.' He bent down, tried to catch her eye. 'I wanted to know how you were doing. Whether there was any-one—'

'You're married. You've got kids.'

He nodded.

'True. I still couldn't help it. Don't regret it either. Don't . . .'

She pulled on her jacket. Got her bag.

'You're on my team,' Lund said. 'Not Dyhring's. When we talk to Ussing . . . anyone in that place . . . you do as I say.'

He nodded.

'So the idea is we pretend it never happened? Is this . . . ?'

She put a finger to her lips.

Went, 'Ssshhhh.'

Robert Zeuthen had summoned a meeting with the heads of his security teams. They were hunting through containers in ships berthed in Zeeland terminals, opening them one by one. It was a protracted process, one that was causing difficulties with their customers.

Eight men round the table, Reinhardt too.

The lead security officer said it could take up to a week to complete.

'Hire more men,' Zeuthen ordered. 'Whatever you need.'

'Men aren't the issue. We have to persuade the shipping companies to let us open sealed consignments. That means they need to go through all the paperwork again. The cost . . .'

'Just do it.'

Reinhardt wanted a private word. They went to the window. The grey ocean outside, piers along the harbour. They could see groups of security officers working alongside the police below.

'I've been liaising with the board. Everyone wants the best outcome for you, naturally.'

Something unspoken hung in the air.

'But?' Zeuthen asked.

'We're rudderless, Robert. The stock price is dropping. Rumours are rife. If it falls any further we could be open to a hostile bid, from the Koreans, the Chinese. Anybody.'

'If they've got complaints tell them to talk to me.'

Reinhardt stiffened, unhappy with the tone of Zeuthen's voice.

'Kornerup's still around. It would help if we allowed him to return on a temporary basis. I'll keep an eye—'

'Just do what I ask, will you? What you're paid for.'

'I've worked here since I was eighteen years old, Robert. Most of that time for your father. He never spoke to me like that. It wasn't necessary.'

'Did my father have to deal with this?'

He didn't wait for an answer. There was a figure in reception. Maja in a powder-blue sweater and black trousers. Zeuthen went to her.

'I can't find anyone who knows what "the gap" is,' she said, coming off the phone. 'I've talked to the nanny. Their teachers.'

'Maybe it's just a game they made up. The TV crew are here. We've got the script written. We can make the appeal now. They'll give it to the news channels straight away.'

They'd talked about it already that morning. Brix had been on the phone.

'The police really don't want us to do this, Robert. They say they'll be inundated with calls. Most of them will be fortune-hunters.'

'The police,' he muttered. 'What have they done for us?'

'I know . . .'

Hand to her shoulder.

'I've never asked for anything. Not before. But . . . please.'

Once she'd have stepped back from him, shook her head automatically. Not now.

'Just this,' he begged.

The room next door. Two chairs in front of the window. Lights. Cameraman. A director, a woman with a microphone.

Nothing to talk to but the single, blind eye of a lens.

Ussing's office, a small, plain room at the back of the Parliament building. He didn't sit. Didn't want to acknowledge Lund and Borch had any right to drag him out of the campaign. An aide sat and listened as a witness.

'This is about finding Emilie Zeuthen,' Lund cut in when he kept on whining. 'I'm sure the electorate will forgive your absence.'

A stocky man with a sly, aggressive face. He glared at her then and said, 'Don't try and pull those tricks with me. I'm not Troels Hartmann and this isn't the Birk Larsen case. You're not throwing me in a cell. I've told you the truth already.'

She went over the questions anyway.

'Peter Schultz was a friend of yours. You met. Your car was in the area when Louise Hjelby disappeared. Do you honestly think we've got no right to be here?'

'Look. I'm appalled by what's gone on. If I could help I would. Schultz and I were just friends—'

'We've got a witness who says he heard you talking about the Hjelby girl,' Borch said.

Ussing laughed.

'Seifert? I threw the idiot out of here for dipping into the campaign budget. He's damned lucky I didn't have him charged with theft.'

'Why didn't you?' Lund asked.

Not a welcome question.

'We didn't need the publicity. You have to watch your public profile . . .'

Lund pulled out a photo of Louise Hjelby, brandished it in his face.

A new picture. Just a week before she vanished. Pretty girl. Long dark hair. Too-pale skin. No smile.

'Did you ever meet her?' she demanded.

Ussing looked at his aide. The man stared at the floor.

'We checked your movements,' Borch added. 'On April the twentieth two years ago you were campaigning in Gudbjerghavn. Where Louise was killed.'

'So was everyone. Zeeland were closing down the port. There was a debate. It was a big issue.'

'Here's a copy of your hotel bill,' Lund added and threw a sheet on the desk.

Ussing sat down, looked at the invoice. Kept quiet.

'You drove a black car,' Borch said. 'BMW. It was seen on the same road Louise took. Same day. Around the same time.'

'I was campaigning!'

Lund grabbed a chair, sat down. A sign that said: going nowhere.

'The girl was raped then murdered. Your friend Peter Schultz wrote it off as a suicide. Emilie Zeuthen could die because of that. So let's be precise here. What did you and Schultz talk about for nearly an hour? And don't tell us it was the weather . . .'

The aide came over. Private whispered words.

'It seems we used the girl in one of our campaigns,' Ussing said finally.

The man placed a brochure on the desk and said, 'It was to try to get people interested in becoming foster parents. A number of private children's homes had closed recently. There was a need. Still is. It was a local initiative . . .'

'And you are?' Borch asked.

His name was Per Monrad. Ussing's campaign manager.

'Anders set up the organization in the first place. We wanted to use the girl as an example of how it could work. Then . . .' He frowned. 'We found out she'd killed herself.'

He tapped the brochure.

'I had thousands of these printed. We had to scrap the lot. It wouldn't have looked good . . .'

Lund skimmed through the pages.

'How was Schultz involved? What did you need him for?'

Ussing shrugged.

'He wasn't really. We heard the girl had killed herself. I had to make a decision whether we ran with the campaign or not. So we talked about what had happened. I was anxious that we hadn't upset the kid by using her in the ad. She seemed a bit shy. Also the agency never got permission from the foster parents or the school for some reason. An oversight I guess. They said she didn't want them to know until it came out.'

A double page photo across the centre spread of the brochure. Anders Ussing and Louise Hjelby. He was smiling broadly, had his arm around her shoulder.

Lund held up the picture, showed it to Borch, then to Ussing. Waited.

He was struggling.

'I didn't even know the girl. I just turned up for the photo. Never saw her before or after.'

Borch nodded as if to say, 'Really?'

'You didn't give her a lift that afternoon?' Lund asked. 'You didn't put her bike in the back of your car?'

'No! Are you suggesting I killed that girl?'

'We're just asking,' Borch told him.

Monrad placed another sheet on the table.

'This is what Anders did that day. A very busy schedule. Meetings throughout. In the afternoon we went to Esbjerg for a debate with Hartmann.'

'Good enough?' Ussing asked and got up from the table, went for his coat.

'I want everything from your campaign logs for that day,' Lund said.

'This is outrageous . . .'

Borch was on the phone already.

'If I don't have what I want by this afternoon I'll be back with a warrant,' she promised.

Outside Borch came off the call. He said the advertising agency had confirmed Louise had taken part in a photo shoot for the brochure one week before she went missing. Ussing had other links with Schultz, to do with a bank loan. They were trying to firm up information on that.

'How the hell did your people miss all this?' Lund asked. 'What were they doing?'

'I don't know. I've asked for copies of all the photographs.'

She nodded at Ussing's office.

'What do you know about him? His private life?'

Nothing.

'Or is that secret too?'

'You do go on sometimes. Ussing was divorced five years ago. He's got two grown-up children. Doesn't see them much. He's heterosexual and likes women. Not girls as far as I know. Anything else?'

'Get people going over his diary with a fine-tooth comb,' she ordered. 'Talk to his campaign staff. Not just his pet monkey Monrad in there. I want to see Hartmann's people. Let's work out if these meetings hold water. And . . .'

Borch wasn't listening. There was a TV at the end of the corridor. He was walking towards it, staring at the screen.

Maja and Robert Zeuthen side by side, comfortable that way for once. Behind them the port and a flat icy sea.

'We're hoping that people will help us,' Zeuthen was saying.

'If someone has seen something, seen Emilie, please come forward,' Maja added, straight off a hidden autocue.

The camera focused on her face.

'She knows we're looking for her. She knows we'll continue until we find her.'

The clip cut to the news presenter. A reward on offer for Emilie's safe return – up to a hundred million kroner.

Lund recalled the Birk Larsens running down the same blind alley, not that they could offer a fraction of that money.

'I thought you had Zeuthen under control,' Borch said. 'The phones are going to be off the hook with every lunatic in the country. This is—'

'Bad,' she interrupted. 'Really bad. Yes, I know.'

Maja Zeuthen went back to Drekar after the TV interview. Carl was there, pedalling up and down the corridors on his trike.

The mansion seemed empty. Perhaps some of the staff had been given leave.

Carsten called and asked, 'Are you two coming home soon?'

Home.

Such a short word. Full of so many complexities and dilemmas.

'Sometime,' she said. 'I'll call you.'

That was it.

She watched the boy race to the fireplace in the study, park the trike there.

'You could always pedal to "the gap",' Maja suggested. 'It's not a secret any more.'

Carl gave her a look and said, 'Mum . . .'

Then picked up a set of cards and started to mess with them.

'I know where it is anyway.' She watched him, saw how at ease he was in the big old house. 'It's in the garage.'

He snorted.

'No it's not!'

'The basement then.'

'No.'

'Then . . .'

'I don't want to ride all the way up to the gap.'

She nodded, tried to imagine where he might be talking about.

'Up?'

The cards. He shuffled them.

'Carl. What do you mean by "up"?'

'Emilie said I wasn't to tell you. She said . . .'

Enough. She came and took him by the shoulders, peered into his young and puzzled face.

'You've got to show me where it is, Carl. Maybe Emilie left something there. Maybe we could . . .' Dreams. That's all they were and they seemed more distant than ever. 'Maybe we could find her.'

He went over and waited for her at the door.

Four floors up in the roof, somewhere in the east wing close to the stone dragon that always fascinated them. Derelict rooms. Places they never needed, never cleaned, never occupied.

A storeroom, plain shelves, cardboard boxes. Things there that pre-dated the marriage, hadn't been touched since Robert's parents were around.

The roof got lower. Carl went straight to a hidden light switch. Crouching she followed him into a narrow division between two walls.

A rug on the floor beneath a tiny window in the roof. He got down, crawled into the corner, found a low lampshade, turned it on.

Maja looked at the circular glass above them, recognized the shape. This was one of the eyes of old man Zeuthen's stone monster. The mythical creature of the Vikings that he made the emblem of Zeeland. Beneath it was the place they retreated when she and Robert fought. A secret refuge from a family falling apart.

Maja got on her hands and knees, sat by the rug. Looked at the scraps of paper. Like her scrapbook. The same simple, childish hand.

Hearts and flowers. The words 'Mum' and 'Dad' joined together as if in hope. She turned the page. A photo from the wedding album stuck with glue. She and Robert looked young. So much in love.

'Does Dad know you come up here?'

He brushed aside his fringe and looked at her. Shook his head.

'We just played. That's all.'

She sifted through the papers. Photos too. Prints of a little cat on long grass. Then, hidden beneath a soft toy, a thin white cable. She pulled on it and an iPad emerged from the rug. It had a leather case, black, like an executive toy.

'This isn't Emilie's. Hers is downstairs.'

He looked blank.

'Where did it come from, Carl?'

The boy hesitated.

'Please,' she begged. 'This is important.'

'Emilie said the man gave it to her.'

Breath short, pulse racing.

'What man?'

He closed his eyes. This hurt.

'*What man?*'

'The man with the cat.' He was crying. Knew he should have said this. Daren't somehow. 'The little cat, down by the fence.'

Maja Zeuthen opened the heavy cover of the iPad. Found the switch. Turned the thing on.

Morten Weber called on the way back from the event at the garden nursery. He sounded happy.

'The press are all over Ussing,' he told Hartmann and Nebel listening in the back of the car. 'I'm putting it round that there's more to come. Here's hoping.'

'Don't push too hard,' Nebel warned. 'Let's leave him to hang himself now.'

A pause then Weber said, 'One can but hope. All those people who were ready to fire you last night are coming round, Troels. Birgit Eggert's clucking like a happy mother hen. My own inclination is to wring her scrawny neck . . .'

'Morten . . .' she howled.

'I said my inclination. Not intention. Not yet. Oh, and I got a message that Rosa Lebech's changed sides for some reason. She's with us again.' Another break. 'I can't imagine what prompted that.'

'I told you it would all work out,' Hartmann declared.

'Was that when you were chopping logs yesterday, ready to quit? One last thing. Lund's been on the line. She's asking for our diaries from the last election. They want to check out Ussing's claims he was on the stump with you when the girl went missing.'

'Give her everything she wants, Morten. Just keep the woman out of my way.'

Laughter.

'I'll do my very best, promise.'

It was Hartmann's turn to hesitate. Then he said, 'And thanks for coming back. I wavered, didn't I?'

'You did, Troels. And you're not the wavering kind.'

'Won't forget again,' he promised.

The call was over. Nebel looked at him as the car headed into city traffic.

'What did that mean?' she asked.

'You don't look a day older, Lund,' Weber said as she and Borch entered the Prime Minister's quarters.

'Is that so?' she said.

Weber seemed much the same too. A short, slightly scruffy man with unruly curly black hair and thick glasses. He seemed to have acquired a badly fitting suit and waistcoat on the way from local to national power but that was it. He'd been bright, cunning, utterly dedicated to Hartmann during the lengthy Birk Larsen investigation. An obstacle when he wanted. Someone who greased the wheels when it was in Hartmann's interests.

'This is Mathias Borch from PET,' she said, introducing the two of them. 'Have you met before?'

They both shook their heads. Lund guessed she believed them.

Brix had been on the phone just before they went into the building. The Politigården was inundated with calls after the Zeuthens' TV appeal. Half of Denmark seemed to think they'd seen Emilie and wondered how to get their hands on the reward.

'Ussing's giving us hell,' Lund told Weber. 'He says you're dropping him in the shit for political reasons.'

'Did he sound convincing when he said that?'

'Not really,' Lund agreed. 'He looked as if he was lying through his teeth.'

Weber smiled.

'But then he's a politician,' she added. 'So what should we expect?'

The smile became fixed.

'What do you want of me exactly?'

'Did Hartmann have a debate with Ussing on April the twentieth two years ago?' Lund asked.

Weber's fingers clattered the keys of the laptop on the desk.

'Yes. He did.'

'That's not just a line in an old diary? You're sure?'

The little man laughed.

'Sorry I forgot. Talking to you is like the proverbial Muslim divorce, isn't it? You have to say everything three times. Yes he did. Yes he did. Yes he did.' Another rattle of the keys. 'It was in a fishmeal factory in Esbjerg. Started at five thirty.'

Another jab at the laptop. He turned round the screen so they could see. A cutting from a local newspaper. A photo of Ussing and Hartmann on a platform.

'Did Ussing act strangely?' Borch asked.

'No more than usual I imagine. He's a thug at heart. You don't expect niceties from the man.'

'And Hartmann?' Lund asked. 'How was he?'

Weber said nothing. Borch was looking at her too.

'I was just interested,' Lund added. 'Did he drive himself that day? Or take a break in the ministerial car?'

'Why would he do that?' Weber replied.

'I don't know. I just wondered if he did.'

'I don't think so.'

'But you don't know?'

Weber leaned back in his chair.

'He has a chauffeur. For security purposes his movements are logged every inch of the way. Ask PET. They do it. Alongside that we have a campaign bus and some support cars. When he's on the road Troels Hartmann doesn't go walkabout unless I say so. When he does someone's always there.'

Borch's phone rang. He walked away to take it.

'Why do you ask?' Weber demanded.

'It's what I do.'

'Lund. I understand you feel Troels didn't do as much as he should have before.'

'He didn't.'

'Fine. He didn't. But he's a decent, honest man. Somewhat prone to hidden shallows on the emotional front. But none of us is perfect. He has a right to a private life just like the rest of us. Is that all?'

She looked at Borch. He had nothing.

'For now,' Lund said.

The latest polls came in at the end of the afternoon. Hartmann preened himself over them. Then Weber brought him up to date on the police investigation.

'I gather you had Brünnhilde in the building.'

Weber gave him a quizzical look and took a seat by the window.

'The Valkyrie of the Politigården.'

'Oh. Opera's not my thing. Sorry. She's just doing her job, Troels. Rather well actually. We don't really think Ussing murdered that girl, do we?'

Nebel was listening from the door.

'So long as the mud sticks. It's not the deed that kills you it's the lie,' Hartmann said cheerily.

'Actually it could be either,' Weber pointed out. 'Or both.'

'I've got Mogens here,' Nebel said, changing the subject. 'With Birgit. I told you they wanted a word.'

'You did,' Weber agreed. 'Send them in.'

All smiles, Rank in a smart suit, Eggert dressed down, they came through the door.

'We had an informal committee meeting,' Rank said. 'After all the fuss last night. They send their regards. Everything's looking good. The polls!'

'We haven't had this kind of support in the provinces in ten years!' Eggert added. 'It's wonderful. And if you look at the detail so much of it's for you personally. Your leadership. Your charisma. Your character.'

'You checked then?' Hartmann asked.

'Well, we have to,' she replied. 'And now it seems your witness wasn't entirely wrong about Ussing.'

She had her hands behind her back. Holding something. Eggert came up to the desk and held out a bottle of red wine. Bordeaux. Old. Expensive.

'I can't apologize enough for what happened. Mogens has been magnificent in clearing up an awkward situation. Putting me right on a few points.' She brandished this bottle. 'I hope this goes a little way towards . . . making up.'

He stared at the label.

'I heard it was one of your favourites,' she added hopefully. 'I was saving it for election night but . . .' She looked round. 'Why not now?'

'Don't bother,' Hartmann said. 'Best save it for when I appoint my new cabinet. You'll need something for comfort.'

'Troels,' Rank said quietly. 'We've all been under a lot of stress lately. Birgit knows what she did was wrong. She's trying . . .'

He stopped when Weber got up and stood next to the two of them, folded his arms, looked them up and down.

'This isn't a matter for debate,' the little man said. 'The Prime Minister doesn't trust you any more, Birgit. Why should he?'

She didn't look at him. Just Hartmann.

'We've worked together for years, Troels . . .'

'All the more reason you should have supported us when we needed it,' Weber noted. 'The Permanent Secretary will prepare the Treasury for your dismissal once the election is over. Until then you'll make no public appearances. Nor should you regard yourself as a member of the government.'

He went to the door, opened it, nodded at the bottle.

'There's a corkscrew in my office. You can borrow it on the way out if you like.'

Closed it after her then looked at Rank, alone, unsmiling, worried.

'Nothing to be afraid of, Mogens,' Weber said and patted him on the back. 'That's the end of it. You may have a shitty memory but at least you're loyal.'

Rank said thank you and meekly left.

'She'll be calling her scheming little pals before she gets to the lift, Troels. You know that.'

'Let her. They're deadbeats. I'm winning. That's all that counts.'

'And Rosa?'

Hartmann got up.

'You can leave her to me.'

Beyond reception, down a long corridor he found her, sitting on a sofa, looking blank in a sharp new suit.

She got up as he approached, was all over him before Hartmann could open his mouth.

'I just came from a party executive. It's a done deal. Even your doubters are getting excited. We can do this now. We can make it public.'

'Really? You're sure this time?'

'Absolutely! The Centre Party will get behind your nomination as Prime Minister. When you win we'll be there, applauding.' She picked up her coat. 'Let's get the press release done and go for dinner. Last night was a bit . . . rushed, shall we say?'

'Can I get a word in here?' Hartmann asked.

'Sorry?'

He shrugged.

'I mean thanks . . . but no thanks. There isn't going to be an alliance. Not politically.' His eyes never left hers. 'Not personally.'

Her face fell.

'I don't understand.'

The briefest of wry smiles.

'However delightful your company, Rosa, however sweet our time together . . . your ex-husband still tried to screw me by leaking documents from the Ministry of Justice. Worse than that you went running to Anders Ussing the moment things got sticky round here. You weren't there when I needed you. And now when I don't . . . well . . .' A sorry frown that wasn't sorry. 'Who gives a . . . ?'

'We mean something to each other. Don't we?'

Hartmann sighed, looked downcast.

'I have to be honest. I'm a simple, affectionate man. I never doubted my own sincerity. The trouble is . . . I just can't convince myself of yours.'

A look of fury on her face. He did that to women sometimes, and it always surprised him.

'What?' she demanded. 'What?'

'This shouldn't affect our work,' he insisted. 'I'll always value your opinion when it comes to matters of policy. Within reason, of course.'

A smile. A handshake, one that surprised her so much she took it.

Nebel was watching from reception when he walked away. She grabbed his arm and dragged him into a corner.

'Dare I ask what that was about?'

'Decisions.'

'I just bumped into Birgit Eggert on the stairs. She's livid.'

'So what?' he asked. 'I don't need her.' A glance back at Lebech, walking out. 'Any more than I need the Centre Party. You've seen the polls, haven't you? We're ahead.' He stabbed his chest. 'I'm ahead. It's me this country wants. Not Birgit. Not Rosa.'

She looked furious.

'So you and Morten put this together? And didn't think to tell me?'

Hartmann put his head to one side, as if puzzled.

'I'm telling you now, aren't I?'

Down in the Parliament garage Lund and Borch were working their way along the lines of vehicles.

Black cars everywhere. Politicians seemed to like them. Information was coming in about Ussing. It looked interesting.

Ten minutes in Borch came upon one that matched. BMW. Still registered in Ussing's name.

They went round it, inch by inch. Almost three years old, Ussing's private vehicle.

'If you're thinking what I think you're thinking, Sarah, forget it.'

She crouched down at the back. The boot was big enough for a young girl's bike.

'He could be the next Prime Minister,' Borch added. 'We need to tread carefully.'

She was down by the tyres. He came and joined her.

'I know he's an obnoxious jerk but that's not against the law. Not yet—'

The lights flashed. Something beeped. They looked up and there was Ussing walking towards them, the car remote in his hand.

'What the hell is this?' he yelled. 'Are you Hartmann's lackeys or what? Get out of there . . .'

He went for the door. Lund stood in the way.

'We talked to your people in Jutland,' Borch said. 'They didn't know where you were on April the twentieth two years ago until you turned up for the debate.'

He was getting irate.

'I have an appointment. I want you to move away from my car.'

Borch pulled out his notebook.

'You're on the board of the Workers' Bank. Schultz was heavily in debt to them over a property deal. The bank never pursued him for the money.'

Mouth open, Ussing shook his head, said, 'What?'

'Was that the deal?' Lund asked. 'You cleared the debt and he wrote down the girl's death as a suicide?'

'That's it!' He went for the car door. 'If you want any more speak to my lawyer.'

He grabbed the handle, started to get in. Lund pushed him away, slammed the door shut.

'You recognized Louise Hjelby,' she said. 'What was it? Stick with me and I can make you famous? Put your bike in the back and we'll head out of town for a little ride?'

'This is ridiculous. I'm going.'

He brandished the car keys. Lund snatched them.

'Not where you think,' she said. 'We're taking the car for examination. You'll have to answer questions . . .'

Ussing started screaming harassment and lots more besides. Lund's phone rang.

Juncker, still at the harbour. It wasn't good. A camera had caught the speedboat as it returned from the bridge.

'There's just one man on it. He's still wearing that mask. No sign of Emilie. Maybe he threw her overboard along the way.'

'That's not—'

'I've got the pictures! Twenty minutes later you can see the red van leaving. Emilie wasn't there.'

She could hear the despair in his voice.

'If that poor kid's dead,' Juncker said, 'it doesn't matter whether we solve the old case or not, does it?'

'It matters. Keep looking.'

When she hung up Ussing was still yelping. She wondered whether to take him there and then.

Then her phone rang again. Brix.

'We're doing this by the book,' she said wearily. 'Whatever Ussing's people say . . .'

'Forget Ussing,' he broke in. 'I need you down at the docks. The Zeuthens have been on. They've found something.'

It was raining when they got to the Zeeland terminal. Cranes and trucks worked the piers, harsh lights reflecting on the flat water. Juncker and Madsen stood outside the portable office Zeuthen had commandeered for the search. The police had been kept at arm's length though Niels Reinhardt had talked to them from time to time, telling them what was going on. An expensive, fruitless exercise by the sound of it.

Lund peered through the cabin window. Zeuthen was there in a work jacket for once, Reinhardt by his side wearing a hard hat. Then the slight figure of Maja Zeuthen, something in her hands. They wouldn't tell Juncker what they'd found. They wanted Lund.

'OK,' she said and led the way inside.

Maja Zeuthen had it. An iPad. Proof, she said of how the kidnapper had made contact with Emilie. Zeuthen stood back while she explained. It had happened at Drekar. Perhaps he felt responsible.

Then she pulled up the video she'd found.

Emilie, happy, excited, looking into the camera. A message for a stranger. A response to an apparent kindness.

'Hi, there! And thanks for the iPad. I'm really happy with it. And I promise not to tell.'

Lund looked closely. The girl was in a nightdress, hair long, beautifully combed. Behind her what seemed to be an attic wall. This was a secret. One to be kept.

'Mum and Dad won't let me go online anyway. They say I can't talk to strangers.' The blonde hair shook. 'But it doesn't matter.'

Zeuthen looked away. They'd seen this before. He didn't want to repeat the experience.

'They don't talk much any more,' Emilie said with a shake of her head. 'Just argue. They don't know what I do. They don't care.' She brightened. 'And thanks for the kitten photos. They all look so cute. I don't know which one to have.'

Juncker swore, looked at Lund.

'You can bring them to the fence so I can meet them.' Nervous hand to hair again. 'If you feel like chatting tomorrow just leave a message on my wall. Bye . . .'

A wave. Zeuthen crossed the narrow office, stared at the maps on the wall.

Lund went to him. Waited until he looked at her.

'I could have stopped this,' he said.

'How?'

He didn't answer.

'You should call off your people, Robert. Emilie never came to the port. We've got CCTV when he got back from the bridge. He was on his own.'

Zeuthen thought for a moment then pointed to the maps.

'He must have put her off on a ship along the way. We'll extend the range. We can . . .'

His wife was still looking at the video. Fingers on the screen. As if the girl was really there.

'You should talk to her, Robert. She needs you.'

So many maps and charts. Inlets and fjords. Ocean routes and weather. A wide world beyond this tiny cabin.

'You can't stop the hurt,' she added, 'but maybe if you share it a little goes away.'

He walked over then, watched the video replaying. Put his fingers on the screen alongside his wife's. Then his arm round her shoulder.

Juncker was getting fidgety.

'Need a look,' he said, pointing at the iPad. 'Just want to check something.'

Maja Zeuthen hesitated for a second then passed it over.

'He gave Emilie this,' Juncker said. 'He knows computers. He must have set it up first so the two of them could talk.'

'Makes sense,' Borch agreed.

Juncker closed the video screen and went to the settings. The thing would keep track of the networks it used to go online. They were there: a series of numbers, IP addresses. One only to begin with. *Drekar.*

Then, at the very beginning of the records, another.

A line of numbers. And a name: *Marigold Cafe.*

Juncker got out his smartphone, typed something with his thumbs.

Showed them: an industrial area somewhere near the water beyond Vesterbro.

'This is where he first went online,' the young detective said. 'He must have had a place there.'

Lund couldn't take her eyes off the map. The river was between the harbour and the bridge where he'd faked Emilie's death. He could have stopped along the way.

Twenty minutes and they were there. A dead factory by the water, empty piers, empty car parks. Juncker had established it had belonged to Zeeland. The one working business was the cafe. Lund sent him to check there while she and Borch took a look around.

Not much to see.

After a couple of minutes Juncker was back with news. Louise Hjelby's mother had worked in the cafe when the area was bustling. People remembered her, liked her. One man even recalled the daughter as a toddler. He said someone had been asking about the mother and the girl not long before.

'And?' Borch asked.

'And that's it. There are a few homeless people living rough round here. Have you made their acquaintance yet?'

It was hard to find anyone who'd talk to them. Borch had tried a couple of men huddled round a brazier but they barely spoke Danish. Lund scanned the empty area in front of the factory. There was a shape in one of the alcoves.

She went over. A woman with long straggly grey hair huddled by the wall, clutching at a bottle.

Worth a try.

'Three nights ago,' Lund said, 'this was around here.' She had a picture of the speedboat from forensic. 'Did you see anything?'

The woman scowled, shook the bottle.

'Night-time's for sleeping. Why don't you go home and try it?'

'Because we're looking for a missing girl, grandma,' Juncker threw in.

He got a mouthful of abuse for that. And a filthy look from Lund.

Borch pulled out a couple of notes.

'Fine. We've established you're not Asbjørn's grandma. Here's two hundred kroner if you can tell us something we don't know.'

She was about to speak.

'Something useful,' he added. 'Have you seen anyone unexpected round here at all?'

'Listen, sonny. There's me. There's that filthy creep round the corner. That's it usually.'

'Pets,' Lund said. 'Anyone keep pets?'

She stopped and thought.

'Cats in particular,' Borch added.

The woman pointed at the far end of the building.

'Some weirdo goes in there sometimes. He's got cats. Stays down in the basement. I don't bother with him.'

'Why not?' Juncker asked.

'He's rude. Doesn't talk to anyone. He's got money too. You can smell it on him and he won't give the likes of me the time of day.'

'When did you last see him?' Lund asked.

She tugged on the long greasy hair.

'Couple of hours ago.'

Borch got directions, gave her the notes.

Empty building. One set of stairs down at the corner. Torches out. Guns too. Borch forced his way to the front.

The place had an earthy, mouldy smell. But from somewhere ahead there was a sound, low and mechanical.

Borch went in first. Found a light switch. No one. Just a small empty room. A ventilation fan working in the ceiling. The place had been occupied.

'Jesus,' Juncker whispered. 'This guy just goes where he likes.'

Lund's torch fell on a pile of bloody tissues and bandages.

Juncker caught his head on a wire dangling from the ceiling.

'Dammit he's got power. Probably a net connection too.'

In the corner was a small pile of clothes. Dark, warm, practical, cheap. Her torch beam stayed on them. Borch looked at the things, then at her.

'That's what Emilie was wearing when we saw her on the boat. Isn't it?'

Juncker had found another heap in the corner. Adult this time. Winter boots, survival gear, waterproofs.

'Looks like he's getting ready for a war.'

'He's in one already,' Lund said and found the inevitable laptop, a cheap Samsung, propped up on a makeshift desk created out of packing cases.

Borch came over, picked up a few of the sheets of paper scattered around the computer. Ship movements. Container numbers. Cargo assignments and schedules.

'You think he could have shipped Emilie off in one of those?' Juncker asked. 'Like the kid was freight or something?'

A map of the world roughly drawn in crayons on a whiteboard. Arrows for shipping routes.

It was too simple. Too obvious.

'No,' Lund said. 'I don't . . .'

The light was winking on the lid of the laptop. Webcam. Working.

Her phone rang and she knew it was him.

'I thought we had a deal, Lund. You're supposed to be looking for him. Not me.'

'Working on it. Zeuthen's offer of a reward's complicated things . . .'

'I don't give a shit about him and his money. You told me you'd solve that case.'

He coughed. Sounded sick.

'Not overnight. We're getting there.'

'Yeah,' he crowed. 'I read the news. You think it's Ussing now?'

Juncker was going through more papers. Borch kept messing with the laptop.

'We're running through some options . . .' she insisted.

'No you're not. You're being jerked around again. Ussing's nothing to do with this.'

'For God's sake give me some time!' she yelled.

A pause then he said in the same croaky voice, 'You had plenty. Here's the truth. There weren't twelve black cars that day. There were thirteen.'

'What?'

'Take a look behind you, in the waste bin. You're in my apartment. Make yourself at home.'

She walked to the packing cases, found the bin, upended it.

Something familiar. The kind of notebook the kid had used in Jutland.

'Got it?'

'Yes.'

'Someone tore out a page before I saw it. Probably your boyfriend from PET.'

Lund held up the book so Borch saw.

'You've disappointed me greatly. I'm going to have to do this myself now,' the man said then hung up.

She stared at Borch.

'There was another car. Someone removed the last page. Was that you?'

'For God's sake, Sarah. Do you believe him?'

Lund held up the book.

'The page is missing. Yes. I do.'

Juncker bent his head round to take a look.

'It may be missing but he's still got the number.'

He took the thing gingerly. Laid it out by the laptop. The boy's pencil had made marks in the back cover. The impression had been outlined in ink: *AF 98 208.*

'This is a joke,' Borch said, snatching the book. 'It's got to be. That car was never there.'

'What car?' Lund wanted to know.

Juncker had moved to the laptop, turned to the browser.

'He's been reading the news, folks. Keeping up to date.'

'What car?' Lund cried.

Borch elbowed Juncker out of the way and started looking through the open windows on the screen.

In a photo app there was a close-up of a rear number plate. The same one. Black Mercedes.

'Talk to me,' Lund pleaded.

Borch's fingers hit the zoom keys, pulled out.

Three figures in the background. Hartmann, Morten Weber, Karen Nebel, smiling, ready to visit the garden nursery that morning.

Juncker placed a slender finger on the screen.

'You said PET checked out Hartmann's car.'

'We checked out his campaign car. As far as we knew that was the only one he was using that day. This is his own. We never . . .'

Lund was on the phone, running for the stairs.

Got Brix as she hit the cold night air.

'It looks like our man's got his eye on Hartmann,' she said, feeling for the car keys. 'We're going to Christiansborg. You might want to think of getting him into the panic room or whatever they call it over there.'

Blue light flashing, Lund's car slewed to a halt on the slippery cobblestones outside the Christiansborg Palace. She'd left Juncker to deal with the latest bolthole. Just Borch with her, making calls to PET along the way.

He claimed they didn't know Hartmann's private car was in Jutland even though it had a tracking device too.

Lund looked at him.

'If it wasn't on the official vehicle list we wouldn't check for it,' Borch pleaded.

'And who ripped that page out, I wonder.'

She got out, strode up the steps to the entrance to the palace. Uniformed security everywhere. Hartmann wasn't in the panic room. He was chairing some kind of meeting inside, refusing to budge.

'We don't see any threat here,' the chief security officer said. 'No one gets in without ID.'

'There's a threat,' she insisted. 'I want this place locked down. I want a list of current visitors . . .'

Borch was still bleating about the book.

'No one at PET touched that bloody page. We need to focus on Ussing—'

'He says it's not Ussing!'

'How the hell would he know?'

'Check the CCTV,' she said. 'Take a look at everyone who's come through these doors over the last hour.'

'They're all kosher,' the security man insisted. 'Proper IDs . . .'

'I want it checked!' she yelled.

Someone came up with a printout of current visitors. The phone rang. Lund walked away to take it.

'What the hell's happening?' Brix asked. 'I've had Hartmann's people on squawking. Ussing's too. They don't like you, Lund.'

'I'll try to live with that. He's here in Christiansborg. I know it.'

'Really. About Ussing . . .'

Hartmann's meeting was with the leaders of three minority parties. Bit-part actors in the theatre that was Danish politics. But if the polls were right he would garner sufficient support to form a government with their backing, paid for with a handful of lesser ministerial posts.

They shook hands on a provisional deal. Karen Nebel watched, smiling, as the men went back to their offices.

'I'm still pissed off you fired Birgit without telling me.'

'There wasn't time. Talk it through with Morten.'

'I can't. He's been called into a meeting with security. Something's up. You could have discussed this with me.'

He didn't like that.

'If people plot they know the risk. Let's draw a line under—'

'Leave the clichés to me, please. You've just gambled the whole election on a hunch. We go to the polls on Friday.'

'I'm aware of the date.'

'We're exposed now. If we lose just a couple of points of support you won't have a majority, not with those three clowns you just talked to.'

He headed back to his office.

'Don't you dare walk away from me when I'm talking to you,' she screeched. 'If—'

'You're paid to make sure we don't get hitches, Karen. Focus on that. I'm finished with Rosa Lebech. Ussing's in shit with the police. Who's going to vote for them? And if we get Emilie back home—'

'I thought Emilie Zeuthen wasn't part of our campaign.'

He looked briefly guilty.

'Also,' she added, 'there's something odd going on. Lund asked for some transport details from the archives. I had the PA complaining the motoring logs for those days in Jutland are missing.'

Hartmann scratched his head.

'You mean our logs?'

'Exactly. And . . .'

Fast footsteps down the hall. Morten Weber scurrying towards them.

'OK,' the little man cut in. 'I just talked to the security people. Lund thinks Emilie's kidnapper is inside the building. Looking for someone.'

'The kidnapper?' Hartmann asked, astonished.

'Exactly. I want you back in your office.' He took Hartmann's arm, started to drag him. 'Right now.'

Downstairs in the security office Borch and Lund went over the CCTV. One monitor, screens from cameras all over the palace.

'Everyone's accounted for,' the local man said. 'No sign of an intruder. No one in the place who doesn't have full ID.'

'This doesn't feel right,' Borch grumbled. 'Maybe he's conned us again and he's going for Ussing.'

'No,' Lund said. 'Ussing's in the Politigården with his lawyer. He's not a suspect.'

Borch's tie was adrift. Hair a mess again. He looked better that way.

'What do you mean he's not a suspect?'

'He's got an alibi. He was in a hotel with the wife of one of his campaign team. She's confirmed it.'

She ran a finger down the list.

'Complicated lives these people lead . . .'

The security officer was moaning about the work, people wanting to go home, catch trains.

'Here,' Lund said, jabbing at a name. 'You had someone come in from the photocopying service four hours ago.'

The man nodded.

'We've got a lot of photocopiers.'

'Twenty minutes ago someone used the same ID to get back in.' She looked at the clock. 'At six thirty. For a photocopier.'

He shrugged.

'They're all security approved. Maybe he forgot something . . .'

'It says here's he's approved all the way to the Prime Minister's quarters. So where is he now?'

The shrug again. Borch asked how to move the video forward. Switched to Hartmann's section of the building.

After a bit of searching he found a figure there, back to the camera, baseball cap, company jacket.

They watched.

'He's limping,' Lund said. 'He's hurt.' A thought. 'He's not carrying a bag or anything. Where does that corridor go?'

'The Prime Minister's private office,' the security man said.

Borch was up and asking directions before she could say a word.

Two floors up the security men with Hartmann butted into the conversation he was having with Morten Weber.

'We need you in the safe room now,' one said.

'Oh for God's sake . . .'

'Best do it, Troels,' Weber broke in. 'No moaning. Where's Karen?'

'She went off looking for something. The transport report Lund asked for. It's missing. She thinks there's a backup—'

'Sir . . .'

Strong hand on Hartmann's arm. They walked to the secure room next to the office. Went in. No windows. Just a few chairs. A desk. A computer. A fridge.

The security men closed the metal door. A fan in the ceiling whirred.

Weber went to the fridge, opened the door.

Whistled.

'Water?' he asked.

Karen Nebel was four rooms away, in the general office, hunting for things on her computer. It was late now. Everyone had gone home. So she worked by the light of a desk lamp and the screen.

Went searching in the archives.

A sudden noise made her jump. Next to the office was the server room for the department. Humming computers and disk drives.

The light was on. Someone was in there.

Nebel walked to the door, saw a man crouching in the dark, shining a torch on the racks.

Uniform. Baseball cap.

'Hello?'

No answer. He moved along the line of servers. Seemed to find something he wanted.

'Excuse me,' Nebel said more loudly. 'This office is supposed to be closed.'

She could just see him pull a hard drive out of the housing, stuff it into his bag. Then he got up and made for the door, hand on his cap, pulling it down. Limping.

'I'm talking to you . . .'

Nebel didn't get closer. Didn't dare somehow.

When he was gone she sat down. Got her breath back. Felt she'd been close to something she didn't understand.

Another noise. Two shapes at the door. Weapons up.

Nebel let out a brief yelp.

Lund and Borch looked round.

'A man was here,' Nebel murmured. 'I think he took something.'

A series of quick questions. Then Lund was on the phone to security.

The briefest description.

A uniform.

A baseball cap.

A limp.

One camera had caught him heading for the service stairs leading down to the ground floor, then the basement.

Borch and Lund ran together. Winding stone steps. After a while they were in darkness. No sign of light switches; nothing to do but take out their torches again.

At the ground floor, nothing. She told Borch to look round. He hesitated.

'Just do it,' Lund whispered, then went for the stairs again, down into the basement.

Alone now. Just a torch and a gun. She walked slowly, carefully. One long cold corridor, white walls, stone floor.

A stain to the right. She looked: blood.

Another five steps. Another stain. The slam of a door in the shadows ahead.

Lund followed. Heating pipes murmuring. The sound of tiny animal feet scurrying close by.

She walked on. The corridor shrank until it was scarcely wide enough for two people next to the rumbling pipe by her side.

Finally a shape, caught in a security light.

'Stop now!' Lund yelled.

A face turned. She couldn't quite see it.

He had a piece of paper in his hands. Was lighting it with a match, raising the flame to the ceiling.

Smoke detector.

A bell rang somewhere. The flaming paper floated on a strong breeze.

Cold winter air.

When she looked again he was gone.

Lund ran round the corner, saw an open window, climbed through.

Rain on her face. Heart pumping. Ahead was the Christiansborg courtyard, cobblestones gleaming in the damp night.

She dashed across it, stood in the centre, turned on her heels, scanned every way there was.

Dark buildings behind. Ahead the city. Lights and traffic.

Someone joined her and she knew who it was. Didn't need to look.

Borch took a kick at an empty beer can left on the ground. Booted it over the cobbles and yelled a few obscenities into the night.

'Did that help?' Lund asked when he was done.

Karen Nebel hadn't seen much. Just a man in a blue uniform, baseball cap down over his face. He stole a hard drive from the server room.

'You let the man go?' she asked when there was a break in the questioning.

'Yes,' Lund agreed. 'That's what we do.'

A commotion at the door. A tall, familiar handsome figure. Troels Hartmann marched into the room, looked her up and down.

'You're never good news, are you, Lund? What the hell was this man doing here?'

Borch stayed back. She didn't.

'He's trying to find out where your car went on April the twentieth two years ago. Any clues?'

Hartmann glared at her.

'I sent through the transport details,' Weber cut in. 'After we talked—'

'But we didn't!' Nebel cried. 'Something's missing . . .'

'The campaign car's tracked, morning to night . . .' he continued.

'We're not talking about the campaign car,' Borch said. He looked Hartmann in the eye. 'It's yours. Your own car he's interested in. So are we.'

Weber got between them.

'OK. That's enough. We don't use personal transport during election campaigns. There's no point—'

'It was there,' Lund told him. 'A young boy saw it. Noted down the number. The day Louise Hjelby disappeared . . .'

'What the hell has this got to do with me?' Hartmann asked. 'Are you pulling your old tricks again?'

'You should be looking at Ussing,' Weber said. 'Not wasting your time here.'

'Ussing's in the clear. He had nothing to do with the girl's murder.'

Weber kept quiet. So did Hartmann.

'Emilie Zeuthen was kidnapped because we never got to the bottom of this case,' she went on. 'We have to follow every lead . . .'

Hartmann smiled. The old look, handsome and infuriating.

'Because this criminal demands it, Lund? Are you seriously saying you think we're involved somehow?'

'I didn't suggest—'

'The fact is,' Borch snapped, 'your fucking car was there. We know that. So just tell us who was driving, will you?'

'I don't like your tone—'

'I don't give a shit whether you like it or not, Hartmann!'

He jerked a thumb back to the server room.

'The drive he took had all the backup GPS records attached to this office. Official cars. Private ones. He's going to know who drove it. Where. When. Would be really nice if we knew that too.'

'I won't take this from the likes of you!' Hartmann yelled. 'Or her. You're accusing someone here of murder . . .'

'We'd like to sit down and talk about this calmly,' Lund suggested.

Weber crossed his arms.

'Forget it, Lund. The circus stops here. No one from this place was driving the car that day . . .'

Borch elbowed him out of the way, got in Hartmann's face.

'Someone ripped out the page with your number on it. We're being screwed around, Hartmann. I swear to God if it's you . . .'

'Don't talk to the Prime Minister like that,' Weber began.

Hartmann turned, started to leave. They followed, Borch dogging him, the security officers trying to get in the way.

One of them tried to put him in an armlock. Borch threw him off.

'Tell us who drove it. Tell us who got Schultz to close down the case.'

His hand went out, took hold of Hartmann's jacket. Borch had just about dragged him round when the bodyguards pounced and pulled him off.

Face red, hand jabbing at the tall man in the smart suit.

'We're going to find out. Don't think you can run from this one, Hartmann. She's not a teenage girl from Vesterbro this time . . .'

Silence.

Hartmann marched into the room ahead, then Nebel and Weber. The doors shut behind them.

Lund closed her eyes. Opened them.

'Oh. You're still here.'

'Maybe I went a bit too far . . .'

'No, no. You? Too far?'

She turned on her heels, went for the stairs.

'It was just terrific. Truly terrific.'

Robert Zeuthen hadn't listened. After Reinhardt reported back on what the police had found at the kidnapper's lair he ordered the search to spread out into international waters.

The Zeeland security people were back in the boardroom, briefing him and Maja, with Reinhardt adding in details he'd gleaned from Brix in the Politigården.

A map on a giant presentation screen showed the shipping lanes around the city. Brix had told Reinhardt that Emilie might be trapped inside a container taken as cargo. The logs showed twenty-three freighters in the Øresund on the night the kidnapper faked her death.

'The problem is, that's three days ago,' the team leader said. He hit a key on the computer. The dots started to fan out, all over Europe. 'The ships have moved, they've reloaded. The number Emilie could be on might have doubled. More. It's difficult—'

'I want every one checked,' Zeuthen insisted. 'Every ship. Every terminal.'

'Most of them are at sea,' Reinhardt said.

'Tell them to call into the nearest port. We'll foot the bill.'

The security men didn't say anything. It was left to Reinhardt.

'Even if the owners agree we can't cover every possibility. She could be ashore already. We have to leave this to the authorities . . .'

'What about the appeal?' Maja asked. 'Has anyone come up with something useful?'

Reinhardt shook his head.

'We've been inundated with calls. So have the police. Nothing of substance. Not yet.'

Zeuthen nodded and said, 'Notify the freighters as I asked. Keep answering the calls. I'll be in my office.'

He left the room. The men there didn't want to talk to her. A shape at the door. Carsten. She wondered how long he'd been listening.

He came in and asked if there was any news.

She asked him to wait. Walked to the office. A place she'd come to hate.

He stood by the window, phone in hand. Black jumper now. Jeans. An ordinary man, out of uniform.

'I'm calling Carl to say goodnight,' Zeuthen said.

He'd been crying. Eyes pink and watery.

'I just felt like hearing his voice,' he said with a shrug and the briefest moment of embarrassed laughter.

Then the tears came again, and so did hers.

'It's not your fault, Robert.'

'I didn't know about the iPad. That place in the attic where she was talking to him. About the cat. The hole in the fence. I let her down. Let you down. Everyone . . .'

Her hand tightened on his arm.

'Emilie was mad at both of us. You were . . . you are a good father.' She took a deep breath. Tried to form the words. 'You told me we'd find her. So we will.'

It happened so naturally. Her arms wound round him, his round her. A long, slow, warm embrace.

She was reluctant to let go. So was he. But there was Carsten Lassen, a sad reflection in the rain-soaked window, watching.

They didn't speak when they went to Lassen's car. Didn't speak as he drove her back into the city. A call from the office. More responses to the appeal. Nothing concrete. Just bounty-hunters.

She listened, said thanks, stared out of the passenger window at the damp night beyond.

The security people had set up a link on her iPad. Names, numbers, comments left by callers to the hotline. She ran through them on her lap.

'So many,' she murmured, mostly to herself. 'I don't know where we can—'

'If you dangle a hundred million kroner in front of people you can guarantee you're going to attract a bunch of lunatics.'

There was a hard, hurt tone to his voice.

He turned out of the docks, onto the main road.

'You can see what he's doing, can't you?' Lassen asked.

'He's trying to find our daughter.'

At that he snorted.

'Robert's the same man he always was. Controlling. Unreasonable. Uncaring . . .'

'Not now.'

'If he'd been a proper father this would never have happened. Maybe Zeeland are to blame anyway. They covered something up.'

The iPad updated. More names. More numbers.

'Robert and Zeeland aren't to blame for anything. The police said so . . .'

'Those idiots? What do they know?'

She kept looking at the iPad. Not him.

'He's using this to get you back,' Lassen said. 'I don't want to lose you. I'd do anything.'

His hand strayed from the wheel, brushed her leg.

'Just drive,' she whispered. 'I'd like to see my son.'

Juncker called from the factory. There were no signs that Emilie had left any clues, a scratch in the wall, a hidden number plate. Juncker thought she couldn't have been in the place long. The toilet hadn't been used. There was no trace of food.

They'd found fingerprints. Nothing on file. No new information from the homeless people living close by. But they had a photograph of Louise Hjelby's mother taken before she fell ill: a smiling woman in a bikini on a Spanish beach.

'He stole a hard drive,' Lund said. 'He's going to need a computer to see what's on it. You think that place was his main base?'

'He had everything here. Power. Light. Internet. I think so.'

'Let's assume he's on his own now. Start with the libraries and Internet cafes. I'll call you later . . .'

Brix was in the adjoining room. Dyhring had turned up. Borch was still livid about the row in Christiansborg. The two PET men had been arguing already.

When she went back they sat round the table, PET one side, police the other.

One piece of news from Dyhring: the kidnapper had broken into the van of the photocopier company and stolen the uniform and the ID.

He glared at Borch.

'I just watched the CCTV. He was limping. He's hurt. Really impressed you couldn't catch the bastard in those circumstances.'

Lund threw an evidence bag on the table. Inside was the notebook they'd recovered from the basement.

'Have we got Hartmann's car movements yet?' Brix asked.

'Still waiting.'

'For what?' Dyhring snapped. 'A few scribbles in a kid's notebook? Why the—'

'I wish I'd known about them this morning,' Brix broke in. 'When you said you'd told us everything you knew.'

The PET man shrugged.

'It was news to us.'

'A lot is,' Brix noted. 'So Hartmann's private car was definitely in Jutland?'

Dyhring threw up his hands.

'It was an election. We were too busy to keep a check on private cars.'

Borch picked up the bag with the book in it, took it out, flicked through to the back.

'Someone tore the page out, Dyhring. They did that for a reason. Someone was trying—'

'You don't know what you're talking about! It could have been Schultz. Could have been the boy.'

'And it could have been someone from PET who saw that book two years ago,' Lund said.

Dyhring waved at her, scowled.

'We need to demonstrate we want to solve the Hjelby case,' she insisted. 'That's the only way we can stay in touch with him.'

'Who's the victim here, Lund?' Dyhring was getting mad. 'Who's the criminal? We're here to find the bastard. Not do his bidding.'

Borch got to his feet, slammed both fists on the table.

'That's what we've been doing, dammit! With no help from the likes of you . . .'

A long silence. Dyhring got up, told Borch to join him outside.

He didn't move.

'Borch! Come with me.'

They went across the corridor. Lund and Brix could see them through the glass, arguing, yelling.

'I need you to go to the commissioner and ask him to approve a full search of Hartmann's offices,' she said.

'On the basis of a young boy's hobby of collecting number plates?'

'Then think of something else. If we're not seen to be doing something we'll never hear from him again.'

'I once nearly charged Troels Hartmann over a murder he had nothing to do with.'

'Because he lied to us. Lied and lied and lied.'

A shape in the door. Ruth Hedeby was there.

'I've had the container numbers sent to Zeeland,' Lund said. 'I'll check out how that's going.'

'Don't go till you hear this too,' Hedeby said. 'Since it's your doing yet again.'

Lund looked puzzled.

'What is?'

'I just got a formal complaint from the Prime Minister's office about your behaviour. Rudeness. Aggression. Unfounded allegations . . .'

'The rudeness was from Borch,' Lund said, pointing to the window. 'He's already apologized.'

'What the hell's going on here?' Hedeby demanded. 'First you try and pin a murder on one of the leaders of the opposition. Now the Prime Minister.'

Lund shook her head.

'No we didn't. We just asked them some questions. Ussing was trying to hide the fact he'd met Louise Hjelby. Hartmann . . .' A shrug. 'We still don't know why his car was in the area.'

She looked at Brix and waited.

'There was a sound reason for everything we did,' he said finally. 'I stand by it. As I stand by my officers.'

Hedeby waited then asked, 'Is that it?'

'What else do you want?'

'I want to hear about the iceberg when you see it,' she said. 'Not when it hits. No more surprises. From either of you.'

Then she left.

Thanks were never easy. For her to say. For Brix to hear.

Lund looked through the window. The office opposite was empty.

'We can do without PET,' Brix said.

It took a while for Hartmann to calm down. The rest of the parliamentary staff went home. A forensic team continued to work in the server room. Weber got a bottle of brandy, made him take a big drink, poured one for Karen Nebel and himself, sat down with the two of them in the study, listened, growing ever more glum.

'I'm not going through this again,' Hartmann complained. 'Lund can't do it to me twice over.'

'The election's on Friday, Troels,' Nebel said. 'I've got every reason to lean on Brix and keep her out of here.'

'Fuck the election!' he screeched. A stab at his chest. 'This is about me.'

'Drink your brandy,' Weber advised. 'Keep your cool.'

Hartmann glared at him.

'You don't know what it's like.'

'Actually, Troels. I do. I was there, remember.'

Favours done, then forgotten. They didn't come out of the Birk

Larsen case smelling of roses. Lund had good reason to resent the lack of cooperation she got back then.

'What the hell's my private car got to do with this?'

The whining wasn't going to stop. Weber could see that.

'Why is someone keeping tabs on it here?'

'Because you're Prime Minister,' Weber said gently. 'They have to.'

'Then work out who was driving, will you? It wasn't me.'

Nebel shrugged. Said the obvious. The transport details were on the hard drive the man had stolen. They were the backup copies. The originals were gone too.

'Back to business,' Weber said. 'I've cancelled all meetings for tonight. Tomorrow you've got to have breakfast with some business sponsors. After that—'

'I want those records,' Hartmann interrupted, staring at Nebel. 'I'm doing nothing until this is cleared up . . .'

'I'm looking!' she cried. 'The original's gone missing. The backups are with whoever stole them. I don't know who else—'

'Find somebody! How hard can it be?'

Weber got up, poured himself more brandy.

'You don't need to ask anyone else,' he said eventually.

Hartmann scowled and said, 'What do you mean?'

'I took the damned report. I got it out of the system as soon as I heard Lund was sniffing round this afternoon.'

He picked up his briefcase, found a printout, threw it on the desk.

'Benjamin was driving your car that day. He took it to Jutland. Sit down. Let's get this out of the way.'

Benjamin.

Kid brother. Almost a son to Hartmann. A pain in the arse. A clown. A joker. A tragedy waiting to happen. Twenty-six years old, acting like a teenager. Drink. Hanging round with left-wing extremists. God knows what else.

Not the kind of relative a man who craved to be Prime Minister wanted around.

'You didn't see him that day,' Weber said. 'I made sure of that. There was a demo in Copenhagen against the banks. PET had picked him up.'

'I should have known . . .' Hartmann whispered.

'You were in the middle of a campaign! Dyhring knew who he was. If it had been anyone else he might have wound up in court. But he talked to me. We agreed to let it ride.'

A sip of brandy. A guilty look.

'Seems Benjamin wasn't happy with that. He came home. Took your car keys. Drove off to Jutland to cause more trouble. He was writing stories, taking pictures for some anti-capitalist website or something—'

'You should have told me!'

A shrug.

'Maybe. But I didn't want you involved. He was in a bad way. Mad as hell. He'd had a few drinks. I didn't want that in the papers. I don't think he did either. He . . .'

The little man put his glass down, closed his eyes.

'He really admired you, Troels. It's hard to explain. I don't think he understood himself. But he loved you. Didn't want to harm you. He was just . . . lost I guess.'

Nebel asked, 'How long did he have the car?'

'All day,' Weber replied. 'I got a call from him around ten in the evening from a filling station outside Esbjerg. He'd run out of money. Run out of petrol. Didn't know what to do.'

'Did he meet the girl?' Nebel asked.

'No! He was just driving round, doing nothing. I put some petrol in the car and got him home. And that was it. Or at least . . . I thought so.'

Hartmann pointed an accusing finger.

'I want a full report on this. When he called. Where he went. Where you found him. Any other lies you want to get off your chest?'

Weber stiffened.

'I didn't lie to anyone. I just kept quiet. I didn't know anything about a murder. Besides . . . Benjamin didn't kill that girl. He was the gentlest human being I ever met. Too gentle. Too—'

'You can tell all that to the police.'

Weber and Nebel exchanged glances.

'We need to think this through,' she said carefully. 'If it comes out the wrong way people will think we've been pulling strings.'

'I don't give a damn. You've got to—'

A knock on the door. One of the media team was there. She looked worried, wanted Nebel to see something on TV.

Weber leapt up and switched on the set in the corner of the office. Brix, a late-night statement from the steps of the Politigården on the Zeuthen case.

'We're investigating a series of events in the Prime Minister's office,' he said. 'This is a routine inquiry. It will continue until we receive some satisfactory answers.'

Shouted questions over the line of TV mikes. Brix shook his head.

'I can't go into details and you wouldn't expect me to,' he insisted, eyes straight into the camera. 'All I can say is we will leave no stone unturned in the effort to get Emilie Zeuthen back alive.'

Nebel got to her feet.

'I'd better get in there for the phone calls. We'll need to make a holding statement.'

Then she left.

'So that's why you wanted to quit?'

The question seemed to puzzle Weber.

'Not at all. I was doing my job. The one I always do. Protecting your back. Last time round I had to save you from yourself. This time . . . it was your screwed-up little brother. All the same—'

'Get out of here.'

Weber didn't move.

'That's not the way to handle things, I'm afraid. I'll be gone soon enough. After you're elected . . .'

It happened so rapidly even Hartmann was barely conscious of what he was doing. He picked up the little man in the cheap, creased suit, dragged him, screaming, fighting to the door.

Threw him out into the Christiansborg corridor. Went to the window and stared out at the riding ground, the cobblestones gleaming in the slick rain.

There was an unexpected face in the Zeeland executive offices. Robert Zeuthen had to think for a moment before he could place the man. Then he went over to Reinhardt, furious, asked what Kornerup was doing there.

'What you've asked for is complicated, Robert. No one knows this business better.'

'I fired him.'

'Technically you didn't. The board haven't ratified anything. They've asked him to stick around and see this through.'

'Do my wishes mean nothing?' Zeuthen asked.

'They mean a lot. But we need experienced people around us. You have to put personalities to one side. If you don't we can't do this effectively.'

Kornerup was a great player of internal politics. More scheming than Zeuthen could ever be.

A call from reception. He walked out to the desk. Lund was there, pale, tired, nervous.

'Unless you're going to tell me you've found Emilie I can't see we've anything to talk about,' he said. 'You let the man go again. Now there's all this crap about Hartmann . . .'

'Forget about Hartmann. I sent you those container numbers . . .'

'The ones in port we've searched.'

'This man knows so much about you, Robert. He has to be a former employee . . . someone who's had contact . . .'

Reinhardt was eavesdropping and came over.

'We've been through all the staff records. I sent you the ones that met the criteria you specified.'

'There has to be someone else . . .'

Zeuthen got a phone call, walked away, angry.

Reinhardt, frowned, apologized.

'There isn't. We're very busy here, Lund. It's stressful. We're doing what we can.'

She still hadn't worked out what Reinhardt did for the Zeuthens. At times he seemed to run the company. At others he appeared to be little more than a servant.

'The murder in Jutland is the key to finding Emilie,' Lund said. 'The man who kidnapped her is the father of the girl who was killed. From what we know he worked in shipping.'

'What else can we send you?' he asked. 'Tell me. I'll do it. But honestly . . .'

'He knows computers. Knows weapons. How shipping works. He's intelligent. He wasn't some lowly sailor. It's in Zeuthen's interests . . .'

'Don't you dare tell me about Robert's interests. I know them better than anyone. I've looked after him since he was little.'

'Then help me! Maybe he's an engineer. A tech person. He didn't know the girl was dead so perhaps he wasn't here two years ago. If there was something . . .'

He had an immobile, passive face. But for a moment something seemed to move him.

'Back then the crisis was really hitting us, Lund. We had to lay off thousands of people. All over the world. We closed some companies. We took over others and got rid of staff.'

A nod, a sorry one.

'If you're really asking me to find you a disgruntled old employee of ours . . . I wouldn't know where to start.'

She thought about it.

'He's in his forties. Got a degree in engineering or technology. He served in middle or upper management. He's Danish. From Copenhagen. The accent . . .'

Reinhardt said nothing.

'Send me the records,' she added. 'We'll deal with them.'

'I'll do what I can,' he agreed.

She was about to go then his long arm came out and stopped her. Niels Reinhardt looked around and made sure no one could hear.

'Just so that we understand one another.'

'Yes?'

'If Emilie loses her life because of some old murder case you couldn't solve this will destroy Robert. His wife too.'

'I can appreciate that.'

'Can you appreciate the consequences?' he asked. 'Because I can't. Not for one moment.'

The call was from Maja. She was in the basement car park for some reason.

Zeuthen took the lift, went down there. Found them by his car. Maja. Carl. A couple of holdalls.

'Hi, Dad,' the boy cried, trying to sound cheery.

Just the sound of his young voice was cheering. Zeuthen smiled, ruffled his hair.

'What's up?'

She didn't want to look at him.

'I wondered if we could stay in the guest rooms.' A shrug. 'Just until we find something else.'

It came as a surprise. He took the bag, said of course.

Eyed Carl.

'We could get pizza from Toni's. Like . . .'

Like before.

He didn't dare say it.

'No anchovies!' Carl cried.

The old argument. A running joke.

Zeuthen folded his arms, looked stern.

'But I love anchovies.'

'No anchovies, Dad! Yeeucch. Extra cheese . . .'

It never palled.

A glassy look in Maja's eyes. She took her son's hand, walked towards the Range Rover at the end of the line.

'Anchovies for the daddy,' she said. A nod to Carl. 'Cheese for the boy.'

Happy.

This was what it felt like. Simple. Inexplicable. Real.

The three of them walked through the dank, airless car park and slowly her free hand reached out, found his.

Lund had pizza too. No anchovies. A very obvious police guard still stood outside her house when she got back. Two men she knew, cheerily asking for a piece.

Brix called as she went inside. Hartmann had been in touch to confirm his private car was in Jutland at the time of Louise Hjelby's murder, driven, without his knowledge, by his younger brother Benjamin.

The house seemed empty. Lund walked round calling for Eva.

'What was the brother doing there?' she asked.

'It sounds like he was a mess. Involved with drink and drugs. Some left-wing group.'

'Doesn't explain why he was in Jutland.'

'He was mad at Hartmann. PET had picked him up at a demo in the city. He wasn't going to be charged. Preferential treatment.'

She thought about that.

'Why didn't Morten Weber tell me?'

'Supposedly someone in admin mislaid the report when he asked for it. They're very apologetic.'

'I bet they are. Do we believe them?'

A pause then Brix said, 'I think so. Weber saw the brother when he drove out there. He took him back to the city. He'd run out of money. Was in a state. He's willing to give us a statement tomorrow.'

'You bet . . .'

On the fridge, above the ultrasound pictures was a note in a scrawled, childish hand. It read: *I've moved in with a friend. A thousand thanks for all your help. Hugs, Eva.*

'Hugs?' Lund said.

Brix asked, 'What?'

'Nothing. Let's bring in the brother.'

A sigh.

'Try and keep up. Benjamin Hartmann's dead. The inquest said it was an accident. He got hit by a train a couple of weeks after his brother won the election. PET say it was probably suicide. They don't think he could have been involved with the Hjelby girl.'

'Why?'

'He was a hippie or something. We'll look into it tomorrow. Keep your phone on. Let's hope our man calls.'

Lund got a beer, looked at the two pizzas. A vegetable one for Eva. Another packed with three kinds of meat for herself.

Eva's went in the bin. She sat down, began to eat from the box, drink from the bottle. There was a rap on the back door. A face there she didn't want to see.

Borch was back in rough clothes, seaman's hat pulled down low.

'I've been freezing out there for an hour. Is that pizza?'

'Only got one.'

He didn't say anything. Perhaps he saw.

'Can we talk for a minute? Or are you too pissed off with me?'

'One minute . . .'

He came in, closed the curtains. There was a document folder under his arm. He looked frozen, starving.

Lund retrieved the vegetable pizza from the bin and said, 'You can have some of that if you want. Doesn't she feed you?'

He eyed the beer. She sighed, got one from the fridge.

'You can't stay . . .'

'I'm not going to. If you've heard about Hartmann's brother you know they're hiding something. There's more to it than—'

'What do you want?'

He put the folder on the table, picked up a bit of pizza in his fingers. Popped the beer open, took a swig.

'This is a copy of our file on Benjamin Hartmann. I wanted you to have it. He was . . . known.'

'Brix said he was a hippie.'

'Yeah. A malcontent. Mixed with some of the protest groups. Bit embarrassing for big brother I guess.'

She put the documents to one side.

'You could have given me this tomorrow.'

'No. I couldn't. I won't be there. Dyhring's taken me off the case. I'm supposed to keep clear of everything to do with it. Hartmann. Zeuthen.' A pause. 'You.'

More pizza. He was always a delicate eater. More so than she was.

Borch looked at her, winced, said, 'I'm sorry I caused you so much trouble. I didn't mean to . . .'

'You don't have to say this.'

'I do, Sarah. I should have told you from the beginning. I really don't know what happened to the page in that notebook. Dyhring had it. It went into the system. When we thought there was nothing to it the boy got it back.'

And there he was again, just the way he'd been at the academy. Boyish, a little naive, desperate.

'I want to know you believe me. It matters. It . . .'

This was how it began so many years before. Lund stepped back, tried not to look at him. Didn't say anything at all.

His arm stretched out. She moved away again. Borch's head went down. He sniffed, took another swig of the beer.

'Thanks for the food,' he said then went out the way he came.

Twenty years they'd been apart. She was the one who brought them back together. It would never have happened without that sudden desperate need in Jutland.

Why?

Lund looked at the little house. The plants. The pictures on the fridge. The message that finished 'Hugs . . .'.

There was an ordinary life to be led, however much it had eluded her, however hard she tried to escape it.

And perhaps there, somewhere, lay happiness.

With Mathias Borch . . .

Her eyes drifted to the table. A folder with a name: *Benjamin Hartmann*. A photo inside of a young man with long hair and his brother's handsome, compelling features. But a different cast to his face too. Hartmann could be brittle, damaged at times. But not like his younger brother.

Perhaps . . .

The idea returned. She pushed it away. Tore another piece of pizza. Flicked through the pages. Buried herself there.

Eight

Wednesday 16th November

At ten thirty the next morning Troels Hartmann was doing his best to pretend it was business as usual. Nebel was with him for a public appearance at a school in the city. A posse of reporters and cameramen followed them from the car into the hall, lobbing questions about the car, his dead brother, the lack of progress in the Zeuthen case.

Hartmann kept quiet, walked into the school, broke into a wide smile for the young pupils lined up to greet him.

Handshakes. No questions from them except a request for souvenir photos while Nebel made some calls.

Afterwards, a brief private moment.

'Morten's with the police,' she told him. 'I'm telling the media it's a briefing.'

He nodded. Waved to the kids.

'I'm trying to get through to Zeuthen's man, Reinhardt. We need to clear the air there. No luck so far.'

'There's nothing to clear.'

'Best we tell him that. Also . . .' She looked down the corridor. 'It seems Ussing's gatecrashed the event.'

A look of fury in his eyes, and it was directed at her.

'Tell me that's a joke. We dictate who we appear with and when.'

'Well he's done it. The school's after money for a refurb. He's making promises. You've got a brief appearance together then some more photos with the kids in the yard.'

She passed him a piece of paper: a draft release from the Socialists about raising the local education budget.

'Spending money we don't have again,' Hartmann grumbled. 'Tell them we'll match it. Any other good news?'

'The police say they can't account for Benjamin's movements for twelve hours.'

'Morten can put them straight on that.'

'He can't. They still don't have an exact satnav record for the car. He killed himself two weeks later. The police are bound to think he's linked somehow . . .'

Hartmann got directions from a passing pupil, started walking for the hall.

'There's no connection, Karen. I knew my brother better than anyone. He was mixed up. Depressed. That's all.'

A smiling woman emerged. The head teacher. She asked Hartmann to wait in a side room for the audience to assemble.

Must have been a young class. The walls were covered with bright, imaginative paintings. Anders Ussing stood in front of them with his aide, Per Monrad.

'Bit of colour always brightens things up, don't you think?' he asked with a broad grin.

'True,' Hartmann murmured.

'Funny old world, isn't it? One minute those idiots in the police believe it was my car that picked up that girl before she was murdered.' The grin got wider. 'And now they think it was yours.'

Hartmann put his head to one side and looked at him.

'You met the girl, Anders. I didn't. Any more than my brother—'

'That's not what Lund reckons. She's on your tail again. Must be scary. Don't worry. I won't mention it.' He looked round the class. 'Not here.'

'Don't hold back on my account.'

Ussing laughed.

'You know that's exactly what my staff said. Morten took his time coming forward, didn't he? He and Mogens Rank are close. Are you sure they didn't lean on Schultz?'

'I'm sure.'

A nod. He finished his coffee.

'I guess you've got to say that. Otherwise things would look really bad with Zeeland and the Zeuthen girl. Two days to voting. How does it feel? As if it's coming your way?'

Hartmann walked to the window, looked out at the dismal playground, the grey, cold day.

Karen Nebel came over.

'You'll have to keep it short,' she said. 'Brix just called. They want to talk to you. They think Benjamin killed the Jutland girl.'

The night team had recovered the file on Hartmann's brother, and his medical record. Ten months before he died he'd been thrown out of college in America after an arrest during the Occupy Wall Street protests in New York.

Lund listened to Brix going through the details.

'He was being treated for depression. Diagnosed as bipolar. Had arrests for minor drug possession . . .'

Twenty-six years old. No real job. Permanent student. He had links with some extreme left-wing groups. Had written for a number of activist magazines and websites. After getting into an argument at a squat in the city he'd come to live in Hartmann's house, not that his brother was home much.

The most recent photo was from the PET files: long hair, a nose ring, tattoos. The punk stare at the camera. The inquest was told that in the last two weeks of his life he'd been disturbed, asking for medical treatment, complaining of headaches. Troels Hartmann had been busy forming a government, knew none of this. Then Benjamin walked in front of a freight train in Nørrebro.

'Morten Weber says he never went anywhere near where Louise Hjelby was in Gudbjerghavn,' Brix went on. 'He'd been driving round the countryside, following some of the campaign cars.'

'Any proof?' she asked.

Lund had been trying to call Eva all morning. Just getting voice-mail.

'None. On the other hand there are no records of violence. Of sexual aggression. He just sounds like a mixed-up teenager who never grew up. Did Zeuthen send any new employee records through?'

She shook her head.

'We can't wait for them. Zeuthen thinks he can handle this on his own. Hartmann's got to come up with—'

'Lund! The kidnapper's not phoned you. I put Hartmann in the frame to help you there. Doesn't seem to have worked, does it? And what are these?'

Scattered over the desk were a stack of files she'd got from the archives. Reports, names, photos from the Birk Larsen case. She should have cleared them away before he came in.

'I was just looking . . .' Lund started.

'That case is long dead. I don't want you trying to bring it back to life. Hartmann had nothing to do with that girl's death . . .'

'Doesn't mean there's nothing to learn.'

'If we put the Prime Minister through the emotional wringer for no good reason heads are going to roll round here.'

'It's got to be the brother!' she cried, jabbing at the photo. 'PET got him off a public order charge. Who's to say what else they hid along the way?'

He seemed to concede that point.

'I'm not arresting Hartmann. It's up to him if he wants to be interviewed. And don't place any great faith in the shit Borch feeds you either. We don't know what he and Dyhring got up to.'

Brix left it at that and followed her back to the office. Juncker had got nowhere tracing the stolen hard drive.

'The guy's got to have another place, Lund. He always has.'

But that was wrong. She could feel it. The man was hurt. Running out of options. Running out of time.

'What happened to Borch?' he asked.

She was looking at the photos on the wall: Emilie Zeuthen, Louise Hjelby, and now Benjamin Hartmann. Two dead. A third in jeopardy.

And a photo of a woman in a bikini, looking happy on a beach a long time ago.

'He's off the case. Did you get anywhere with Louise's mother?'

'Monika Hjelby. She lived by the yacht harbour. I'm trying to track where exactly. About Borch . . .'

'Forget about Borch! I told you. He's off the case. That's all I know.'

She went to the table, started sifting through the documents for no good reason. He followed.

'Was it because of you?'

'What?'

'Don't get mad. I just asked. Did you get him bumped because he screwed us around in Jutland?'

'I . . . don't . . . know. OK?'

'OK.' He shrugged. She could yell at him now and it made no difference whatsoever. 'I just asked because his wife's outside and she says she's not going anywhere until she's talked to you.'

A slight woman with a pale drawn face sat alone on a bench in the corridor. Looked up nervously as Lund came out, introduced herself, held out a hand that wasn't taken.

'I'm on my way to an appointment,' Lund added. 'If you'd called ahead—'

'Mathias came home late last night.'

Straight stare. Accusing. Miserable.

'He didn't come to bed.' Head to one side, eyes fixed. 'I found him in the living room. On the sofa.'

Lund looked at the door, tried to think of excuses.

'At first I thought he was obsessed with this case the two of you had.' A bitter, sarcastic smile. 'But it wasn't that, was it? He says he's in love with someone else. It's you, isn't it?'

No answer.

'You went to Jutland together. What happened then?'

'I didn't—'

'Don't say anything if it's just a lie. Don't . . .'

Silence between them. Only one voice to break it.

'Do you love him? Do you even know him? I don't give a shit you were a couple once. I don't care what was unfinished between the two of you.'

She started to cry, to shake. People nearby could hear. Looked embarrassed.

'We've got two little girls. He's their dad. Don't take him from us.'

One moment waiting for an answer. When it never came she turned and left. Angry footsteps down the long Politigården corridor.

Then Brix breezed in.

'We're on. Hartmann's willing to talk. Christiansborg.' He peered at her. 'You all right?'

'Yes,' she whispered without thinking.

*

303

Kornerup was back at his desk when Zeuthen came into the Zeeland offices that morning. He looked as if he'd never been away.

'Everyone sympathizes with you, Robert,' he said. 'But there's still a business to run. And all these demands you're making. They're exceedingly complex.'

'You'll do what's necessary then clear out.'

Kornerup smiled.

'Your fellow directors have asked me to . . . stand guard in the meantime.'

Along the corridor a door opened. Men in suits, a couple of women walked out. The board.

'There was an informal meeting this morning. It seemed best not to engage you and Reinhardt. You were busy, understandably, with trying to find your daughter.'

'I can block this,' Zeuthen said.

'True. But that's all you can do. You don't have the votes to force through an alternative. If you force a stalemate the markets will hear. We'll be easy meat for a predator. The share price is dismal enough already.'

Reinhardt was arguing with two of the men who'd left the meeting. Angry words there.

A hand went to Zeuthen's arm. Kornerup's beady eyes shone through the owlish glasses.

'You take care of your family. Leave the rest to me. We can see this through then assess the situation in a week or so.' A pause. 'Though it may be that we have to offload some operations more quickly than that. The stock . . .'

Zeuthen blinked, fought to keep hold of his temper.

'We've a deal in place with Hartmann . . .'

'And what's that worth?'

'Zeeland stays here.'

'Hartmann's being investigated. I wouldn't place much faith in him frankly.' He checked his watch. 'You must excuse me. I have a conference call with Shanghai.'

He walked off. Back in harness.

Reinhardt came up, still furious.

'I knew they were muttering behind your back. I'd no idea they'd go this far.'

'You let him in, Niels.'

The accusation hurt.

'To help us with the shipping! That's all.' He shook his grey head. 'Perhaps I should have realized. He's a cunning old bastard. I'll make sure he keeps out of your way. He talks to me only from now on.'

The shipping monitors were alive again. Security estimated Emilie might be on any of fifteen different freighters at sea, or six terminals around Europe. Most of the ports had been checked but Rotterdam, Hamburg, Stavanger and St Petersburg were refusing to open up shipments without the permission of the owners.

'The police won't help, I'm afraid,' Reinhardt added.

'We'll approach them directly. I can take Hamburg and Rotterdam. You go to Stavanger and St Petersburg.'

'Robert . . . is it really feasible he could have done this? I know the police found those papers. But . . . why?'

'What else should I do?'

'I don't know. Perhaps something here.'

'The board don't listen to me. Kornerup doesn't. Are you joining them?'

Reinhardt shook his head.

'I served your father through thick and thin. I do that for his son too.'

Zeuthen slapped a hand on his arm. A brief smile.

'Then sort out the plane.'

A grand room in Christiansborg, winter sun through leaded windows. A landscape of the old harbour. A marble fireplace and walnut bookcases. Lund sat one side of the table with Brix and Dyhring. Hartmann on the other, next to Karen Nebel. No Morten Weber, which seemed odd. The man seemed a little lost without his political adviser, kept looking round the room as if counting the furniture, the paintings, the fittings, like someone about to be dispossessed of a home he loved.

Then he pulled himself together, looked at her and said, 'I never knew Benjamin was in Jutland that day. He took my car without my knowledge. Not that I believe for one moment—'

'So why didn't Morten tell you?' she asked.

'For Benjamin's sake. In case I got mad with him. For my sake in case I worried.'

There was something in Hartmann's gaze she hadn't seen before. A touch of self-knowledge. Of doubt.

'I wish he had. Morten wishes it too. But we were stuck in the madness of an election. You don't think about anything but the result. Friends. Family . . .'

Lund looked at the two men next to her. Neither wanted to speak.

'Louise Hjelby was raped and killed in a boatyard. Your brother was in the area—'

'The Prime Minister's aware of the case,' Dyhring said abruptly. 'You don't need to waste his time going over old ground.'

She looked at the PET man. At least she and Brix now knew where they stood.

'Benjamin was being treated for depression. He'd been diagnosed as bipolar. Arrested at a demonstration in the city. Kicked out of America for much the same—'

'Lund!' Dyhring said. 'We know all this.'

'Then you know why I'm asking.' She turned to Hartmann again. 'How was he after the episode in Jutland? Did he change?'

A shrug.

'It was an election. I was on the road. We barely spoke.' He closed his eyes, grimaced. 'There was no time. Never was. Even before.'

A short note of laughter.

'I told him if I lost we'd go on holiday. The Alps or somewhere. Barricade ourselves in a hut up the mountains and just walk, hour after hour, day after day.'

He leaned forward, hands together, eyes on her.

'I knew Benjamin wasn't well. He knew it too. We were trying to work on it. He was seeing specialists at the hospital. They all said the same thing. It was going to take time.' Hartmann frowned. 'We didn't have it.'

'What did he do all day?' Brix asked.

'He listened to music. Watched TV. Messed around on the computer for hours on end. And . . .' A sour glance. 'You know what he did. He was hanging round with some of these left-wing, anarchist creeps. That's where PET picked him up.'

'Embarrassing for you,' Lund observed.

'Not really,' Hartmann shot back. 'It's hardly unusual to have a troubled adolescent in the house. It's just that mine was twenty-six and didn't want to grow up. He was never violent. Not even aggressive really. He was just lost and I didn't find the time to help him. That's my cross to bear . . .'

Nebel tapped her watch.

'We've answered all your questions. The Prime Minister has important engagements—'

'Benjamin killed himself!' Lund cried. 'Don't you want to know why?'

'He was depressed,' Hartmann whispered.

She pulled out a sheet of paper bearing the logo of the university hospital.

'It was more than that. The day before he died he asked for an urgent appointment with his consultant. This is the report. He wanted extra medication. He said he was suffering from anxiety attacks. He wanted to know if the hospital would admit him.'

'May I see that?' Hartmann asked.

She handed over the report.

'They wanted him to come back with you and discuss it. But when they said that he told them he'd done something you'd never forgive. Do you have any idea what that might be?'

The room was so still, so silent. Hartmann could do nothing but stare at the medical record.

Then, in a low, uncertain voice he said, 'The day before he died I did come home. Very late. I just . . . just thought he was asleep. No music. No TV. I thought that was a good sign.'

He grabbed the carafe, poured himself some water.

'I was in the kitchen. Benjamin came downstairs. He had these brochures for Switzerland. Some catalogues for mountain clothes. Tents. All that stuff . . .'

'Troels,' Nebel said and put her hand on his. 'You don't have to do this.'

'No. This needs saying.' He looked at Lund. 'I knew there was something he wanted to talk about. But I think he could see I was wiped out. So in the end he said it didn't really matter. He just wanted to show me the travel brochures.'

Hartmann almost broke then. Had to wait for a moment to compose himself.

'But we'd won, hadn't we? I told him I couldn't make it that year. Not with the work we had on. Maybe another time.' He shut his eyes in anger. 'As if . . .'

A nod of the head. A moment of self-hatred.

'I got up the next morning. I was going to make him breakfast. I thought we were getting somewhere finally. But then I went to his room and his bed was empty. He was gone and that was the last . . .'

Nebel's hand squeezed his. A man came to the door. Dyhring got up and spoke with him in the corner.

'I let him down so badly,' Hartmann said. 'But he didn't hurt that girl. He could never have done something like that. It's not—'

'We need the car,' Lund cut in. 'Forensics can find traces going back years—'

'This is ridiculous!'

High voice, pained eyes, Hartmann glared at her and she saw him now the way he was in the Politigården six years before, bringing down the wrath of a murder inquiry simply to avoid the revelation of another personal tragedy.

'Benjamin would never—'

'This has to end here,' Lund said, getting cross. 'What did he say that night? Did he mention the girl? There was something on his mind . . .'

Dyhring walked over. He had an iPad from the man who'd come in.

'It doesn't matter what he said. Benjamin's innocent.'

He placed the tablet on the table. There was a map there, and a car route.

'We've recovered the stolen hard drive from an Internet cafe in Vesterbro. The satnav tracks show exactly what we've been told. The Prime Minister's private car went nowhere near the boatyard, nowhere near the harbour.'

Lund grabbed the iPad, looked at the map.

'I want everything you have, Dyhring. I want to go over—'

Hartmann swore, got up, walked out. Karen Nebel leaned over the table.

'I expect a full and public apology. If it's not out there within the hour this will go further.'

She left. Then Dyhring. Then, after a single bitter glance, Brix.

*

308

Outside with nothing but her folder, no idea where to go next, who to call.

He was standing by the palace steps, leaning against the wall.

'Not now,' she whispered, looking at him.

Then Borch was on her.

'What happened? What did Hartmann say?'

She walked to her car. He dogged her every step, pleading.

'Sarah . . .'

'Hartmann's Mercedes was nowhere near Louise. The satnav proves it.'

'What satnav?'

'Dyhring's people found the hard drive. I haven't heard from the kidnapper. We don't have a clue where Emilie is.'

She looked at him.

'They did you a favour pulling you from this one. We're in for a kicking.'

He was shaking his head.

'Dyhring can fake satnav records if he wants. He can do anything he damn well likes. Did you ask Hartmann about his brother—?'

'Yes! Yes!' She turned, gestured at the palace. 'Go and interrogate him yourself if you don't believe me.'

Then she climbed into her car. He was in the passenger seat before she could lock the door.

'Have you still got the kid's notebook?'

'We've checked all thirteen black cars listed on that day. Nothing fits.'

Borch held out his hand and said, 'Gimme.'

Lund growled. Did it anyway. Borch flicked through the pages, and the reports that came with them.

'Hang on. One of the people you chased was a woman who said she's never even been to Jutland.'

Lund looked through the window, kept quiet.

'Maybe the kid got the date wrong,' he went on. 'Or the number or something. Sarah . . .'

Still staring ahead at the lifeless day she said, 'Your wife came to see me this morning.'

Borch clutched the notebook to him, kept quiet. She turned and looked him in the eye.

'I don't want you to ruin everything . . . your family, their lives . . . over me.'

He shut up then. Her phone rang. Juncker.

'I heard about the hard drive, Lund. He's going to be very pissed off when he finds he's been wasting his time.'

'True,' she agreed.

'I've got a name for someone who knew Monika Hjelby. Birthe. She lives at the yacht harbour. Expecting a visit. I'm going to check out what PET found at the Internet cafe. Can you handle her?'

'Text me an address.'

'Thanks.'

The message came through straight away. Asbjørn Juncker never waited on anything. Lund reached over and popped open the passenger door.

'He won't give up, Sarah.'

'I've got to go now.'

Borch got out. She drove off. It was only when she was in traffic that Lund realized he'd kept hold of Jakob's notebook.

Reinhardt had fixed the plane for Rotterdam: flight plan filed, fuel and pilots booked, arrangements made at the other end. He went through the details in Zeuthen's office.

'I'm going to have another word with Kornerup after that,' he added. 'Make sure the man doesn't step out of line.'

'Good luck,' Zeuthen said, got up, nodded, smiled. 'And thanks. I appreciate it.'

'Don't mention it, Robert. It's why I'm here.' A short laugh. 'Why I live on the job.'

They were by the window overlooking the port. Ever since Zeuthen could remember Niels Reinhardt had a house and an office in the grounds, not far from the water. Another sign he was part of Zeeland, and seemed to have been for ever.

'Take a break some time,' Zeuthen suggested.

'Not till we've got Emilie back. Besides Annette's in the house in France, staying there with the girls. I'm just a bachelor boy. I want to do what I can. I'll call with any news.'

Zeuthen got his jacket and his briefcase, was about to leave for the airport when one of the security team came in. Someone had turned up in reception. A yachtsman claiming he saw something the night Emilie disappeared after the incident at the bridge.

'We've talked to him as much as we can. He's demanding to see you. I think . . .' He rubbed his fingers. 'It may just be for the money. We've got him next door.'

Zeuthen asked his assistant to tell the airport he'd be late for the flight then went to the empty office where they'd taken the visitor. He wore a green oilskin jacket in spite of the heat. Thick heavy glasses. A woollen hat. The face was coarse and weather-beaten, unshaven, not quite a beard. A stocky man, powerful. Unusual.

The story.

Four nights before he'd been sailing the Øresund in his dinghy. It was three in the morning, freezing cold. He was sitting at the helm.

'All of a sudden I heard a speedboat going by very quickly.' His voice was Danish, local. Cultured. 'It didn't have any lights which I found a bit odd. You've got to have lights.' The man pointed out of the window. 'You're shipping people. You know that.'

'And then?' Zeuthen asked, glancing at his watch.

'Not long after I passed a coaster. Not a big vessel. Then I saw the speedboat again. It had berthed by the side. They put down a ladder. I saw a child walk up ahead of a man.'

'Four nights ago?' the security officer asked. 'And now you come to us? Not the police?'

His head went to one side. He peered at Zeuthen through the thick glasses.

'I've been sailing. I didn't know till I got back. Then I tried to phone the police but it was impossible to get through. You don't seem grateful.'

Zeuthen shook his head.

'Let me understand this. You say you saw my daughter on the Øresund while you were out on a yacht. At three in the morning. In the dark. The winds were strong that night . . .'

'They were,' the yachtsman agreed.

Zeuthen got to his feet, glanced at the security officer and said, 'Show him out. I'm going to the airport.'

The yachtsman laughed, shook his head. Smiled.

'Why's it so hard to be believed when you're telling the truth, Mr

Zeuthen? She was about a metre and a half tall. I'd guess around forty kilos.'

Zeuthen stopped, listened.

'She had long blonde hair. Straight. Very blonde I'd say. Black trainers. Blue raincoat. No life jacket.'

Robert Zeuthen came back, took the chair again.

'I couldn't help but see,' the man insisted. 'I was bobbing up and down thirty, forty metres away. They had lights on the deck. Lights to help that little girl up the ladder. And the man. They knew what they were doing. It was very clear.'

He leaned back, stretched his arms, looked to one side.

'I don't know if I should say this. It's a bit embarrassing.'

'Say what?'

'It looked as if she was waving. At me. Children do that, of course. I should have realized something was wrong.'

Heart in mouth, Zeuthen asked, 'Did you see the name of the coaster.'

A nod of the head.

'Oh yes. Of course.'

'What—?'

'I'd like to tell you. But you're a businessman. You understand we have to deal with the practicalities first.'

The security officer stiffened, glared at him. Zeuthen waved at him for silence.

'If what you're telling me's the truth you can have the reward as I promised. I'm a man of my word.'

A laugh. A nervous finger scratched at the woollen hat.

'I don't doubt it. All the same I would like some kind of guarantee. A token of good faith.'

'Such as?' the security officer asked.

He thought for a moment then said, 'A written contract, properly witnessed. And two per cent of the reward up front. In cash. That'll do.'

'We don't have that kind of money here,' Zeuthen told him.

He relaxed back into the chair, looked out of the window at the ocean.

'No rush.'

Zeuthen snapped his fingers at the man next to him. Told him to make the arrangements.

When he was gone he looked at the yachtsman.

'This is my daughter we're talking about. Every minute matters.'

Not a flicker of emotion.

'I understand that,' the man replied. 'All the same I'd rather wait.'

He rolled the chair from side to side.

'A cup of tea would be nice. Milk. No sugar.'

They got a PA to fetch one and left him there.

Alone. A cup of tea. He went to the computer. The last user had logged off. So he typed in a new user name, a fresh administrator password. Found himself staring at a wide-open network, wondering where to roam.

The yacht harbour had seen better days. Lund parked next to a rotting rowing boat on a deserted quay and double-checked the address. It looked like a maritime junkyard not a home. Lifebelts, ropes, anchors, broken masts. At the back, next to a two-storey corrugated-iron building with a few plant pots on the stairs, was a woman in a long work jacket, sorting through boxes.

'Birthe?' Lund asked, pulling out her ID.

She had shoulder-length black hair, and swept it back from a suspicious face.

'If you're here about the pilfering you're too late.'

'I'm not. You knew Monika Hjelby. Louise's mother. We're looking into the girl's death.'

'Too late for that too.' She nodded at the stairs. 'I let Monika the flat up there for ten years. Long gone now.'

'All the same,' Lund said. 'Can we talk?'

Inside it was tidy, clean, organized. The two women had met through the cafe where Monika worked.

'She was pregnant. A bit posh. No money. She said she needed a place for a couple of months. After that the father was going to be back. But . . .'

Birthe sighed.

'Men,' she murmured. 'So Monika stayed.'

'You never met Louise's dad?'

'She went on about some guy. He never showed up. She reckoned he had money. Was a class act.'

'In what?'

'I don't know. She used to get all secret if you asked. I'd tell you but then I'd have to kill you. All that stuff.' She laughed. 'I liked Monika but really . . .' A finger twirled at her head. 'She was away with the fairies mostly.'

Lund wanted it straight.

'So she never had a man stop by?'

'Not while she was alive. Some guy called a couple of years ago. Said he was an old friend. Wanted to see her.'

'And?'

A shrug.

'I told him to look in Amager cemetery.'

'And Louise?'

'He didn't know she had a daughter. Big surprise I think. She was in the children's home by then.'

Lund asked what he looked like. The woman frowned.

'Just kind of ordinary. I don't really remember. He definitely didn't know Monika had a kid. I never saw him after that. Never gave it much thought.'

Phone call. Lund took it and an urgent voice said, 'This is Eva Lauersen's midwife. I need to talk to your son.'

Birthe was starting to look bored.

'This isn't a good time,' Lund said.

'Eva was brought in last night with severe abdominal pain. The baby could be premature.'

She went to the window.

'Is it serious?'

'We really need to talk to Mark.'

'I'll try and get hold of him.'

Grey water. Dead land.

When she turned the woman had gone back down the stairs, was sorting through the boxes again. Looking for pennies in a pile of junk.

On the way to the car Lund said, 'Do you know which children's home Louise was in?'

Birthe stopped for a moment.

'It wasn't a council home. I know that. They were all full. Monika went to a charity when she knew she was dying.'

Keys. Phone. She wondered where Mark had vanished to.

'What charity?'

'She wanted things to be right for Louise. I helped her write lots

314

of applications.' The woman scowled. 'Why do I call them that? Begging letters. That's what they were. For a dying mother who just wanted to do the right thing for her kid.'

Her gnarled hands pulled at a piece of netting, threw it to one side.

'Only one of them was interested. Zeeland. Monika was dead happy. Apparently they liked unmarried mothers.'

Lund came back.

'Zeeland? You're sure?'

'I'm sure. They've got the money, haven't they? I still feel sorry for that poor couple though. That girl of theirs . . . They help all those kids and have to deal with this shit.'

'Where was the home?'

She thought for a moment.

'Jutland somewhere. I think.'

On the way back from another debate Karen Nebel turned on the TV in the car. The interview hadn't gone badly. Ussing kept making the same points over and over again, about hidden agendas and cover-ups. But he had no ammunition and knew it. If anyone came out on top it was Hartmann.

'I heard from Zeeland while you were on air,' she said. 'They're still behind us. The polls continue to look good. You don't need to be downcast.'

Another evening in Copenhagen. Traffic. People struggling through the rain.

'Is that all there is? Polls?'

'No,' she answered, trying not to get cross. 'There's an election the day after tomorrow. A weekend forming a government. The chance to start again. You've got the public behind you. Zeeland. Your team—'

'That time in Jutland . . . did you know? Did Morten mention it at all?'

'For God's sake . . . can't we leave that behind? The police understand it's nothing—'

'Did you know?'

'He never mentioned it. I'd no idea Benjamin was out there. Why?'

He turned off the TV.

'Lund was right. He did change. I don't know why I never noticed. It's clear to me now.'

'It's called hindsight, Troels. No great mysteries there. Don't let that woman get to you. Morten's made a statement. You've got nothing to worry about.'

A dry laugh.

'This is politics, Karen. There's always something unpicking itself in the background. It's just that we can't see it yet.'

Ten minutes later. A reception in one of the city halls. String quartet playing, waiters with champagne and canapés. Donors to be thanked. Supporters to be greeted.

First face when he came through the door: Weber in a dinner suit, black bow tie, untidy hair, taking him to the line of guests.

Small talk. A speech, off the cuff. He could do that so easily now.

Then Weber got him in a corner, raised his glass.

'I watched you on TV with Ussing. You wiped the floor with him.'

'Don't mention it.'

Weber caught something in his answer, didn't speak.

'What I meant was,' Hartmann added, 'don't mention the argument we had last night. The fight. The reason. That's what you do, isn't it? Bury yesterday, just think about today and then tomorrow.'

'Seems to work.'

They were alone. No one could hear.

'What really happened in Jutland?' Hartmann asked.

Weber hesitated.

'Haven't we done this one to death?'

'No. Something changed. Benjamin was different. I'd like to know what that was.'

A waiter came up. Weber grabbed for a fresh glass.

'Just leave this alone, will you?'

Hartmann bent down, stared into his face.

'What happened, damn it? I want to know.'

Weber looked round, guided him out to the lobby.

No one there. Just polished stone and the dead faces of august statues.

'He called me from the bus station. He was really upset.'

'You mean he did see the girl?'

'Forget the girl. Benjamin was in a mood. He'd been driving round taking pictures for one of those stupid websites. They wanted him to cause some trouble in front of the press.'

'No,' Hartmann insisted. 'He wasn't like that.'

Weber nodded.

'He wasn't. Which is why he felt so bad that he nearly did it. It wasn't his fault. He'd been hanging round with all those lunatics and swallowed their propaganda. About how we were brown-nosing big business by reaching an accord with Zeeland. I'd talked to him about this before. Told him it was crap—'

'You?' Hartmann jabbed a finger in his face. 'He was my brother. He should have had that conversation with me.'

'Yeah, well. You weren't there. And I needed you to focus on the campaign. He could have screwed things up for us. We worked too hard for that election for Benjamin to ruin it.'

'So what did you do?'

'I told him to shut his trap and drove him back to Copenhagen. He was hysterical. Going on about how they were planning to run to the press with this story he'd given them. Honestly, he was as mad as a—'

It happened without a second thought. Hartmann slapped him hard in the face, bent down, said, 'Tell me what he saw.'

Weber didn't step back. A quarter-century of friendship, of struggle between them. It seemed distant at that moment.

'He thought Karen was in Zeeland's pockets. She was organizing meetings behind your back. Cutting deals . . .'

'What meetings?'

Weber shrugged.

'I wasn't a part of this. Don't ask me. Benjamin said someone came down from Zeeland HQ and had a chat with her. He saw them. He didn't know who he was scared of the most. Those nutters from the website who wanted to run the story. Or you if you found he'd been spying on us. So I took him home and I told him to shut up and forget about the whole thing.'

'That's it?' Hartmann whispered.

He could see her in the hall. Smiling, glad-handing the crowd.

'That's . . . it.' Weber raised a finger. 'Apart from one thing.'

Hartmann waited.

'We were a week away from the election and running out of budget when we went to Jutland. When I got back to the office there was cash in the bank.'

It took an hour and a half to make arrangements for the money. Zeuthen waited in his office. Got a message from Reinhardt saying he'd persuaded Kornerup to back off on company issues for a while. Then he called Maja, told her, and she was there straight away, demanding to see the yachtsman.

'There's no point,' Zeuthen said. 'He won't talk until we give him something.'

'What kind of man is he?'

'We think he saw her,' Zeuthen said. 'His description . . .'

The head of security walked in, didn't look at him, said, 'The police are here to interview the witness.'

Asbjørn Juncker stood behind him.

'I didn't call them!' Zeuthen yelled.

The man didn't budge.

'I'm sorry, sir. I had no choice.'

'We're here to help you get Emilie back,' Juncker added. 'It's up to you where you throw your money. We can verify his story . . .'

'He described her blonde hair, blue raincoat . . . He knew . . .'

Juncker took a deep breath.

'He couldn't have seen her in a blue raincoat. We found those clothes at the place he'd kept her. I saw her at the window when he was taking her out of that factory down the docks. Saturday. The same day. She was wearing something dark.'

Zeuthen swore, dashed down the corridor. Into the room. Empty.

Juncker went to the receptionist. The yachtsman had asked how to get down to the basement.

'He said he had to pick up something from his car,' she added. 'I saw him using the computer. Was that OK?'

Juncker checked by the chair. There were a few splashes of blood.

He looked at the security man and said, 'Close off the building.'

Over to the lifts: Zeuthen, Maja, Juncker together.

It seemed to take for ever to get to the basement. Bare parking area, half full of shiny cars, mostly black.

Juncker was running, gun in one hand, phone in the other, trying to get Brix.

Maja stood and stared at Zeuthen, scanning the rows.

'Why's he here, Robert? What does he want?'

'I don't know . . .'

The place looked empty. He'd vanished again.

Arms folded, she leaned back against a pillar, looked at him.

'I don't know!' Zeuthen said, half-shouted, again.

Half a kilometre away in a low building by the waterfront Lund was pushing a doorbell. Odd place. Half office, half home by the looks of it. Tidy flowers and shrubs maintained around the front door. Computers and a large desk in a room behind. And just a few steps away the harbour, a short pier, black water, waves rippling in the moonlight.

An answer finally. The tall, erect figure of Niels Reinhardt came to the door. He seemed surprised to see her.

'Your PA said you were here.'

'I usually am. What more do you want, Lund? We've sent you all the personnel records we could find.'

She looked behind him. Waited. A polite man.

'Come in,' Reinhardt said, opening the door. 'But please be brief. I have to go to Kastrup.'

It wasn't what she expected. More modern. More stylish. Reinhardt had the outward appearance of a genial, elderly uncle. But there were abstract paintings on the walls, wooden statues that looked as if they came from Africa. A personal touch that seemed somewhat against the grain.

She wondered about his age. Sixty? Sixty-five? Not as old as she first thought. And he moved easily, briskly.

'It's about the Zeeland Children's Fund. I gather you're involved . . .'

He walked into the office, turned on more lights.

'The fund? Why do you want to know about that?'

'It's probably just a dead lead. I want to rule it out.'

He looked at her for a moment then pulled open a filing cabinet and took out some brochures.

'Robert's father was a good Christian. He believed in charity, helping the weak. Zeeland developed a corporate social responsibility long before such things became fashionable.'

He fanned out the brochures.

'We've got clinics and homes for children. In Denmark, of course. But also in Africa, the Middle East. Asia. It's quite an investment. One we've had to prune a little lately but . . .'

They stopped by a long window with a view back to the pier and the sea beyond.

'Why's this relevant?'

'Louise Hjelby was in one of your homes for a while. It was called Majgården.'

He nodded.

'I remember the name.'

'It closed three and a half years ago. There are no records left.'

Reinhardt frowned.

'As I said these are hard times. We don't keep records here I'm afraid. You really must excuse me. Robert wants me to take a plane to St Petersburg. There's a ship there . . .'

He got his briefcase.

'Emilie was taken by Louise's father. For some reason he didn't know he had a daughter. I think he went to the children's home to try to find her. Then . . .'

Reinhardt listened, looked interested.

'How can I help?'

'If there's someone he might have talked to. Left a name.'

A shake of the grey head.

'I need to get to the bottom of this if I'm going to find Emilie. Just a contact for Majgården . . .'

'Let me see what I can find. I'll look in the secretary's room. You wait here.'

When he was gone she started to poke around.

On the desk more wooden statues from Africa. On the sideboard behind a line of souvenirs. Chinese. Indian.

And photographs. She always had to look at those.

There were six in a line. She bent down to look.

The phone went.

'It's Borch.'

The first picture was of a group of children. Girls mainly. Black. Africa judging by the dry bush behind. Eight kids, grinning for the camera. Reinhardt stood in their midst, arms around two of them, holding them tight. Laughing in a way she'd never seen.

'There's a reason you couldn't find the car, Sarah.'

'What's that?'

The second photograph. Indian girls. Reinhardt among them. One was sitting on his lap.

'The numbers were written down by a seven-year-old kid. He made a mistake.'

Next shot. This one had a caption: *Guatemala.* Kids in native dress. A young girl behind Reinhardt, her arms winding round his neck.

'He reversed the first letter. He wrote a Z when he meant to write an S. That's why we were chasing a woman who'd never been to Jutland.'

Every photo looked innocent. It was just a kindly old man with orphans in a children's home his company funded. They all seemed happy. No sign of apprehension. Fear. Concern.

'Here's the thing.' A pause. 'If you reverse the letter you get a Zeeland car. It's not hard. If I can see this our man surely can.'

Fourth photo along. Denmark. A sign: *Majgården.* A group of girls, none of them more than twelve. Blue and white smock dresses. Pretty faces. Not quite so happy. But it was a cold, dull day, and the only smile was the tall, grey-haired man at the back, his hand on a young girl's shoulder.

Possessive. That was the word. Lund looked more closely. It wasn't Louise. She was two along, unsmiling, dark-haired, dark-eyed. As if she knew already.

'I checked the number,' Borch went on. 'It's—'

'Niels Reinhardt,' she cut in.

Lund picked up the photo, held it, tried to think.

'He's been hiding behind Robert Zeuthen all along,' Borch said.

A sound from behind. Lund slipped the picture back onto the shelf.

He was there, looking directly into her face. Black suit, black tie. No smile. She wasn't a child.

A note in his hand.

'I've found you a name and a phone number.'

Borch in her ear asking where she was. Lund cut the call.

'The head of the fund secretariat,' Reinhardt added. 'She may be able to help. I can't guarantee it, I'm afraid.'

She took the paper.

'Now I really have to go,' he said.

A routine. He went to the wall, turned on some kind of security.

'You knew about Majgården,' she said. 'You went there.'

He picked up his briefcase.

'I'm the chairman of the fund. I don't have much time. But I always try to get out and wave the flag when I can.'

She retrieved the photo, pointed to the picture of Louise Hjelby.

'Did you know this girl?'

'No. I visited all the homes when I could. Who is it?'

'She's—'

A siren drowned out her words. The whoop of a burglar alarm. Reinhardt's eyes went straight to the security panel on the wall. One red light flashing.

'I'm sorry,' he said. 'The basement circuit plays up sometimes. There must be an open window.'

'Stay here,' Lund ordered, opened her coat, took out her gun.

Four steps towards the window. The lights went out. Every last one of them. Torch in her hand, eyes adjusting to the darkness. Black water making a pattern beyond the glass.

Lund looked. Heard something. Walked forward, down the steps, into the shadows below.

Hartmann left the reception with Karen Nebel. She'd had a briefing from Brix. The kidnapper had got into the Zeeland building and demanded money, then vanished.

'Again?' he asked.

'We've got a meeting with the Agricultural Council next. The vote's a bit weak in that sector. It might be an idea—'

'I don't want to be talking about horseshit when Emilie Zeuthen's life's on the line.' He glanced out of the window. A modern hotel was coming up. It looked like just about every other stop along the way. 'This election hangs on that girl. Not the Agricultural Council. Get Mogens Rank to bring me up to date.'

'You don't need Mogens for that. The man told Zeuthen he was a witness. Said he'd seen Emilie. He checked something on the computer and then he was gone.'

Hartmann looked at her, astonished.

'Why did he go to Zeeland?'

'I . . . don't know . . .'

Her phone rang. The screen said it was Weber. Hartmann saw and told her not to bother.

'Are you two OK again? Doesn't look like it.'

'Get a new round of polls organized.' A pause. 'If we've got the money.'

'We've got the money. Did Morten say something about Benjamin?'

Hartmann turned to her.

'He said he saw something.'

'Where?'

'In Jutland. Where else?'

She shook her head.

'Saw what?'

'Doesn't matter right now. Get Mogens. I want to know what's going on at Zeeland.'

Lund walked round the basement, saw nothing but an open window. Found a signal, got a call. Brix.

'We're at Zeeland. You should be here.'

'I'm in the grounds. Reinhardt's place. It's near the pier.'

'The man's been in the offices. He could still be in the building. He's looking for someone.'

'I'm with Reinhardt. The lights went off. The security alarm—'

A dog barked. She could near the noise of a busy team in an echoing room. Garage, she thought, could see it.

'Tell me later,' Brix ordered.

'Borch called. He said one of the car numbers was wrong. The boy made a mistake—'

'Borch's off the case.'

'Listen—'

'You made a fool of me in front of Hartmann, Lund. Get over here now.'

Then he was gone.

She closed the window. The alarm had stopped already. Walked up the stairs and said, 'Reinhardt. You need to come back with me to the offices.'

The room was empty. A porcelain statue lay shattered on the floor. The long windows giving out onto the water were open.

Torch to the ground, gun in hand, she went outside, searching. Finally on the pavement near the pier she found a spot of blood. Another.

Took out her phone. Was about to call when she heard a single soft footstep, the sound of a handgun being racked. Felt a cold nose of metal press against her neck.

'Put it down, Lund,' said a familiar voice. 'You don't need that now.'

Brix was in the executive offices, yelling at the team for more, Zeuthen and his wife following him, nagging constantly.

A single CCTV image suggested the man had got out of the building by a service entrance close to the water. That was all they had.

'He was looking for one of your staff,' Brix said. 'We've been telling you this for days—'

'And we've been giving you names!' Zeuthen cried.

'Not the right one . . .'

Juncker raced in, clutching a couple of sheets.

'We've something from the PC he used. He went through the vehicle directory looking at registration numbers. The last one he saw was . . .' He read from the page. 'ZE 23 574. It's like one of the numbers in the book the kid had. With just one letter changed.'

Brix blinked, asked Zeuthen a question even though he knew the answer.

'There are just initials here. Who's NJR?'

'Niels Jon Reinhardt. My assistant . . .'

'Why's he looking for Reinhardt?' Maja asked.

'Where is he?'

'Getting ready to catch a plane,' Zeuthen said. 'He's got a place in the grounds. Down by the old pier. He . . .'

Brix called Lund.

No answer.

This was a kind of justice so he wanted a witness. Needed someone to see him deliver a verdict, a sentence, carry it out.

Hands tied behind her back, gun two strides away, Lund watched, struggled against the ropes.

Niels Reinhardt was on his knees on the pier getting pistol-whipped slowly, carefully by a burly figure in a green yachtsman's jacket.

'What do you want?' he croaked and then the arm came down, a fist punched into his face, sent him whimpering to the cold concrete.

The water shimmered. An old dock bollard lay next to him, rope curled lazily round the base.

The man crouched, said in a calm, controlled voice, 'You saw Louise at the school. You pulled up next to her and stopped. You asked if she wanted a lift.'

Her gun wasn't so far away. If she could slip quietly towards it, free her hands . . .

'See this now, Reinhardt,' he said. 'Live it again. She was tired from walking. She knew you from the home. So she said yes. You put her bike in the boot . . .'

'I don't know what you're talking about—'

The arm flew back, a punch, then another.

'Was she scared when you turned down the wrong road? When you threw her into that workshop?'

Lund rolled round, got a clearer look, yelled, 'You don't know it's him! You killed three innocent sailors. Do you want another . . . ?'

A face turned to look at her. Ski mask: two holes for the eyes, one for the mouth.

'You can't know for sure,' she said weakly. 'Think about it.'

'I've done nothing but think about it, Lund. Nothing . . .'

He kicked Reinhardt in the gut. Waited for the groans to end.

'Then you took her to the harbour. Threw her in the water. Like a piece of rubbish.'

He walked close to Lund, found a chain, a lump of concrete.

Looked down at her, said, 'What's justice, Lund? Do you know? Have you ever—'

'It's not stealing an innocent girl from her parents,' she cut in. 'Or killing a man . . .'

The ropes were loosening. The gun getting closer.

'You don't *know*!'

He walked away from the chain and the concrete. Threw something in front of her.

The photograph. Majgården. Louise Hjelby looking glumly at the camera. Reinhardt behind. In control. Triumphant.

'Do you think she was the only one? Where's your justice there?'

Back to the stricken man on the pier, dragging the chain and the heavy lump behind. He tied them round Reinhardt's ankles, started yelling again.

'Was it like this?' he demanded. 'Was she alive when you threw her in the harbour?'

A punch. A kick. A wave of the gun.

'No answer?' A wry laugh. 'Then you go in the same way. Think of it. The water . . .'

The block was attached now. When he pulled it Reinhardt moved with the thing, closer to the edge. To the cold sea and oblivion.

'Think . . .'

'This has to stop,' Lund said and her voice made him look.

It took a while but she'd shrugged off the ropes. They weren't that tight. He was in a hurry, careless. Now she was standing on the small pier, gun in hand, sights straight at him.

'Put your weapon down. Move away from him. Do this now . . .'

In the dim beam of the jetty light she could see the look in his eyes: surprise.

He stood upright, straight-backed like a soldier. Walked through the shadows, away from the bloody Reinhardt.

'Stop there now,' she ordered. 'In the light.'

He was. Just.

'Hands on your head. Down on your knees.'

A shake of the masked head.

'Oh, Lund. So much single-minded dedication. Yet so little attention to detail.'

The gun shook in her hands. She edged round until she was between the man and the stricken, panting Reinhardt.

He watched then said, 'I emptied the magazine when I took it from you.'

The smell of marine fuel and the ocean. A bone-chilling breeze coming in off the water.

His right hand went to his pocket. Scattered shells on concrete, rattling like toy bells.

Reached into his other pocket, took out the gun again. Held it straight at her.

326

'Get out of my way,' he said.

Lund pulled. The trigger clicked on empty.

'Move,' he said. 'I'm tired of you now.'

Reinhardt whimpered behind. She tried to focus. To think of the right words.

But there was nothing.

Just two shots out of the darkness, tearing the night apart.

Lund stood. Lund shook. Looked ahead.

The man was down. Another shape behind. She could just make out Mathias Borch.

'Deal with him,' Lund ordered and ran to the edge of the pier, dragged the bleeding Reinhardt back from the edge.

A thought as she did so. Body armour.

Turned, saw two legs kick up from the floor, take Borch in the shin.

Not quick enough. The PET man kept his balance, crashed the weapon hard on his skull. Got him down again, knees over his chest, right arm flailing.

'Don't kill him!' she shouted.

Raced across, yelled it again, caught Borch's hand as it came back.

Removed the gun.

Something shiny protruded from the top of the green jacket. Plastic. Like a military vest.

'Get up, Mathias,' she said and helped him.

Breathless, speechless, he stood there, knuckles bleeding from the blows.

Sarah Lund bent down, removed the black ski mask they seemed to have been chasing, staring at for a week now.

An ordinary face. Bloody. Eyes closed. Everyman, sleeping. No clues what might lie in his head.

The Agricultural Council was boring. When the news came through of an arrest Hartmann cut it short and went back to Christiansborg where Mogens Rank was waiting, looking happy.

The papers were starting to call the result of the election. Ussing, never a popular figure with women voters, was losing ground. If Emilie were found alive Hartmann could expect a landslide in which he might pick his coalition partners with ease.

'What's he saying about the Zeuthen girl?' Hartmann asked as Rank walked with him into the palace.

'Nothing yet. He was shot during the arrest.'

Hartmann looked alarmed.

'He'll be fine,' Rank added. 'He was wearing some kind of bulletproof vest. They're taking him to the Politigården from hospital . . .'

'I want to know everything. Who he is. How he was arrested. What his motives were . . .'

Rank was silent.

'Any clues?' Hartmann asked, wide-eyed.

'His name's Loke Rantzau. Forty-three. He was in Navy special forces for a while. Then left to become a security consultant. Zeeland used him on a freelance basis for several years—'

'Why the hell didn't they give his name to the police?'

'Like I said he was freelance, not staff. Apparently it was . . . delicate. He was involved in ransom negotiations for a couple of hijackings in Somalia. It seems on the last one . . .' Rank opened the door to Hartmann's office, looked round, made sure no one was listening. 'He became a hostage himself. Hans Zeuthen handled the situation personally I gather. Even we weren't involved.'

'You're saying we had Danish nationals held hostage and the government didn't even know?'

'It's still a little unclear, Troels. I'm working on it. Rantzau was the father of the murdered girl in Jutland. He was captive for nearly four years before he got himself out of that hole. When he came back to Denmark . . .' A shrug. 'It's not a pretty tale any way you look at things.'

Weber came dashing in from the outer office.

'I just heard. Has he said anything? When will they get the girl?'

'Talk to Karen, not me,' Hartmann muttered, then walked into his room and slammed the door behind him.

Mogens Rank straightened his tie, adjusted his glasses.

'I thought he'd be a bit happier than that.'

Weber nodded, told him he could go. Then followed Hartmann into the office.

He was on the phone, talking to someone about the Zeuthen case. When he came off Weber said, 'This has to stop, Troels. I know you can't accept Benjamin took his own life but you've no right to blame me. I tried to help him. More than you know.'

'Fuck you! He was having a breakdown. Instead of telling me back then you whipped up some cock-and-bull story about Karen and Zeeland to save your own hide.'

Weber waited a moment then said, 'Our hide, Troels. Our hide.'

A knock on the door. Mogens Rank hadn't left.

'This is dreadful,' he said. 'Rantzau claims Zeuthen's personal assistant Reinhardt had something to do with killing the girl. I've met the man. I've had dinner with him. Rantzau nearly killed him apparently. I—'

'Was he in Jutland?' Hartmann asked.

'Rantzau? Well we know—'

'No!' Weber yelled. 'Reinhardt?'

'I've no idea. Why?'

Morten Weber sat down, took off his glasses, rubbed his eyes. Didn't look at Hartmann. Didn't look at anything.

'Best get Karen in here, Mogens,' he said. 'We need to work out how we're going to handle this.'

They kept him in a secure interview room, guarded constantly. No windows. Lund for the interview, Borch by her side. Brix had insisted on it. Without him Lund would be dead, and Reinhardt too.

Cameras. Brix watching from the observation window on the other side.

A few details had emerged already, from the Navy where he served until the age of thirty after gaining a degree in electrical engineering from Copenhagen University. From Zeeland's accounts department, not that the records there were complete. As far as they could work out Rantzau had spent the last thirteen years working as a freelance security consultant. A mercenary of a kind, rarely in Denmark, no family that anyone knew of. He'd helped develop and commission Zeeland's own security networks. Trained guard teams for company ships travelling through dangerous shipping lanes. Negotiated ransom deals with Somalian pirates. And been a hostage himself.

Not that any of the recent details were certain. The man himself was saying nothing.

'Are you in pain?' Lund asked after all the other questions failed.

The hospital had examined him. Impact bruises from the body armour. A cut on the leg. He'd told a nurse he'd caught it on some rusty metal in Jutland. Probably when Lund shot at him she guessed. A shoulder flesh wound from Borch's gun.

No answer.

'We're getting there, Loke,' Borch said. 'According to your Navy records you're fluent in four languages. Just one will do right now.'

He placed a photograph on the table. A younger man, shorter hair, no lines on his face. A Navy uniform. Smiling.

'Hans Zeuthen dumped you, didn't he?' Lund said. 'You were negotiating a ransom for him. Somalia. It went wrong. The men got out. You stayed.'

He sat up stiffly, like a soldier, looked straight ahead. Saluted. Kept quiet.

The door opened. Dyhring marched in. Brix furious behind him.

'I didn't authorize this,' the PET man moaned.

'You didn't need to,' Brix said. 'He's our prisoner. And besides . . .' He nodded at Borch. 'You're represented.'

'This is a PET case,' Dyhring yelled. 'I want this interview ended now. I want Borch out of here. I want—'

'Out,' Brix said, jerking a thumb at the door.

The burly PET man's eyes narrowed.

'Are you serious?'

'Very,' Brix barked. 'If you like I can tell the Ministry of Justice you've been putting road blocks in the way ever since this began.' He nodded at the battered, silent man at the table. 'Which is why he's still got Emilie Zeuthen hidden somewhere. I'm not handing that task over to you—'

'Borch!' Dyhring barked. 'Come with me.'

'He's with us now,' Brix said. 'If you want to fire him I'll pick up his wages. Now . . .'

Madsen was at the door looking ready for an argument.

'I've got Robert Zeuthen on the way here to talk about his daughter,' Brix added. 'I don't want you spoiling the atmosphere.' A nod at the burly detective. 'Either Dyhring walks or we remove him.'

The PET chief took one look at the grinning detective then disappeared down the endless corridor.

Brix went back to the one-way glass. Listened, watched, checked the cameras were still working.

Borch throwing container numbers on the table. Shipping schedules. Photographs.

Still Rantzau stared forward at nothing.

'Loke,' Lund said. 'We need to find Emilie. The longer we spend looking for her the harder it gets to nail the man who killed your daughter. I want to see him in front of a judge. I want to put him there. Watch him go to jail. Don't you?'

Something changed. His head turned. His dark, troubled, intelligent eyes focused on her.

Not a word. Just an expression and it was one of contempt.

Borch broke, was on him, yelling, fists up. Grabbing his neck. Forcing him to look at photographs, the documents.

'Which ship is it, Loke? Which container?'

'Stop it!' Lund yelled and dragged him off.

Grumping, Borch went back to his seat. The three of them sat in silence. Then she said, 'I know what she went through, Loke. I know you see it in your head all the time. Day and night. I can't take it from there. But I can find him. I will . . .'

He looked straight at her. Amused almost. She stopped. Listened.

'They'll never let you, Lund. Don't you understand that? You've already made sure he'll go free.'

'What if I prove it was Reinhardt? If he's arrested . . . charged?'

Rantzau looked at his hand, dabbed at the blood there. Shrugged.

'Then you'll have to get a move on. Time's short. It always was. It gets shorter by the minute.'

He went quiet.

'Meaning what?' she asked. 'Loke? *Loke?*'

Later, in a room along the way, Lund saw Robert and Maja Zeuthen. For the first time there was a glimpse of hope in their eyes.

That didn't cheer her.

'He's the man,' she said. 'He's adamant Emilie's still alive but he won't say where she is. We'll continue to talk to him. If I can convince him we're working on his daughter's case . . .'

'Let us see him,' Maja pleaded. 'We can . . .'

Lund shook her head.

'It won't help. He seems to have reason to hate Zeeland. He believes you covered up his daughter's death.' She watched Zeuthen as she spoke. 'He worked for your company. There were some hostage negotiations in Somalia. They went wrong. Rantzau ended up being held there. When he came out . . . that's when he found out about his daughter.'

'We know nothing about this,' Zeuthen said. 'Why should he take it out on us?'

'Trust me,' Lund insisted, 'you can't ask for his sympathy. It's not there. We need to investigate your assistant, Niels Reinhardt.'

'Reinhardt?' the mother asked.

'He'd met the murdered girl. His car was in the vicinity. There are questions we need answered . . .'

Zeuthen was getting mad.

'This is ridiculous. Niels has been like a member of the family for as long as I can remember. You've got this man. Surely—'

'If we find his daughter's killer, hopefully we can get to Emilie before it's too late.'

Silence.

'Too late?' Maja Zeuthen saw it straight away. 'What do you mean by that?'

'We need details of your children's charity—'

'Lund! What do you mean . . . too late?'

Tired, confused. Stupid. She felt all those things. It had just slipped out though they had to know anyway.

'Rantzau says that four nights ago he shipped Emilie out of Copenhagen for a foreign destination. He won't say where.'

'And?' the woman persisted.

'He claims she's in an airtight tank inside a container. He showed us . . .'

She opened her notebook, passed the page over.

'It's a decompression tank for divers.'

Drawings of a metal tube with a door on the side.

'We'd know if something like that was on board,' Zeuthen insisted.

'That's what he says.'

'How long?' Maja Zeuthen asked.

'There's nothing to say any of this is true—'

'How long?' Robert Zeuthen repeated.

'Forty-eight hours. Maybe less. We need all the information you can provide on the charity. Reinhardt is back in his house at Zeeland. He's not badly hurt. He was lucky in—'

'Let me understand this,' Maja Zeuthen cut in. 'You think Niels Reinhardt raped and murdered that girl? And if you can prove it this Rantzau man will tell us where Emilie is?'

'That's about it,' Lund agreed.

Mogens Rank found Nebel in the office. The four of them sat down to listen to his account of the case so far. Reinhardt's connection with the children's home. The fact his car had been seen in the area.

'Is there anything else that connects him to the girl?' Weber asked.

'It seems he met her once. There's a photograph. He was running the children's charity. There's no great surprise there.'

Weber wouldn't leave it.

'Is there any suggestion . . . any evidence to show he pressured Peter Schultz into shelving the investigation?'

Rank shook his head.

'Who's saying anyone from our side leaned on him? Ussing had reason to. He had the Hjelby girl in the campaign. He was photographed—'

'Anders Ussing's in the clear,' Weber cut in angrily. 'The Politigården say so. He didn't know the girl had been murdered. Schultz was doing someone else a favour there.'

Rank rolled his eyes.

'It wasn't us! If I thought someone here did that I'd tell you. Believe me.'

Karen Nebel had sat silent throughout. Hartmann looked directly at her and said, 'Unless there's something we don't know about. What do you think, Karen?'

'About what?'

'Do you know Niels Reinhardt?' he asked abruptly.

'I've met him. We all have. He was our point man when Hans Zeuthen was alive. For his son too.'

'Did you meet him that day in Jutland?'

She met his gaze.

'It was election time. I met lots of people. A few from Zeeland. If—'

'Answer the question,' Weber begged. 'Did you meet Reinhardt that day in Jutland?'

She put down her pen, leaned back in the chair, looked round the table.

Yes. I did.'

'Why?' Weber wanted to know.

'Because the party needed it. Because we had no choice . . .'

Hartmann got up, pointed a finger at the adjoining room. Went there. Poured himself a brandy. Waited.

One minute later she came in, sat down opposite. Weber followed, closed the door, stood there, listened.

'Is this formal, Troels?'

'If it was we'd be having this conversation in front of Mogens. Do you want him in here? He is the Justice Minister after all.'

A shake of her blonde hair.

'No. I don't need Mogens. I was doing my job. We were down in the polls. All the talk of crisis wasn't helping. We needed Zeeland on our side.'

'And?'

'Robert Zeuthen had just taken over after his father's death. Their CEO Kornerup was trying to steal the company from under his nose. If he'd managed that we'd have had Zeeland announcing mass redundancies the week of the election.'

She got a glass, poured herself a drink.

'Reinhardt called and asked if he could come out to Jutland to talk. He said he could keep Kornerup at bay, keep Robert in position, if we promised them a few sweeteners. A freeze on some taxes. Birgit Eggert was fine with that idea. So were you when she mentioned it. We announced it the next day.'

'Benjamin saw you,' Weber said.

'So what? It wasn't secret. Wasn't illegal. They're one of our biggest companies. Everyone knows they lobby politicians for what they want—'

'I never asked you to take that meeting,' Hartmann objected.

'I don't bother you with every appointment I make. We were in the middle of a campaign.'

Weber nodded.

'And he gave you money.'

'Zeeland made a political contribution, through the usual channels. It wasn't as if he handed over a bag of cash in a car park.'

'Benjamin thought we were sucking up to big business already,' Weber told her. 'When he caught you two together—'

'That's not my fault, Morten. I didn't do anything wrong.'

He came to the table, grabbed a glass, poured himself a drink.

'But Reinhardt did. He murdered that kid afterwards. Or so Lund thinks. If it turns out that's true Ussing's going to crucify us. Who's going to believe we didn't lean on Schultz to kill it? We had Reinhardt's money in the bank.'

'You think I helped Reinhardt cover up a murder?' she yelled. 'Just for money?'

'You could have told us you met him that day,' Hartmann said.

'Why? It never crossed my mind. Why would I connect some murdered teenager with an old guy from Zeeland? What am I? Psychic?'

'You're paid to be,' Weber complained. 'Not to—'

'Enough,' Hartmann pleaded.

Head in hands. Fingers kneading his brow. He eyed the drink, nothing else.

'Do you honestly think I had something to do with burying this case, Troels?'

She waited. He didn't look at her. Didn't answer.

Nebel got to her feet, walked straight out.

When she'd left Hartmann turned to Weber.

'She has to make a full statement to the police. After that find her a desk in the secretariat somewhere. She can photocopy stuff or something—'

'We need Karen,' Weber interrupted. 'Tomorrow's the last day of campaigning. Your final debate. She's too well connected . . .'

'Benjamin must have talked to someone else. Not just you.'

Weber stayed quiet.

'Tell me, Morten.'

'He was hanging out with those protest friends of his. That's why he was taking pictures. They were supposed to be for their website.'

'What website?'

Weber scowled.

'It's called *Frontal*. The usual extremist conspiracy crap. They never ran anything. I kept an eye out.'

He went quiet.

'And?'

'He said there was a girl there. He liked her. Sally. I offered to pay for him to take her away for a holiday but . . . that was the capitalist bastard trying to bribe him again.'

'Find her,' Hartmann ordered.

Niels Reinhardt was back from the hospital. Head wounds. Cuts on his face. Bruised ribs. Lund and Borch were in his apartment in the block by the water outside Zeeland, watching uniform officers and forensic start a search.

'My phone's ringing,' Reinhardt said. 'It's probably my wife. She's coming back from France. Am I allowed to answer—?'

'You can do that later,' Lund told him. 'Your diary says you were in Jutland the day Louise Hjelby disappeared.'

Borch put the book on the desk.

'Do you remember if you stopped in Gudbjerghavn?' she asked.

'I don't think so. We'd shut the port there the year before.'

'Where were you going?'

'To Esbjerg. I had a few meetings first thing in the morning.'

'Who with?' Borch wanted to know.

'Politicians. It was during the election. We were lobbying them all to try to gauge what their support for industry truly was. I met with someone from Hartmann's camp. Ussing's too.'

He struggled to do up his tie. Abandoned the idea. It hurt too much.

'What people say in private differs from their public stance sometimes. We were struggling with the economy. Trying to find some way to help the company . . . help Denmark through the worst of it.'

'You remember that?' Borch asked. 'Two years on?'

'Yes, I do, actually. Robert's father had died not long before. There was a lot of turmoil in the company as a result. Also April the twenty-first was my wife's sixtieth birthday. I had a large party to organize.'

Lund looked at the diary. It was blank for the following day.

'So you had your interviews and left Jutland?'

'No. I didn't feel well. My wife insisted I stay at a hotel. I went there in the middle of the afternoon. Didn't leave.'

Borch asked for the name of the place. Reinhardt shook his head, gave him the name of his PA, said she'd have it.

'You had access to the charity files,' Lund said. 'You knew Louise Hjelby's address in Gudbjerghavn. You'd met her in the children's home . . .'

'I didn't know she was the girl you were talking about.' He gestured at the pictures on the shelf. 'Would I keep a photo of her in my living room if I had something to hide?'

She looked at the frames lined up next to one another.

'You might if you wanted a trophy. A souvenir.'

Reinhardt spat out a quiet curse.

'So no one can confirm what you did after these early morning meetings in Esbjerg?'

'If that's what you say . . .'

Borch brandished some phone records.

'And your mobile was turned off from two in the afternoon. Went dead twelve kilometres from Louise's home? Didn't come back on until you were in Copenhagen the next day?'

'The battery must have run out! This is absurd. I'm sixty-four years old. Do I look like the kind of man who goes round raping and murdering young girls?' His voice broke. He looked ready to weep. 'I can't believe you think I could do such a thing!'

Borch told him they'd need DNA and fingerprints. Reinhardt's car was being taken to the Politigården garage.

'I want your passport,' Lund added. 'You won't leave Copenhagen without our permission. Breach any of these conditions and we'll take you into custody.'

Her phone rang. Lund walked to the long double windows to take it. The little jetty where she and Reinhardt had nearly died was now lit up like a miniature seaside pier.

It was the hospital, asking again for Mark. Eva was sick, needed support, needed clothes. She phoned him, got voicemail, left another message.

Borch was listening to Juncker moan again, asking this time why they were searching Reinhardt's home, not looking for Emilie Zeuthen.

When she came off the phone he asked what was happening.

'We need to search Reinhardt's place in France,' she said. 'And anywhere else he has. If he killed Louise he must have been abusing other kids in these homes. Maybe he wasn't the only one.'

'Leave this to us, Sarah,' he said. 'Go and find Mark.'

'Have we tried giving this Rantzau bloke a good kicking?' Juncker asked.

'There's work to do here!' she pleaded.

'Yes. And we'll do it,' Borch replied. 'Take a break.'

Maja was upstairs in Drekar making phone calls, talking about getting her passport, looking abroad herself. Then Kornerup turned up. Confident. Not quite a smirk on his face. But it wasn't far away.

Zeuthen stood in front of him at the foot of the grand staircase.

'Why are you here? I don't want you in my home.'

'I'm sorry, Robert. I understand fully. But we need to discuss the police's interest in Reinhardt.'

Zeuthen groaned.

'It's ridiculous. They've fouled up again. Niels has been around for ever. I want—'

'It's not just about Reinhardt. The charity's been a very public venture for Zeeland. If the media get hold of this story—'

'They said this man Rantzau worked for us,' Zeuthen broke in. 'Did Niels know him?'

Nothing.

'Did you?'

'I want our best lawyers to help Reinhardt. He's an innocent man. He's owed that.'

'You didn't answer my question.'

'No. I didn't.'

'Well?'

Kornerup winced, looked at the study. The two men went and sat down.

'Your father dealt with ransoms personally. We just did as we were told.'

'Which was what?'

'We kept clear of direct negotiations. We used go-betweens. It seems Loke Rantzau was one of them. I didn't know. I'm sure Reinhardt had no idea. The man was barely on the books.'

'He was captured. We did nothing.'

Kornerup frowned.

'It's a dangerous business. I gather he has a military background. He'd know the risks.'

Zeuthen was staring at the secure cabinet ahead of him. He knew what was in there. Had thought of it for some time.

'The point is, Robert, we should be leaning on the Politigården. They have to stop interrogating Reinhardt as if he's a criminal and focus on this Rantzau creature. Why aren't they putting pressure on the man? He knows where Emilie is. No one else.'

Footsteps at the door. Maja was there in a long coat, from her old wardrobe, one she wore when they were together.

'How can you be so sure Reinhardt's not involved?' she demanded.

'Maja . . .' Zeuthen began.

'I know you think he's an uncle or something. But Lund must have a reason to suspect him.'

He went to the cabinet. They kept the family paperwork there. And a weapon. A silver handgun. Just in case.

Zeuthen got her passport, walked over, handed it to her.

'You asked Reinhardt to find out if anyone in Zeeland knew about that girl's death,' she said. 'Why didn't he . . . ?'

Kornerup was on his feet, hand extended. Looking at them both.

'Everyone at Zeeland wants the best for you both, and Emilie,' he insisted. 'If I can help in any way just ask.'

The hand stayed out. Zeuthen took it.

'We've had our differences,' Kornerup said, 'but they're forgotten on my part. You lead this company, Robert. Tell us what to do.'

When he left she went upstairs, sat on the bed in the guest room. The passport was on the pillow.

Zeuthen came in, sat next to her.

'Where do you want to go?' he asked.

'I don't know.'

'The plane's ready. I heard from Hamburg. There was nothing there. Maybe St Petersburg. Reinhardt was supposed to go . . .'

She stiffened at the name.

'If something had gone wrong in the company I would have known about it,' he said.

No answer.

'I'll go to the office and see what I can do. When you decide where . . .'

Her hand crept out, took his.

'Stay here. Stay with me. And Carl.'

He saw now. On her lap was one of Emilie's scrapbooks. Drawings of the family. A photo of a kitten.

'We'll get her back,' he said. 'When she comes home everything will be different. That's a promise. If—'

'They don't tell you everything in the company. I can see it in Kornerup's eyes. You're a figurehead, Robert. Your father's son. They do what they like behind your back. They—'

'I don't care about Zeeland! I just want the four of us, together again. We can go somewhere. Stay away for as long you like. As long as the kids can bear looking at us.'

She laughed a little at that, held his hand more tightly, moved her head towards his, whispered, 'Did I leave you? Or you leave me? I don't remember.'

'Bit of both I guess.'

This was how it was before. Close. Full of a simple, unquestioning love.

'How stupid could we be?' she said. Then kissed him.

He was a shy man. Not passionate yet full of emotion.

She smiled, felt the tears prick at her eyes.

Put a hand to his head, pulled him close.

'It's your turn now. Remember?'

Eva was sleeping. The doctor was talking in low, concerned tones about something called meconium aspiration syndrome. Lund looked blank.

'The baby's amniotic fluid is contaminated,' the woman explained. 'If it gets any worse we may have to induce labour.'

She looked at Lund.

'To be honest she didn't want me to call you. But you're the only relative I could find.'

They'd given her a room of her own in the maternity ward. Gentle cries down the corridor. White figures scuttling around with bundles held in careful arms.

'Is the baby OK?'

A pause then, 'We're keeping an eye on it.'

No direct answer. Never a good thing.

'Does your son know about Eva's condition?'

Lund had brought a bunch of flowers. They seemed pointless now.

'I've tried to get hold of him. I don't know where he is.'

A nod. One that said: nothing new.

'She needs support. She's scared. Can't blame her.'

With that the woman walked off.

Lund found a vase, put the flowers next to the bed. The sound made Eva stir. She rolled on the sheets, young face flushed with the hospital heat, the drugs perhaps.

Big belly in a white gown. Shuffling, wriggling. Uncomfortable. Lund remembered that. And the fear.

A nurse came in and said, 'Excuse me. You left a bag in the corridor. It's not allowed—'

'No. I didn't.'

'It says Eva Lauersen,' the woman added. 'I'll leave it here anyway. If you . . .'

Lund rushed past her, looked down the corridor. A tall figure in a worn parka heading for the exit. She caught up with him just before the door.

'Mark?'

He looked worn out.

'Don't start, Mum . . .'

'I won't. I think Eva's going to be OK. But there could be a problem with the baby. She needs you here.'

He had his hood pulled low over his brow. The way they looked on the street.

'I told her the two of you can stay at my place. For as long as you want . . .'

'Yeah. Like the last couple of nights. And look what shit we're in now . . .'

All the apologies. All the pleas. And still he could throw this nonsense at her.

'You can't blame me for everything. A lot. But not . . .'

A teenage sneer and for a moment he was young again.

'I know I failed you,' she added. 'I don't need reminding of that. If I had the chance to do it all again—'

'No!' he cried. 'Don't say that. You never wanted me. I never interested you. There was always the work. Some . . . dead girl or something. Never me. I was alive and that bored you.'

She wanted to argue, couldn't find the words.

'And now you've got a little house and a little garden. A little job behind a desk. So you've finally earned the right to tell me how to live.' He shook his head. 'You don't know who you are. And you want to—'

'You live your own life!' she cried. 'I don't want to tell you how. Mark . . . you're smarter than me. Stronger. God knows you had to be.'

She was crying and that held him.

'The only good thing I gave you was a lesson in what not to do. You can use that. You and Eva . . .'

Something new in his eyes. Maybe it was hatred.

He turned, started to walk away, down the tiled corridor into a sea of bodies in gowns, white and blue and green.

'Mark,' she whispered and knew he couldn't hear.

Her phone rang.

'I've been checking up on Reinhardt,' Borch said. 'He used his credit card at a newsagent's. Half an hour before she disappeared. Two kilometres from the school.'

She thought she saw a tall hooded figure disappearing through the distant doors.

'Sarah?' Borch asked.

Her son didn't look back. Maybe never would.

Nine

An early start. Lund was in the office just before seven. Brix looked as if he'd never left. Zeeland's lawyers had been on the phone already, screaming Reinhardt's innocence from the rooftops.

'You need to find something more incriminating than a man buying chocolate frogs at a newsagent's,' he said as they went down to the forensic garage.

'There's a picture of him with the girl in his study,' Borch noted, sipping at a coffee by a black Mercedes on the ramp.

'More than that too.' Brix nodded at the car. 'Well?'

'It gets regular cleans and valets,' Borch said. 'Executive car. Executive treatment.'

He went round to the boot. Pointed out an area in the interior ringed by forensic marks.

'There are scratches in the paint that match Louise's bike. It's a common form of paint. And white too. They can't say conclusively the two are linked.'

The bike was next to the Mercedes. Brix looked ready to kick it.

Lund went to the photos on a desk. They were the ones from Lis Vissenbjerg's original, hidden autopsy. There was a new report there.

'Forensics have taken a new look at the pictures of the body. She fought. Injuries prior to death. He would have had blood on him.'

'And is there any in the car?' Brix asked.

'I said.' Borch was getting tetchy. 'It gets valeted and cleaned constantly. The fact we can't find it doesn't mean it wasn't there.'

Lund kept going through the latest findings.

'She had some broken teeth. They seem to think they could have come from a watch.'

Picture in hand – dead mouth open, blood, shattered teeth – she came over and showed him.

Brix nodded at one of the forensic team.

'We saw that three hours ago. We've got Reinhardt's watch.' The scene of crime man held up an evidence bag. 'Hasn't got a scratch on it.'

Borch tried to argue. No one had seen Reinhardt after his morning meetings in Esbjerg. Or at the hotel.

'Not much use is it?' Brix commented.

'Oh for God's sake,' Lund barked. 'There's a whole day missing in his life. He leaves Esbjerg in the morning. Twenty-four hours later he picks up his wife after a flight from Paris at Kastrup. No one goes off the radar that long . . .'

'Where did he change his clothes?' Brix asked. 'If he'd killed her he'd want the car cleaned straight after. Where did he do that?'

'We're looking! It's not easy—'

'Emilie Zeuthen's trapped in a tank somewhere and time's running out. We need—'

Borch's phone rang. They kept arguing. When they were done he said, 'Annette Reinhardt's upstairs. Let's ask her.'

A blonde woman in an expensive silk dress, a smiling, confident face. She was happy to sit in an interview room, saw the camera straight away, smiled at it and said, 'This is the stupidest thing I've heard in my life. My husband nearly got killed last night. And now you're putting him through hell.'

'Emilie Zeuthen's missing,' Lund said. 'We need to find her.'

The smile vanished.

'Do you think Niels wouldn't help if he could?'

Details. They asked about the birthday party. She said it was a surprise. The family had gathered at the house and leapt out from the shadows when she came home.

'Our two girls and all our dearest friends,' she said. 'Typical of him to keep it quiet like that.'

'He picked you up in his own car?' Lund asked. 'The black Mercedes.'

'Of course he did.'

'And you put your suitcase in the boot.'

A shake of the head.

'Where else?'

Borch asked, 'How was he?'

'Wonderful. He made the most beautiful speech.'

Lund shuffled some papers.

'He wasn't stressed? Or tired?'

'No. He'd gone to bed early the night before. Niels has high blood pressure. I told him to stay in Jutland. Go to a hotel.'

Juncker's team had come back from the house with some photos of the party. Reinhardt in evening dress, bow tie, glass of champagne. Making the speech. The sleeves covered his wrists.

'Did he wear a watch at the party?' Lund wondered.

'I should think so. Niels loves his watch. It was very expensive. I gave it to him when he turned sixty.'

The smile seemed more fragile. Lund noticed the woman fiddling with her wedding ring.

'Tell me about the children's charity.'

'It's a small part of his time,' she said. 'He goes to board meetings. Monitors the finances.'

Borch threw another set of photos on the table. Ones from the homes. Reinhardt with children. Girls mostly.

'He looks in on them too. Not what you'd expect of a board member really.'

'You would of Niels. He's very particular. Very . . . caring.' A pause. 'It's important they get a chance in life. And—'

'You've got two daughters,' Borch interrupted. 'How was he with them?'

The smile was gone entirely.

'When they were small?' he added. 'Were you ever . . . concerned?'

Reinhardt's wife leaned back, folded her arms. Pursed her lips. Stared at the pair of them.

The door opened. Madsen asked for him, urgently. He went out.

Lund stayed.

'You've two summer houses. One in France. One on Anholt.'

'What of it? Are you going to tear those apart as well?'

'Not unless we have to. Is there anywhere else you spend time? The place you have near the Zeeland offices . . .'

'Hans Zeuthen gave that to Niels in his will. It's ours.'

'Where else do you go? Country cottages? Boats?'

'There's a nice little flat in London but we rent that out. And his gallery.'

'His what?'

Lund listened. Made notes. Left her there. Borch was back in the office looking lost.

'Reinhardt's got a place in the city he never told us about,' she said. 'He calls it his art gallery. Let's go.'

He didn't move.

'Get your coat, will you?'

Nothing. She turned. A woman there. Fair hair. Thin, angry face. The wife.

'I'm busy,' Lund said. 'Not now.'

'Yes! Now!'

She had a bag over her shoulder. Threw it on the floor. Shirts and pants scattered everywhere.

'It's your fault we're standing here, Lund.'

Borch came over, shook his head.

'It isn't, Marie. You know that.'

'He's been bleating about moving out. So here . . .' She kicked the clothes. 'You can do his dirty washing for him.'

Every officer in the place was scuttling away, trying not to hear.

'What am I supposed to tell the girls?' She looked at Borch. At her. 'Will they see him in a week? A month? Ever?'

Lund kept quiet, took a long deep breath.

'Say something, you bitch! I've a right to know. You two shagging in Jutland . . .'

He put a hand to her shoulder. She threw him off.

'What the hell are you thinking, Lund? You dumped him years ago. What do you want him for now?'

'It's not just about Sarah,' Borch said. 'We both know that—'

'No. I don't. You . . .'

Little fists flying against his chest. His hands against hers. Curses. Tears.

Lund left them there, crossed the office, went out into the corridor, leaned against the wall.

Then pulled out her phone, got the map, typed in the address for the place Niels Reinhardt forgot to mention.

Underground, his wife said. A funny place for art.

Zeuthen was in the office, couldn't stop looking at the clocks. Seven more shipping companies had opened up their cargo holds. Not a trace of a tank in any so far.

He sat at the table, casual jacket, white shirt, open at the neck. Maja next to him. Reaching out, touching his hand from time to time.

It helped, a little.

Then the door opened and a tall figure walked in, stiff and in obvious pain.

Zeuthen got up. His wife stayed where she was.

'Come with me,' Robert Zeuthen said, taking Reinhardt's arm.

They went next door, talked alone by the window over the harbour.

'I've explained everything to them,' Reinhardt said with a shrug. 'They're the police. We know what they're like. Annette's talked to them too. I'm afraid I'm one more victim of their incompetence. It's strange . . .'

A secretary came in, brought them coffee. He took it with the mannered politeness Zeuthen had known since he was a child.

'They kept throwing all these stupid questions at me and all I could think was . . . why aren't you looking for Emilie? Why waste time on me? Still, the worst's over.'

He put a hand to his neck, winced.

'I want you to go home and relax,' Zeuthen said. 'Don't even think of the office until this is over.'

'That's not easy, Robert. For heaven's sake . . . Brix and Lund are wasting so much time. Emilie's out there somewhere.'

'Go home,' Zeuthen repeated. 'Stay there with Annette. The police may want to talk to you again.'

Reinhardt looked uncertain then. As if reluctant to say something.

'What about Maja?' he asked. 'She wouldn't look at me when I came in. She surely doesn't think . . .'

'No. Of course not. We both know—'

'That would be the worst thing. If—'

'We don't,' Zeuthen cut in. 'That's it.'

Reinhardt's art gallery turned out to be the basement of an unused warehouse on a distant stretch of the harbour, a fifteen-minute walk from his home. Lund and Borch parked by the water, used the keys from his office.

A bare grey room, canvases stacked against the walls, not hung.

There was a Bauhaus chair in the middle on a rug. A low table next to it with a glass and an expensive bottle of whisky. His wife said he liked to be alone when he looked at his paintings. The unit was supposed to be turned into a shopping mall but the owners had gone bankrupt. Reinhardt, a man of some wealth, had bought the freehold, along with the land on both sides.

'He certainly had the place to himself,' Lund said.

Borch looked at a canvas of an abstract nude and scratched his head.

'Why didn't he buy himself his own home instead of living on the job in the grounds of Zeeland?'

'I don't know. I need to get back.'

He stood in the way.

'Sarah. I'm sorry I got you mixed up in all this . . .'

'I really don't want to talk about it.'

'We've had problems for a long time. It wasn't just down to you . . .'

'I said I don't want to talk about it.'

She knew that look on his face: hopeful.

'I know. You're right. I just think—'

'Stop thinking, Mathias!' Lund yelled. 'There's no point. It didn't work before and it won't work now.'

He stood there silent, eyes on her.

'I think we should just forget the whole thing . . .'

'I don't want to. I can't.'

She turned round, confused. Went to the wrong door. Then another. Couldn't remember which way they came in.

'If we work at it this time. We're older. Smarter . . .'

'Ha! You think?'

She dodged behind a big canvas, one of the few on a frame. Tried another door, locked.

'I lost you once,' he said in a loud, firm voice. 'I'm not letting you run away again.'

With a brisk step she went for another corner, stopped. Borch caught up.

'I just think if we talk things through honestly. Spend a little time together. Maybe a holiday . . .'

'Not going back to bloody Norway,' she whispered.

A tall canvas was turned the wrong way round. Paint to the wall. It was the only one like that. She walked to it, moved the thing to one side.

There was a door behind. Lund tried the handle: open.

Looked down a long dark staircase with a metal banister to one side.

Borch's head appeared around the frame. He pulled out a torch and aimed the beam down the steps.

She did the same then got in front of him and said, 'Me first.'

It was a garage, set beneath the building one level below the basement. No windows, even on the metal door that led to a winding drive at the end. A high-pressure washer at the back. Polish. Cleaning material and liquids.

At the far side was a set of storage units. Plastic sheeting over the nearest. Beneath a large cardboard box.

Gloves on, she opened it, aimed the torch. He came and joined her. Tugged out some more boxes.

Every one full of printouts from children's homes. Details of children, photos, dates of birth, addresses of foster homes, medical records.

'This whole set is from Majgården,' he said.

His torch flashed to the next corner. Borch got up, took a look. 'Sarah?'

She came over. He'd found a workbench. Spanners and drill heads. Socket wrenches. Cleaning fluid.

And a watch.

It was a short drive back to the Zeeland offices. Reinhardt barely looked up as they came in. But Maja Zeuthen was eyeing them from the next room. Lund noticed that.

'You own a building across the harbour,' Borch said. 'You never told us.'

He got up, looked tired and hurt.

'It's just a place I keep my paintings.'

'You don't just keep paintings there,' she told him. 'You've got records from the children's homes. Louise's at Majgården among them.'

Robert Zeuthen marched in, started complaining the moment he reached them.

But he went quiet when Lund asked for it.

'Why do you have records of children hidden away in the basement?' she asked.

Reinhardt was looking at Zeuthen, no one else.

'This is enough,' Borch asked. 'We're taking you in for questioning. I don't imagine you'll have to look far for a lawyer in this place. They'll know where we are.'

He walked forward, put a hand to Reinhardt's back.

'Let's go.'

The squat was in Nørrebro, not far from the Ungdomshuset, the radical meeting house that caused riots when it was torn down a few years before. Hartmann had never been. It was the source of too much conflict. But he guessed it looked much like this: an old building, semi-derelict, covered in graffiti. The wrong place to visit in his ministerial car the day before an election. Still he needed to know.

Morten Weber was nagging as they drew up.

'This last debate's going to be crucial. The polls are narrowing. We need a strategy. We have to bring Karen back. She knows TV better than any of us.'

'Karen could bring us down . . .'

Weber scowled with disgust.

'Oh don't be so ridiculous. She took a donation from Zeeland. I bet they were giving Ussing a sweetener at the same time. Covering their bets. Don't get high and mighty . . .'

Hartmann started to get out. Weber's arm stopped him.

'Do you really want to do this? PET are going crazy. These people hate us. It's not somewhere to be seen right now.'

Hartmann strode to the building, two bodyguards rushing to keep up. There was a racket that got louder when he walked through the door. Someone was thrashing a set of drums on a stage set up at the back. A girl singer with plaits was yelling tunelessly into a mike. The place was almost in darkness. It smelled of sweat and dope smoke. The walls were covered in wild graffiti. Tables at the edges, laptops on them, bottles of water and beer.

The people there looked at him, a man in a suit, as if an alien had landed. But Hartmann walked on and eventually a young woman with bright-blue mascara, red lips and a ring through her nose, came up and said, 'Do you want a cup of tea?'

He said no thanks, asked for Sally.

The girl's eyes, flickering to a figure in black at a laptop in the shadows, told him.

Hartmann went to her, bent down and said, 'I'm Benjamin's brother.'

A cigarette at her lips she kept tapping at the computer.

'I'm trying to find out what happened. I was hoping you could help.'

'You're the Prime Minister, aren't you? Why ask me?'

There was a rickety chair. He pulled it up. Sat down. Told the two bodyguards to make themselves scarce.

'Because I was too busy for Benjamin when he needed me. I feel . . .'

She had dark eyes, black mascara, a face made white with make-up. But she was looking at him.

'I feel I let him down and I don't know how. He came out to Jutland when I was campaigning there two years ago . . .'

'I remember. He was mad at you. PET picked him up after we had a flash mob outside the bank here. Instead of throwing him in a cell like they did with the rest of us your people kicked him out and told him to keep quiet.'

A cup of tea turned up anyway. He was grateful for it.

'It's true,' he agreed. 'I never found out till now. He took my car. Did he say what he did out there?'

The girl with the tea vanished. Sally said, 'Why should I tell you?'

'Because it's important to me.'

'Benjamin didn't think so, did he?'

'I don't know. He told a doctor he'd done something unforgivable out there. I need to know what he meant by that.'

She stubbed out the cigarette, thought for a moment.

'Benjamin saw one of your cronies sucking up to Zeeland. He'd been working on that story for weeks.'

'What story?'

'About where your money came from. But you put a stop to that, didn't you?'

Hartmann shook his head.

'No I didn't. I didn't even know.'

'Oh come on. He was going to crap on your election . . .'

'I loved my brother. I would have done anything to help him.'

'Except be there.'

He looked round the place. There didn't seem to be anyone over the age of twenty or so.

'Is that why you encouraged Benjamin? So you could hurt me through him? He didn't fit in here either. You used him. He was the one you damaged.'

She nodded at the door and said, 'You should go. Your monkeys are getting restless.'

'He felt guilty,' Hartmann said. 'For chasing that story. Guilty for chasing me. Guilty for disappointing you I guess. So we're both responsible, Sally. Don't fool yourself otherwise.'

There was a look of doubt in her young face. He wondered if any of that had got through.

The bodyguards were chattering into their phones. Then Weber pushed his way through and said they had to leave.

'The press have got wind of this. Unless you want to be on the news surrounded by joints and herb tea we need to get out of here.'

Hartmann stood up, looked at the girl.

'Long time since I had a joint. It's really easy you know . . . shuffling off your responsibilities. Passing on the blame. Someone's got to try to run things. Take responsibility. Maybe one day you'll appreciate that.'

He scribbled his number on a scrap of paper and threw it in front of her.

'All I want is to understand why my brother died. If you change your mind and think you can help—'

'Troels!' Weber cried.

Hartmann tapped the paper.

'Call me whenever you like.'

Reinhardt was in an interview room, camera on, Lund and Borch on the other side of the table.

'An art gallery with a garage underneath,' Borch said. 'What do you do in there?'

'Not much,' Reinhardt answered. 'Clean my car. Fix it.'

'It's a company car,' Lund pointed out. 'They do all that for you.'

Nothing.

'We found a little bathroom too. A bed. Do you spend nights there?'

A shrug.

'I like to look at my paintings. Study them. Sometimes it gets late . . .'

Borch flicked through some records from the Majgården files.

'Seven boxes with photos of little children. Do you study them too?'

He groaned, as if the question were idiotic.

'Louise's details were in there, Reinhardt. The address of her foster home. Where she went to school.'

'They were there for convenience. I didn't even look at them.'

Borch picked up an evidence bag. The watch.

'You know what this is?'

'It's my old watch.'

'You like watches, don't you? Your wife said. Couldn't bear to throw it away even though it was broken.'

Lund pushed another bag in front of him.

'This is the watch we took from you yesterday. It's identical. You broke the old one. The watch your wife gave you. Then you replaced it with another.'

'I didn't want her to know. I was moving some things around and I caught it on a metal railing.'

'Where?'

'In the garage,' he said straight away.

'We're going to check, Reinhardt. It was just after the girl died, wasn't it? You broke the thing smashing her teeth—'

'No!'

Temperature rising, more pictures.

'This is your birthday party,' Lund said. 'The night after Louise was raped and murdered. There isn't a single photo of you wearing a watch.'

He didn't say anything. Just shook his head.

Borch took up the questions.

'You said you drove straight past Gudbjerghavn. But we've got your credit card being used in a newsagent's there. How come?'

'I don't . . .'

Hand to head. A look of pain.

'I don't deserve this . . .'

Another photo on the table. His car boot, the white paint scratches.

'You tracked her,' Borch went on. 'You picked her up. Turned off your phone. Drove her to that boatyard. Tied her up. Raped her for hours . . .'

Lund pushed a photo of the dead girl's mouth in front of him. Three teeth smashed, bloody lips.

'Did she fight, Reinhardt? Is that why you hit her?'

Chains and manacles. Blood on the single mattress on the floor.

'Wasn't she obedient like the other girls? Is that why you kept hitting her? Didn't she do as she was told?'

'These are lies . . .'

'She was alive when you dumped her in the harbour. Drowned her with that lump of concrete you tied round her legs.'

A pause. She waited, then asked, 'What are your daughters going to think? Will it be a surprise? Or . . . ?'

There was a flash of anger and heat in his eyes and Lund thought: *Now I see him.*

'You didn't go to any hotel,' Borch went on. 'You drove straight back to your garage. You cleaned the car. Took a shower. Then what? Poured yourself a drink. Pulled out her record from your files. Thought . . . had that one now?'

'I haven't done anything!'

They were out of photos. Out of ideas. Apart from one.

'We know you were there, Reinhardt,' Lund told him. 'We know we can prove this. The only question is . . .'

He knew what was coming.

'Are you going to tell us now so we can find Emilie Zeuthen alive? Or just screw around like this until she's dead?'

'I would never do anything to harm Emilie,' he spat back. 'She's a Zeuthen. A beautiful child. You should take that beast Rantzau into a room and force it out of him . . .'

The door opened. Brix there, beckoning.

'Busy,' Lund told him.

'Out!'

Back in the office by her desk. A lawyer called Keldgård. Donald Trump hair and the same smile, a lackey with him and lots of files. Dyhring too.

'You have no right to subject an innocent man to any further questioning,' Keldgård said. 'I want Niels Reinhardt—'

'Piss off,' Borch snapped. 'We've got a pile of evidence building against this bastard. He's been stringing us along from the start.'

The man glared at Brix.

'See! Just like I said. Your people keep insinuating that Zeuthen and Zeeland are somehow incriminated in this matter. That they pressured your prosecutor . . .'

'We never said that,' Lund pointed out.

'What is it you're after?' the lawyer asked. 'Good headlines? A multinational company picking on a penniless orphan from Jutland . . .'

Borch stuck a finger in his face.

'This girl was raped and murdered . . .'

'Not by Reinhardt,' the man interjected. 'Your conspiracy theories are ridiculous. It's a scandal no one has stopped you before now.'

'Peter Schultz . . .' Lund started.

'Was covering his own mistakes. Nothing more than that.'

Keldgård threw some documents on the desk.

'We've been making our own inquiries. He was trying to nail the sailors for the crime. Then when he realized he'd screwed up he logged it as a suicide. He did that, Lund. No one else.'

Her finger pointed back to the interview room.

'Reinhardt has questions to answer . . .'

'This kid's notebook's useless. We talked to him too. He only wrote down Danish licence plates. The road's not far from the

German border. Any tourists, any foreign workers going home . . .
he ignored them.'

He smiled.

'You mean you didn't know that?'

Keldgård turned to Dyhring.

'Reinhardt was in his room at the Hotel Royal Prince when
Louise Hjelby went missing.'

'We confirmed this,' Dyhring said. 'We looked at the hotel
registration records. The key logs. Reinhardt used his card to go in
the room at twenty-five past three. He didn't leave until eight thirty
the next morning.'

She tried to catch Brix's eye.

'We need to check this.'

'Why?' Dyhring asked. 'Don't you believe me? It wasn't him,
Lund.'

The lawyer retrieved his papers.

'This is the last time you target Reinhardt and Zeeland with these
ludicrous accusations. I can only pray you do a better job trying to
find Emilie Zeuthen.'

Brix snapped his fingers. Reinhardt came out of the interview
room, shook hands with the lawyer and his assistant. The three of
them walked off. Dyhring followed.

'If it's not him then who the hell is it?' Borch wondered.

Brix was staring at the documents on Lund's desk.

'Why are you still looking at the Birk Larsen files?'

'I wasn't. I just haven't had time to put them back.'

He folded his arms, long face, disappointment written all over it.

'The Justice Minister wants us to handle the interrogation from
now on,' Dyhring announced. 'Understandable. Borch?'

'What?'

'We need to talk. In thirty minutes Rantzau's ours.'

She got in there first, just as a warder was bringing some food. Lund
took the tray off him, placed it on the bed. Rantzau was in a blue
prisoner suit. He didn't look well.

'Are you OK?' she asked.

He said nothing, got the tray, put it on his lap, started to eat
with a slow deliberate precision, as if to a steady rhythm.

Lund waited a while and then said, 'It can't be Reinhardt.'

The fork went up, went down.

'We weren't so smart with the notebook, Loke. The boy only made a note of Danish numbers. Reinhardt's got an alibi.'

Nothing.

'We're reopening the investigation. Full staffing. Looking back at everything we have. Sending people out to Jutland again.' A pause. He still didn't look at her. 'It's going to take some time.'

Eyes on the tray. He kept eating.

'I'm going to find out who killed your daughter. I promise.' He picked up a yoghurt pot, sniffed at it. 'Don't make Emilie Zeuthen die for this.'

Spoon in the pot. He tasted it. Wrinkled his nose.

With the warder watching from the door she got up, knocked the tray off his lap, sent everything crashing to the hard stone floor. Thrust a sheaf of papers under his nose.

'Read it for yourself. He was in his hotel room. All sorts of cars drove past that day.'

He took the papers, looked at them.

'Maybe you're the one who's blind. You're obsessed with Zeeland. Maybe you're what they say . . . a crazy.'

Silence.

'Oh fuck it,' she snapped and turned to go.

'There's a wisdom in craziness, Lund,' he said in the same flat, tired intelligent voice. 'Sometimes. You have a son, right?'

'I told you this . . .'

'Then why's Zeuthen's little girl so important to you? Don't you want to look after your own? You have your nice little house. The plants in the garden. A good life.'

'You don't know my life! Whatever point you wanted to prove is made. If you want to give Louise justice—'

His fingers went up. The sign of a devil's horns.

'Justice . . .' Rantzau hissed. 'You talk of justice? It's the only damn thing I can give her. I was working for those bastards night and day for years. Hardly came home. Never knew I had a daughter. Trapped in some stinking Somalian hole getting kicked and tortured day in and day out. When I come out? Old man Zeuthen doesn't want to know me.'

The hate in him diminished for a moment.

'Monika . . . we broke up. She never told me she was pregnant.

Then I get back and look for her. She's dead. And she had a daughter . . .'

'I talked to her foster parents, Loke. They said she was a sweet, bright girl. She wouldn't want—'

'Louise isn't here. I am. I gave her nothing while she was alive. Zeeland . . .' A hard stare full of hatred. 'You ask me to show consideration for something you call justice. My child was raped and thrown into the harbour. You had every chance to find out why. And what did you do?'

A prison guard came and said PET wanted to talk to him in the interview room. Bent down, started to unlock his shackles.

'If Emilie dies,' Lund said, 'your daughter's going to be forgotten. A record in a file no one opens. Not because I want that. I'd like anything but. Because you stopped us, Loke. No one else. You.'

They took him away.

Lund sat on the bed in the empty cell. After a while Juncker came in.

'I just took a call from the hospital. Your son's girlfriend just had a baby.'

She got hold of the tray, started to pick the broken crockery and bits of food off the floor.

'Did he say anything, Lund?'

'No.'

She put the tray on the bed, stood up. The warder could do the rest.

'So what do we do now?'

It was getting dark outside.

'I've no idea, Asbjørn. Sorry.'

Hartmann didn't talk much on the way back to Christiansborg. At six Weber called a briefing with Mogens Rank.

'Lund's colourful conspiracy theories have flown out of the window,' he told them. 'There'll be a reckoning there. All this nonsense about business interests and political interference has been laid to rest.'

'So did Schultz act under pressure or not?' Hartmann asked.

'No,' Rank insisted. 'I've already said . . . when we met he simply wanted to close the case. I had him confirm Zeeland weren't involved. After that he was trying to hide his own incompetence.

It was nothing to do with us. Nothing to do with Ussing. Just one small man and his blunders.'

Weber started to scribble something.

'We need a press release. Before the debate.'

Rank nodded.

'Agreed. If you want me to hold a conference I can make all this clear. Ussing's accusations about us covering up for Zeeland have no basis in truth and we should say it. This is good news . . .'

Hartmann shook his head.

'Don't start cheering until the girl's found. Lean on PET all you can.' He checked his watch. 'I need to see someone.'

He went down the corridor to the media department. Found her collating papers by the photocopier.

Busy room. Boring work. Someone had to do it. Karen Nebel had given up a career on national TV. For this.

Hartmann looked round, gestured at the others in the room. Watched them leave.

Got a filthy look from her.

'Karen. I had to pull you out of the team while everything was being checked out. We now know there's nothing—'

'I told you that. You didn't believe me.'

He grabbed a chair, rolled it beside her, sat down.

'You've every right to be angry. I was a fool. I should have been more trusting.'

'True.'

'I need you. More than ever now.'

The practised smile of a politician, importunate, knowing, expectant.

She groaned.

'Oh for God's sake don't try that stunt on me. I'm not Rosa Lebech. You can't screw your way out of this one.'

'Can't I?'

Nebel blinked. Then put a hand on his shoulder, stroked his cheek, briefly ran her fingers through his hair.

'Not while I'm conscious, dear. Are you ready for the debate?'

'I think so.'

'In that case you're not.' She picked up a couple of sheets of paper. 'Here's what you're going to say.'

He reached out. She pulled them back.

'Don't ever do that to me again. Understood?'

Morten Weber came round the corner with their coats.

'Are we all comrades in arms again?' he asked cheerily.

She laughed at that. He went over and to her surprise pecked her cheek.

'I missed you, O wise one,' Weber said. 'And so did this idiot. Didn't you . . . ?'

Hartmann was taking a phone call.

'I'll see you in the car,' he said when it was done.

The girl was in the shadows near the steps. Black hat, hair hidden. Face without make-up this time.

Growing up, he thought. They all did it. Benjamin was just late. He would have got there one day.

Hartmann told the bodyguards to stay where they were and went over. She dropped a cigarette onto the Christiansborg cobbles, ground it with her heavy boot.

'I lied about Benjamin. He didn't hate you. He didn't want to hurt you.'

'Thanks.'

'To be honest he was proud of you. He said you were a decent man. But the world you were in was like that. He didn't want to be a part of it. I suppose . . .'

Someone walked past. She went quiet.

'What?' he asked.

'I suppose we did use him. He was a nice bloke. He didn't really belong with us.'

She reached out and pointed a finger at Hartmann's chest.

'But someone did put pressure on him. If it wasn't you it was someone else. He was worried. He wanted us to get rid of the photos.'

'Wait, wait, wait,' Hartmann interrupted. 'What photos?'

'In Jutland he took a lot of pictures. He put them on his web account. He was going to publish them in *Frontal*.'

'Photos of what?'

'I never saw them. His account got deleted. Benjamin freaked out when it happened. He lost everything.'

Hartmann tried to think back to those last few days.

'I don't remember him mentioning anything like this.'

'Well, he wouldn't. He was using Delta for the web. They're owned by Zeeland. He thought . . .' She shrugged. 'I don't know. He was getting paranoid. He said there was a backup somewhere.'

'Where?'

'He never told me.' She pulled a set of keys out of her pocket. 'He asked me to hold on to these. I don't know what they're for. I don't know why he kept them really.' A pause. 'Hartmann?'

He didn't know what to say.

'I'm sorry I made you feel bad. That was mean. Your brother was a nice guy. Bit too gentle to be hanging round with us. Maybe we're the ones who should feel guilty.' She looked at the palace ahead. 'I don't know.'

The girl called Sally turned on her heels and was gone.

Hartmann looked at what she'd left him: two keys on a piece of string.

The Zeeland offices were emptying at the end of the day. Zeuthen was alone in his room, trying to think. Security had called with the latest news from the Politigården. No new leads on Emilie. Nothing on the Jutland case.

He'd phoned Brix and asked for a personal meeting with the kidnapper. A chance to make a direct plea. The answer was non-committal. But if Zeuthen turned up they could hardly refuse him.

And face-to-face . . .

He had the silver handgun from the mansion. Took it out of his briefcase. Checked the magazine. Reminded himself how to use the thing. Security had taught him when he first succeeded his father at the helm of the company. A precaution, nothing more.

A sound at the door. Zeuthen hastily stuffed the weapon into his jacket pocket. Maja came in, looked at him suspiciously.

'What are you doing?'

'I'm going to the Politigården. Maybe if I can persuade Brix to let me talk to him he'll say something.'

She always had a way of seeing through him.

'Let me come too. If we're both there . . .'

'It's going to be hard enough to get Brix to let me in, love.'

Her curious eyes stayed on him.

'It'll be fine,' he said, then came and quickly kissed her. 'We'll get her back.'

361

On the way out the PA caught him.

'I checked Reinhardt's records like you asked,' she said. 'There's nothing here that connects him to the Jutland girl.'

'Thought so,' he said, waiting for the lift.

'Right after he was with you at the crisis meeting.'

There was something she wanted to say.

'It's odd.' The woman looked uncomfortable. 'I don't really understand . . .'

'Can this wait?'

She shook her head.

'I think you ought to see it now.'

Back at the hospital, walking down the long corridor, headed for the room where she'd last seen Eva. The same doctor was on duty, standing by a wall phone, checking some records.

'I told you to call,' Lund complained. 'You could just leave a message or—'

'We had to induce in a hurry,' the woman said. 'There wasn't time.'

She had such a casual, relaxed manner. It was infuriating.

'I didn't want her to be on her own when it happened. That's the worst . . .'

The doctor looked puzzled.

'I'm sorry?'

'You shouldn't be alone . . .'

'Eva wasn't. Your son came this morning. He's been here the whole time.' She smiled. 'He really helped. Nice lad though . . .' She laughed. 'I thought he might pass out when I said he could cut the cord. He managed it, mind.'

She went a couple of doors down, beckoned Lund to follow.

'Go in if you like.'

Through the window, Eva on the bed, a baby in her arms. Mark next to her, holding a tiny hand. He touched Eva's hair, kissed her.

'They both did brilliantly,' the doctor added. 'The baby's fine. No problems.'

She held out her hand.

'Congratulations. You're a grandmother.' Her bleeper went. 'Sorry.' She nodded at the room. 'Stay as long as you want.'

Alone Lund watched, unseen behind the glass. Saw Mark take the little girl in his arms, a look of pride and wonder on his young face.

Six years ago a surly kid turning into a surly teenager. Now a father. A good one too. She was sure that would be the case.

And he'd found his own way here. Without her help. In spite of her. Lund knew she could leave and they'd never see. But she'd walked out on him so many times before.

Hand on the door, deep breath. A smile, not forced, one of joy.

As she was about to walk in her phone rang.

'Lund? They said I had one phone call. You're it.'

A voice she'd never forget. Calm. Rational. Controlling.

'Loke.'

'I'm willing to take a risk. If you promise my daughter's killer will be punished I'll show you where Emilie Zeuthen is.'

'You know I will.'

'Then come and get me.'

She walked away from the door, tried to control her temper.

'Make this easy for us just this once, will you? Tell me where she is and—'

'No,' Rantzau interrupted. 'I make the conditions. I lead the way. Take it or leave it.'

Nothing was ever simple with this man.

'I can't make that call.'

'Then find someone who can. There are no other options.' He paused for effect. 'You need to do this now, Lund. Time's running out. You don't want to pick up a body, do you?'

There was a sound. Other voices. Then Borch came on the line.

'I don't like this,' he said. 'He's up to something.'

Through the window she watched them. Mark still had the baby in his arms, eyes on nothing but the tiny bundle. Eva's hand on his.

'On my way,' she said.

Zeuthen read the printout the PA had found, asked where Kornerup was. Found him in the basement garage, getting back from an appointment.

'What the hell were you doing checking up on this case in Jutland two years ago?'

363

He scattered the pages on the bonnet of the black Mercedes.

'I've just read the files from the archive,' Zeuthen said. 'You wanted to be kept informed. Why?'

The look on Kornerup's face told him the temporary truce between them was over.

'Why are you digging up the past, Robert? There's nothing that concerns you there.'

Zeuthen jabbed a finger at him.

'You were looking—'

'I'm more than happy to go upstairs and discuss this if you wish. There was the possibility one of our sailors was involved . . .'

'Don't lie to me! They weren't even charged. So why were you interested?'

Kornerup folded his arms and leaned back against the car.

'I'm the CEO of this company. Your father wasn't long in the grave. It was my job—'

'You thought Reinhardt was involved?'

A snort of disgust.

'Of course not. Don't be ridiculous.'

Zeuthen took the collar of his coat.

'I want to know what you've been up to. This is my daughter's life we're talking about. If I find you've protected Reinhardt—'

'The only person I've protected is you! I promised your father. He knew you weren't up to it. The crisis. Negotiations with the government. We needed him, not you. And since he wasn't there I acted as he would in the circumstances.'

'I want to know—'

'If you doubt Reinhardt ask him to his face. He's served this company and your family all his life.'

Kornerup nodded down the garage, to a tall figure standing by the lift.

'I think he's owed that, don't you?' he said and brushed past.

Niels Reinhardt glanced at Zeuthen, then looked away. The cuts and bruises on his face were still livid. Yet he was immaculate again. White shirt. Dark tie. He walked over, the ever-present servant.

'I should have told you Kornerup was informed about the Jutland case, Robert. It was simply because our sailors were involved. I was the one who passed him the file. That's why my name's there. I'm sorry. What with everything . . . it slipped my mind.'

Zeuthen nodded, said nothing.

'I'd do anything to get Emilie back home,' Reinhardt added. 'I hope you know that.'

The phone rang in Zeuthen's pocket.

Maja, excited, tense.

'He's talking to them, Robert. He says he'll show them where Emilie is.'

'Where?'

'They don't know. They're on their way to the airport.'

Zeuthen snapped his fingers at Reinhardt, threw him the car keys.

'I'll talk to Brix,' he said. 'Stay by the phone. I'll get back as soon as I can.'

Ten past eight, Kastrup. Brix had approved the helicopter charter. A white AS365 Dauphin.

Five hundred and fifty kilometres to Stavanger in Norway. Flight time one hour and forty-five minutes. Local police to meet them on arrival.

Rantzau went in the back on his own, cuffed and shackled. She sat on the bench ahead, across from Borch. Seat belt. Safety briefing from the pilot. The sound of the engine, the steady rush of the rotor blades. The Dauphin lifted from the black asphalt, rose over the lights of Kastrup, flew into the cold, damp night.

Just before ten Ruth Hedeby came down for a briefing with Brix. Dyhring was with her.

'Where are they going?' she asked.

'Stavanger.'

'I know that. But where exactly?'

'Once I have the details I'll give you a full briefing.'

The bitter smile.

'Upstairs want it now. How do we know the girl's in Norway?'

Brix picked up his notes.

'He says he shipped her there in a container. He told Lund he'd prepared it for his own escape. It looks plausible.'

Hedeby stared at him.

'Plausible? Is that the best you've got? So she's not inside this tank like he said?'

Brix was getting bored with this.

'He says she's in the tank, inside the container. That way nobody can hear her if she starts yelling. If—'

'Well find the bloody container then!'

'We're looking. But there are hundreds of them shipped to Norway over the past few days. Some have landed. Some are in transit elsewhere. Some still en route.'

She waved a hand at him.

'You've got nothing, have you? You've chartered a helicopter. Sent Lund and Borch out of Danish jurisdiction with a murderer? All on the promise that we'll find his daughter's killer?'

'We will,' Brix insisted. 'What would you have done in the circumstances?'

Dyhring shook his head.

'Loke Rantzau doesn't believe in your investigation. He hasn't from the start. It's just one more game . . .'

Hedeby ordered him into the adjoining empty office, leaving the PET man to make a call.

'You need to understand the situation, Lennart. Mogens Rank just held a press conference. He hauled us over the coals. Lund's been a disaster throughout and you've let her do whatever she wanted.'

'When I asked you what you'd have done differently . . .'

'I wouldn't have pissed off every last person along the way. I've got Zeeland and the government on our backs. Whether Hartmann wins the election or not we're screwed unless we get that kid back safely.'

He closed his eyes, took a deep breath, then said, 'Hard as this may be for you to understand, Ruth, that isn't why we're looking for her.'

Brix went back to the office. She vanished into a huddle with Dyhring. Juncker was moaning that he hadn't been included in the trip to Norway.

'You'll get a helicopter ride one day,' Brix grumbled.

'It's not about the bloody helicopter! Here I am going through Zeeland personnel files . . .'

'What?'

'Something Lund asked for,' Juncker explained.

'Did you get hold of Robert Zeuthen as I asked?'

'I can't find him . . . I could still fly up there—'

'What do you mean you can't find him?'

Juncker stopped, thought about something.

'I mean he wouldn't get back to me when I left messages. That helicopter—'

'For God's sake, Asbjørn. Forget the helicopter.'

The young detective was flicking through his notes. He passed Brix the flight details, pointed to the fine print on the bottom of the charter order.

'You know who owns the company, don't you?' Juncker asked.

Towards the end of the flight her phone rang.

'Where are you?' Eva asked. 'It sounds like—'

'I'm working. How's the baby?'

A squeal of delight.

'Forty-four centimetres and three thousand five hundred grams. And she's got all her fingers and toes. She's beautiful. When are you—?'

'And Mark was there.'

'Yeah. He's been really sweet. He's holding her now. Do you want to talk to him?'

The pilot was signalling at her to cut the call. The landing pad was ahead. They were going down.

'I've got to go. I'll be home tomorrow. Send me a picture of her.'

'Sure,' Eva said. 'I think she just woke up.'

Over the racket of the helicopter Lund could just make out a high-pitched cry.

She looked at her messages. Found the one from Brix and showed it to Rantzau.

'This is confirmation we're investigating your daughter's case. We're checking traffic cameras on the main road. Going through border records . . .'

He was back in the green sailing jacket he'd worn at Zeeland. Glanced at the email, unmoved.

'Does Zeuthen know we've left Copenhagen?'

'The parents are being kept informed,' Lund said. 'I'll keep you updated about everything that happens in Louise's case. You know the deal, Loke. Let's get Emilie now.'

He nodded. Then after a while said, 'We need to go for a drive.'

'Where?' Borch wanted to know. 'Around Stavanger?'

'Bit further than that.' He nodded at the window, the sea marked by street lights along the waterfront. 'Up the coast.'

'Wait,' Borch said. 'You sent the container here and then shipped it somewhere else?'

Rantzau looked at Lund.

'He catches on quickly, doesn't he? If you do as I say I'll lead you to the girl.'

Borch shook a fist in his face.

'Drop this shit and tell us where the container is.'

Rantzau closed his eyes, leaned back on the seat. Looked asleep. Lund's phone rang again. She looked at the screen. Still no picture.

'We've a problem,' Brix said. 'Zeuthen found out where you were going. That helicopter firm belongs to him. One of his planes just landed in Stavanger ahead of you.'

They were coming down. She looked out of the window. A single executive jet was parked near the helipad. Nearby was a fleet of police vehicles, blue lights flashing.

'What do you want me to do?'

'Keep him away from Rantzau. But keep him happy.'

Not long after they were down Borch went to talk to the Norwegian police.

Thirty seconds. That was all it took. Then Robert Zeuthen strode up, winter jacket, open-necked shirt, Niels Reinhardt in overcoat, suit and tie behind him.

He looked at Rantzau. Rantzau at him. Then they led the man in shackles to the back of a secure van.

'What did he say, Lund?' Zeuthen asked. 'Where is she?'

'We're going up the coast. I need you to wait here. We'll bring Emilie straight back.'

'Screw that!' Zeuthen yelled. 'She had two days' air and you wasted one of them pestering Niels here.'

'We're on top of this . . .'

Zeuthen shook his head.

'Do you want me to call Troels Hartmann? See what he says? We know this area. We can help.'

'We'll stay in the background,' Reinhardt added.

'I'm going to be there, Lund,' Zeuthen said. 'Best get used to it.'

Borch was back, shaking his head.

'I need you to follow instructions, Robert,' Lund said. 'Get in my way and you're gone.'

'Whatever you say,' Zeuthen answered and told Reinhardt to get them a car.

Maja had brought Carl to the office. He was playing with his cars on the table while the security officers tried to track ship movements around Stavanger. It seemed impossible. Thousands of fjords, most of them navigable with small docks scattered everywhere.

Then Kornerup came in. A man she'd never liked.

'Any news?' he asked.

'Not yet. I need to go home for a while. Carl's bedtime. We need a helicopter and a doctor on standby in Stavanger for when they find Emilie.'

Kornerup nodded.

'Of course. I looked at some of the work Rantzau did for us. He was in Norway regularly, putting in IT systems and security networks. He must know the coast and the fjords very well.'

She looked at him.

'Have you told the police?'

'We will, Maja. Don't worry.'

It needed saying.

'I suppose there are plenty of places to hide someone there. Empty buildings. Old boatyards. Now you've moved so much out to Asia.'

He stifled a smile.

'I'm sorry if I've offended you somehow. We're doing everything we—'

'Carl!' she cried. 'Come on. Let's go home.'

'The board and I are putting pressure on the government to get Emilie back home,' Kornerup added.

She shook her head, told Carl to put his toys away.

'When this is over I'll make sure we look at your security,' he promised. 'The kids in particular.'

'You're fired, aren't you?'

He did smile then.

'It was a misunderstanding. I assure—'

'You couldn't care less about us. All that matters . . .' She glanced round the flashy office. '. . . is this. Zeeland. Money. Power. Greed.'

'Drekar's a very fine mansion, Maja. Where do you think it came from?'

She went to the boy, scooped up his toys, put them in her bag. Kornerup followed.

'I would like you to know—'

'When we get Emilie back things are going to change here,' she snapped. 'As for your misunderstanding . . .'

A little hand came up and took hers.

'Mum,' Carl said. 'Let's go.'

The TV studios for the last debate in an interminable election. Hartmann fought hard to concentrate, to get Benjamin out of his head. The girl Sally. A set of keys.

'Can you confirm that the police are on their way to Norway to get Emilie?' the presenter asked at the outset of the programme. 'I know this is an unusual way to start a debate. But all of Denmark wants an answer . . .'

'We do,' Hartmann said without a second thought. 'We all want the agony of the Zeuthen family to end. The Justice Minister will be making a fuller statement shortly. But I can say that it appears the kidnapping's over. The criminal who seized Emilie has agreed to tell police where she's being kept.'

Ussing, Rosa Lebech, the minority party leaders all in a row.

'Here we go,' Ussing cut in. 'Hartmann's selling his hollow optimism. How long before we realize it's just a pack of lies again?'

'This is a child's life,' Hartmann shaking his head.

'Yes and you've played it for your own advantage,' Ussing retorted. 'Because none of your promises are worth a cent without your friends in Zeeland. Is it true they're withholding money from your campaign funds until Emilie Zeuthen's found?'

'Not that I know.'

'So you won't deny it . . . ?'

'Oh for pity's sake, Ussing. Where are you going with this?'

'Who leaned on the deputy prosecutor, Hartmann? Who set those goons of PET on me?'

Ussing was losing it. Getting loud. Gesticulating.

Hartmann looked straight at the camera. Kept calm. Didn't waver.

'Someone's behind this!' Ussing yelled. 'Someone . . .'

Fifteen minutes later back in the make-up room Karen Nebel was pacing up and down.

'He managed to sow some doubt there. We're two points down in the polls.'

Mogens Rank was on the monitor, giving an interview about the hunt in Norway.

'There isn't a woman in this country who'll vote for him after that,' Hartmann said. 'What's Lund up to?'

'Doing what this bastard Rantzau asks. He won't give them an address. They have to go wherever he says.'

He leaned back and looked at himself in the mirror.

'For how long?'

She shrugged.

'They seem to believe him. Robert Zeuthen's with them too.' She came and sat on the make-up table, looked at him. 'How about we pull in some of the little people on the right for a beer?'

He laughed.

'I'm not that desperate.'

'You are, Troels. With margins like these it could go any way.'

A rap at the door. Morten Weber came in. Damp coat from the wet night. Downcast.

'Anything?' Hartmann asked.

'No joy,' Weber said dangling the keys. 'I tried the people at that place he went to. They don't know anything.'

'They fit somewhere. Benjamin gave them to that girl. He had a backup of some photos from Jutland. Give me the keys.'

Weber handed them over.

'He must have got photos of Karen talking to Reinhardt. It doesn't mean a damned thing.'

Hartmann shook his head.

'Then why did someone from Zeeland delete them from the server?'

'Because Zeeland closed that company down. Lots of people have lost their stuff . . .'

Nebel sighed, got their coats.

'I want to see what he had,' Hartmann insisted. 'There must be someone you haven't asked about the keys.'

'Like who? The election's tomorrow. Why are we wasting time on this? Have we given up already? I'm sorry about Benjamin. But you're getting obsessed—'

'Give me the keys,' Nebel snapped and took them out of Hartmann's hands. 'If it's so important I'll take care of it.'

'For God's sake Karen . . .' Weber whined.

'It's done,' she said brightly, pocketing the things. 'Let's get out of here, shall we?'

An hour outside Stavanger, travelling down narrow winding roads. The Norwegian police were in the front. Next came Lund and Borch in a small van with a secure unit at the back. Loke Rantzau was in there, cuffed to a metal bar attached to the seatback. The medics had given him painkillers for his wound, which he popped from time to time. Zeuthen and Reinhardt followed behind.

Brix called. He'd set Juncker working on shipping records in conjunction with Zeeland's security people. Seventy containers had passed through Stavanger during the window they were looking at. Every last one went in a different direction.

Nothing cross-referenced with the lists they'd found in the underground lair he'd been using. The *Medea*, where he'd tortured the three sailors, had been searched again in the hunt for useful paperwork. Nothing so far.

Borch was driving. Lund told him what was going on.

'Doesn't matter if he leads us to the girl,' she added.

It wasn't easy to see the surrounding countryside in the dark but it must have been hilly and wild.

'If,' Borch muttered. 'He could still be jerking us around. There's no guarantee she's still alive. If he put her in this tank. Jesus . . .' He glanced back. 'Who could do something like that? To a kid? Bloody hell . . .'

'She has to be alive.'

'Yeah.' He looked at her. Grinned. 'By the way . . . congratulations, grandma.'

Lund laughed.

'Thanks.'

'A girl.' She'd told him this already. 'That's good. The important thing is for them to have another kid soon. You need eighteen months, two years between them. That way they team up. Become their own little army.'

He glanced at her.

'You were an only child. Look where it got you.'

'Thanks!' She tried to remember. 'You were an only child too.'

'Yeah. Maybe that's why we hooked up in the first place. Like attracts like. Screwed up together.'

She put down the map she'd been using.

'You were never screwed up.'

'I was when you left me.'

Lund didn't say anything. Just liked the sound of his voice.

'Let's say we find Emilie alive,' he went on. 'And this all has a happy ending. You go back to being a granny in Copenhagen. Pushing paper in OPA.'

That would be good, she thought. That was a life she could take.

'I like that idea,' Lund said.

'So will you move in with me? You still owe me the deposit for that flat we never took. I'm willing to take that as a downpayment. You won't have to give me a penny.'

Her hand went to her forehead. He was looking at her. The puppy expression again. Full of need and longing.

'I'm not moving in with anyone. And besides . . . you're married.'

'Not for much longer. That was falling apart anyway.'

'Mathias . . . I don't want to hear—'

'You're a grannie!'

'So you keep saying.'

'It's about time you settled down.' He took his hand off the steering wheel and tapped his chest. 'With me. We could live in that little shed of yours I suppose . . .'

Her phone rang. Borch kept nagging. She told him to shut up.

It was Juncker. He said they'd got some mobile phone data from the masts in Jutland on the day Louise was snatched. Fifty black cars on the road besides those in the notebook. German, Polish, Swedish . . .

'Talk to the drivers,' she said. 'Check their alibis.'

'Fine but are we sure about the date? In the prosecutor's report it says April the twenty-first . . .'

'Forget that, Asbjørn. He changed the date. It's April the twentieth you need to look at. Check the watchmakers like I asked. The pathologist thought the damage to Louise's teeth came from a watch. Find out if any of the motorists handed one in for repair.' She glanced at Borch. He was still lost in his imagination. 'And keep going with the old files.'

A noise from behind. Rantzau was banging on the window separating them from the secure compartment.

'Can we stop?' he asked over the intercom. 'I'd like a cigarette.'

'We're not stopping till we get there,' Borch told him.

'Fine,' Rantzau said. 'Take the next left, then up the fjord. Just where it runs inland. You need to drive to the end.'

Lund checked on the map.

'That's got to be another four hours or more,' she said. 'The road goes nowhere. There's no town—'

'I know that,' Rantzau said. 'Wake me up when we arrive.'

She looked in the mirror. He'd rolled his head back, closed his eyes, looked ready to sleep.

It was almost midnight. They'd be lucky to reach the place he'd indicated by dawn.

'We'll get there,' Lund said. 'We'll find that girl.'

Borch nodded.

'Also . . . my house may be small but it's not a shed.'

'Could use some work,' he suggested. 'An extension at least.'

She snorted.

'Oh, yes. And I remember how good you were at that. Screaming at screwdrivers. Drilling through pipes . . .'

That got to him.

'Hey. That was back then. I'm pretty good now. Lots of practice.'

Headlights punching through the black Norwegian night. Trees by the side of the road. Forests to get lost in. She hadn't been in one of those since Nanna Birk Larsen went missing six long years before. And now Mark, little Mark, was a father. The elusive bonds of family were finally beginning to fall into place.

'OK,' Lund said. 'You can build us an extension. I want radiators in it though.'

And left it at that.

Mathias Borch let out a little whoop and then a drum roll on the steering wheel. His fingers drifted towards hers.

A tunnel loomed up. He had to swerve to keep in line.

'Eyes ahead,' she said. 'On the road.'

Then patted his hand on the wheel and went back to the map.

Ten

Election day. The formal campaign was over. Nothing for the politicians to do but smile for the cameras, vote for themselves then sit back and wait for the verdict of the public.

When Hartmann walked to the polling station near Christiansborg the mob of reporters around him didn't want to know about the economy or his rescue package. Every question was about Emilie.

Was she alive or dead? Could he offer any prospect of the miracle the whole nation sought? That she might come home safe, be reunited with her family?

His answers were anodyne and non-committal. Talk of hope and prayer. Little else.

Inside Weber briefed him. The opposition parties were still on the fence, waiting to know what would happen in Norway.

And from there . . . no news. The convoy had driven deep into the remote, empty hinterland, travelling through the night. Whenever the police thought they were approaching their destination Rantzau gave them fresh instructions. Ten hours they'd been on the road and still it went on.

Hartmann went for the door.

'Hang on.' Weber grabbed his arm, nodded at the voting hall. 'Ussing's in there.'

'I'm not waiting for Anders Ussing,' Hartmann said and marched inside.

The Socialist leader was putting his paper into a ballot box, beaming for a line of photographers.

'Sorry we turned up together,' Hartmann said. 'Bad luck they say.'

'For you,' Ussing replied happily. 'Enjoy today, Troels. It's your last in Christiansborg.'

Hartmann kept quiet, went into the booth. Looked at the paper with the names, the pencil. His phone went.

'It's Karen . . .'

'Anything on the keys?'

'One of Sally's friends saw him buying a padlock. He had a place where he kept his basketball things and some stuff he brought back from America.'

'Benjamin never played basketball. That can't be right.'

'She said it wasn't far from the railway. Where he died . . .'

Outside he could hear Ussing braying as usual.

'Perhaps he doesn't know who to vote for!'

A round of laughter.

Hartmann came out, placed his paper in the box, was gone before most of the photographers caught it.

'Another picture,' a couple cried.

'Even the Prime Minister only gets a single vote,' Hartmann told them with a brief smile and went for the stairs, Weber hard on his heels.

On the steps the little man started whining.

'This is our last chance to turn the tide. Can you just stop and smile for the cameras please?'

'Karen's found a place Benjamin was using to keep things. Maybe those keys fit—'

'Oh for God's sake. Not today . . .'

'Cancel all my appointments,' Hartmann ordered. 'We're going to Nørrebro.'

After the serpentine rural roads through Norway Rantzau had led them back to the coast and a small container terminal north of Bergen. Borch was fuming. The man himself was silent, had slept seemingly peacefully most of the time.

When they arrived the modest dockside was stacked with containers from all over the world. He said the one they were looking for was green and numbered 67678. It wasn't there.

Lund was on the phone to Brix. He was getting nervous.

'Why the hell can't you find it?' he demanded.

'Borch's checking out the shipping logs with the manager here. I'll let you . . .'

An angry figure came out of the office. Sheets in hand. Two Norwegian uniform men had Rantzau by both arms near the waterside. He kept looking at the grey sky and yawning.

She followed Borch as he crossed the jetty, trying to get him to talk.

They got to Rantzau.

'You had the container picked up from here yesterday,' Borch said. 'Where is it?'

The yawn again then Rantzau asked, 'Did I?'

It happened in a second. Borch's right hand came up and slapped him in the face.

'Where the hell is it?'

A laugh. Another slap. The Norwegians were getting nervous.

Lund got between them, told him to cut it out. Rantzau looked sicker than ever. A red weal was working up on his right cheek. He was unshaven. Pale. Unsteady on his feet.

'Where's the girl, Loke?' she asked.

He shot a glance at Borch.

'You can tell your boyfriend if he does that one more time we may as well all go home.'

'He won't,' she promised, pushing Borch back. 'You've had us running all round Norway on a wild goose chase. You said time was running out.'

Rantzau looked at the water, coughed.

'He had it picked up by a truck,' Borch said, thrusting some paperwork in front of her. 'There's no record of where it went.'

'Loke.' She stood closer until he looked at her. 'We've got a deal. Copenhagen won't keep chasing Louise's case if you won't help us.'

He nodded.

'The truth is I arranged for it to go somewhere quieter than this. I didn't know they'd pick it up yesterday.'

Borch pushed his way in.

'Who did you use for the transport? Give me a name or I swear to God I'll slap you again, and it's going to be harder this time.'

Rantzau looked at him, looked away. At Lund.

'We're going up the fjord,' he said. 'You'll need a boat.'

A commotion behind. Zeuthen was there, hands in his pockets, trying to barge in.

Lund yelled until two Norwegian officers intervened, keeping him back.

'Loke. This has to be for real,' she said.

'Everything I do's for real, Lund. What's the point otherwise?'

He nodded at a small white pleasure cruiser, moored by the pier.

'That'll do.'

Half an hour later they'd chartered the boat and were heading up the bare fjord. There was snow on the slopes, breaks of sunshine between heavy, threatening cloud. Rantzau stood in the lee of the cabin, out of the icy wind, handcuffed to the metalwork, smoking as many cigarettes as he could beg.

After an hour their generosity ran out.

She joined Borch, Reinhardt and Zeuthen at the stern where they were poring over charts.

'We used to have small boatyards up here,' Reinhardt said. 'Rantzau visited quite a few setting up their IT systems. He must know the area very well.'

Borch looked dubious. The fjord seemed empty.

'Where the hell could you put a container ashore here?'

Reinhardt thought it was possible. There were several small harbours, a few of them with roads linking back to the coast.

'We don't have time for this,' Zeuthen said and tapped his wrist.

She left them and called Juncker. They'd come up with nothing new on the foreign cars.

'We can't find any driver who's been near a watch shop,' he added. 'Except for Niels Reinhardt. He bought a new one in Fisketorvet, first thing in the morning after Louise Hjelby was killed. Except it can't be him, can it? He wasn't in Copenhagen. He was at that hotel in Esbjerg.'

Lund looked at the tall man standing alongside Zeuthen at the back of the boat, patiently going over the charts.

'You're sure it was Reinhardt?'

'Looks like it. I called the shop. It was a very expensive watch. They don't sell many like that. There's a credit card slip. The man he described sounds like Reinhardt.'

It looked as if Rantzau was saying something.

'Also,' Juncker added. 'Brix caught me checking that old Birk Larsen stuff which didn't go down too well, I can tell you.'

'You have to keep looking, Asbjørn. Nothing happens if you stop.'

'I'll try to remember that. Where are you headed? Don't even think of hanging up on me . . .'

She cut the call. Borch was coming.

'The latest fairy story is we're heading for an empty pumping station. I'm going to get the Norwegians to bring in more men. You can talk to Loke if you like. I swear I'm going to kill the bastard if he jerks us around one more time.'

'The hotel . . .' she said, 'did you check the lock-system data?'

'What hotel?'

'Reinhardt bought his new watch the day after Louise was killed. In Copenhagen. First thing in the morning. When he was supposed to be in the hotel in Esbjerg. Are we sure he's got an alibi?'

Borch shrugged.

'Dyhring had someone on it. They said the lock-system records showed he went into the room that afternoon and stayed there till the following morning. PET went over his alibi really closely. Maybe the watch man got the date wrong.'

'It's on his credit card.'

'He couldn't have changed the hotel lock records. It's not possible . . .'

The boat turned into a small bay. Rantzau was pointing. There was a jetty, bigger than she'd expected. A series of low grey buildings nestled in a rocky inlet, a narrow winding road behind. The place looked deserted, abandoned. Empty.

'If she's not there,' Borch said, 'I swear . . .'

'Yes,' she said and briefly patted his arm. 'I've got the message, thank you.'

Just before midday Hartmann's Mercedes pulled into a grubby cul-de-sac in Nørrebro, two bodyguards from PET in the car behind.

Morten Weber was on the phone getting a briefing from Mogens Rank.

'Still no news,' Rank said. 'They've hired a boat. He's taking them up a fjord now.'

'What is this? A holiday?' Weber demanded.

'Rantzau says he's leading them to the girl.'

The PET men came up with umbrellas. Hartmann stepped straight beneath his, looked around. Benjamin had died under a train behind this place. The track wasn't even fenced. Next to the buildings was a basketball court, a few youngsters playing on it.

'No one's going to touch us with a barge pole if we can't get the Zeuthen girl out of there alive,' Weber said.

'Don't worry,' Rank insisted. 'We're on it. Tell Troels I'll gladly fill Agger's boots at the Treasury if he wants. I did economics at university.'

Weber muttered something caustic and finished the call. Karen Nebel was there already, leaning against the third door of a set of lock-ups.

'You've found it?' Hartmann asked.

Weber was getting agitated.

'We don't have a single coalition partner. Ussing's ringing round. Can't we do this another time?'

Nebel had the padlock in her hands.

'That might not be a bad idea,' she suggested.

Hartmann shut his eyes for a moment. Then said, 'I need to see.'

She stood aside and threw open a rusty metal door. There was a storeroom beyond. Nebel found the light switch. An ancient desk. Behind it cuttings from the newspapers. All about Hartmann and the party. Notes stuck to each story. A big sheet over them that read, 'Where does the money come from?'

'I never knew he played,' Hartmann muttered as he looked at a pair of basketball shoes and some sports gear thrown in the corner.

Pictures of Hans Zeuthen and his son. Weber. Nebel. Hartmann himself.

Weber started to go through them methodically.

'OK,' he said. 'Here. You've got it.'

A photo of Nebel with Reinhardt, next to his car.

'So Benjamin got a shot of Zeeland promising Karen some cash,' Weber said. 'And Karen saying thanks.'

She was looking at the floor. Papers scattered everywhere. A chair turned over.

'Someone's searched this place. Then shut it up afterwards. The padlock was on the door when I found it.'

'Yes, well . . .' Weber looked at his watch. 'We've seen what there is to see.'

Nebel came and looked at the old photo from Jutland.

'That can't be what they were after. If it was they'd have taken it.'

Hartmann walked to the desk. A packet of cigarettes. An old lighter. Papers everywhere. Old bus tickets. An ancient laptop. And a baseball cap. 'Harvard' on the front. Something he must have brought back from America when they kicked him out of college.

'Benjamin was really screwed up,' Weber said in as gentle a voice as he could manage. 'You can see that. We shouldn't be here.'

Hartmann picked up the cap. Couldn't remember his brother ever wearing it.

'He got mixed up in a kind of politics we don't listen to, Morten. That didn't kill him.'

A train ran past. Noisy. Fast. So close it shook the room. Hartmann put a hand to his head, couldn't think straight.

'I'm really sorry I dragged you out here. It's up to me to bury my brother. Not you.' He took one last look round the grimy room. 'Can you get someone to pack up his stuff and put it in storage somewhere?'

'Of course,' she said.

'Morten. Get in touch with the party leaders and find out how long they're willing to wait on news from Norway. You're right. We need to get moving.'

The cap was still in his hands. Not much worn at all. Hartmann stuffed it into his jacket pocket and walked back to the car.

Maja Zeuthen had gone to the Politigården and made it clear to Brix she wasn't leaving.

Things were happening, not that they were about to tell her. So she retreated into a corner and waited for him. Listening.

He was on a tense call, to Lund she guessed. Pumping her for information. Getting little back in return. The previous night Robert had told her he'd forgotten his car charger for the phone. She'd never managed to raise him again or got a message back.

Then, that morning, putting the passport back into the secure cupboard in Drekar, she'd noticed something was missing. The silver handgun she hated. A box of shells too.

'So what if no one saw Reinhardt in the hotel?' Brix barked. 'We packed in looking at him when we knew he had an alibi. Focus on finding the girl . . .'

He caught her listening, grimaced.

'Maja Zeuthen's here,' Brix said. 'She insists on speaking to her husband. She hasn't been able to get through herself. Put him on the line.'

Then he handed over the call.

She went out into the corridor to take it. Robert's voice was tired and anxious.

'We haven't found her yet,' he said. 'I'm sorry. This man Rantzau . . . I don't know . . . I have to go.'

'Robert,' she whispered. 'I know what you've got there. I saw what you took from the cupboard.'

Silence then, sounding a little cross, he said, 'I really have to hang up.'

'What good's that going to do us?' She blinked, realized the tears were coming. 'We've enough hurt already without . . .'

A click. The line went dead. Brix was behind her.

'What is this?' he asked.

A tall man. Polite mostly. But forbidding when he wanted to be.

'I asked you a question, Maja. What the hell's going on?'

It took fifteen minutes to check the jetty and the storage sheds. There wasn't a single container at the pumping station.

'He's been stringing us along from the start,' Borch said.

Rantzau stood by the dockside, handcuffed, trying to beg a cigarette from anyone who passed.

She watched him and said, 'There must be somewhere we haven't tried—'

'Sarah, Sarah! Stop this. He's screwed us over. We're going to have to get the bastard back to Copenhagen right—'

'Lund!' Rantzau cried, trying to point with his cuffed hands. 'There it is.' He smiled at Borch. 'I told you.'

An articulated truck rounded the headland travelling slowly down the narrow, winding road. There was a green container on the back.

Zeuthen came out from behind the warehouses with Reinhardt.

'I didn't deal with details,' Rantzau added. 'I'd no idea they'd bring it here by road.'

It took another ten minutes for the truck to reach them. Then the Norwegians got the driver to unload the container onto the pier and took him in for questioning.

The heavy doors were locked and chained. They had to find cutters and that took time. All the while Zeuthen got more frantic. Calling to the girl inside. Shouting they were nearly there.

Just before one thirty the last chain was broken and the sliding retainers pushed up.

'Emilie!' Zeuthen shouted and pushed his way to the front, stared at the blackness ahead.

Walked inside.

Borch pulled out his torch. Something at the back against the corrugated steel wall.

Zeuthen dashed to it, pulled at the dark shape. It moved. Flew beneath a flurry of kicks.

An industrial plastic bag. Empty. That was all.

The Norwegians had taken Rantzau into one of the warehouses. She left the container, found him sitting on a bench in front of a young and nervous Norwegian uniformed cop.

Lund bent down, looked into his bruised and battered face.

'You lied to me, Loke. You promised me Emilie.'

'Everyone lies, Lund,' he said with a shrug.

Borch wasn't far behind.

'What was the point of this?' he demanded.

Rantzau shook his head, puzzled.

'The point? Isn't that obvious? I had to do it.' Settled, relaxed. He grinned. 'If I hadn't you might have found her.'

Lund shrieked. The scream echoed round the building.

His manacled hand came up. A bandaged finger jabbed at her.

'You don't want to find the bastard who murdered my daughter—'

'I'm trying,' she cried. 'I will. I promise . . .'

Rantzau shot to his feet, wild and bellowing.

'Then why did you let him go? Why's he sitting out there laughing at me every time I look?'

The watch. The hotel. The black car. But most of all the sly way Reinhardt had of evading Zeuthen's gaze whenever the subject of Emilie – not Louise Hjelby – came up. She couldn't speak.

'You had him,' Rantzau said more calmly. 'Then you set him free and brought him here. To watch.' He leaned towards her. 'You owe me, Lund. Much more than I owe you. I'm the cheated party. No one else.'

Footsteps. Zeuthen, Reinhardt, two more Norwegian cops.

For the first time Loke Rantzau looked Emilie's father in the face. 'There's still time to save her. But you have to tell me the truth.'

'What truth?' Zeuthen screeched. 'I don't know anything.'

Rantzau nodded at Reinhardt.

'He does. Get your man to tell me how he killed my daughter. How your people managed to bury the case. Like you buried me . . .'

Zeuthen stared at him. Rantzau's head went to one side, a look of amazement.

'You really are a fool, aren't you? Just a dupe like the rest of them? Have they—?'

'If it's Reinhardt he'll be punished,' Lund said.

He laughed.

'Why should I believe that? Do you ever listen, Lund? They won't let you—'

'I'm telling you, Loke. I'm telling . . .'

She stopped. Something silver, familiar, stood in Zeuthen's hand. A rich man's semi-automatic. In one short violent movement he dashed it hard against Loke Rantzau's temple.

Then to one side. Hand shaking, Zeuthen loosed off a single shot into the darkness.

Hearing it dance around them Borch tried to move forward, saying all the words.

Robert. Relax. Keep cool. Don't . . .

'Tell me where she is!' Zeuthen roared.

The gun was back in the manacled man's face. Lund felt she'd never seen Loke Rantzau so calm, so resigned. As if this was the place he'd wanted to be all along.

'Tell me . . .' Zeuthen began.

'I know how you feel,' Rantzau said in a jaded, casual tone. 'We're the same. You and me . . .'

'Drop the gun, Robert,' Lund begged. 'We'll never find her this way.'

Rantzau closed his eyes for a moment. When he opened them he wasn't looking at Zeuthen any more. Just the tall grey figure of Reinhardt opposite.

Frightened.

Silent.

Doubt in Zeuthen's face.

'Just do it,' Lund pleaded. 'We're not finished here.'

Slowly Zeuthen lowered the gun. Had it to his waist when Rantzau flew at him, taking the two of them tumbling to the grimy floor.

The silver weapon fell from Zeuthen's hands, rattled on the cold concrete. The shackled man's fingers lunged for it, grasped the handle, started to take hold, to aim at Niels Reinhardt.

One shot.

Two.

The nervy young Norwegian cop had his gun out before any of them.

No body armour for Loke Rantzau this time. Prone on the floor his body leapt with each impact.

Borch was down first, dragging Zeuthen out of the way, kicking the silver gun into the shadows. Lund was next, crouching by Rantzau.

Blood on his chest. Eyes opening. Blood seeping from his mouth.

A word. Or a ghost of one. She put her ear to his lips. The softest of whispers, 'Lund . . .'

'If you'd wanted Emilie dead you'd have killed her long ago, Loke. For God's sake where is she?'

Her fingers were in his greasy hair. His eyes on hers, lips shifting towards something like a smile.

'There's a god?' Rantzau croaked.

Mouth to his ear, so close she could smell the sweat and dirt on him.

'I promise you, Loke. I swear . . . I won't forget Louise. I'll see this through . . .'

Fragments of words.

'Won't . . .'

The breath fading, and the light in his eyes.

'Let . . . you . . .'

'They won't stop me,' she swore. 'They never have.'

The man was dying. She knew what that looked like.

Lund took his manacled hands, held them, pleaded, 'Emilie . . .'

One word, half heard, as much a final groan as anything. Then the hard spark of hatred vanished from his eyes and his head fell to one side.

Lund got out her phone, fingers trembling, walked to the door, out into the languid winter day.

Zeuthen behind, throwing all the questions she couldn't answer.

No time for argument or explanations.

'Lund?' Zeuthen cried. 'What did he say?'

No time for Brix either. She got straight through.

'Asbjørn. Get Madsen. Get all the good men you can find.'

'Yes?' said a young, surprised voice a long way away.

'Then find yourself a boat.'

Hartmann was in the conference room in the Prime Minister's quarters with Mogens Rank and Karen Nebel. Fine paintings. Old furniture. A long polished table. He tried not to think how much he'd miss it.

'We need something, Mogens.'

'I know,' Rank said. 'I'm sorry.'

Weber came in with a couple of sheets of paper.

'This doesn't look good. We're halfway through the day and the polls are against us. If you don't get out there, talk to the party, do something . . . we're screwed.'

Hartmann shook his head, looked out of the window. He would miss Christiansborg. Such a long journey here. No way back.

'Here's an idea,' Weber suggested. 'Let me try and patch things up with Rosa. If we throw the Centre Party some cabinet posts . . .'

'I'm not crawling,' Hartmann retorted. 'Neither is she.'

'Actually she is,' Weber said and took out his phone. 'I've had two messages in the last thirty minutes.'

He held out the handset.

'Come on. This is what we do. Haggle. Trade. Barter. Just call her.'

Hartmann took the phone, went to his office on his own.

'You wanted me, Rosa?'

'I was trying to get Morten. But you may as well hear direct. We're going to back Ussing as the new Prime Minister.'

'Oh.'

'Unless you have an interesting offer. And some good news about Emilie Zeuthen.'

Benjamin's baseball cap was on the desk. Harvard. He was smart enough for college. The will wasn't there somehow.

'For us to support you we'd need to be in government on equal terms.'

Hartmann turned the hat round in his fingers.

'But you don't have anything like equal votes.'

'That's the deal,' she insisted. 'Ministerial posts divided fifty-fifty. Give us a strong alliance and we could make this work.'

'This isn't negotiation. It's blackmail.'

A pause, then she said, 'That's what you get when you dump on people.'

There was something hard beneath the brim. Hartmann fumbled inside, found it. A USB memory stick hidden away.

'Troels?'

He cut her off without another word. Nebel was at the door.

'Did she offer anything worthwhile?'

'She just wanted me to surrender. Any news from Mogens?'

'Nothing. Is Morten still here?' she asked.

Hartmann shrugged.

'If you didn't see him on the way in I guess not.'

She hesitated, only spoke when he pressed her.

'I talked to some kids playing basketball when we went to the lock-up today,' Nebel said. 'Gave them my card. One of them just called me back.'

She closed the door. Sat down.

'He was asking why we kept going back there.'

Hartmann turned the USB stick in his hands, wondered what was on it, how long it might take to find out.

'Going back?'

'Two years ago, around the time Benjamin died, he saw one of us before.'

Asbjørn Juncker was in the bows of the police inflatable, face to the chilly winter wind. Black clouds building to a storm. An ambulance wailing on the waterfront. Cars screeching to a halt there. Brix had been engaged in a heated row with Hedeby and Dyhring when the young detective went to talk to him about Lund's call. So he hadn't waited. Told Madsen, got some men, ordered the boat.

Phoned back to the Politigården on the way and didn't much listen to Brix's instant fury at all.

But when Juncker looked back at the shore he could see a familiar tall figure striding up and down the growing pool of vehicles. Brix was there now. A blonde woman too. Maja Zeuthen, waiting. The way she had throughout.

This was the last throw, Lund said. No more options. Loke Rantzau was dead, gone before he could give any precise instructions. All he'd said was a single word: *Medea*. On the basis of that they'd have to pray that somewhere in the rusty belly of the decrepit freighter now bobbing in front of them a young girl was trapped, still alive.

Even though, as Brix had yelled at him already down the phone, they'd searched the place twice before.

Four men in the inflatable, Juncker first up the steps. Straight into the doors behind the bridge, on the phone to Norway.

'Where am I supposed to look, Lund?'

The entrance led to a vast internal chamber that ran from the upper deck to the bottom of the hold. Rooms and storage space on every deck. He'd no idea how to start.

'Do you know where they searched before?' she asked.

'Sure. I was here.'

'Then don't look there.'

Madsen and the other men were fanning out, taking the first level.

He'd watched Lund working, tried to learn the way she thought. It wasn't easy. There was a hard, almost cruel logic to her sometimes. She had a way of setting emotion to one side, cutting through the personal, human side of the problem, going straight for an answer most people didn't want to contemplate.

'We gave up when we found those dead guys the first time,' he said. 'The second time we were looking for the man. For computers. For somewhere he worked.'

'Good,' she said. 'So where didn't you look?'

He thought about this.

'What do you call the bottom of a ship?'

A long sigh.

'I don't know, Asbjørn. Will you just get moving?'

There, he thought, and started to run down the winding iron stairs.

A grubby engine room. Dead machinery he didn't begin to understand.

His torch flashed into the shadows.

'There's nothing here.'

'It has to be soundproof so we couldn't hear her if she's yelling. Try to think like him, Asbjørn.'

'I'd rather not . . .'

'Then start. A cold store. A small hold somewhere.'

'We checked those out!'

'Not all of them. You said so yourself. He looked after her. He fed her . . .'

At the end of the engine room was another door. They hadn't been here. He was sure of it. Heart pumping, torch up, Juncker walked through.

'Nothing, Lund,' he said into the phone, and didn't know if she could hear.

Lund.

Just saying her name made him wonder how she'd work this place. He remembered again what she did, and in this last desperate moment tried to copy it.

Deep in the hull of the ancient listing freighter Asbjørn Juncker turned on his heels, three hundred and sixty degrees, trying to see something that ordinary people couldn't. Perhaps shouldn't because that kind of vision, a damaged and individual perception, came with such a price.

At the last moment the torch beam caught a flash of colour. Pink and white.

He walked forward, looked.

A yoghurt pot. Raspberry. Empty. Plastic spoon inside.

Behind it the smallest of doors, one that fell short of the ceiling and the floor. Juncker opened it. Went in. A tiny room, barely big enough for modest storage.

'Asbjørn?' Lund was a tinny voice in his ear. One he barely heard.

There was a shape on the floor. Small, in a black coat. Not moving.

He put down the phone, reached out with his arms.

On the pier Brix got the first call. Madsen saying they'd found her. The inflatable was on the way.

He told Maja Zeuthen. Saw the fear and hope in her eyes.

Next to the medics they stood, watching the dull water, a small boat bobbing up and down on the choppy sea.

The doctor ordered a stretcher with blue plastic sheeting, oxygen, checked his bag.

All eyes on the waves, the inflatable rising and falling.

Soon they could see her. A shape in Asbjørn Juncker's arms. At the jetty Madsen and the others stood back, let Juncker lift her light frame, carry her up the metal stairs, carefully, one step at a time.

Someone spoke.

Emilie.

It took Brix a moment to realize it was the mother, hand on mouth, tears in her eyes as she followed the still form in Asbjørn's arms.

The shiny blonde hair of the pictures was dirty and lank. Her face filthy too. She seemed asleep. Or dead.

Juncker lifted her onto the gurney then did something Brix never expected. Got down on his knees. Eyes closed, fingers raised together, whispering a quiet prayer.

Maja Zeuthen's hands were over her daughter's. Tears welling. Sobbing. The doctor forced her out of the way. Oxygen mask. Pulse. A medic talking about hypothermia. Wrapping her in a blue insulation jacket.

'Emilie, wake up,' Maja cried. '*Wake up!*'

Asbjørn Juncker stopped, came and stood next to the mother, both of them watching the immobile face on the stretcher.

A weak burst of moisture began to mist the transparent plastic of the mask, like shining pearls of life.

'Wake up,' Maja begged.

The cloud grew. Emilie Zeuthen's eyes opened. Around the bleak jetty, over the grey water, a shout, a round of sudden joy, police and medics, all.

Brix turned and stared at the dead ship, crooked in the harbour. No words just then.

And Asbjørn Juncker half-staggered to a capstan, sat on it, took out the phone, resumed the call he'd never ended.

'Bloody hell, Lund . . . we've got her,' he said in a voice breaking with every syllable. 'She's alive.'

She's alive.

Robert Zeuthen listened to the news from his wife. What the medics said. Hospital. Nourishment. Gentle care.

Emilie was safe at last.

Stood by the cold Norwegian fjord, not far from the body of Loke Rantzau getting loaded into a police van.

Tried to speak through the tears as she told him, 'I'm holding her, Robert. I'm holding her . . .'

A stiff and reticent man. Not easy with emotions. It took a while.

'I'll be with you as soon as I can,' he said finally. 'I'll . . .'

The water seemed to mock him. Everything Zeuthen possessed came from that chill, uncaring source. And it meant nothing.

'I'll never let you go again,' he whispered, cut the call, put a shaky hand to his face.

She's alive.

Hartmann was alone at his desk, sketching out his resignation letter when Nebel walked in and broke the news.

Alive and in Copenhagen all along.

'You're sure this time?' he asked. 'No mistakes. No—'

'She's alive, Troels.' Nebel looked as if she'd been crying. 'She's with her mum, on the way to hospital. They say she's going to be fine. The man who took her . . .'

Hartmann picked up the sheet of paper he'd been scribbling on, screwed it into a ball, threw it into the bin.

'Best get the news out there, Karen,' he suggested. 'No delay.'

'Done already,' she said. 'I know my priorities.'

'Have you got anything back from the technical people yet? Do they know what was on that USB stick?'

'Priorities,' she repeated.

'I asked for it.'

'Then I'm sure it's on the way.'

'She's alive,' Borch said as they stood next to one another, watching Robert Zeuthen alone on the quay, weeping with relief, lost to the stark, bare landscape around him.

Lund looked at her phone, wondered if this was the right time to call.

'You did it, Sarah.'

Mathias Borch wore a broad smile. Seemed young again, the way he had when they first met. The puppy look. She'd fallen so heavily for that.

'We did it together,' she insisted.

He laughed. Kissed her cheek, would have come back for more if she hadn't retreated.

'No. You did it. You were always so much better than me.'

She nodded.

'At some things anyway.'

Reinhardt strode over. She steeled herself to deal with him.

He broke into a diplomatic smile and said, 'Robert's aware he broke the law by bringing along that gun. He's deeply sorry. He would never have killed Rantzau . . .'

'Loke's still dead,' Lund said.

Reinhardt nodded at the local police.

'They shot him.' He didn't look in the least sorry. 'Blame the Norwegians. What I suggest is this. We call in a helicopter for Robert. It's important he gets back to his family as soon as possible. I'll stay and deal with any formalities.'

He looked at them.

'Is that acceptable?'

Lund stayed quiet. Borch said OK.

Reinhardt strode back to Zeuthen, slapped him on the shoulder, got nothing in return. The younger man walked off towards the end of the jetty alone.

'It can't be him,' Borch said. 'We checked him out. It's impossible.'

Lund didn't take her eyes off Reinhardt and he knew it.

'I want him checked out again. Everything from the hotel to the watch to . . .'

Borch shook his head.

'Dyhring won't wear that. They won't let Brix get involved either. We've spent a lot of time on this. Emilie Zeuthen's safe. Rantzau's dead . . .'

She glared at him. The moment between them was gone.

'Niels Reinhardt travelled the world for Zeeland's charity. He's been doing this for years.'

'Sarah,' Borch said with a pained, worn expression. 'Stop this. You're just guessing.'

'And he's still doing it,' she added. 'Loke Rantzau realized that. Why didn't we?'

The polls didn't close until eight in the evening. Long before then it was clear Emilie Zeuthen's rescue had transformed the election. Mogens Rank was left to make the announcement of her safe release. It was being replayed on the giant TV screen in the Parliament building when Hartmann arrived for the victory party.

For once Rank was full of praise for PET and the police. Their steadfast work had brought the case to a satisfactory conclusion. Emilie was now being treated in hospital and would be allowed home to her family later that night.

There was no more talk about Zeeland withdrawing from Denmark. All the indications were that Hartmann would be free to choose the coalition partners he wanted, and decide how lowly or otherwise their ministerial positions might be.

None of this mattered to him at that moment. He was intent on tracking down Morten Weber in the crush.

It took ten minutes, dodging handshakes and congratulatory pats on the back. Then he found Weber amidst a throng of party workers by the window over the square.

The little man raised his glass as Hartmann approached.

'We're headed for a dream result, Troels. The best we've ever achieved thanks to you.' The others toasted him on cue. 'Rosa

Lebech's been on the phone. She'd like to talk. I said . . . when we have the time. When the hangovers have receded.'

That got a laugh, but not from Hartmann.

He grabbed Weber by the collar and dragged him into the corridor.

'Oh for God's sake, Troels. What is it now?'

'You were at that lock-up of Benjamin's around the time he died. Someone recognized you.'

Weber leaned back against the wall, folded his arms. Didn't look concerned.

'And?'

'What were you doing out there?'

A shrug.

'What I'm paid for. Watching your back. Someone tipped me off Benjamin had been taking pictures of Reinhardt and Karen. I just wanted a word with him. That was all.'

'Who told you?'

Weber put down his glass.

'Look. This is a great night for us. Let's not spoil it. I explained to Benjamin it was pointless publishing those photos. He didn't want to know. He told me to get lost and that was it. I didn't steal any pictures from him—'

'Who tipped you off?' Hartmann repeated.

Weber shook his head.

'We're not going there again.'

Hartmann grabbed his jacket with both hands, pinned him against the wall.

'People are starting to look,' Weber whispered. 'This is no way to start your second term . . .'

'Tell me or I'll break you. I swear—'

'Mogens,' Weber said. 'Dyhring called him. PET found out Benjamin had uploaded those photos to his web account. They were watching out for us. Mogens wondered if I could have a quiet chat . . .'

Hartmann let him go. Weber brushed at his jacket.

'For God's sake, Troels. Nothing happened. I would have told you but the next day he was dead. You were in a state.' He shook his head. 'I didn't want to make things worse telling you your own brother had been trying to stir the shit behind the scenes. I was looking after your interests—'

'Not any more you're not.'

'No,' Weber agreed. 'Not any more. I told you that already, didn't I? But you know what . . . ?'

He straightened his jacket. Looked across the corridor. Karen Nebel was there, watching them, worried.

'If it makes you feel better blaming me then do it. If it means you don't have to look at yourself and ask why Benjamin was falling apart, hanging round with druggies and creeps while you were too busy to notice—'

The slap came. Weber took it.

'That's twice now. We're done.'

He headed back for the party. Hartmann was about to follow when Nebel stopped him at the door. The IT people had got into the USB key. It was full of photographs.

The crowd was getting bigger, happier with every fresh result going their way. Hartmann wanted to be among them. Drown in their shared pleasure. Wait until he was on his own and get stinking drunk.

Nebel kept going.

'I know, I know,' he said finally. 'Benjamin took some photos of you and Reinhardt. We've been through this, Karen.'

'He took more than that. He followed Reinhardt after he left me. Look . . .'

She had the pictures from Benjamin's USB stick on her iPad, skimmed through them with a finger.

Photos of Zeeland's man filling up his black car. Going into a newsagent's and coming out with a magazine and some sweets.

'Then these,' Nebel said.

Hartmann looked. Couldn't hear the room any more. Couldn't care less what was happening in the polls.

Brix was watching the party start up in the Politigården when she called.

'We need to start again with Reinhardt. Check the garage. The hotel. His watch . . .'

He closed his eyes. Wondered at her persistent ability to ruin his mood.

'Listen, Lund. As long as he's got a cast-iron alibi we won't get a warrant for anything. I won't ask for one either. Emilie Zeuthen's safe. Her kidnapper's dead. That's the end of this story.'

Juncker was chatting happily to Ruth Hedeby on the other side of the room. Someone would probably bring in beer soon.

'We still don't know who killed Louise Hjelby,' she said. 'Reinhardt's our best suspect. I think he's done it before. For all we know he'll do it again.'

A long, pained sigh.

'What's this to you? I thought you were turning up at OPA on Monday?'

'I promised Rantzau—'

'That means a lot to me. I've got the paperwork here. Reinhardt stayed in room one eighteen. The lock registered when he came. Then when he left the following morning.'

'I'll double check that . . .'

'No! You won't. You'll come back here and get a commendation. And on Monday you'll start at OPA. You know how I tried to stop you?'

'Reinhardt . . .' she began.

'I'm not going to stand in your way any more,' Brix added. 'This investigation's closed. The Hjelby case has run into a dead end. You've nothing on Reinhardt. Even if you're right we can't bring him to court. He's wrapped in Zeeland lawyers. There's nothing I can do . . .'

Silence then she said, 'You mean you won't let me?'

'If you prefer to put it that way . . .'

He listened for the next objection. But it never came.

'Lund?'

Someone had opened a bottle. Hedeby on the other side of the office. It was champagne and she was pouring.

The wrong sort, Brix guessed. She was never good with wine. But still . . . he'd drink it.

Lund came off the phone, kicked a rock on the jetty, watched it go over the side, heard a splash as it hit the water. It was getting dark. Robert Zeuthen had been picked up by helicopter. He'd be back in Copenhagen before his daughter was home in Drekar. Reinhardt had hung around making arrangements. Borch had been . . . nice.

He came over, phone in hand.

'I don't know what's going on in the office. I can't get hold of Dyhring.'

'They're all slapping each other on the back and getting pissed.'

'Hartmann won the election,' he added. 'We won't hear from him again. Busy day, eh?' He put a hand to her arm, smiled. 'A good one too.'

'I doubt Loke Rantzau would have agreed with that.'

'Rantzau was a murdering bastard.'

The Norwegian police had taken away the body. There was no need for them to stay around.

'His daughter thought he was a hero,' she said. 'In a way he was. Navy special forces. The man Zeeland turned to when they needed some dirty work done. I promised . . .'

The smile vanished.

'A promise to a man like that means nothing, Sarah. Besides Reinhardt's alibi's unbreakable.'

His hand strayed to her hair. She shook him off.

'I know you don't want to let go of this. But honestly . . . it could have been any one of a hundred cars that went down that road. You found Emilie. That's what this was all about.'

A tall figure strode over. Reinhardt cheery again.

'I'm finished here,' he announced. 'The Norwegians are content to let us go.'

He looked at Borch, not her.

'We're all very grateful to you for finding Emilie. I've ordered an air taxi back to Copenhagen. A little airport. It's just thirty minutes from here.'

Lund kept her eyes on him.

'You're welcome to join me,' Reinhardt added. 'But we need to leave now.'

She didn't stop staring, didn't say a word.

'That would be good,' Borch said and watched him walk off to arrange a car.

'We're done here, Sarah.' His hand gripped her, left when she didn't respond. 'Let's go.'

Hedeby called Brix into her office. He was right. The champagne was terrible. Something on his face must have betrayed the fact.

'God you're a snob,' she said.

'Just picky.'

'Management are having a celebration later. I'll let you choose for that. I'll pay too.'

'Management?' Brix asked. 'Does that by any chance include those shits from PET? Because if it does . . .'

She winced.

'Be political, Lennart. It's important we keep in with them. Dyhring won't be joining us. He rushed off to the Ministry of Justice. Mogens Rank summoned him for some reason. So . . .'

Her fingers brushed his collar. Then his cheek.

'You look good. I was wondering whether to send you home to change. But this'll be fine.'

Brix raised an eyebrow, kept quiet.

'I'm sorry if I've been a bit bad-tempered,' she added. 'It got a bit heated round here.'

'Ruth . . . is there something I should know?'

'Why are you always suspicious?'

'Because events merit it. What's up?'

'Nothing!' She stroked his close-cropped hair. 'Except tomorrow the commissioner's going to announce he'll be retiring in six months. The board will sit in two weeks.'

Her fingers left him, went to her own head.

'Once upon a time I thought maybe I'd stand a chance. But . . .'

A smile.

'You'd look good in that uniform.' She squeezed his hand. 'Just a thought.'

They were almost ready to go to the airport. Borch and Reinhardt had gone off to talk to the local police.

Lund phoned the hotel in Esbjerg, asked for the front desk.

'I'm calling from Zeeland,' she said. 'I'm Niels Reinhardt's new secretary. He's asked me to make some travel arrangements. I'm not sure . . .'

'It's OK,' the woman replied. 'We know Mr Reinhardt well. How can I help?'

She looked round, made sure no one was near.

'He asked me to book a room but I can't remember what sort he wanted.'

'Mr Reinhardt always stays in three twenty-two. It's a suite. There's a nice view of the sea. What dates are we talking about?'

They'd be gone in a few minutes.

'I thought he said one eighteen. I've got a booking here from a while back. It says that too.'

'That can't be right,' the woman insisted. 'He's been coming here for years. He always has three twenty-two. Let me check.'

Reinhardt came out of the office, shook the hand of one of the Norwegian officers, looked at the rainy night, then went and sat in the front of the car.

The receptionist came back.

'Actually you're right. He did stay in one eighteen. That's odd.'

'Why?'

'It's in the old wing. Not so good. We take care of the owners. We wouldn't put him in there ordinarily. But if it says so . . .'

Lund closed her eyes for a moment, felt the rain on her face.

'The owners?'

'The chain's part of Zeeland. Didn't you know? Usually they book straight through the computer system. I mean . . . you run it in Copenhagen.'

She looked at Reinhardt in the passenger seat of the car, eyes closed. At peace.

'Hello?'

Lund ended the call, phoned Juncker. He sounded happy. Wanted to be congratulated, so she obliged.

When his bubbliness died down a touch she asked if there was anything new.

He went somewhere quiet. The raucous noise of an office party had receded.

'You could have got me in big trouble . . .' he moaned. 'I had to shove those Birk Larsen files in a drawer every time Brix was hanging around.'

'Did you find anything?'

'No.'

Someone was laughing close by.

'Oh. Apart from one little thing. Probably doesn't mean a lot . . .'

'Just tell me, Asbjørn.'

'You mean . . . Juncker.'

'Juncker,' she sighed.

He did, all in a single sentence.

Borch came out of the police van, climbed into the driver's seat of the car next to Reinhardt. Parped his horn.

Mouthed a word, gestured with his finger.

In.

Mogens Rank was in his office with Dyhring when Hartmann and Karen Nebel barged in.

The champagne was open already. Rank looked a little giddy.

'Oh come on, Troels! Lighten up. I know there are still a few votes to be counted. But all the same . . . we won.'

Dyhring was sliding away.

'You're going nowhere,' Hartmann said. Nebel booted the door shut.

He had her iPad. Put it on the desk. Pulled up the photos. Niels Reinhardt by the side of the road. A girl with a white bike behind him. The whole sequence was there. Reinhardt talking to Louise Hjelby. Putting the bike in his boot. Then opening the door, smiling, as she got in the passenger seat looking a little wary.

Rank was about to speak when Hartmann said, 'Whatever you do, Mogens, don't tell me this is the first time you've seen these.'

The smile vanished from Rank's face. Dyhring came over and looked at the iPad. Said nothing.

Hartmann jabbed a finger at the photos.

'You both knew Zeuthen's assistant murdered that girl.'

Rank glanced at Dyhring.

'Was this the two of you?' Hartmann demanded. A nod at Rank. 'You leaned on Schultz and got him to cover up the case? Then cleaned up my brother's pictures as soon as you learned about them?'

Rank took off his glasses, fiddled with them, put them back on.

'Nothing's ever quite as simple as it seems. Let me explain . . .'

'I don't need an explanation!' Hartmann yelled. 'It's obvious. You told Zeeland about the photos. They deleted them from Benjamin's account. When Morten came back without the originals you set PET on him. And now he's dead . . .'

Dyhring came over, stood next to Rank.

'It wasn't like that.'

Hartmann waved a fist at them.

'Who killed my brother?'

'No one.' Dyhring looked at Mogens Rank. 'The Justice Minister can tell you—'

'Out with it!' Hartmann roared. 'Before I get in a car to the Politigården and send you both to jail.'

Rank scowled. Looked sick of this.

It was Dyhring who started to talk.

'We knew about his lock-up. We searched it late that night. We couldn't find those photos. While we were there he turned up. I tried to talk to him, to explain what we were doing. He got scared, ran off.'

The PET man thrust his hands deep into his pockets.

'The train line there's unfenced. I don't think he knew where he was going. There was nothing—'

'You murdered him.' Hartmann, jabbing a finger in Dyhring's face.

'No we didn't. We don't kill people, Hartmann. We protect them. Or we try to.'

'Don't give me that shit . . .'

'I didn't go out there because I wanted to,' Dyhring objected. Another glance. 'I was sent.'

Mogens Rank nodded.

'True. By me. It's easy to say I regret it now. Which I do. What happened to your brother was terrible. A dreadful, unfortunate accident.'

Hartmann leaned on the table, listened.

'We'd had so many problems with Benjamin,' Rank added. 'The demos. That day he stole your private car and careered drunk all over Jutland. I didn't want you to be bothered by any more nonsense . . .'

'Tell that to the judge,' Nebel snapped.

Rank sighed, as if impatient with them.

'This was about much more than a few photos, Karen. We'd just won the election. The credit crunch was biting. We all know the trouble Troels went through with Lund six years before. One loose accusation against a senior executive of Zeeland could have brought down the entire government . . .'

'A loose accusation?' Nebel cried. 'It's proof he killed that girl.'

'No, it's not.' Rank brushed the photos away with his fingers. 'They're just a few pictures. And it was made very clear to me that Zeeland wouldn't forgive such a suspicion being placed at their door.'

'By whom?' she demanded.

'That's irrelevant. I had a choice to make and I made the right one. The case was closed. Why risk everything for the sake of an orphan girl in Jutland no one really missed?'

He looked at Hartmann and shrugged.

'It was the right decision, Troels. Think about it. Benjamin . . . none of us knew or wanted that. His death was a tragic accident. If there was some way we could turn back the clock . . .'

'Come on,' Nebel said, and grabbed the iPad. 'Let's get out of here.'

'We can't run the country without Zeeland!' Mogens Rank bellowed. 'They won us the election back then. Emilie Zeuthen's winning it for us today. The girl's alive. Her kidnapper's dead. How is this a disaster?'

He got to his feet as they started to leave.

'Tell me how!' Mogens Rank yelled at their backs.

Five minutes through the winding corridors of Slotsholmen. Past the busy election party, through all the glorious rooms. Back in his office Hartmann sat, tie gone, hair a mess, sweating, wondering.

The TV was calling a historic victory. The greatest gap between the majority party and its rivals in modern history. He sat at his desk, going through the iPad again.

'We'll go and see Brix,' Nebel said. 'We'll show him the photos. Tell him everything.'

He didn't move.

'It's important we do this before Mogens has the chance to clean up his files,' she added. 'After that we can have a party committee meeting and decide what to do.'

She took his arm again. Before long they were walking down the stairs.

'I can distance you from this. We can escape the damage.'

He was almost at the door when a figure came out of the shadows.

Anders Ussing, smiling as always, hand extended. Hartmann stopped, had no choice.

'Well, Troels. Congratulations on your victory. Here's to . . .'

Hartmann stared at the outstretched hand, brushed past. Ussing yelled an obscenity down the stairs.

By the side door, peering into the rainy night, Karen Nebel checked round and said, 'There's no reason you can't still meet the Queen tomorrow and form a government. We can ask for a judicial review of Rank's actions and PET too.'

In the windows opposite he could see the party. Faces at the bright windows, beneath the great chandeliers. People were laughing, dancing. Creatures of Slotsholmen, puppets in the great charade.

A woman by the leaded panes caught sight of him. Talked to some of her friends. Pointed. Waved. Cheered.

Pretty, all of them. Part of the make-believe.

He stopped, smiled, waved back. It all came so naturally.

'Troels,' Nebel said. 'We have to go.'

He didn't move. Mind turning.

'Mogens is right, isn't he?' Hartmann said. 'Of themselves the photos prove nothing. Reinhardt had an alibi. It wasn't just PET said that. It was the police too.'

'What the hell are you talking about?'

'There was no proof. Just a few pictures. The damage to the country if they'd pursued an innocent man like Reinhardt—'

'If he was innocent where's the problem?'

He wasn't listening.

'Benjamin wasn't well, Karen. I don't want to reopen that wound. I owe him that. If anyone's to blame for his death . . .'

Her hands gripped his shoulders.

'Stop this. Stop this now,' she pleaded. 'Don't you see? It's what they're after. They want you to keep quiet. To give in. Accept they can screw with little people's lives as much as they like. This isn't you, Troels . . .'

The faces at the window were still there. Fascinated. Perhaps thinking this was another of Hartmann's trysts.

'I'm going to find a driver. Then we're off.'

She headed for the car pool round the corner.

The women were waving again. Raising their glasses.

Troels Hartmann broke into his best smile. The one from the posters. Asked himself where he wanted to be.

The moment Robert Zeuthen landed he called Maja. She was still at the hospital, waiting for Emilie to be discharged. There'd be a doctor coming home with her. Counselling in the days to come. But she was fit, had been reasonably well treated until Rantzau left her trapped in the tiny room in the *Medea*. There never was a pressurized tank or a deadline. In the end he probably meant to free her anyway.

'Give me an hour,' Zeuthen pleaded.

'We'll be home by then,' she said. 'Maybe the four of us can get away together.'

Silence. He stood in the lift in the black glass Zeeland office, seeing in his mind's eye the dragon flit past outside, trying to find the words.

'Can't wait,' Zeuthen agreed. 'Wherever you want. For as long as you like.'

She said goodbye and then he went looking.

Kornerup was in his executive office on his own, going through charts and reports. He looked up when he heard the door open. Leapt to his feet. Strode across the office beaming, pumped Zeuthen's hand.

'What a result, Robert! We're all delighted. The board met while you were in Norway. They send their best, naturally. If there's anything—'

'Before I kick you out of here one final time you can tell me whether Reinhardt murdered that girl in Jutland.'

The hand came back. Kornerup's face froze. A look of disdain behind his big, round glasses.

'You're tired. It's understandable. Go home and get some rest. Don't rush. We can cope.'

Zeuthen looked around the office. It had once been his father's. He didn't recall how Kornerup had acquired it in the confusion after his death.

'I talked to that lawyer you brought in. I know you briefed him yesterday when Reinhardt was under suspicion.'

'Niels is a senior executive of the company,' Kornerup objected. 'He deserved our support.'

'By giving him a fabricated alibi? From our own hotel chain?'

Kornerup laughed.

'You don't think we could have got it from someone else's, do you?'

Furious, Zeuthen took a step towards the man.

'I want answers.'

'No, you don't.'

'Did Reinhardt kill that girl?'

Kornerup thought about this.

'To tell you the truth . . . I honestly don't know. It's hard to believe. He was your father's personal assistant for many years. I thought I knew the man but . . .' A shrug. 'It's irrelevant. We've had so many crises around here of late. There was no need for another.'

'Get out,' Zeuthen ordered, pointing at the door. 'Leave now before I call security and have them throw you in the street.'

The laugh again.

'You've no evidence against Reinhardt. Why bring down a scandal on your own head? It could ruin Zeeland if we allowed it. Think of the positives. You've got Emilie and Maja back. Hartmann won the election. The board's behind the idea we stay in Denmark, for now anyway.'

'I fired you—'

'No you didn't. You couldn't. You're a name on the notepaper, Robert. That's all. The board confirmed me in post this afternoon. That's not going to change. Though Reinhardt . . . I think it's time he retired. Don't you?'

He leaned forward, then added, 'I'm asking on a personal basis, you understand. Not an executive one. Think of yourself as an occasional ambassador for us from now on. A figurehead, nothing more. You really don't need to turn up here at all. Not unless I ask for it.'

A short, ironic smile.

'And enjoy the weekend with your family. On Monday I'll get my PA to fit you in for a chat about your future. Does that sound OK?'

Zeuthen started to lose it. Kornerup stood his ground, listened for a moment, said, 'No. That didn't require an answer. I'm busy. Let yourself out.'

Then returned to his desk, to the reports, the charts, the business.

On the way to the airport the phone rang. Vibeke, Lund's mother, full of pride and delight.

'You should have been here. Mark and Eva are doing brilliantly. And the kiddie's a real sweetie . . .'

She sat in the back of the car, Borch driving, Reinhardt in the passenger seat.

'Is that nice Mathias Borch still working with you?'

'He is.'

'Send him my love. He was always my favourite. Yours too, I think, if only you knew. Let me pass the phone to Mark.'

She could hear the baby cooing. Picture a cot, Eva doting over her. All in Lund's little cottage. Borch's 'shed'.

'Hi, Mum,' he said, and sounded happy, relaxed, exhausted. 'She's really cute. Sleeps all the time. Is it OK if we stay in your place for a couple of days?'

They must have been past the fjords. Barely any traffic. Just the occasional farmhouse in the bleak winter dark.

'As long as you like, Mark. And congratulations.'

'I forgot to send you the photos. It was all so busy. I'll do it—'

'No need right now,' Lund said. 'I'll be back soon. I want . . . I can't wait to see you.'

She said goodbye. They were driving over a long bridge. What looked like a runway on the other side, lights marking the outline in the dark.

'Did someone have a little one?' Reinhardt asked from the front.

Her phone beeped. She looked at the pictures that had just come in. Mark, Eva and the baby. Her mother pleased as Punch.

Lund ignored the question, went back to staring out of the window.

'The plane's paid for and ready,' Reinhardt said when he got no answer. 'They just need some signatures and ID.'

Borch pulled into the car park. A line of light aircraft stood on the apron. The place seemed deserted apart from an office near the tower beyond some hangars.

'I'll deal with it,' he said and got out.

The night was clear. No rain. Bright stars. A waning moon. The sharp tang of snow on the way. She took out the notes she'd made from the last phone call with Juncker, when he'd been looking at the old Birk Larsen case files while keeping out of Brix's sight.

'Does the name John Lynge mean anything?'

Reinhardt didn't bother to turn.

'Should it?'

'You tell me.'

'Not that I can think of.'

'Six years ago he was one of Hartmann's drivers. He murdered the Birk Larsen girl.'

A long, thoughtful pause.

'That was a nasty case,' Reinhardt said. 'From what I recall you thought Hartmann killed her for a while. And then . . . wasn't it one of the family friends?'

'That's what went down on the records,' Lund said. 'But it wasn't. It was John Lynge.'

He laughed.

'You always seem to know more than everyone else. Why is that?'

'Because I know how to look.'

He checked his watch. Outside Borch was still hunting for a way into the office.

'Lynge had form for child abuse. Do you stick together?' she asked. 'Is it like a club or something? Do you do each other favours? When we tear apart your so-called gallery will we find the member-ship records too?'

'I really don't know why you keep pursuing this.'

'We checked John Lynge's work history. Before he got a job with Hartmann he was employed by Zeeland. He was your driver for the children's fund. That must have been convenient. Did he watch? Help out from time to time?'

Reinhardt sighed.

'Do you honestly think I remember all my staff? Is this relevant, Lund?'

Such a slim connection. But it was there. If Brix let her she could work on it.

'Were you surprised when that lawyer came up with the alibi yesterday?' she asked.

His head turned. No answer.

'Someone from Zeeland made it look as if you stayed in room one eighteen. The computers are run from your Copenhagen office. They changed the data for the lock records so it seemed you were in the clear.'

Borch had finally found a way inside. She could see him talking to someone there.

'You never stay in room one eighteen. That's for ordinary people. It's always the suite in three twenty-two.'

She leaned forward from the back seat, got closer to him.

'I know you killed Louise Hjelby. She wasn't the first, was she?'

He took a deep breath, relaxed into the seat, yawned.

'What's Robert Zeuthen going to think when he realizes you'd have let his daughter die to keep that secret?'

Brief laughter, a shake of the head.

'You might as well tell me. As soon as we get back the case is alive again. I'm going to put you in jail.'

Reinhardt reached up and adjusted the mirror so that all she could see were his eyes, grey, knowing, unworried.

'I don't think that's going to happen,' he said in a measured, easy tone. 'We wouldn't be having this conversation if that were the case.'

'I'll—'

'No.' His eyes were on her in the mirror. Reinhardt put a finger to his lips. 'Listen to me for once. Let me make myself absolutely clear. I admire your tenacity. Your precision. Your . . . correctness. I'm grateful you've reminded me how necessary these qualities are. You've taught me a lot.'

'Don't push it . . .'

He didn't look directly at people often, she realized. And knew why too. In this full, frank gaze the friendly uncle vanished. In its place came the real Niels Reinhardt: cunning, intense, determined.

'I will, of course, take full note of this for the future, Lund. You've no need to worry. I won't trouble you in Denmark again.'

He shuffled round in the seat then looked her up and down.

'We must all know our place. When will you learn yours?'

Head spinning. Imagining. Searching for questions no one else would ask.

She took out her phone, looked at the pictures there.

Her mother, Mark, Eva. The baby in his arms.

Then she stepped outside, got the gun from its holster, racked it. Walked round to the front of the car.

Borch was out of the office. He saw, realized.

Shouted, 'Sarah?'

Lund got to the passenger door. Reinhardt wound down the window.

'Sarah!' Borch yelled, racing towards her.

Gun up. Barrel to the grey head. Reinhardt turned and stared, a look of puzzlement, distaste on his face.

One shot.

Somewhere in the night birds rose on invisible wings.

Blood on the windscreen.

Borch shrieking.

A figure in a dark coat and suit slumped against the dashboard.

Lund stepped back, looked at the body. Borch was on it, checking, not that there was much point.

'What the hell have you done?'

The gun dropped from her fingers, clattered on the ground.

'Get in the car. Sarah! Get in the car, dammit.'

In the back, the smell of blood and munitions. Borch thinking.

'Right. We'll say he tried to grab your gun. You had no choice. If we can . . . Oh Christ!'

A long pained shriek. He stared at her, eyes full of pain.

'He told me it was him,' Lund said. 'She wasn't the only one. Any more than he was . . .'

Borch was barely listening.

'OK. This is what we do. You take off your coat. Dry the blood.'

He reached over, rifled through Reinhardt's jacket, retrieved a wallet, money, credit cards.

'No one's expecting us in Copenhagen for a couple of hours.' He gave her the cash. 'I'll think of something to say here. The pilot's booked. He can take you to Reykjavik. Get the first flight out of there.'

He pulled out an ID card.

'This will give you security clearance. Tell them your husband's in PET.' He closed his eyes, struggling. 'You . . . you're on your way to see a sick aunt. You'd forgotten your passport. So they let you travel on my clearance. OK? Sarah? OK?'

The glass was smeared with blood and brain. Reinhardt's body had somehow tipped half out of the car.

'I can give you the girls' medical cards. That'll help. Tell them to call me if you like and . . .'

She didn't move.

'Get your damned coat off, will you?'

Nothing.

'It's not a great plan, love. But if you just sit here they're going to come along soon. Then you're going to jail for a long time. Doesn't matter what you say. What I say . . .'

He shook his head, punched the seat back.

'Dammit, Sarah . . . why? We could have . . .'

Her hand went to his cheek. He looked close to tears.

'Get out of here now,' Borch pleaded. 'We'll work something out. We'll . . .'

She leaned forward, kissed him. Bristly cheeks. Cold lips.

Fear and love. Regret and determination.

He was crying then, got out of the car, ran to the office.

The pilot was in a back room checking charts, looking at the weather, his watch.

'I've got to stay here,' Borch said. 'Just one passenger. My colleague.'

'Are you all right?' the pilot asked and stubbed out his cigarette in the bin. 'You don't look too good.'

'She's not going to Copenhagen either. She has to go to Reykjavik.'

The man shook his head, laughed, said, 'Really?'

'Change of plan. Rey—'

'You think we're going single engine over water? At night? In this weather?'

'Somewhere else then . . .' Borch stuttered.

'What is this?'

'My colleague . . .'

He walked to the window. So did the pilot.

'What colleague?' the man asked. 'There's someone flat out in the car park. Looks hurt . . .'

Borch dashed out of the door. A body on the ground. Tyres squealing on wet asphalt. Red lights vanishing into the dark.

Brix got bored with the lazy, self-congratulatory chatter. Found he couldn't stop thinking about Niels Reinhardt and a dead girl in Jutland with a name no one had uttered all evening.

He avoided Ruth Hedeby's glittering, come-on eyes. Found a quiet corner.

The watch. The dates. Reinhardt's odd manner, both servile yet evasive. It wasn't a lot to go on. They'd have to be quick. They'd need to break the alibi too.

But if anyone could do it . . .

He phoned Lund's mobile, waited, wondering what to say.

Then something odd. An answer. The sound of a car driving at speed.

'Lund?' he said. 'Can you hear me?'

A long silence. The line went dead. He tried again, got voicemail. Was thinking about how to proceed in the morning when Hedeby came round, took his arm, forced another glass on him.

'Upstairs now, Lennart,' she said with a broad, happy smile. 'There are people you need to meet.'

On the damp Christiansborg cobbles Karen Nebel waited in vain. Hartmann was inside the party already, smiling at his happy followers, shaking hands, high-fiving those who wanted.

The flash of cameras. Morten Weber clapping. Rosa Lebech lurking, smiling hopefully.

Hartmann turned, waved, raised a toast, a smile, triumphant again.

Back in the game. Part of the rush.

On the stairs of the cold, grand mansion Robert Zeuthen sat with his family. One arm holding the silent Emilie. The other round Maja and Carl.

A single suitcase on the floor. That night they'd sleep in the little cottage in the grounds where the magic that was family first began.

Then in the morning take the car to Kastrup. Fly south. Somewhere warm beyond the wings of the Zeeland dragon. A place where they could discover what was lost. Then think about the future.

The little airport in Norway, Reinhardt's corpse a crumpled bloody heap on the asphalt.

A sudden rustle of wings. A crow came out of nowhere, glossy in the harsh airport lights, waddled towards the shape on the ground. Black beak sharp. Ready to peck.

Seventeen days later

On the first Monday of December Brix sat down for breakfast as usual in the quiet, elegant cafe near Nyhavn, close to his flat. His former wife had discovered the place. Ruth Hedeby had liked it too after she split up with her husband. That relationship was gone now, soured by work, by his need for distance.

So he ate alone most mornings and felt happy that way. A moment of solitary reflection before the working day began. He needed it now more than ever.

Coffee and orange juice. A pastry from the fancy selection cooked on the premises. He was about to start when a woman walked in and took the seat opposite. She had short, straight hair, dyed somewhere between glossy copper and chestnut. The cut seemed considered, perhaps expensive, and out of place with her clothes: a cheap shiny black anorak, a sweatshirt bearing the name and logo 'Cambridge University', black jeans.

A joke, he thought. Unreal. Like the rest of her. He was about to say the seat wasn't taken anyway when he looked at her pale, blank face and bright, large darting eyes.

'Coffee, Lund,' he said. 'Something to eat . . .'

'That would be good.'

'Where've you been?'

'Travelling. I'm amazed you couldn't find me.'

Brix leaned back and stretched his long arms behind his head.

'We've been busy. Didn't you get the chance to read the papers?'

She was staring out of the window. Christmas lights and decorations in the street. A seasonal market not far away in Nytorv where

414

Peter Schultz had fallen to his death only a few weeks before. The city kept turning even if the country appeared to be living on the edge of a precipice.

'Something to eat,' he said, pointing to the counter and the rich range of pastries.

Lund called over the waitress and asked for ham and eggs and toast. White toast. And ketchup. The woman blinked, glanced at Brix. He nodded.

'What's happening?'

Lots, he thought, and told her. Reinhardt's very public death had opened the floodgates. Complaints about sexual abuse in Zeeland's homes had started as a trickle two days after he was shot. Within a week the Politigården was inundated with them. Brix, now favourite to be next commissioner, had set up a dedicated investigation team, headed by Mathias Borch seconded from PET.

'I haven't seen any arrests,' she said.

'We start this week. It's a big job.'

The coffee turned up. The toast, ham and eggs. She started to tuck in, with a gusto that made him think she hadn't eaten properly in days.

'But that's what you wanted, wasn't it? Why you shot him. So all those children would find the courage to come forward.' He raised his cup. 'Not that many are children any more. We've got cases going back almost forty years.'

'Anyone I know?'

He wondered whether to tell her, then decided she was owed.

And it wasn't just the victims who came forward. There were other, innocent, decent people appalled by what had occurred. Robert Zeuthen had returned from Bali with his family three days before and immediately asked for Borch to make a statement about undue influence within Zeeland. Hartmann's spin doctor Karen Nebel had resigned and produced a series of incriminating photos that had led to the suspension of Dyhring from PET and the resignation of Mogens Rank as Justice Minister.

'The chances are Hartmann's government won't last till Christmas. Not that Anders Ussing's going to benefit.'

'He was in on it too?' she asked.

'I doubt that. But we've got his aide, Per Monrad, named in several accusations. I'm having Asbjørn pick him up later today.

After that some people inside Zeeland. A few other parliamentari-
ans. Some men in industry. The media. Show business. You may
know a few of the names. I doubt their wives are going to believe
one word of what they're about to hear.'

'Asbjørn's got promise,' she said then went back to eating.

'True. Hartmann didn't do anything wrong by the way. He's as
appalled as anyone.'

She jabbed a finger at him.

'Troels Hartmann didn't do anything. That's the point. We don't
have a nice, comfortable place between right and wrong. There's
one or the other. Jan Meyer told me that. I should have listened.'

'You did, didn't you? And now the government's doomed.
Zeeland looks as if it's going to fall into the hands of the Chinese
or the Koreans. Thousands of jobs gone . . .'

'They were kids! If we don't protect them, who does?'

He pushed back what remained of his breakfast. Appetite gone.

'You always were very Old Testament, Lund. Desperate to pull
down the pillars of the temple. Perhaps that's why I indulged you.
I was fascinated to see what would happen. And here we are.'

The shorter chestnut hair suited her. Some nicer clothes . . .

'Was it worth it?' he asked.

'Do you think I had a choice?'

Lennart Brix leaned back in his chair, closed his eyes, thought
about this. Then put his wallet on the table, took out all the money
he had, pushed it over.

'We can stop off at a cash machine. I can get you more.'

Lund stared at the notes, didn't move.

'I've got plenty of work to be going on with,' Brix added. 'You're
smart enough to vanish again. Just do it, will you?'

She wrinkled her nose at him, disappointed.

'You want me to run away? That's what Borch said. I don't . . .'
She chopped at her breakfast with the knife and fork. 'I don't do
that.'

'No,' he agreed. 'You don't.'

'On the other hand . . .'

A glint in her eyes. His hopes rose.

'I'd like another fried egg,' she said. 'Before you take me in. And
a drive. Not a long one.'

*

Forty-five minutes later they were in the modest suburb of Herlev. He'd never been there. Never been close to this woman's strange and private life at all.

It was a modest wooden bungalow, painted red. Brix slowed the car as they approached. Festive lights winked beneath the guttering. There was a bright-blue Christiania trike by the front door, with what looked like a fitting for a cot.

A black car stood outside. Had been there ever since Lund went missing. A bored-looking Madsen sat behind the wheel, turned and stared as they drew near.

Brix brought the car to a stop by the kerb, waved at him to move on. The two of them watched him scratch his head then drive off down the road.

Her keen and glittering eyes were on the little cottage. Brix could see what she was looking at so closely. Through the window a man and a woman, standing. He was lifting a baby by the arms, kissing the child held between them. Then an embrace.

A family of three. Close. Content. A happy picture.

'We've got a few minutes. If you want to go in and see them . . .'

'Plenty of time for that later,' she said, shaking her head.

Brix folded his long arms.

'Sarah. They're the only reason you came back. Aren't they?'

Lund nodded.

'Mostly, Lennart. But at the risk of repeating myself . . .'

She pointed through the windscreen at the city spreading out before them.

'Can we go to the Politigården now? Like I said?'